# PRAISE FOR JERUSHA AGEN

"Jerusha Agen once again delivers top-level suspense and thrilling action. Fast-paced suspense at its best."

DIANN MILLS, BESTSELLING AUTHOR OF *CONCRETE EVIDENCE* ON *COVERT DANGER*

"Fast-paced, explosive thriller. I couldn't turn the pages fast enough."

CARRIE STUART PARKS, AWARD-WINNING, BESTSELLING AUTHOR OF *RELATIVE SILENCE* ON *RISING DANGER*

"*Rising Danger* grabbed me from the first chapter and never let go. Don't miss this edge-of-your-seat story of suspense and romance."

PATRICIA BRADLEY, AWARD-WINNING AUTHOR OF THE *LOGAN POINT* AND *MEMPHIS COLD CASE SERIES*

# WASTED

# BOOKS BY JERUSHA AGEN

### GUARDIANS UNLEASHED SERIES

*Midnight Clear* (prequel novella)

*Rising Danger* (prequel)

*Hidden Danger*

*Covert Danger*

*Unseen Danger*

*Lethal Danger*

*Terminal Danger*

### WINDY CITY WESTONS SERIES

*Waylaid*

*Wasted*

*Watched* (2026)

### SECURITY LEAGUE SERIES

*Protected* (prequel novella)

*Introverted* (second prequel novella)

*Rescued*

*Trapped*

### SISTERS REDEEMED SERIES

*If You Dance with Me*

*If You Light My Way*

*If You Rescue Me*

# WASTED

WINDY CITY WESTONS | BOOK TWO

## JERUSHA AGEN

SDG Words, LLC

© 2025 by Jerusha Agen
Published by SDG Words, LLC
www.JerushaAgen.com



Library of Congress Control Number: 2025909336

ISBN 978-1-956683-47-9

Scripture quotations are from The ESV® Bible (The Holy Bible, English Standard Version®), copyright © 2001 by Crossway, a publishing ministry of Good News Publishers. Used by permission. All rights reserved.

This book is a work of fiction. Names, characters, places, and incidents are the product of the author's imagination or are used fictitiously. Any resemblance to actual events, locales, or persons, living or dead, is coincidental.

# ACKNOWLEDGMENTS

The classic advice for writers is to "write what you know." But how incredibly boring would a story be if I only stuck to repeating my own knowledge and experience?

Good thing I'm not afraid to ask others what *they* know. And then the fun begins as I get to learn new information and let my imagination run wild.

Thank you to Matthew Agen for sharing harrowing true stories of the little-known dangerous side of home health physical therapy.

Thanks to Bob Severson for telling me about death wobbles and teaching me how to sabotage someone's ride. Don't worry, you are innocent of anything I may do with this information. Hugs!

Sarah Hamaker, thank you for being the supportive and inspiring writing buddy God knew I needed.

Barbara Diggs, your prayer support and friendship continues to be invaluable. Thank you doesn't say enough.

A huge thank you is due to my excellent betas and proof-readers who don't mind when I send them a messier than usual manuscript. Thanks to J.E. Grace, Natalya Lakhno, and Vickie Watts for helping me clean up the mess and for being the first to love Victoria's story!

To my first Leonberger, the inspiration for Max. You'll always have my heart.

Mom, thanks for being exactly what I need to get through my blocks, sad times, happy times, and trials in writing and in life. This book would never have been possible without you!

*Soli Deo Gloria*

*Blessed are the peacemakers,*
*for they shall be called sons of God.*

Matthew 5:9

# CHAPTER
## ONE

"WHAT DO YOU WANT?"

Victoria Weston's smile slipped away at Jamica Trent's unfriendly greeting.

So much for the hope that this home health visit would entail less drama than Victoria's initial evaluation visit. She hadn't even made it inside the house out of the freezing cold yet. And might not anytime soon with the way Jamica held the door halfway open and blocked it with her body.

But as Victoria took in the weariness around Jamica's angry eyes and the tears on her one-year-old baby's dark cheeks as the boy slid down her hip, compassion replaced any irritation. "I'm here to see your mother for physical therapy."

"You ain't the therapist." Jamica surveyed Victoria as if she was a solicitor or con artist. "She's a short, chubby chick."

Not the kindest way to describe Ginny Lenton.

*Lord, please give me patience and compassion.* After repeating the same request she had prayed when she'd approached the Trents' house, Victoria forced a smile. "I believe you're thinking of Ginny, my PTA."

Jamica's eyes narrowed. "PTA?"

"My assistant."

1

"Jamica!"

Victoria nearly closed her eyes in relief, although she could have done without the sharpness in Delilah Trent's tone.

"Let the woman inside for Pete's sake! You want me laid up forever? Don't think so, the way you been carrying on."

Victoria held back a smile. Delilah evidently still had as much lively spirit as the day they'd first met.

Jamica rolled her eyes and left the door to hang open on its own.

Deducing that was an invitation to enter, Victoria stepped inside, switching her therapy equipment bag to her left hand so she could close the door with her right. Her gaze jumped ahead to find Delilah.

The sixty-two-year-old patient sat up with both legs extended in front of her on the brown sofa in the living room. A television blared across from her against the far wall.

The path to reach Delilah was littered with clothing, toys, empty soda cans, and boxes. All potential fall hazards.

Victoria would evidently need to discuss fall prevention again, though Ginny had said she'd already been emphasizing the problem at each of her visits. "Hello, Mrs. Trent."

The woman waved a dismissive hand as Victoria picked her way across the living room. "Told you to call me Delilah last time."

"Of course." Victoria hadn't forgotten, but since she had only met Delilah one other time at the initial evaluation appointment, she didn't want to presume the invitation to be informal still held. "It's good to see you, Delilah." Victoria smiled as she reached the sofa. "How are you feeling?"

Delilah harrumphed. "Depends on how much Jamica's been gettin' on my nerves."

Victoria laid a disposable pad under her bag before setting it on the nearby wooden chair that looked like it had once been part of a dining set. "Family dynamics can be tricky at times." She retrieved a pair of nitrile gloves from the outer pocket of her bag and pulled them on. "Did Ginny tell you what we'll be doing at my visit today?"

"Seein' if I pass the test, I guess." Delilah chuckled.

Victoria smiled again. "No test, I promise. We're only going to assess how you're doing and determine if we need to make any adjustments to your exercise and treatment program. I'll go over your meds with you, too, and make sure everything is good there."

Delilah shrugged one shoulder under her pink cable-knit sweater. "It's all the same."

"Good. Then there shouldn't be any surprises." Victoria gently drew up Delilah's loose cotton pant leg until she could see the dressing covering the incision. Thankfully, Dr. Tennison had agreed with Victoria's recommendation that Delilah keep the wound covered longer than normal due to the questionable sanitation of her living conditions. "How do you feel about your progress since your knee replacement?"

A snort from behind Victoria prompted her to look over her shoulder.

Jamica stood about eight feet away with her baby, glaring at her mother. "I can tell you. She just lays there and says she can't do nothin'. And she moanin' and groanin' all the time."

"Don't you tell them lies, girl." Delilah's dark eyes flashed as she craned her neck to see Jamica past Victoria. "And you be polite now. We got company."

"She ain't company. She a therapist. And why you need her anyway? I thought the surgery supposed to fix you. Ain't you supposed to *go* to therapy like everybody clsc? You don't gotta bring a bunch of strangers in here."

Victoria straightened and stepped to the side so Delilah could see her daughter. Better not to try to check the incision in the middle of an argument.

"Why you so edgy?" Delilah's eyes narrowed at Jamica.

The girl tried for a shrug, but the obvious tension in her shoulders wouldn't cooperate enough to convince anyone of nonchalance.

The notes of Chopin's *Nocturne No. 9* broke through the tension. Victoria's ringtone. "Excuse me." She peeled off her glove and grabbed her phone from another pocket in her bag. She'd have to thank the caller who had such perfect timing.

Relief slid through her as she stepped out of the line of fire and glanced at the caller ID.

*CareFull Home Health.*

She pressed the phone to her ear. "Victoria Weston."

Delilah and Jamica restarted their verbal sparring before Victoria could clearly hear the voice on the other end of the line.

She covered her left ear with her fingers. "Ginny?"

"Hey, yeah. What's with all the noise?"

"I'm at the Trents'."

"Oh, gotcha. At it again. At least you know I wasn't making it up."

"I was aware of that from my first visit." Victoria chose her words carefully, though with the shouting match going on, it was doubtful Jamica or Delilah would hear a word she said.

"Yeah. They sound pretty heated this time. You good alone there?"

"I believe so." Though Victoria wouldn't mind wrapping up the visit as soon as possible. "What did you need?"

"Oh, Dr. Tennison's office called with a question about—"

A slam cracked through the house.

Victoria jerked to see the front door bounce back from where it must have been smacked into the wall.

A tall man in a dark jacket stood in the doorway, a red bandana layered under a black winter hat on his head and fury twisting his features.

Light glinted off something in his hand.

Was that—

The long, silver blade left no doubt. He was holding a knife.

# CHAPTER
## TWO

"AND THIS IS the office area where we all..." Racquelle Leath, the CareFull Home Health clinical manager, let the sentence stall as she led Cillian Doherty around the corner. Probably listening to the high-pitched, female voice infused with what sounded like fright.

"Are you there? Victoria?"

The name pierced Cillian's chest. Victoria. The woman who had brought him here.

"She just hung up. What should we do?" A young redhead standing by a long desk aimed her panic at a seated brunette, her eyes bugging out of her head.

"Ginny?" Racquelle hurried toward the two women. "What's going on?"

"It's Victoria."

Cillian's chest clenched. "What about Victoria?" The question launched as quick as a reflex. Why was the girl scared and talking about Victoria?

"I was on the phone with her, and then there was a loud noise and shouting." Ginny wrung her hands as words tumbled from her mouth. "And she told me to be sure to file the yellow folder. Then a guy yelled, and she hung up. Or got cut off."

"You're sure she said the yellow folder?" Racquelle's dark eyebrows dipped as her forehead creased.

"Is that your code for somebody to check on her?" Cillian looked down at the shorter woman.

"No. That's the purple folder. Yellow is the code to call the police."

"Did you?" Cillian transferred his gaze to the nervous redhead.

She glanced at the administrator, confusion mingling with the shock that shaped her features.

"He's our new social worker. Cillian Doherty. Did you call the police?"

Ginny swallowed visibly, strangling her hands. "I wasn't sure what—"

Cillian pointed at Racquelle. "Call 9-1-1 now." He landed his gaze on Ginny as she started to back away. "Where is Victoria?"

"The Trents' house...Um, 2401 Blackmore Lane. It's on the West Side."

Cillian had already swung away, breaking into a run to the exit. He wouldn't need directions to that part of the city. Rough neighborhood. Not quite as bad as the one he'd grown up in, but enough to mean Victoria could be in serious danger.

Cillian reached his jeep and yanked the door open, jumping in behind the wheel and screeching out of the parking lot. He hadn't come this far to have something stupid happen to her before he could even say *hello*.

At least she was close. With the shortcuts and ignoring the speed limit, he'd make it in five minutes.

He didn't slow down until he reached Blackmore Lane. He checked every address, some on the houses and some on mailboxes.

There. 2401.

He glanced at the dashboard clock as he drove past the

little one-story brown house. *Four minutes, forty-three seconds.* Not bad for not having driven these roads in sixteen years.

He pulled up to the curb beyond the house, far enough away that his jeep shouldn't be spotted from inside. He got out, scanning the property.

A recent model gray Honda Civic was parked on the street off to the side of the driveway. Victoria's? An uncomfortable pinch grabbed his chest.

The driveway held two cars. A dark blue nineties two-door Pontiac and less ancient Toyota Camry. But the Pontiac grabbed his attention. Because the driver's door hung open.

Voices carried from the house. Shouts. A man and a woman.

The yelling woman wasn't Victoria. But she was probably still in there.

Cillian walked toward the house, ears perked and head on a swivel.

The shouted words became clearer as he neared.

"I'll see whoever I want!" The woman's scream blew out the open front door.

"Yeah? I'm the last face you ever gonna see!" The man's shout held enough hatred and anger to tense Cillian's muscles as he slowed by the doorway. "The kid and then you!"

"No!" The terror in the woman's shriek spiked adrenaline through Cillian.

"Hey!" He launched himself through the open doorway with the shout.

"What—" Expletives spewed from the loser who held a toddler dangled from one arm and an overly dramatic kitchen knife in the other.

A girl stood six feet away from him just inside what looked like a living room, her cheeks soaked with tears.

Two women were in the room behind her. One on a sofa and one standing near her. The elegance of the second woman couldn't be missed, even in a split-second glance. Victoria.

Awareness surged Cillian's pulse double-time, his gaze

wanting to linger. But he jerked his attention back to the troublemaker who was endangering Victoria and three others.

"Who are you? You better get out of here while you can walk."

"Wow." Cillian straightened to his full height, several inches taller than the knife-wielding punk. "I've never seen such a show of real manhood." He raked a derisive gaze over the guy and the toddler. "What are you gonna do after this? Beat up some old ladies?"

Anger flared the punk's nostrils. "Maybe. If it's your old lady."

Cillian laughed. "What do 'ya know, he can make a joke. Guess that means you're a brainy kid. No brawn."

The guy's eyes narrowed like a flinch. Another hit to the dude's ego. One or two more insults should do the trick.

"That's why you take on toddlers and women. Awesome flex, dude. Bet the bullies picked on you all the time, didn't they?" Cillian laced his tone with exaggerated pity.

"You better shut your mouth, you—" The punk added a string of unflattering names and expletives.

Cillian grinned. "You sure talk a lot. I'm beginning to think you've never used a knife before, have you? Definitely not on a real man. Somebody your own size."

"I'll use it to cut out your heart, you—" More colorful words followed as Cillian met the punk's gaze, keeping his grin.

"Go for it." Cillian waited. Senses sharp, ready.

The guy would drop the kid for a better attack.

The toddler slipped a micro-inch.

The punk was starting to loosen his hold as he stared at Cillian. The fear in his eyes was a clear tell. He wouldn't have the guts to go for a lunge. He'd try a slash instead.

There. His grip on the knife tightened, the shift of the blade giving him away.

Cillian kept his hands at his side, fingers loose.

A tiny movement, a slight lean in the punk's torso.

Now.

The toddler fell to the floor as Cillian met the punk more than halfway.

Cillian darted around the predicted path of the knife, swiped the attacker's hand away. Gripped his wrist. He twisted the arm around the punk's back, ready to dislocate his shoulder.

"Ah, I give up." The attacker opened his hand behind his back, letting the knife drop to the floor.

"And that's supposed to make me not break your arm?" Cillian twisted a little farther. The punk deserved to feel a little pain. Might make him think twice before attacking women and children again. But probably not.

"Come on, man!" The punk twisted his head, trying to see Cillian behind him.

"Freeze! Police!" An officer stepped through the doorway, his gun raised.

"Looks like the cops are your friends today, pal." Cillian murmured the words by the punk's head before he met the officer's alert gaze. "This man used a knife to threaten assault and harm to the child and these women." Cillian continued to hold the punk as he talked over his shoulder. "I've disarmed him, and the knife is on the floor between us now."

The cop nodded. "Phil." He angled his head to signal to the officer behind him, who walked around his partner toward Cillian and the punk. "You can let him go now and back away."

Cillian did as the first cop instructed, watching until they had the punk cuffed and the knife in their possession.

Then he let his attention go where it had wanted to since the moment he'd entered the house. Since the moment he'd arrived in Chicago again. And long before.

Victoria. Man, the woman made even scrubs look gorgeous.

Her hazel eyes locked onto his across the distance of the small living room.

His heart crashed into his ribs.

He had come back to rescue her. But this wasn't the kind of rescue he'd had in mind.

———

It couldn't be him. Victoria stared across the cluttered room at Cillian Doherty. At least, she thought it was him, though the concept seemed like a scientific impossibility.

He told his version of what had happened for the third time to another officer who seemed intent on visually mapping out the events. Cillian's voice—the deep, impressive tone he'd had as a seventeen-year-old—carried to her, fluttering her pulse in that way it always had.

Sixteen years. Sixteen years without seeing or hearing anything about him. And now, he'd suddenly burst into a client's house during an altercation?

She'd nearly had a heart attack when he had appeared out of nowhere. Because it was him. Her first and only crush.

She'd thought she must be hallucinating for the first few seconds, until he'd quickly scanned the room.

The power of his presence, the intensity and heat, and those coal-dark eyes as they'd briefly touched on her were unmistakable.

But why was Cillian Doherty here? In Chicago, the place he'd been desperate to leave behind forever?

After sixteen years, he'd stepped into her client's home right at that moment, in time to save her and the others from an attack. The implausibility of the situation was nearly too much for her to process or comprehend.

Shouts from outside the house pierced her confused stream of thoughts. Jamica. Already trying to plead for her boyfriend's innocence, from the sounds of it. Never mind that the man had threatened to kill her and her young son only moments ago.

Delilah still sat on the sofa, now behind Victoria since

she'd moved a bit closer to the entryway earlier to relate her version of the events to one of the officers. Delilah argued for the opposite outcome than her daughter, demanding that the officer she spoke with arrest Jamica's boyfriend immediately and throw away the key.

But the Trents' family troubles, their high-volume complaints indoors and outside, sounded like white noise in the background of the moment.

Perhaps Victoria was experiencing some degree of shock. After all, this was the second hostage situation she'd experienced in only four months.

But the odd, almost muffled sounds and her lack of awareness of the people around her contrasted with the extremely heightened awareness she had for one person. One man.

No, she wasn't in shock. At least not from the danger she had survived again.

Cillian kept looking her way as he talked to the officer.

She noticed every glance, each one like a jolt to her nervous system. Why was he here? How could he be?

He abruptly turned away from the officer. He was walking her way.

She wasn't ready. She swallowed, the unnerving feeling of watching a ghost from her past crawling through her.

But he wasn't exactly the same. Her mind seemed to latch on to his appearance for something to think about as a defense against his approach.

The thick black hair he'd let grow to his shoulders as a teen was now tamed into a flattering style that was medium length on top and not too short on the sides. The shoulders she'd thought were broad when they had dated had filled out along with the rest of his muscular physique, matching his increased height. He was taller than either of her brothers, perhaps six foot three, judging from how far she had to tilt her chin to see him—when he stopped directly in front of her.

His dark brown eyes landed on her, full of the intensity and heat that emanated from him. Still.

Her breath caught.

She'd forgotten. Forgotten how handsome he was. How her heart tried to smash through her ribs when he was near. How his presence and attention made her feel things she never had before and hadn't experienced since.

"Victoria Weston." His deep voice oozed like hot lava through her insides. His mouth angled in the lopsided grin she hadn't forgotten, though she'd tried. Oh, how she'd tried, telling herself he was a boy of her youth. Her first crush. He was simply a part of her coming of age that could be left behind as a distant, forgotten memory.

But the man standing before her was no teen memory. He had come of age, as well. The results were enough to scatter her senses and—

"Looks like you're still getting yourself into trouble." His grin and tone said he meant it to be humorous.

But the remark rang with echoes of other words she hadn't left behind. *"You're going to be in worse trouble if you don't stop letting him control you."*

She clenched her jaw against the memory, the pain of it. The many reasons she'd shut out those days came rushing back, the reasons she'd had to close the vault of her heart to Cillian Doherty. And it seemed he hadn't changed as much as his appearance suggested.

Whatever his reason for the sudden re-appearance, she didn't need to know what it was. She needed to excuse herself from him before he led her into trouble again.

"And you called me a thrill-seeker. If this is what your job is like every day, I guess I should've become a PT." Teasing twinkled in his admittedly hypnotic eyes.

But it wasn't working on her. He was clearly still the person she'd known before. Flippant, flirty—a charmer focused on fun and adventure. He'd always preferred to bail on real life, never taking anything seriously, even when her—

No. She would not walk down that memory lane. She didn't have to worry. She was no longer an adolescent girl with her first crush. She was an independent, thirty-one-year-old woman who knew better than to be charmed and led astray by any man, no matter how handsome. Ironically, she had Cillian to thank for her first lesson in resisting such men and her own misguided feelings.

She should make clear to him, as soon as possible, that his wiles would no longer work on her and were not welcome. "I'm sure it still wouldn't be what you're looking for. We focus on patient care, not self-centered fun and games."

Surprise flickered in the depths of those dark orbs. Likely astonished she had the gumption to answer him back, since she never had when they were teens.

But then his grin widened, stretching across his face. "I see I have a lot to learn. I may have to shadow you for a while so you can teach me what that patient care looks like." His suggestive tone curled a shiver through her. Or was it a tremor of trepidation?

"What do you mean?"

He folded his arms over his mock-neck blue sweater, challenge glinting in his gaze. "Well, clearly you're the expert on how to not have any fun and how to take care of everyone perfectly."

She resisted the urge to take the bait, the reference to their shared past. Her more alarming concern at the moment was his inference that she still didn't understand. "Why would you shadow me?"

"I told you." His mouth formed a smirk that she itched to wipe off. But that would require physical contact.

She harnessed the mental control she usually had in spades and focused on the more pressing question. "Why are you here?"

"To rescue you, of course."

Honestly, he had a knack for getting under her skin. She had to fight not to roll her eyes like the teenager she was trying not to be. "And you knew somehow that I was in danger at this particular client's house?"

"Yes."

She pinched her lips together. She would not meet him at his level. She instead gave him the silent stare that worked on her younger siblings, even Spring. The one that said they knew their behavior was inappropriate, and she would wait for them to do the right thing.

He chuckled, lowering his arms to land his hands on his hips. "I heard it at the office. I was there when you called in. Or right after anyway."

"The office? You mean CareFull Home Health?"

"What other office do you have?"

She held back a frustrated grunt. "Do you want to tell me what you were doing there sometime today? Or should I leave now for my next client?"

He laughed again, a low and familiar sound that threatened to undermine her irritation. "You're looking at CareFull's new clinical social worker."

The statement hit a wall in her brain, stopping it from being absorbed. That couldn't be. But Racquelle had mentioned they'd finally found a candidate for the social worker position. Victoria had been too busy to inquire further about the candidate at the time. A fatal mistake, apparently.

But even if she believed in chance, the odds would be too ridiculous for such a coincidence to be possible. Cillian couldn't have happened to return after sixteen years and end up taking a job at the very business where she was employed. And he'd never had any interest in becoming a social worker when he was seventeen.

"Are you telling me you didn't know I worked there?"

"No." He didn't look away or blink. The man's confidence, or arrogance, was unshakable. He suddenly leaned toward her, shrinking the space between them. "I took the job *because* you work there."

She blinked, stomach twisting as her pulse thrummed in her ears. Either from his closeness or from the alarming admission he hadn't even tried to hide.

She should probably be grateful for his honesty. He'd had plenty of vices, but lying was never one of them and, apparently, still was not. "Why—"

"How about I fill you in over lunch?" He glanced at their surroundings. "This probably isn't the best place to rehash old times."

She pulled her gaze from him, taking in the police officers, Delilah, and others who still talked and gathered evidence. How had she not heard or seen them from the moment Cillian moved close to her?

Her reaction to him didn't matter nearly as much as what he'd admitted. He'd come to Chicago, even taken a job at her workplace, because of her. What did he mean?

*"Expert on not having fun and taking care of people perfectly... Still getting yourself into trouble."*

What he'd said in their brief exchange returned like sound bites of evidence, clicking into place. References to their past. To the worst part.

The memory, the thought of what he knew—the secret—squeezed her lungs as if it might choke her.

She had kept the truth to herself all these years for good reasons. For her family.

Only one other person knew the secret. And he was standing in front of her, seeming to taunt her with it.

Was that why he had returned? To expose what had happened as some sort of delayed revenge?

The possibility robbed her of words, of air.

"Come on. You're not afraid to have a little lunch with me, are you?" The daring technique. Always his next tactic when she didn't acquiesce to what he wanted immediately.

Well, that kind of persuasion didn't work on her anymore. "I'm late for my next client as it is." She pointedly checked her wristwatch, breathing a little easier as she broke from the pressure of his gaze. "I couldn't possibly meet for lunch."

"Dinner, then."

She lifted her chin, her strength returning as she thought of an easy answer. "I don't date coworkers."

His grin returned. "Drinks."

She should've known he'd keep trying. He never did give up until he got what he wanted. "I don't—"

"You don't drink? You know you're an adult now, right?" The amusement in his gaze irked her enough to solidify her resolve even more.

"That is why I choose not to consume alcoholic beverages."

His lips twitched as he watched her, the grin gone, but apparently not for long. "Okay. Dessert or coffee, then."

She couldn't say she didn't consume dessert or coffee, since that would be a lie.

"I promise I'll tell you everything you want to know about why I'm here." The confidence in his eyes said he knew that would convince her.

Which should make her turn and run the other way. She should at least stand her ground and refuse to meet with him or speak to him again.

But as irritating as it was for her to admit, even to herself, he was right. She needed to learn what he was doing here, what he wanted, and what his intentions were. She had to know if he planned to reveal her secret.

It still wasn't the right time. The division and problems the revelation could wreak in her family were unthinkable. She couldn't allow him to expose the truth. She needed to share that at the appropriate time herself, if there ever was a need to do so.

"Very well. I will meet you at Mason Grill at eight p.m." Choosing the time and place herself gave her the modicum of control she desperately needed. She could not have him thinking she was as easy to persuade as her fifteen-year-old self, the young girl who had let him lead her into making the most tragic mistake of her life.

"It's a date." He'd likely said that to bait her. Yes, the amusement in his eyes left no doubt.

But she bit her tongue and stepped around him, holding her head high as she left the house without looking back.

She had only agreed to learn why he was here. She would likely need the knowledge to counteract whatever he had in mind.

Cillian Doherty may have materialized at the perfect time to save her life, but she had the feeling his next move would be to upend it.

# CHAPTER
# THREE

VICTORIA INHALED DEEPLY, then slowly exhaled as she pulled into the driveway of her next client.

She braked in front of the wrought iron gate that blocked entry into Thomas Briscoe's estate. An intercom and button to buzz for entry stood to the left of her window, but she opened her door instead of using them and got out.

Though it was later in the day than she usually came, already noon now, Thomas likely still wanted her to retrieve his mail.

A cold wind bit her cheeks as she walked to the cranberry red, ornate mailbox at the side of the road.

Her foot slipped. She lifted her hands out from her sides for balance.

Her pulse spiked, but she managed to stay upright, reaching for the mailbox to ensure she stayed that way.

She glanced down to see the reason for her suddenly poor traction.

Of course. A thin layer of ice coated the end of the driveway by the mailbox, likely a result of the recent snowmelt and refreeze they'd had. The joys of winter.

Good thing Thomas always asked her or Judy Kline to

retrieve his mail. The housekeeper disliked the task enough, especially in winter, that Victoria was happy to bring in the mail during her twice-weekly visits.

She'd have to ask Ned Parker about applying salt to melt the ice, if she saw the reclusive groundskeeper today.

She removed a few envelopes and a flier from the box. Keeping an eye on the slippery pavement, she went to the keypad next to the intercom and entered the access code.

The gate clicked and slowly retracted, giving her enough time to return to her car and drive through before it closed behind her.

Tension stood her nerves on end as she followed the driveway to the front of the Victorian mansion that was slightly larger than the house in which she had been raised.

*Breathe.* It wouldn't do to enter her client's home with frazzled nerves and unease she could spread to others. She wished she could blame the hostage situation—the second she had survived—for her tender emotional state. Perhaps that explanation would make for an interesting story.

But she knew better.

The memory of Cillian's handsome face escaped her efforts to keep it at bay, partially obscuring her view as she followed the curve of the driveway. The dark stubble lining his jawline, the deeper furrows on his brow that only increased the intensity he'd always had. And those eyes.

A shiver skidded through her. If only the sensation was merely a delayed reaction to stepping into the cold by the mailbox.

She sighed as she pulled her car to a halt in the parking area past the portico. She shouldn't let him get to her so much.

But he was working at CareFull Home Health now. At her workplace. And he'd done so because she worked there.

Had he returned to expose her secret? The one only he knew.

But why would he? Why after all these years? If he'd

wanted revenge, he could've told her father what he knew then, right after she had said she wouldn't see—

She pinched her lips together, halting the spiraling thoughts. It didn't matter. Not right now. She needed to do as she always did while working—set aside her personal life and concerns to serve the client one hundred percent.

And she was already late, in this case, though she had called Thomas to explain and ask if she should still come at a later time. She'd been relieved he'd said yes.

She needed the excuse to avoid meeting with Cillian until she could order her thoughts and regain control of her emotions. She could also use the distraction of seeing one of her favorite clients.

Pushing open her door, she left the car to greet the frigid air once again.

Two cars were already parked next to hers. Brenda and Ryan must be visiting. Thomas would not be in a good mood with his niece and nephew at the house. But their presence would also mean he'd be even more pleased than usual to see Victoria.

She walked under the stone portico and took the four steps to the grand double-door entrance that was framed by pillars.

Seemed odd that an edifice with such a classic, historic grandeur would have an electronic keypad alongside the heavy wooden doors. But Thomas Briscoe was surprising in several respects, including the complete trust he'd placed in Victoria soon after she had begun physical therapy for his recovery from hip replacement surgery.

She entered the passcode, and the lock clicked as it released. Pulling open one heavy door, she slipped inside, scanning the foyer for any of the visitors evidenced by the cars outside.

The foyer appeared empty and quiet, the brown and cherry wood and intricately patterned encaustic tiles gleaming from Judy's conscientious care.

"Stop your hovering, woman." Thomas's irritated voice carried to the foyer.

Victoria smiled as she followed the sound.

"I'm not an invalid, and I never will be, no matter how much you and that brother of yours would love it if I was."

Victoria's smile transitioned to a wince as she neared the open doors of the library. Sounded like she would have her work cut out for her today if his relatives were getting on his nerves that much.

Footsteps clinked across the library's parquet-patterned hardwood floor toward the doorway, and Brenda appeared, muttering under her breath as she glared ahead. Until her gaze landed on Victoria.

The transformation was quick and smooth as Brenda stopped in front of Victoria, a polite smile shaping her red-lipstick-covered lips. "Ms. Weston. So glad you could make it after all. Uncle was so disappointed when you missed your appointment."

As always, Brenda's apparent friendliness was undergirded by barely disguised criticism.

Victoria smiled. "No more than I was, I'm sure. But I won't keep him waiting any longer." She watched Brenda, hoping the woman would take the hint and step out of the way.

Victoria could go around her. But such an action would only irritate Brenda and make any peacemaking efforts Victoria might need to attempt all the harder.

Brenda's mouth tightened at the corners as if she was tempted to say something more.

"Did you need anything before I go in?" Victoria delivered the question in a professional tone.

"No, of course not." Brenda moved aside and extended her hand toward the library. "Please."

Victoria let out a quiet breath as she entered the room, inhaling the scent of old books as she took in the floor-to-ceiling shelves packed with early editions and favorites she and Thomas shared.

"So, you finally decided to show up."

Victoria laughed and crossed the room to the distinguished gentleman who sat in an armchair in front of the grand fireplace, facing away from her. His tone assured her his remark was the opposite of Brenda's—critical words that disguised fondness, welcome, and humor.

She rounded the chair and gazed upon the client she'd come to think of as a friend.

His gray beard and hair refused to thin with his eighty-four years, though his slight body, shrinking stature, and pale, milky skin tone made him hard to recognize in the portrait of the young, strapping shipping magnate that hung above the mantle.

But his eyes twinkled through his glasses with more merriment and kindness than the serious, cold young man he appeared to have been when the painting had been completed.

"Yes, I did. Despite the welcome I knew I would receive." Victoria gave him a smile.

A single laugh burst from Thomas, and he slapped the leather arm of his chair. "About time somebody with some wit arrived. I've been having to put up with these imbeciles and their simpering all day."

Victoria cast a glance beyond the chair.

Brenda still lingered at the library door, looking in their direction. She could probably hear every word her uncle said.

"I believe Brenda can hear you." Victoria lowered her voice as she set the mail on the nearby end table, then placed a pad under her bag beside the letters.

"I hope she can." Thomas raised his volume louder. "Maybe then she and her brother will stop their sickening patronizing and find something to do instead of waiting around for me to die."

A predictable response from Thomas. But Victoria still frowned as Brenda turned away and left, disappearing from sight. Knowing Brenda, she was likely going to remain somewhere within hearing range.

"Perhaps she has better intentions than you think." Victoria returned her attention to Thomas.

He harumphed. "The only intentions she and Ryan have are to see me dead within the year so they can get their hands on my fortune. They might even want to help it along if either of them was smart enough to think of how to do it."

"Thomas." Victoria stared at him. He often criticized his niece and nephew, but he'd never suggested they would do anything to harm him, beyond pestering him to death. "You don't mean that."

"Don't I?" He placed both hands on the arms of the chair and leaned forward. "You are the only one I can trust, Victoria." His voice lowered to a secretive tone she hadn't heard him use before.

She had never seen such urgency shape his features either. Her chest pinched, and she took a step closer. "What do you mean?"

"Are they watching? Listening?"

She checked the doorway. "I don't see anyone."

"Come closer." His voice dropped in volume even more as he beckoned her near with his fingers.

She crouched in front of his chair. "Thomas, what is it? Are you all right?"

"No." He glanced to the side, then locked his gaze on hers. "Well, I may not be. I can't trust anyone. They're all after money, and they'll do anything to get it. *Anything*." He hissed the last word.

Had someone threatened him? It was hard to believe his own niece and nephew, practically Chicago royalty in their standing among the wealthy families, would engage in anything sinister or criminal. Perhaps Thomas was simply being dramatic. It had to be difficult that his two heirs only pretended to care about him.

"But what about Mr. Glenn?" Victoria had met the museum

curator once when he'd arrived to meet with Thomas after a PT session. Thomas had acted friendlier and more pleased to see Clinton Glenn than anyone she had observed Thomas with before. "And your attorney, Mr. Neely. Surely, he's trustworthy?"

"Bob? Yes." Thomas looked off to the side, as if staring at the fire without seeing it. "I think so. I may show him what I discovered."

Discovered? Victoria held back more questions. It wasn't her place to pry into a client's personal life. "I'll pray for wisdom in the situation. Whatever is happening, the Lord can help you navigate it. 'The fear of the Lord is the beginning of wisdom.'"

"'...all those who practice it have a good understanding.'"

Victoria smiled. At least he wasn't so disturbed as to not finish her Scripture quote, as per usual. "Well, shall we get started? I'll have you come to stand." She moved closer in case he needed any assistance, though she didn't expect him to. He'd made excellent progress in his balance. More than he seemed to realize.

Thomas leaned his upper body forward and stood as she had shown him, minimizing effort and ending with better skeletal alignment.

"Well done. I have a new exercise I'd like you to try today that will focus on your balance when—"

A grand two-toned bell rang through the mansion. The doorbell.

Thomas's body stiffened. He reached for Victoria and gripped her wrist.

"Thomas? What is it?"

"Not now."

Voices carried from the hallway. Two males.

Thomas darted a glance over his right shoulder toward the open doorway. "Will you come back tomorrow morning?"

"I was planning on Wednesday, since we're having a session today." Their usual schedule was every other weekday.

"No. You can't stay. I need to do this."

Victoria followed his gaze to the foyer outside the library. And to the figures that appeared there.

Two men entered the library and strode toward Thomas and Victoria. Ryan Briscoe and Clinton Glenn. Why was Thomas acting almost…afraid of his nephew and the curator she'd thought was his friend? Or was only one of them making him so tense and uncomfortable?

"Please, come back tomorrow at nine." Thomas whispered the request with a fierce squeeze of her hand. "I'll explain everything then."

"Uncle, your friend is here to see you." Ryan gave the unnecessary explanation as if his uncle was blind as he and Mr. Glenn paused halfway into the large room. "But I see you're busy with your therapy." Ryan seemed unable to help the condescension that laced the word, *therapy*. No wonder Thomas so easily saw through his and Brenda's supposed affection.

Thomas looked in the new visitor's direction. "Victoria was just leaving." He returned his gaze to her, his eyes peering deeply into hers, full of urgency she'd never seen in him before.

"Yes." She returned the squeeze, her hand still in his. "I'll be back." She said the words in a normal tone, looking directly at Thomas so he would know they were meant for him—her promise she would return in the morning as he'd asked. Good thing tomorrow was her day off, or she might have had to refuse due to already scheduled appointments.

She scooped up her bag and the disposable pad. Giving a nod to the two men, she passed them and headed for the library doorway.

"Thomas, so good to see you." Mr. Glenn's tone was as warm and friendly as the last time she'd seen him visit Thomas at the estate. Perhaps there was nothing wrong, and she had misread the situation.

Relief eased some of the tension in her chest as she neared the foyer.

"Leave us, Ryan."

Victoria paused at the almost unrecognizable voice.

Thomas had never sounded so cold, so grim. Not even when discussing his disappointing niece and nephew.

Should she turn back? See if Thomas needed her? Perhaps if she understood the problem, she could offer her help.

"I'll see you out." Ryan's statement at her shoulder made her pulse jump.

She glanced at him, catching the disapproval in his eyes, as if he thought she was intending to eavesdrop.

He was apparently judging her in the light of his own character, at least from the two times she was sure she'd caught him listening outside his uncle's office when Thomas had been on the phone. But confronting him on that point would do no good at the moment.

She allowed him to lead her to the front door and shut it behind her. Her thoughts, however, remained inside, with Thomas. And she did the only thing she knew could enable her to let go of worry and the things she couldn't control.

*Lord, You know what Thomas meant. You know what trouble he's facing. Please give him wisdom and Your peace. Help me to leave this matter and all things in Your hands.*

The last request in her silent prayer was one she should have prayed earlier. She would need the Lord's help to make it through the rest of the day, knowing that in seven hours and forty-six minutes, she would meet with the man she had never thought she would see again. The one she had allowed to occupy her heart, only to regret it for the rest of her days.

She would have to be very careful this evening. She could not let herself commit the same error twice.

# CHAPTER
## FOUR

CILLIAN COULDN'T TAKE his eyes off the woman seated across the table from him. It was obvious why she'd picked Mason Grill. Essentially a sports bar and grill, the counter in the center of the restaurant was filled with boisterous drinkers. The restaurant's music was louder than Cillian guessed it would be during the day, when families probably occupied the booths along the outer walls. The large TVs ratcheted up the noise level even more with the sports and other channels they displayed.

There was nothing romantic about the location, that was for sure. And the loud environment made conversation a challenge, even where they were seated in a small booth by the wood-paneled wall. The restaurant was perfect for Victoria to pick since she apparently didn't want to talk or chance anything that could be interpreted as a date.

Her already perfect posture had been straighter than normal, basically rigid, since the moment she'd walked in, and he'd waved at her from the booth. Surprise had lifted her eyebrows. Probably expected him to be late, since he'd never prized punctuality as a teen.

But he'd intentionally arrived ten minutes early, predicting she'd arrive five minutes before eight. He'd been right. At least this way, he could start showing her he'd changed in some ways. In the ways she would want him to.

She'd barely said a word after she'd joined him in the booth, clearly taking great care to be sure her knees and feet didn't touch his beneath the table. A real trick, since the tiny space didn't at all allow for his long legs.

But he tried to oblige, angling one foot out into the aisle. He couldn't help but remember a time when she hadn't tried to avoid contact. When she'd actually enjoyed the tame touches, the hand holding. All firsts for the innocent fifteen-year-old she'd been then.

Did she have more experience now? The idea of other guys getting close to her squirmed in his belly. But judging from her prim and proper, almost laughable attempts to keep her distance from him now, maybe she still hadn't dated much.

She had changed her outfit for this non-date, though, which could mean she wanted to look nice. Or she just didn't want to wear scrubs to a restaurant. Her slim-fitting burgundy turtleneck and long, flowing skirt that skimmed heeled boots were completely modest, completely Victoria, and insanely attractive. Kind of like the way she always wore her hair up in a perfect bun that begged him to undo the clip like he once had and run his fingers through the auburn silkiness.

His heart thumped against his ribs so hard it was probably audible. His blood rushed in his ears. If he didn't stop thinking like that, he was going to do something impulsive and send her running. He reached for his coffee to make sure his dry throat didn't sound croaky when he tried to say something.

After a quick gulp, he looked at Victoria again. Or tried. She still wouldn't make eye contact, angling her head to supposedly observe the men at the bar instead. "If I didn't know you so well, I'd think you were checking out the other guys."

"Excuse me?"

His mouth twitched at her polite response. The restaurant was loud, but not that loud.

She'd heard him. At least she finally looked at him, her gorgeous hazel eyes aiming at him across the table.

Those eyes. Still had the ability to shoot heat behind his ribs and make him want to move way faster than he should. Made it so easy to remember why as a junior in high school, he'd chosen to date a freshman.

Well, at first he'd wanted her as another conquest. He'd gotten tired of the wild and shallow girls he'd won over and then discarded when he had become bored. But Victoria, her goodness and wholesomeness, offered a fresh attraction and new challenge.

He'd never expected to fall in love. For the first and only time in his life.

Even then at only fifteen, she'd had something special. A grace and elegance that made her seem almost untouchable. Unattainable.

It was more than physical. More like a quality that emanated from her core. And lured him to her.

It wasn't enough when he'd gotten her to fall for him. He'd wanted more. Wanted her love forever. Wanted to marry her, when they were old enough.

But she'd never belonged to him. Never even gave him her heart. She had proven that when she'd ended it. When she'd chosen her father over Cillian.

*"I can never see you again. I'm sorry."* Her words, raw and strangled by tears over the phone, were captured in his memory forever.

They had filled him with fury at first, an anger and pain that drove him from Chicago to wander across the country for years. But now, they motivated him like nothing else.

She hadn't wanted to reject him. She'd said she was sorry, and he knew she had meant it. She'd been controlled, made to do it by someone who held her captive. Who probably still held her in his grip.

The server appeared with Victoria's cheesecake and Cillian's multi-layered slab of carrot cake. The teen boy asked on autopilot if they needed anything else, then swung away and trudged off before they would've been able to answer if they'd wanted to.

"You had questions for me, right?" Cillian dug into his cake with a fork and casually glanced at Victoria. Better to put the ball in her court if he wanted her to let her guard down. Right now, she still held herself as rigid as the wooden back of the booth's uncomfortable seats.

Her eyes narrowed slightly, her tiny piece of plain cheesecake sitting untouched in front of her. "Why are you really here?"

He munched his mouthful of cake, then reached for his coffee to wash it down. "I told you. I came for you." The straightforward approach had always been best with Victoria. Knocked her back on her heels a little.

A hint of pink color flushed her cheeks.

He tried to hold back a grin. Still could make her blush. Very good sign.

Though that expression was new. The pinched lips and stern stare. "What precisely do you mean by that statement?"

He let his grin through. She always had been the most grammatical speaker he'd ever known, though he'd succeeded in getting her to relax the rules a bit when they had dated. "Just what I said." Though he knew as well as she did that there were multiple meanings and interpretations to his wording.

"I don't recall asking you to return to Chicago and accept a job at my workplace."

He chuckled. That was new, too—the sarcasm and spunk she'd surprised him with at her client's house. It made her even more attractive than when she'd only been sweet and agreeable to everything he'd wanted. He always enjoyed a challenge. "I never wait to be asked to do anything. You know that."

She met his gaze, unflinching. As if she was studying him and his motives. "It's been sixteen years. I don't know you anymore, and you don't know me." The definitive tone of her statement, the finality of it—almost like an order her father might give—rang in Cillian's ears like an irresistible call to battle.

"I bet I know a lot more about you than you want me to."

She looked away then, reaching for her fork.

What was she thinking? He couldn't tell quite as well as he used to be able to. Though even as teens, she'd been hard for him to predict. She viewed the world so differently and had different priorities. The classic opposites-attract relationship. But man, did they ever attract.

The sixteen years since he'd seen Victoria hadn't dimmed her beauty one bit. They'd only made her more stunning. The baby fat in her cheeks had disappeared, heightening her perfect features, high cheekbones, and large hazel eyes. The lines appearing just slightly at the edges of her mouth and corners of her eyes suggested she must smile and maybe even laugh sometimes. She used to with Cillian. A lot. At least once he could get her to relax and forget about what her father was going to do.

Was that still what held her back? Her father's control? Cillian would bet money on it. But he should confirm that his instincts, and the whole reason for coming back, were correct. "For example, you became a PT because your dad wanted you to."

Her gaze shot to his, giving her an excuse to lower the tiny clump of cheesecake that she didn't appear to want to eat anyway. Either she was full or nervous.

He'd bet on nerves. Which also meant he still had an effect on her. Definitely something he could build on.

"The work interests me and enables me to help people. I enjoy that."

He quirked a closed smile. So like Victoria. She didn't like to lie. But she would dodge a question and leave something out.

"And gives you a doctorate in a medical field. That's Daddy's standard, right?"

She dropped her focus to her plate, her tight swallow visible in the muscles along her smooth jaw.

He was hitting close to the mark. Maybe a bullseye. "I bet all your brothers and sisters are doctors, too, right?"

She cleared her throat. "No. Spring was a pro cyclist, and now she's studying to become a teacher." Victoria reached for her water glass. "And Treese is an athletic trainer."

Cillian laughed. "Bet your old man threw a fit."

Victoria finished her sip of water and lowered the glass, her attention flitting to Cillian's face as if uncertain she was safe to land there. But she did, a hint of pain in the depths of her eyes.

He dropped his smile and held her gaze. "Sorry. I shouldn't joke about it. It's probably been rough for them and you." And meant he'd been exactly right about her father not changing, still demanding and bullying his children into doing everything he wanted.

She didn't look away for a few beats, her eyebrows dipping slightly as she studied him. "It was difficult with Spring, but I'm hoping he'll come around, given the circumstances."

Was Victoria actually confiding in him? About her family? The encouragement pumped his pulse a little quicker. This was faster progress than he'd thought he might make. He had realized it could take a while to get back to where she would confide in him like she used to, when she'd poured out her hurting heart about her father, and Cillian had been her shoulder to cry on. And then when her mother was dying, he'd been her support and escape, too. At least until...

"Treese is his favorite, so he seems to have given her a pass."

Anger from the memory he'd accidentally stumbled into surged to the surface. "You should be his favorite, Vicks."

Her eyes widened, and her mouth parted slightly. Probably from the nickname he'd given her years ago. The one that would make her smile and melt like butter.

"You've done everything for him. You're perfect. You do everything he wants." Including dumping Cillian. Though he kept that reminder to himself.

"That's not true." She gripped her water glass on the table like she needed something to hold on to and look at. "I've... displeased him plenty of times. He only wants what is best for all of us. He loves us."

That was new. Cillian stared at her as she refused to look up. She'd always done what her father wanted, but she hadn't defended him. She would share how hard it was, how she wondered if he loved her at all, how she wished he wasn't so harsh and difficult to please.

Now, she sounded like a brainwashing success story. Her father's brainwashing. Years with a manipulative bully could do that to a person.

Cillian had seen it plenty of times as a social worker, especially during his years rescuing children in family social work.

She was still Daddy's girl, controlled and trapped under his thumb. But now it was worse. Now she thought she wanted to be.

Cillian had to find a way to fix that. "Have you ever stopped to wonder what you want? How you want to live your own life?"

Her features tightened as something flickered in her eyes. She grabbed her purse off the bench and stood, somehow avoiding the inelegant slide most people had to execute to exit a booth.

"Victoria, wait."

She angled toward the booth and glared down at him. "I

am no longer an impressionable fifteen-year-old you can charm or influence. It's good our jobs will not bring us into contact with each other frequently. I expect you'll maintain professionalism at all times and keep our shared past to yourself."

"Is Victoria Weston asking me to lie?" He only half-succeeded in holding back a smile. He couldn't help it. Her new fiery spirit and strength were amazing, making her even more beautiful and maddeningly attractive than ever.

"Of course not." She gripped the purse strap she'd placed over her shoulder. "If someone asks you about it directly, you should answer truthfully. But you don't have to offer unnecessary information. I certainly hope you didn't come here to hurt me or my family by dredging up past mistakes."

Ah. There it was. So she did blame him for what happened. He'd always thought so, though she'd denied it when she had called to break up with him.

Well, he'd have to deal with that obstacle, too, if he was going to succeed in rescuing her and winning her back. He sobered and met her accusatory glare. "No. I didn't come for that." With the exception of her father.

"Good." She pressed her lips together in that pinched expression. "If you've truly returned in connection with me for some unknown reason, then I suggest you leave again and forget about me as you did before. We'll all be better off."

He stood, quickly, so she wouldn't have enough warning to leave.

She barely got in one step back in the second it took for him to stand in front of her, forcing her to look up at him instead.

"I never forgot you, Vicks. Never."

She stared up at him, frozen with her elegant brows pushed together and a battle of emotions playing out in her eyes. Fear, confusion, anger, and what he hoped was longing. For him.

She spun on her heels and left, the fear or anger apparently winning out. For now.

He wouldn't leave this time, even if she asked him to. He'd changed in that way, too. He had learned how to fight bullies and win.

Her father would not control her for the rest of her life. No matter what it took, Cillian would set her free.

*"I NEVER FORGOT YOU, VICKS. NEVER."* Cillian's voice echoed in Victoria's mind as she turned onto her street.

She blinked at the light rain that smattered her windshield, blurring the darkness beyond.

But the image of Cillian's eyes when he'd said those words appeared more clearly in front of her mind's gaze. So intense. So...passionate.

Her heart twisted behind her ribs. Did he mean it?

She'd imagined he had forgotten her the moment he'd left Chicago. The moment he found another girl to date, which wouldn't have been long, given his looks and charm.

His list of conquests before her had been long, according to high school gossip and judging from the multiple girls who had threatened her to leave Cillian alone, until Cillian had learned of their threats. Then the girls mysteriously began to give her a wide berth in the school's hallways.

He'd always been protective. And her fifteen-year-old self had, of course, wanted to believe everything he told her, including that she was the only girl he had ever loved.

Her chest pinched so hard it hurt. She would never be able to sleep tonight if she didn't let go of the tension that seemed to be winding her as tight as a rope. Not that she could sleep anytime soon. Despite the exhaustion weighing heavily on her shoulders, she had at least two hours of documentation left to do that evening. It was the consequence of getting so far behind on her appointments, thanks to the situation at the Trents'.

She slowed at her driveway, releasing a calming breath through her nose. Her gaze caught on the red pickup truck parked in front of the garage door.

Hank.

A smile upturned her lips despite the fatigue that still sagged her limbs. It was like her mother used to say. She always had time to spend with her treasures.

As the baby of the family and the sweetest of them all, Hank was indeed a treasure. His truck stood empty, so he had apparently arrived long enough ago to have used his key to let himself in. At least Hank was one of the few people Max wasn't afraid of. Victoria's giant dog was likely reveling in his attention right now.

She pulled into the left stall of the garage and closed the overhead door with the remote. As she exited her car and opened the back door, she heard the door to the house open behind her.

"Help you with your bag?"

She turned to see Hank close the door behind him and send her a smile.

She smiled in return. "It does feel heavier by this time of day." She wasn't about to undo the training she'd given him in being a gentleman and helping others.

"You do look beat." He peered at her, his smile fading. "Probably still have documenting to do yet, too."

"Correct."

He winced, then reached to grab her bag from the back seat. He closed the door and met her gaze. "I'm sorry. I really have to talk to you." Turmoil swam in his blue eyes.

She could guess the cause of that anxiety. They'd discussed

it several times already, but he was still clearly struggling. "Of course." She stepped toward him to touch his arm. "Let's put on some hot chocolate, and we'll talk."

As they entered the house, Max rushed at them. The massive Leonberger nearly knocked Victoria over in his exuberance to reach Hank again, even though Hank had already been inside before she'd arrived.

Victoria laughed, then went to the kitchen to make hot chocolate while Max and Hank enjoyed each other some more.

She brought two mugs of Hank's favorite comfort drink into the living room, where they sat on the sofa.

Max joined them a few feet away on the carpeting, lying down and panting from his exertion.

Victoria chuckled as she glanced at her tired but happy boy. "Well, Max is certainly glad you came."

Hank grinned. "Max is the best. I really have to get a Leo myself. Once I figure out my life, that is." His mouth turned down at the corners, and he lifted his mug to take a sip.

"Tell me what's bothering you." Victoria was ready to catch her brother's gaze when he looked up.

"Oh, you know." He glanced away again, then set the mug on the coffee table in front of them. "This whole thing with Dad."

"Are you still doubting if you want to be a neurosurgeon?"

"There's just so much pressure, you know?" Hank leaned back against the sofa cushion and pushed his fingers through his chin-length blond curls. "I just wish he wouldn't act like it's my only option. Like I have to do it."

Victoria pressed her lips together to hold back her instinctive response. She didn't want to push or be too insistent and firm. Given what had happened with Spring, Victoria now realized the dangers of pushing so much that she did more damage than good. She would never want to make Hank believe he was of less value if he didn't fit into their father's mold. She'd unknowingly made that mistake with Spring and would not repeat it with another sibling.

But Hank had both aptitude and interest in the medical field. His intelligence made him perfectly suited for neurosurgery.

Most importantly, he was the one in whom their father had placed his highest hopes. From the moment he'd given Hank his own name—Henry Abraham Wilson, Jr.—their father had planned Hank's future as the one who would follow in his footsteps, becoming a premier neurosurgeon. His investment, expectations, and dreams had all been placed on Hank. It would absolutely devastate their father if Hank didn't follow that plan.

Their mom never would have wanted Hank to disappoint Dad so deeply. It would hurt both men so much, in different ways, damaging their relationship forever and potentially creating a rift in the family. No, Mom would have gently and tenderly guided Hank to do as their father wanted.

Victoria would do the same. She scooted closer to her brother and rested her hand on his knee. "It's completely normal at your stage of life to have some doubts and even to be afraid you might miss a wonderful opportunity elsewhere if you choose the wrong career."

Hank gave her a sidelong look. "I'm twenty-one, Vicki. Not eighteen."

She smiled. "I know. But you're about to start at Johns-Hopkins in the fall. It's a big step and a long-term commitment that might seem daunting right now."

His head turned, his attention aiming toward the brown and black dog on the carpeting. "I think it only feels like that because I don't really want to do it. I mean, I want to do something...*worthwhile* with my life. Something important." He brought his attention back to Victoria. "That's why I wanted to switch to physiatry after Spring's injury." His lips smashed together. "But then Dad shot that down."

"Oh, sweetie. I know it seems like that. And we both know Dad is not very delicate or tactful with his advice."

Hank gave a little snort, his mouth angling into a half smile. "Is that what you call it?"

She chuckled. "He really does love you and wants what's best for you."

"Which is whatever he wants."

She paused, thinking a moment before continuing. "In a way, yes, but what he wants is truly what he believes is best for you."

"What if he doesn't know what's best for me?"

A viable possibility. But Victoria kept the thought to herself. In this case, she wasn't convinced Hank's sudden change of mind about neurosurgery was a good thing either. "Drink your hot chocolate, and let's think this through."

At least that returned the light of a smile to his eyes. "Okay, sis." He reached for his mug and took another sip of the hot brew.

"You've always wanted to be a neurosurgeon since the time you were a child. You played that game where you pretended to perform operations."

"Lots of kids like that game, Vicki."

"All right, but when you reached middle school and high school, you were drawn to science and always said you wanted to become a neurosurgeon."

"Yeah." His gaze drifted to the wall, as if he was far away, lost in thought. "But what if I only believed that because Dad programmed me to think that way?"

"Hank." She sent him a skeptical gaze. "Please. You know you weren't programmed or brainwashed. You can check with Robert, if you don't believe me."

"No." A self-deprecating smile shaped his expression. "Sorry. You're right. I did want to. But now...I just started to see things differently recently."

"When Spring had her accident."

His blue eyes shot to Victoria's face. "Yeah, exactly."

"Hank," Victoria leaned closer and rested her hand on his shoulder, "you are the most compassionate person I know. It's truly a gift, and you will make a wonderful doctor because you have that empathy and compassion."

His lips tugged up at one side. "I hear a *but* coming."

She smiled. "But that compassion can also sway you to make sudden decisions or perhaps poor decisions that are based on the emotion you feel at the moment."

"You think I only want to switch to physiatry because I want to help Spring."

Victoria nodded. "And others like her, yes. That's a good thing. But you must remember that you would have a huge impact on people's lives as a surgeon, too. You would save lives every day."

"True." His mouth worked as it always did when he was deep in thought. "But it doesn't seem like enough somehow." Discontentment weighted his voice, cinching her ribs.

She wanted to see him happy and fulfilled. But more than that, he needed to do the right thing. Praise the Lord, Hank was a Christian as Spring and Victoria were. She could go deeper with him and give him the kind of help that would truly make a difference. "Have you prayed about this?"

Surprise lifted his eyebrows. "You mean about Dad? You think I'm not honoring him the way the Bible says I should?"

"Well, that is a point, and you'd need to pray about that. But I was actually thinking of your vocation. Have you asked God to show you what *He* wants you to do for your career? That's so much more important than what I think or even what Dad wants."

"Right, as usual, Vicki. I can't say I have been praying about it, at least not as much as I should. I'll take more time to do that." He shot her a glance that looked almost guilty. "And you're right about my emotions running all over the place. Yesterday, I actually thought I might switch to pediatric oncology."

"What brought that on?"

"I read an article about a three-year-old girl who's suffering from a rare form of acute leukemia. They haven't found a successful treatment for it yet."

"See?" She squeezed his shoulder. "You're compassionate."

"And confused, I guess." He let out a laugh as he set his mug on the table and stood. "Anybody told you lately that you're the best and wisest sister ever?"

She rose and smiled at her little brother, who now towered over her. "I believe you just did. I love you, Hank."

"Love you, too, Vicki." Hank bent and enveloped her in a hug with his long arms. "Oh." He pulled back. "I should've asked—how was your day? You look beat."

The urge to share pressed against her lips—about the hostage situation at her client's, Cillian materializing out of the past, and the brief meeting with him she still couldn't forget. The anxiety that was making itself at home in her stomach and mind. The unease about Thomas's odd behavior and his hints of some kind of danger.

But she hadn't had the luxury of pouring out her heart and thoughts to anyone since she was fifteen. She had a much more important purpose and duty to fulfill.

She smiled. "It was fine. Now go home, go to bed, and don't give this another thought until you've had a good rest."

"Roger." Hank chuckled as he said goodnight to her and then Max before leaving through the garage.

Vicki went to retrieve her work notebook computer and begin the long night of documentation. She would do her best to take her own advice and not give her clients' personal problems or her own—Cillian included—another thought.

The Lord's mercies were new every morning. She would rest in that promise to face tomorrow. Whatever her heavenly Father had in store, He would provide all she needed to weather it in His strength.

# CHAPTER
## SIX



Dr. Henry Weston malpractice suit.

Cillian glanced at the open doorway to his new office as he typed the search terms into the computer's Internet browser.

The hallway was empty. Not that anyone could see his screen, since it faced away from the door. But better safe than sorry.

These people were Victoria's co-workers. Probably had a high opinion of her father, the famous Chicago neurosurgeon.

But everyone had secrets. Especially bullies like Victoria's father, people that always got what they wanted, that climbed ladders to success and pushed down anyone who got in their way.

Dr. Weston's days of getting away with those tactics were over, at least with Victoria.

Cillian had about thirty minutes between the early morning orientation meeting that had just ended and the next meeting with Racquelle to sign more paperwork. He wasn't about to waste another second before working on the real reason he'd come back and taken this job.

Given his observations during the all-too-short dessert meeting with Victoria last night, there was no question she

43

was still under her dad's thumb. It was way past time to cut her loose and let her live her own life.

And Cillian knew how to do it. Since she was obviously not going to free herself, he'd have to go to the source—her father. Cillian would have to force him to let her go.

A tall order, but not an impossible one. Cillian had developed more than one technique for handling bullies and power abusers in his years as a family social worker. With a guy like Henry Weston, persuasion was out, as was intimidation. The only thing that would work was leverage.

Cillian scanned the results of his search on the screen, hoping to find the leverage he needed. Most physicians, and especially surgeons, seemed to encounter a malpractice suit at some point in their careers. Victoria's dad had been practicing for decades and was one of the two best neurosurgeons in the country, according to the Internet. Some disgruntled patient had to have sued him.

Sure enough, the search results showed three—no, four—malpractice suits brought against Dr. Henry Weston, Chicago neurosurgeon. Cillian clicked on the public records result first and skimmed the information.

Not very helpful, other than giving him the name of the plaintiffs. He backed up to find the news media coverage. Handy that Dr. Weston was so well known, especially in Chicago. The coverage was more detailed than for most mal—

The beat of his smartphone's ringtone cut into his thoughts.

He glanced at the caller ID. JaKobe Riley, requesting a video chat.

Cillian accepted the video call and picked up his phone as the boy's face appeared on the screen. "Hey, bud, how are you doing?"

"Hi." The frown tugging the nine-year-old's mouth wasn't a good sign.

"I can tell something's wrong. What's up?"

The boy shrugged his small shoulders under his blue shirt.

"Is it your mom?"

"I haven't seen her in like forever."

"You didn't get to see her last week?" The arrangement for parental visits meant JaKobe's mom could have supervised visits every other week.

"I guess."

"Oh, good." Cillian kept his expression as serious as the boy's. "It's not your mom, is it?"

JaKobe shrugged again. After they'd initially met, it had taken Cillian about two weeks to get the boy to say anything to him. That happened when a kid grew up getting smacked whenever he cried or talked too much around the adults in his life. Any communication at all was a victory and showed how much JaKobe had healed and grown.

"Let me guess. You're worried about your new foster family."

JaKobe finally looked at the screen and gave a small nod.

"They're good people, JaKobe. I made sure of that. You know I wouldn't put you anywhere that wasn't safe." Cillian had also stayed in Philadelphia long enough for JaKobe to move in with the Hamakers and start adjusting before he'd left for Chicago.

"We gotta eat dinner together, and I have to go to church."

Ah, so it was the structure and rules—things that would give JaKobe the stability and security he didn't know he craved. It was a hard adjustment for a kid who thought neglect was normal.

Cillian leaned back in his chair, holding the phone in front of him as he settled in to help JaKobe through the shock of experiencing a stable family for the first time in his life.

He'd given JaKobe and the other kids he'd worked with his personal phone number for this very reason. So they had one person they could count on to help them whenever they needed it.

They would never again experience his fate. They would never be alone and vulnerable, having to fight to survive and free themselves from the dysfunction and misery their parents created. He would make sure of that. And he would help more kids as soon as he could get back to family social work.

But for now, he would calm JaKobe's fears and then return to another kind of rescue. Saving Victoria from the father who'd kept her as his prisoner for so many years, she didn't even want to get free.

Apparently, God's mercies in the new day didn't mean Victoria would successfully keep Cillian Doherty from her thoughts.

She gripped the steering wheel a little tighter as she turned into the wealthy neighborhood where Thomas lived. She had hoped not having to stop in the office that morning, since it was her day off, would enable her to avoid bumping into Cillian, but her mind crashed into him at every turn.

*"I never forgot you, Vicks. Never."* The memory of his statement and his expression when he'd said it sent a shiver down her spine.

What kind of outlandish declaration might he make next? And what if he did so in front of her coworkers or Racquelle, her boss?

Perhaps Victoria should've stayed longer at Mason Grill instead of letting fear get the best of her and fleeing like a flustered young girl. Thanks to her impulsive escape, she still didn't understand why he had returned out of the blue. He couldn't actually mean he intended to rekindle their romance, could he?

The thought twisted her stomach. But if he supposedly hadn't forgotten about her and still had romantic interest, then what had he been doing for the sixteen years of silence?

On the other hand, she had made it very clear that she would no longer date him or see him. Ever. She'd been surprised how easily and quickly he had respected her wishes at the time. Nothing like the bad-boy rebel he was then.

He hadn't tried to call, hadn't appeared outside her bedroom door, throwing pebbles against it as he had many nights when he'd wanted her to go on some adventure with him.

She never had gone with him in the middle of the night, despite his persistence. Not until...*that* night.

A night she definitely did not need to remember at this moment. She needed to be calm and ready to hear Thomas's concerns, or whatever was weighing on him, without being distracted by her own problems.

The large ash tree that stood outside his fence, barren of leaves, caught her gaze, guiding her to his home and her thoughts to a less unnerving subject than Cillian.

No one would have retrieved the mail from the box yet since it was only a few minutes before nine. Though she could have beaten the mail carrier, as well. She would check anyway.

She looked ahead at the closed, wrought-iron gate as she pulled into the driveway, then shifted the car into park and opened her door.

She planted her heeled boots on the ground, her gaze going to—

A man lay flat on his back by the mailbox. Silver hair and beard.

"Thomas?" The name nearly choked in her throat as she launched from the car toward him, her feet slipping on the icy patch where he lay.

She knelt on her long wool skirt and felt his neck for a pulse. Something oddly textured met her fingers. She bent to see behind his ear.

Blood, frozen and dried, tracked down his neck from somewhere behind his head.

His face was white as snow, his lips tinged blue.

She moved her fingers on his cold skin. She could have misjudged where the pulse should be.

Horror and disbelief surged up her throat.

No. There had to be a pulse. There had to be.

She pushed to her feet and hurried to the car, fumbling for the phone in her purse on the passenger seat.

Pressing the emergency button for 911, she rushed back to Thomas.

"9-1-1, what is your emergency?"

Victoria put her phone on speaker and laid it on the ground as she answered the operator and began CPR. But as she performed chest compressions, her eyes and even her heart knew she was too late.

He was dead.

# CHAPTER
# SEVEN

Victoria pulled the blanket the EMT had given her tighter around her shoulders, but it was no use. She couldn't get warm.

The heat in Thomas's mansion was probably working normally, set to the temperature she usually found much too hot. She couldn't tell. Cold seeped relentlessly through her limbs as she sat on the settee near the stairs in the entryway.

Thomas was gone.

She couldn't believe it. And yet, she could. Hence, the grief —the early, denial stage of grief, Robert would tell her if he was there.

But no one comforting or helpful was there, only police officers who didn't know Thomas, traipsing through his house. At least that meant they were looking for evidence of the person who had...done this. The word was hard for her to think, even in her own head. *Killed* him. Killed Thomas.

Her throat shrunk as tears filled her eyes again. *Oh, Lord. I pray he came to repentance and faith in You before it was too late.*

He had asked her about her Christian faith once, giving her the leeway despite job regulations to share the Gospel. But he had only said she'd given him a lot to think about.

What if—

"Victoria Weston?" A middle-aged man with brown hair and a mustache approached Victoria. His brown blazer instead of a police uniform indicated he must be higher ranking than the uniformed officers on the scene. "I'm Detective McCully. I understand you were the one to discover the body?"

The body. He had been Thomas Briscoe only yesterday. Last night. Even hours ago, depending on how long he had—

"Ma'am?" The detective's gruff voice drew Victoria back to his decidedly unhappy expression as he looked down at her. "You found the body?" Impatience laced his tone.

"Yes." She would get to her feet to avoid having him glower down at her, but he stood too close for her to do so gracefully.

"Since this is an unattended death, I need to ask you some questions."

"Of course. And I'm sure you'll want the timeline and details of what I saw for your investigation." She looked at the empty hands he planted on his hips. Shouldn't he be ready to take notes from her account of what happened?

"Investigation?" His already furrowed brow gained some additional lines.

"Of Mr. Briscoe's death."

"We're not investigating, ma'am. This is an accidental death. We just need to dot the *i's* and cross the *t's*, and then you can go."

"Accidental?" Alarm filtered through her, sending a tremor across her shoulders and into her arms.

"A slip and fall."

"No." Victoria started to shake her head slowly from side to side. "That can't be."

"He was an old man. Happens all the time."

Victoria stared up at Detective McCully, trying to meet his gaze with a firm one of her own. "I'm a physical therapist, Detective. I understand the risks of age, balance, and limited mobility. And I can assure you he did not slip and fall by the mailbox.”

“I'd believe her, Detective.” The deep voice swung Victoria's head to the right. Cillian stepped close to her, looking tall, handsome, and strong.

How had she not seen or heard him enter the house? The same way she hadn't seen the detective or the other officers as she had sunk into grief and deep thought.

But she couldn't possibly ignore him now, not with the way everything in her wanted to lean toward him. Or even to rise to her feet and sink into his arms, to depend on his strength for a moment. The call of an old habit when she'd been a lost, hurting girl.

“I came as soon as Racquelle told me what happened. Are you okay?” His gaze rested on her, genuine concern reflected in his dark eyes.

“And you are?” Detective McCully's tone sharpened even more, as if he was annoyed by the interruption.

“He's a coworker.” Victoria jumped to respond before Cillian. Who knew what shocking answer he might give, especially if he did intend to rekindle a romance.

“Cillian Doherty,” Cillian extended his hand to the detective, “clinical social worker with CareFull Home Health.”

McCully dropped the handshake quickly and returned his attention to Victoria. “I just need to confirm what time you arrived and found the body.”

“Eight fifty-six a.m.” Her mind cycled through the points she could make to show the detective Thomas's death wasn't an accident.

“And what did you do when you found the body?”

“I called 9-1-1 and felt for a pulse. There was none. Then I performed CPR, but I believe he was already deceased when I arrived.”

The detective gave a grunt, not confirming or denying her statement. “That's all I need. You're free to go.” He sent Cillian a suspicious glance, then turned and stalked away.

"There's a man who needs to get out more." Wry humor colored Cillian's observation.

She stared at the detective's retreating form. Should she go after him and try to convince him he was wrong about Thomas?

"You look pale. And cold." Cillian suddenly squatted in front of her, filling the space far more effectively than the detective had. Heat from his body seemed to wrap around her. Or perhaps it was his gaze so close to hers, his eyes penetrating and intense.

His heat found the cold spaces inside her, tingling like sparks, sending energy and life to where she needed it. "You're not okay." His observation felt like a doctor giving a diagnosis after the patient had begun to heal.

"No." She moistened her lips with her tongue. "They're saying this is an accident."

His black eyebrows lifted. "You don't think it was?"

"Absolutely not."

"You mean you think he was..." Cillian glanced around as if checking earshot, "murdered?"

She gave a small nod. "I know it sounds far-fetched, but I don't believe for a moment that Thomas went out to get the mail and slipped. He would never have done that."

Cillian studied her face, then stood. He didn't believe her.

That shouldn't sink her heart, disappointing her far more than the detective's disregard.

"You'd better tell the detective before he leaves."

Her gaze shot far up to Cillian. He did believe her. More warmth poured in behind her ribs, warming her all over. But it wouldn't do for Cillian to have even an inkling that he still had such a powerful effect on her.

She pushed the blanket off her shoulders, letting it drop to the settee as she stood. Very close to Cillian.

She tilted her chin up from his chest to meet his gaze, trying to squash her skipping heartbeat and regulate her breathing despite the visceral response she apparently still had to him. "I was about to tell him before you interrupted."

Cillian angled his head down toward her without moving any closer or farther away. His coal-colored eyes roamed her face, then paused...on her lips.

Her breath caught.

His mouth slowly tugged up at one corner. "Don't let me stop you." The flirty, amused twinkle in his eyes woke her up.

"I would never let you stop me." The words spewed out with the irritation that flared in her stomach. She marched away, searching for the irascible detective.

Honestly. How could she have fallen under Cillian's spell again, even for only one moment? Cillian Doherty was trouble. She knew that. She was mature enough that she shouldn't be swayed by attraction, no matter how handsome he was.

And apparently, he thought she needed his prodding to speak with the detective. He probably thought she was still the shy, quiet girl who'd followed his lead in everything. Sixteen years of being the only mother figure to the strong-willed Weston siblings had cured her of all hesitation and timidity.

A brown blazer caught her eye near the front door. Detective McCully stood there, speaking with a female uniformed officer. Good. Victoria would have a chance to make her case.

"Detective McCully."

He turned her way as she approached, his mustache following the deep frown of his lips.

No matter. She wasn't trying to make a new friend. She was attempting to see that justice was done for Thomas. But she had to take the correct approach, or the detective would never listen to her.

She gave him a smile as she stopped in front of him. "I'm so sorry to bother you, but I can tell you're a thorough detective. I'm sure you would like to have all the facts related to what happened to Mr. Briscoe."

The sound of a small grunt reached her ears, but she held on to her sincere expression, pretending she hadn't noticed.

"As Mr. Briscoe's physical therapist for the past eleven months, I would be willing to give expert testimony that he would never have walked out to the mailbox on his own to retrieve his mail."

A smirk curved McCully's lips. "This isn't going to court, Ms. Weston. Like I said, it's a slip and fall."

She worked to keep her voice even. Showing her rising irritation wouldn't help. "But my point is that he could not have been outside of his own free will."

"Are you saying he wasn't able to walk that far? Some physical disability?"

"Not precisely, no."

The smirk grew.

She pressed on quickly before he could cut her off or leave. "He fell and broke his hip eleven months ago, which is when I began to see him. He healed from the hip replacement but lost his confidence. His balance was fine, but he didn't believe it was. That's the reason he wanted to continue physical therapy. I was helping him with balance exercises, but they were mostly to improve his confidence, rather than compensate for a deficit in function."

Her senses heightened at the sound of footsteps over her shoulder. The tingling through her body told her who it was before she checked, spotting Cillian as he stopped by her side.

Her stomach twisted with sudden nervousness. Good grief, she wasn't competing in a debate competition in high school. She was a professional, experienced PT giving her clinical opinion to a detective. If Cillian wanted to listen, that wouldn't bother her.

The inner pep talk didn't have the calming effect she'd hoped, especially when she caught the look of victory in the detective's eyes.

"So you're confirming he was capable of walking to his mailbox."

Victoria restrained the exasperated breath that tried to escape her throat. That's what happened when she let Cillian distract her. She pressed her lips together and gave the detective the stern look she used with argumentative siblings. Perhaps that would garner more respect. "What I'm confirming, Detective, are two facts that contradict the theory that Mr. Briscoe slipped and died accidentally. First, he had no balance issues that would have made a fall likely if he had walked to his mailbox."

McCully's mouth opened, but she held up two fingers.

"Second, and most importantly, he absolutely never personally retrieved the mail from the box in any season of the year. He asked me to retrieve it for him on the days I was visiting, and he knew I was coming today, as we had made an appointment. Additionally, whenever I was not coming for an appointment, he had either his housekeeper or groundskeeper bring in the mail."

The detective's eyes narrowed. "That's interesting information, ma'am." His begrudging tone said he didn't want to give her even that much. "But there could be a hundred reasons we can't know of to explain why he departed from his routine today. He could've wanted to get the mail because he was expecting an important package or letter. Maybe something that shouldn't freeze outside in the box. We'll never know."

"Don't you think that's a stretch, Detective?" Cillian's deep voice beside her jumpstarted her pulse. "She makes a strong point. If the man never walked that far outside because he was afraid to, he wouldn't have done that today, especially when it's freezing and slippery outside."

McCully tilted his head up to look at the taller man. "Exactly. It was slippery. That would make anybody fall, balance issues or no."

"Really, Detective?" Challenge edged Cillian's tone. "You're going to ignore—"

Victoria touched Cillian's arm to stop him. "I understand

you want to be certain, Detective. I'm sure there must be a great deal involved in declaring something a...murder, rather than an accident." Applying the word *murder* to Thomas, her kind friend, ballooned a lump in her throat. But she pushed through, blinking rapidly to prevent the moisture that rushed to her eyes from pooling into tears. "I'd like to help you as much as I can by telling you about two more details I noticed, if you'll be kind enough to give me a few more moments of your time."

Cillian's sculpted triceps tensed under his leather jacket beneath her fingers.

She shot him a glance.

He looked down at her, heat emanating from his eyes, but whether from irritation at her placating the detective or a reaction to her touch, she couldn't tell.

She pulled her hand away and focused on McCully. "Since I've been here so many times, I can tell you there has always been a Victorian-era Persian rug over there at the base of the stairs." She angled to point in the direction of the staircase near the settee where she had sat. "It's missing."

"Yeah, I can see it isn't there." McCully's tone was as gruff as his expression. "That doesn't automatically mean it's missing. It could've been sent to the cleaners. Or maybe he decided to throw it in the trash. We'll never know."

"The rug was extremely valuable." She had to work hard to maintain a peaceful tone in the face of such blatant disregard for facts that indicated foul play. "And then there are the paintings." She pointed toward the two framed paintings on the wall near where they stood. "These are in the wrong—"

"Ma'am," the detective held up a hand, "I'm sure you have plenty of little problems you're noticing because you want to make sense of this death. I see it all the time. Some people feel better if their friend got killed on purpose instead of a freak accident." He shook his head. "But either way, it doesn't change the fact that Mr. Briscoe died today, and that's just what it is."

She opened her mouth, but frustration blocked the response she was trying to form. Something that wouldn't be rude or offensive but still make the detective listen to basic reason.

"Now hold on. You aren't even hearing the evidence." Cillian folded his arms across his black jacket. "What are you afraid of, Detective? Or are you trying to hide something?"

McCully's eyes flashed as he glared up at Cillian.

Wonderful. Now he was far too angry to listen to anything.

"I suggest you and your friend here stop trying to play amateur detectives and leave this to the professionals. This isn't a movie. This is real life, where the detectives determine what happened, and civilians are not allowed to interfere." He hit Victoria with his glare before he spun on his heels and stalked to the door. He paused by an officer and gestured toward Victoria and Cillian.

"I think we're about to get kicked out." Cillian sent her an unbothered smile. Clearly, his insides weren't knotted into an anxious wad like hers.

She shouldn't have pushed the detective to the point of making him so angry. That never worked with people like him and only created a difficult environment for everyone. Hopefully, she hadn't made the rest of the day too unpleasant for everyone who had to work with McCully.

"Let's spare them the trouble." Victoria started for the door, sending the female officer McCully had just spoken to an apologetic smile.

"You should keep after him." At least Cillian waited until they were past the officer and out in the cold, open air before sharing his opinion. "You're right. You've convinced me this wasn't an accident, and you didn't even get to finish telling him all the things you noticed." Cillian swung in front of her, stopping her progress as he faced her.

His admission shouldn't warm her inside, despite the frigid air. It shouldn't matter that he believed her. But it apparently did. She looked up to meet his gaze. "Detective

McCully will never take my observations seriously. You heard him. He's determined to declare this an accident."

"Then go above his head."

"That would only make him angrier."

"So what?" Cillian pushed his bare hands into the front pockets of his jeans. "He could be trying to hush it up for some personal reason. Or maybe he's one of those cops who likes power too much and will never admit he could be wrong."

She scanned the driveway. Hopefully, none of the officers had heard his characterization of police. But the closest officers were outside the open gate, where she had found Thomas.

The memory of his pale, lifeless face sent a pang through her. Perhaps the detective was right, in a sense. Whether an accident or intentional attack, Thomas was still gone.

Either way, she wasn't a member of the police force. She could do no more than she'd already attempted. "I've told the detective my suspicions. I'll have to let him decide what to do with his own job and his own case." She stepped around Cillian without risking another look at his face.

"Still always following the rules, I see." His accusation followed her, causing her to pause mid-stride as he hit the old wound that had never quite healed.

*"You keep doing what you're told, and you're going to hurt more than me."*

She kept going, trying to outpace the painful echo of Cillian's young voice from the past as it chased her, carried on the icy wind.

# CHAPTER
# EIGHT

How COULD she have changed so little after so many years? Cillian ran the fingers of both hands through his hair as he stared at the computer screen. But he didn't see the phone number and address there.

He saw Victoria as she had dropped her gaze and hurried around him outside the Briscoe mansion, as if she knew she'd better run instead of having to admit she was still ridiculously tied to following rules. Doing whatever people in authority told her to do, including the clearly mistaken Detective McCully.

Cillian had tried his best to break her free from that habit when they'd dated. He'd arguably been the opposite extreme back in those days, but even now as an adult, he could still see she had a problem.

Rules were fine when they were good ones and protected people. But to blindly acquiesce and submit to every person with authority, no matter how stupid or wrong they were, was ludicrous. He couldn't figure out if it was fear, some kind of cowardice that made her do that, or just a brainwashed instinct thanks to being raised by Henry Weston. The man made sure there were hefty consequences anytime he didn't get his way.

Nothing physically abusive, as far as Cillian had been able to figure out, but he had an unhealthy psychological hold on Victoria. Even when she'd been away from him with Cillian on dates and there was no way he could've known what she was doing, Victoria had still never crossed him. Except for that one night. Which majorly backfired because she wouldn't break free from her father. She would only follow his rules to the letter, to the bitter end.

And now she was doing the same thing with the police. Well, Cillian couldn't force her to be more persistent with Detective McCully, but he could end her father's control over her.

He blinked at the screen, clearing his concentration to see the phone number of one of the plaintiffs in a malpractice suit against Dr. Henry Weston. One of the four suits he'd found evidence of online was clearly a dud. The claim was flimsy, a transparent attempt to claim trumped-up psychological damages that hadn't made it to court or any kind of settlement.

The other three suits had all been dropped. Could be they lacked enough evidence to go to court or even to induce the insurance company to settle. But knowing Dr. Henry Weston, Cillian was banking on another explanation.

Weston couldn't have much of a bedside manner and didn't care about people. But he was an expert neurosurgeon who would never botch a surgery if he could help it, if only to keep his reputation and pride intact. That said, everyone made mistakes. And Dr. Weston was only human, despite what he'd programmed his daughter to think.

If he had made a mistake and someone sued, Weston wouldn't be above using unethical and maybe even illegal tactics to quiet the scandal before it could come out. He would do anything to protect his career and reputation. To get what he wanted. Cillian had proof of that firsthand when

Weston had made his daughter reject Cillian against her will.

There had to be a skeleton in one of the closets of these lawsuits. Maybe more than one. All Cillian had to do was gather enough evidence that Weston had intimidated, threatened, or harmed a plaintiff, and he would have the leverage he needed to make Weston do the right thing. To let his daughter go.

Cillian copied the phone number from the screen into his smartphone. Maybe he'd get lucky, and the first plaintiff he called would be the winner.

The rings stopped at two and a half. "Rebekah Leeland."

"Hi, Mrs. Leeland." He smiled to inject an approachable sound into his tone. "You don't know me, so I know it's a little strange for me to call you. But my mother was a patient of Dr. Henry Weston as I understand you were. She had a brain tumor."

"Oh?" Puzzlement colored the woman's tone, but she didn't sound closed off. "I'm sorry to hear that. Is she all right?"

"Yes, ma'am, she is. But I'm afraid that isn't thanks to Dr. Weston, if you know what I mean."

"Did something go wrong?"

Cillian sighed. "Well, let's just say she's considering suing him for malpractice thanks to what happened. I was hoping you could offer some advice that might help her. I understand you had to sue him, too?"

"Yes. Yes, I did." Rebekah's voice warmed slightly. Her defenses were coming down.

"That must have been a difficult situation. Is there any advice you could give my mom and me?"

"Well, I'm afraid I won't be of much help."

"Anything you can offer would be greatly appreciated."

"I wanted to go to court, but my lawyer ultimately talked me out of it."

Great. If that was true, there wouldn't be any smoking gun

here. Cillian swallowed the disappointment and forced pure curiosity into his tone. "Oh, why was that?"

"She said I wouldn't be able to win since we couldn't prove that my poor results after the surgery came from a mistake on Dr. Weston's part. She said I would lose all the money I invested if I tried to keep going."

"I'm sorry to hear that. So we should make sure we have conclusive evidence if we move forward."

"Oh, yes. I thought my slow recovery, and the fact I needed another surgery when I'd been told it would be corrected with only one, was enough. But my lawyer said the opposition was saying the fine print covered that additional surgeries might be required and recovery depended on my own effort. I couldn't get into therapy right away, you see, and then I felt so tired and sick on most days."

Ah. A case of the patient not doing all she could for the recovery. And Weston was sure to protect himself against different recovery rates. He wouldn't be foolish enough to guarantee any results.

This plaintiff was a dead end. Unless… "I really appreciate you sharing your experience with me. This is really helpful. Just one more question—did Dr. Weston or anyone from his staff, or maybe his lawyers, contact you directly while you were suing?"

"Oh, no. That wasn't allowed. They could only contact me through my lawyer."

"Right. That makes sense." And left Cillian with nothing to use. "Thanks, again. You take care now."

"Thank you. And my best to your mom."

His fabricated mother. But a little white lie was worth it if he could help Victoria. He ended the call with a few more nice words, then glanced at the clock on his computer.

Time for another meeting, this one with the other social worker on staff at CareFull.

Freeing Victoria would have to wait. But not for long. Since he'd become a family social worker, he had a perfect track record of freeing victims from their abusers, from those who controlled them or dictated their lives in various ways.

Victoria and her father were his next, self-assigned task. He wouldn't give up until he had completed the job.

———

Was Cillian right? The question swirled in Victoria's mind and tangled uncomfortably in her stomach as she pulled into the parking lot at Life Pregnancy Care Center. She parked her car in the row of vehicles by the sidewalk that ran the length of the brick building.

Ever since the morning's events and Cillian's parting shot, doubt wouldn't let her rest. She'd spoken with Max about the dilemma when she'd stopped at home to eat lunch, as well as to feed Max and let him outside. Though highly intelligent, the dog hadn't been able to offer much insight into whether or not there was truth in Cillian's inference that her adherence to rules was a problem.

More to the point, her chat with Max also hadn't shed any light on the question of whether or not she should take another run at the skeptical detective. She hadn't told Detective McCully about Thomas's concerns yesterday when she'd seen him. Thomas had been so unlike himself—nervous and even frightened when he had said he couldn't trust anyone.

She should've told Detective McCully that. She probably still should. Perhaps that information would make him reconsider his belief that Thomas's death was accidental.

She glanced at the dashboard clock. She had texted ahead that she would be late for her volunteer shift today, since she had needed to fit in the appointment with…Thomas.

Her heart squeezed. If only they'd had the appointment. Now she would never have one with him again. Never see him again.

The reality of his death, his absence and what it meant, set in a little more. Pain pressed into her ribs under the weight of it. A tear fell down her cheek. She would miss him very much.

But she couldn't walk into the pregnancy center with tears running down her face.

She dug a tissue from her purse, dabbed away the moisture, and quickly checked her reflection in the visor mirror to ensure no evidence remained of her sadness.

She opened the door, and cold air slammed into her. Her thought boomeranged back to her at the same time. Evidence.

If she was right that Thomas's death was not an accident, that meant it had to be a murder. And if it was a murder, the killer had to have left some evidence at the scene. Evidence the police likely wouldn't have found since McCully was so determined the death was accidental.

Victoria walked briskly toward Life Center's entrance, the wind biting her cheeks. What if the killer was someone with access to Briscoe's estate? He or she could remove all evidence before the police could return to the scene.

Should she—

"Victoria, good to see you." Kathleen Burns' friendly voice bumped Victoria from her thoughts.

Victoria had apparently walked inside without consciously thinking about doing so. She directed a smile at the founder of the local Christian pregnancy center who was restacking children's blocks in the lobby. "Hi, Kathleen. I'm so sorry I'm late today."

Kathleen straightened and pushed her long brown hair, streaked with lovely silver strands, behind her shoulders. "You are by far the most punctual volunteer I have ever had. And you told me first thing this morning that you had to see a patient, so you aren't even late at all." Kathleen pointed toward the hallway past the welcome desk. "Sydney, however, has been waiting for you quite impatiently."

"Oh. I didn't see Warren's pickup outside." Though Victoria could have easily missed it with how deeply engrossed she was in her thoughts.

"He said he had to get to work at the plant, so he couldn't wait to take her home after the prenatal class this time."

"That's understandable." Victoria was just grateful Sydney had someone to drive her to the pregnancy center and her doctor's appointments. As Sydney's mentor through Life Center, Victoria chauffeured the pregnant teen whenever she could, but her work schedule made her unavailable most weekdays. Thank the Lord, Sydney's brother cared enough about his sister to help her.

"Do you think you could take her home?"

"Of course." Victoria met Kathleen's gaze, which stayed on her with a peculiar expression dipping the woman's eyebrows.

"Are you all right?"

Victoria hesitated before answering. She wouldn't lie and say she was fine. "What makes you ask?"

"You seem…" Kathleen's head angled slightly to one side, "sad."

A small smile touched Victoria's lips. "I can see why Jada says your people-reading skills are legendary."

"So I'm right." Kathleen's mouth pressed into a line as concern shaped her features.

"I lost a friend today."

"Oh, Victoria." Kathleen stepped closer and touched Victoria's arm. "I am so sorry." She watched Victoria for a silent moment, sincere grief in her eyes. "Was your friend ill?"

"No." Victoria shook her head slowly. Thomas's face when she'd found him—cold, dead—blocked her vision. "He was killed." The words escaped before she'd meant to say them. So very unlike her.

She blinked and straightened, meeting Kathleen's gaze as her own cleared. "I'm sorry. I didn't mean to share that."

"Honey, we all need to share our burdens. And you are carrying a very heavy one. You have nothing to apologize for."

Victoria mustered a small smile. "Thank you."

Kathleen nodded. "The passing of a loved one is hard no matter how it happens. But to have life taken through crime—

murder—is the hardest. I'm so sorry." Kathleen spoke as one who knew from experience.

Oh, yes. Kathleen had shared in her testimony at a fundraising event that her son had been murdered.

Dismay pushed up Victoria's throat. "Oh, I didn't think. I'm sorry, Kathleen. I didn't mean to bring up bad memories for you."

"Stop right there." Kathleen shook her head, the set of her jaw firm. "We share our burdens and hurts here. I know you haven't needed that from us so far, but I am always here to listen and encourage you."

A guilty flush rushed to Victoria's cheeks. Kathleen had all she could do to provide that service to the unwed expectant and new mothers who came through Life Center's doors. She didn't need to waste her time on Victoria.

"I appreciate your kindness." Victoria mentally pulled herself together. Her troubles were unimportant compared to the burdens Kathleen already carried—her own and others'. "But I had better find out what Sydney wants to discuss with me and drive her home, if she's ready."

Kathleen gave her a smile that was a little too knowing, then looked over her shoulder. "She was just back—"

"Victoria!" Sydney Morris burst into view from the hallway. The normally skinny sixteen-year-old looked ready to pop at thirty-five weeks into her pregnancy. She rushed toward Victoria and stopped in front of her, dramatically thrusting her slim arms into the air at her sides. "What am I gonna do?"

Victoria waited a moment before answering, trying to be the calm in the emotional storm Sydney often seemed to stir up to a frenzy, whether warranted or not. "Why don't we go to my car, and you can tell me what happened while I drive you home?"

"No. I can't." Sydney clamped her hands on her belly, shaking her head side to side.

Victoria glanced at Kathleen, hoping for a sign to indicate

whether or not the situation was as dire as Sydney seemed to believe.

Kathleen put a calming hand on the girl's back. "Why don't the two of you sit down here? No one else is in the lobby right now, so you can have a private chat."

And Sydney could calm her system before she did any damage to the baby.

"Good idea. Let's sit for a while." Victoria nodded to Kathleen as the older woman guided Sydney into a chair, and Victoria pulled out another one from the row along the wall. She set the chair in front of Sydney and sat down so they could face each other.

"I'll be in the classroom if you need me." Kathleen sent Victoria a sympathetic look before she turned and headed for the hallway.

"I think my mom's going to kick me out." Sydney's voice tightened with panic. "Like for real this time."

So that was it. Sydney's mother had held the same threat over her daughter's head since the day Sydney had announced she wanted to keep her baby. "Tell me what happened."

"She said, 'If you have it today, don't come home.'"

*It.* As if the beautiful baby girl growing inside Sydney was an *it.* No doubt Sydney's mom was trying to hold on to the idea a baby was a meaningless clump of cells. Sydney had shared that her mother had aborted several babies. Pretending the baby wasn't human was one way to cope with the guilt of that decision.

"I'm so sorry she said that to you." Victoria leaned forward and rested her hand on Sydney's in the girl's lap. "That's awful, and I know how much it must hurt to have your mother say something like that. I think from what you've told me, she's hurting, too, through all this."

Sydney looked away and shrugged one shoulder. "I guess."

Victoria's heart warmed. Not all teenagers in Sydney's position would even be willing to consider the idea that their parent could have feelings. "It's probably a reminder to her of things she'd rather forget."

Sydney met Victoria's gaze. "You mean the babies she…"

Victoria nodded.

"Hadn't thought about that. But she still shouldn't kick her own daughter out of the house. And her granddaughter." Sydney pulled her hands out from under Victoria's to rub her round belly.

"I know. You're right. But we all do many things we shouldn't." Speaking of which…Victoria chose carefully how to approach the truth she'd been trying to persuade Sydney to reveal for months. "Have you contacted your little girl's father? Has he said if he'll take you in or offer you support?"

Sydney dropped her gaze before Victoria could read anything in her eyes. "He's not answering my texts."

Same answer as the last time Victoria had asked Sydney about the unidentified man. "Have you tried calling him?"

The teen's chin dipped a microinch with what Victoria assumed was an affirming nod.

"If you give me his name, I might be able to help you reach him." It was the same offer Victoria had made three times before. But she didn't know what else to try.

Sydney shook her head from side to side as she folded her arms above the baby inside her.

"Sydney," Victoria kept her tone calm and patient, "you know who the father of your baby is. Many of the girls who come to the center don't know that. It's a gift you can give your daughter, to be able to tell her the name of her dad. Why won't you tell us who he is?"

The teen finally lifted her gaze. "I told you. He doesn't want anyone to know."

"But you say he loves you."

"Yeah." She nodded emphatically. "He totally does. He's going to marry me."

"Then why wouldn't he want anyone to know he's your baby's father?"

"It's…" Sydney shifted in the chair, "complicated."

Victoria held back a sigh. What secret was the girl so intent on keeping? The man or boy who'd fathered the child must have quite a hold on her. If only Victoria could figure out how to shake Sydney free of that hold. "You said he supports your choice to give birth to your daughter?"

"Uh-huh." Sydney avoided Victoria's eyes as she gave the answer that seemed incongruent with the rest of the story. But at least it meant there wasn't another person in Sydney's life pressuring her to abort her child.

"Then I would think he would want to support you in raising her and financially, as well."

"Oh, he's going to. We're going to get married."

Victoria watched Sydney, trying to figure out the puzzle. Was the girl simply engaging in wishful thinking? Or making things up? If Robert were there, he could tell Victoria if Sydney was lying. Having a brother who was a psychiatrist could be handy in some ways.

Victoria took in a breath. "Okay, when do you think that will happen?"

Sydney shrugged both shoulders. "Sometime after she's born, I guess. But he said he loves me and wants to marry me. So I know he will."

And Victoria knew a dead end when she reached one. "Well, in the meantime, I don't want you to worry about your mom and your living situation. The rooms here at Life Center are all full right now, but I've gone through the process to become an approved temporary foster home. You can stay with me if your mom does evict you. Okay?"

"Really?" The teen's blue eyes widened. "Oh, that would be awesome." She pressed her hands to both sides of her face as a smile blossomed.

Victoria returned the smile. "I wanted to tell you the news at an appropriate time. You don't need to worry about a place for you and your little girl to stay."

"Thank you so much." The breathlessness in Sydney's voice expressed the joy and gratitude written on her face.

"Don't get too excited before you see my house. It's tiny and nothing fancy. But it'll do if needed."

Sydney giggled. "It'll be so cool. I know it."

"Let's get you home for now. And you know you can always text or call me if you need me."

Sydney nodded, still smiling as she scooted out of the chair and stood. "You're like the nicest person in the world."

"That's Christ in me, Sydney. I'm not nice or good on my own."

Sydney squinted slightly. "Oh, right. Like how you said Jesus lives inside you and changed you to want to do good things. It must be cool to always know what's the right thing to do."

Victoria fell silent as she helped Sydney put on the winter coat that couldn't quite close over her extended stomach.

If only Victoria did always know the right thing to do. Even with the guidance of the Holy Spirit, she wasn't always sure, as in the situation with Detective McCully. Or perhaps, she was letting fear or timidity keep her from sharing more of what she knew about Thomas.

By the time she closed the passenger door of her car for Sydney and walked around to sit behind the wheel, she knew what she must do after dropping off the teenager. She needed to pay a visit to the police station.

# CHAPTER
# NINE

"DETECTIVE MCCULLY?" Victoria paused outside the open doorway of the detective's office at the police station.

He angled his brown-haired head to see past the computer monitor on his desk. His eyes narrowed, seemingly at the moment he realized who she was. Not exactly pleased to see her, apparently.

She mustered a smile and stepped inside. "The lady at the desk said I could come back to your office."

"Did she?" The question sounded rhetorical, and decidedly unhappy.

Perhaps this had been a bad idea. But if Thomas was murdered, and she had evidence the detective didn't, she had a duty to share that information. She would simply do so in a manner that was as kind and non-threatening as possible.

"May I borrow a moment of your time?" She walked farther into the office, pausing at the chair that stood opposite the desk. "I realized that, in my shocked state this morning, I forgot to give you some information. I know detectives like to have all the facts to do their job, so I must apologize that I forgot to tell you everything earlier." She paused, but he still didn't ask her to sit.

He simply stared at her. At least his expression appeared to reveal he was thinking, not about to shout at her or send her away.

Hesitation could be helpful. Victoria stepped in front of the chair and sat before he could tell her not to. "I forgot to tell you what Thomas said to me the day before his death."

"You saw him yesterday?"

"Yes. I'm sorry I didn't think to tell you that. I was sure you'd want to know."

His lips pressed together.

Taking his silence as a sign she could continue, she carried on. "Thomas was highly anxious. Normally, he was a self-assured, confident, and commanding person. But that day, he seemed rattled and told me expressly that he couldn't trust anyone." He had also told Victoria that she was the only one he could trust, but she wasn't sure the detective would like hearing that. It sounded too self-aggrandizing and might make her seem to be trying to trick the detective into trusting her, as well.

"A lot of people say things like that, Ms. Weston. It's not evidence of murder."

"I understand that." She kept her response even and unbothered. "But it was the way he said it that was concerning. He was nervous and almost frightened, which was very uncharacteristic for him. When I asked him specifically if he couldn't trust even his close friend, he confirmed by implication that he could not."

"By implication." McCully's mustache angled with his smirk.

"Yes. He indicated that he thought he could trust his lawyer, but also said his nephew and niece were waiting around for him to die."

McCully picked up a pencil from his desk and rotated it between his fingers as if he was bored. "Did he give you evidence of any of these…suspicions?"

"No, but he clearly had some or he wouldn't have been so

upset. And before I left, his friend came to the house, and Thomas sounded so angry with him. I'd never heard him speak in that tone to anyone before, not even his niece and nephew."

The detective dropped the pencil on the desk and leaned onto his elbows. "Look, Ms. Weston. People not liking their relatives and having arguments with friends—none of that is evidence of a crime, okay?"

Disappointment sank in her stomach. "But I believe he thought he was in danger. He said he was going to explain everything to me this morning." The last words caught in her throat. Was it really only that morning that she had been going to see Thomas, to talk to him, to try to help?

"It's like I said. I get that you want to make sense of what happened, but all deaths are hard and all of them are senseless." McCully pushed to his feet and walked around the desk to stand by her chair. "I'm afraid I just don't have time to listen to everyone talk through every death I deal with in my job. There are therapists that I'm sure could help you."

Victoria blinked. Had he actually told her to go see a therapist because she thought her friend was murdered?

McCully extended his hand toward the doorway. "I do have to get to the investigations that are ongoing right now, so..."

She lifted her purse off her lap and stood, trying to meet the detective's gaze.

He looked away, directing his attention at the door he apparently expected her to hurry through.

She walked at a normal pace, weighing the risks of trying to say more. She paused by the doorway and turned back. "Thomas was also—"

"Look, miss." McCully cut her short with his gruff tone as he crossed his arms over his white shirt. "There's going to be an autopsy because that's standard in unattended deaths like this. And I'm confident it will confirm his death was an accident. I can't do anything else for you, and you need to stop taking up this department's valuable time with your theories.

Good day." He swung toward his desk and marched behind it without another glance her way.

Pinching her lips together, she left his office. So much for Cillian's suggestion she try again with the detective. She'd known he wouldn't listen to anything she had to say. What a completely futile exercise.

At least they were going to perform an autopsy. Perhaps the results would be the evidence needed to convince the detective that Thomas had been—

A vibration in her coat pocket halted her thoughts. She paused in the hallway to pull out her phone and check the text message.

*We need to talk. Come to the house tonight at 8:00.*

Dad. She could guess what he wanted to discuss. Hank's waffling on his education and career would be making their father very unhappy.

Unless he had heard about the death of her patient that morning. Her father was well-connected, but he didn't usually hear news sooner than media outlets. And he wouldn't likely know that the wealthy shipping magnate was Victoria's client, since she'd never mentioned him.

This urgent text must be about Hank. She responded with confirmation she would be there, though she'd have to hurry straight to the house from Pilates class.

Hopefully, she would have more success smoothing things over and keeping the peace with her father than she had with Detective McCully.

---

Cillian pulled his motorcycle into the driveway of the middle-class residence and parked alongside a black Nissan outside the closed garage.

Good. Should mean someone was home.

Cold calling Rebekah Leeland had gone pretty well, despite having to talk over the phone since she lived out of state. But asking about a malpractice suit was a pretty delicate topic. Face-to-face would be much better. Cillian would be able to gauge expressions and reactions to better tell if the plaintiff was telling the truth. And he'd know how to adjust his own approach if needed.

This plaintiff, Marsha Faint, and the other plaintiff Cillian intended to contact, both lived in Chicago. Hopefully, Marsha would be as willing to share as Rebekah was.

Cillian swung his leg over the Harley-Davidson Road King and removed his helmet, taking off his gloves to run his fingers through his hair. Pretty nippy ride tonight. Just the thing to give him some added energy for this conversation. The chance to get one step closer to saving Victoria.

He strode up to the door and rang the bell. No dog barked from inside. Good. A nervous dog could've cut the interview short much too quickly.

He resisted the urge to punch the doorbell again, though it felt like an eternity. Wouldn't help to irritate anyone inside.

The door finally swung open. A woman with short gray hair peered up at him through round glasses.

Cillian gave her his friendliest smile. "Hi, are you Mrs. Marsha Faint?"

Her eyes widened slightly as she craned her head to look at him from her petite height. "Yes."

"I'm so sorry to interrupt your evening like this, ma'am. I hope you weren't in the middle of dinner." Though he'd actually chosen six o'clock as the time to arrive since it was likely she would be home.

She just stared at him.

"My name is Cillian Doherty, and I have sort of an unusual question for you. It's a delicate matter about my grandmother." A grandma seemed like a more relatable choice for this plaintiff. "She was a patient of Dr. Henry Weston, but things didn't go well. I learned you had a similar experience, and I wondered if you could offer some advice to help my grandma. She's thinking of suing Dr. Weston for malpractice, but we don't know if we should or how to go about it. Can you offer any advice?"

Her pale lips disappeared further as she mashed them together. Her gaze darted past him into the darkness.

Interesting. Was she afraid someone was out there?

"No. I can't. I don't know how you got my name." She was headed toward closing the door on him. That was obvious just from her tone.

He jumped in quickly to try again. "I'm so sorry to intrude on your personal life. Someone who wanted to be kind to my grandma let us know about what happened to you. And how you were brave enough to sue for malpractice. It's so courageous, and I just wondered if you could share how it went. What the results were for you, and maybe what you would suggest my grandma should do? She would really appreciate your kindness."

"I can't help. I don't know anything." Marsha's response was terse, almost robotic as she darted her gaze back and forth beyond him, like she was checking for something or someone.

But she hadn't settled out of court. Cillian knew that from his research. So she wouldn't have to keep quiet because of a non-disclosure agreement.

"Anything at all would help my grandma. Please, Mrs. Faint?"

The *please* drew her attention up to his face. She stared at him for a few beats, then dropped her gaze.

"I really can't." She backed away. "You'll have to go."

"Ma'am, are you okay? If someone has frightened you—"

She started to swing the door shut as she shook her head. "No, no. I can't talk. You need to leave."

The door closed. Deadbolt clicked into place.

Cillian restrained the instinct to knock or ring the doorbell again, just as he'd held himself back from bracing the door open when she'd tried to close it. This wasn't the right moment for force, even if all he wanted to do was talk to her longer.

She was the one, the key to the leverage he needed.

Because when she'd looked at him that last time, fear had filled her eyes. She must have been intimidated, threatened, or blackmailed into silence. Which meant Dr. Weston had been guilty of the malpractice she'd tried to sue him for.

And he was guilty of illegally dissuading her from going through with the suit.

Now all Cillian had to do was find the evidence to prove it. Then he could force Henry Weston to finally set his daughter free.

# CHAPTER
## TEN



Victoria finished zipping her duffle bag before she turned to cast her youngest sister a confused glance. "Where was I?"

Treese folded her slim arms across the thoroughly immodest cropped and low-cut athletic top. Paired with her skin-tight leggings, the outfit left nothing of Patricia's fit body to the imagination. No wonder two men had joined the Pilates class she taught. "I mean, you obviously weren't here. You did a spine twist when I said to do a swan dive. You never make a mistake like that. I've never seen you anything but focused and pushing yourself in class."

Victoria sighed as she picked up the bag by the long strap and hung it on her shoulder. "I've had a challenging couple of days."

"Oh?" Treese lifted her sculpted dark eyebrows.

Wonderful. Victoria would have to give her some tidbit of information now. Treese's curiosity was legendary and could be dangerous if not quenched. "A patient of mine died suddenly. I found him."

Treese's brown eyes widened. "That's awful. Who was he?"

Victoria hesitated. "I'm not sure I should say. I don't know if the family has been notified yet."

"I'm *your* family." The chip Treese usually wore on her shoulder around Victoria was definitely present tonight.

Unfortunately, Treese also wasn't the soul of discretion. "I don't think the police would like me to discuss it with people. At least not until it's public."

"Fine." Treese's small jaw tightened. "I see you changed." She aimed her gaze at Victoria's long wool skirt and turtleneck.

It was true, Victoria usually wore her fitness clothes to and from Treese's Pilates class. "Dad asked me to come to the house at eight." She checked her watch. "I'd better hurry, or I'll be late."

"I'd say I'll see you there, but I'm going to close down here and then I'm going out."

Victoria tried to keep from narrowing her eyes at her baby sister. "A new boyfriend?"

"*Boyfriend* is a strong word. Meeting a guy, but maybe I'll find another guy, too. We'll see what happens." Treese's mouth angled in the little defiant smirk she had worn when she first started challenging Victoria's authority at the age of twelve.

Victoria bit her tongue. She would be less controlling. Less hands-on and micromanaging. Less scolding. She had pushed and chided Spring too much and had caused significant emotional damage without realizing it. She didn't want to make that mistake again.

Treese was two years younger than Spring, but still almost twenty-seven now. She needed to make her own decisions, good or bad, and suffer the consequences. At least Treese didn't cross their father. There was no danger she would disappoint him or create strife in their family—much worse possibilities than displeasing Victoria.

"Then I guess I won't see you until the birthday party." Victoria turned and headed across the nearly empty studio.

A few women and one man—a new student that evening—chatted by the counter where Treese sold energy drinks and bars. Victoria waved at Donna, the student she was usually next to in class.

The man was only interested in watching Treese, of course. Handy that someone who loved attention so much managed to attract every male within sight, even when she wasn't trying. Although the skimpy outfit could be her way of trying.

"Is the party at eight?" Treese's voice signaled she was following Victoria to the glass door at the front of the studio.

"I'm going to verify with Dad tonight, but I believe so."

"Okay. I can help with the decorations. Probably put them up Sunday night."

"Good." Victoria pushed into the door, angling toward Treese slightly. "Have a good evening. And be careful." She threw a glance at the man ogling her baby sister, protectiveness and discomfort tangling in her torso.

Treese glanced in the man's direction, then chuckled as she moved closer to Victoria, hurrying her out the door. "Don't you worry, sis. He's not even my type." Though the pleased glint in her eyes said she wouldn't mind indulging in the flirtation anyway. "Goodnight!" She waved at Victoria and turned away.

The cold slap of the night air on Victoria's cheeks wasn't unwelcome as she turned left and started up the sidewalk at a brisk pace. She probably needed the chill to combat the frustration boiling in her stomach.

That girl. Victoria never had been able to get a handle on parenting Treese. She'd done her best, but Treese had decided at twelve that Victoria was not her mother and couldn't tell her what to do. It hadn't helped that Spring set the example for that way of thinking. But Treese was two years younger. And unlike Spring, Treese also rejected Victoria's God—their mother's God—in favor of worldly, secular ideology.

Victoria blew out a breath that puffed as a cloud in front of her face in the light of streetlamps. The popularity of the coffee shop and restaurants in this area, and the nearby condos, meant Victoria usually had to park several blocks away from Best You Fitness, Treese's studio.

Tonight was no exception. She'd better step up her pace or she would be late to meet her father. She wasn't about to let that happen.

At least the sidewalk was well lit and the neighborhood fairly safe.

A well-dressed couple walked arm in arm toward her, huddled close in their winter coats. "Good evening." Victoria smiled at the redheaded woman who returned the greeting.

The man with her gave a quick, "Hello," as they passed.

The biting temperature likely explained why the couple appeared to be the only other pedestrians. Only two weeks ago, Victoria would've seen at least thirty people on the way to her car. But now, an empty sidewalk stretched in front of her.

Everyone was wisely staying indoors in the plummeting temperatures. Everyone but those who had parked what felt like a mile away.

Victoria slid her hands into the pockets of her coat, her thin, dressy wool gloves not providing enough warmth for fifteen-degree weather. She tucked her chin into the coat collar that should really come up much higher on her neck.

Trying to forget the cold starting to cut through her coat, she focused on the click of her heeled dress boots as they sounded out the steps to her car.

But what was that other noise?

A different kind of click and a different rhythm.

She glanced over her shoulder.

Shadows and patches of light from the streetlamps created a patchwork design across the empty sidewalk.

No people.

A shiver tracked down her spine. She spun away and looked ahead, walking faster.

Her imagination must be more active tonight than usual.

She'd found her friend, the victim of a murder, only that morning. It was no wonder her nerves were on edge, and her mind was conjuring danger where there wasn't any.

She turned the corner to the next block.

Loud music blared from the bar ahead, its yellow signage flashing. At least the intoxicated customers that loitered outside the bar in the summertime were indoors in the warmth. Although even their unruly presence might be helpful to calm her imaginings of a nighttime phantom.

The pounding bass beats from the music inside the bar thudded loudly as she passed, drowning out any chance of hearing a follower.

But why would anyone be following her? The logical question paused the rapid trot of her pulse.

Even if Thomas had been murdered, that wouldn't mean she was suddenly in danger. There were no greater risks to her now than on a normal evening when she walked the dark Chicago streets.

Come to think of it, the risk of danger when walking alone in Chicago at night was always quite high.

She kept up her quick clip as she left the bar music behind and strained to hear past the cold wind that singed her ears.

The fading music was all that was audible for several minutes.

Wait. There it was. The same sound behind her.

Footsteps.

Her pulse sprinted. Adrenaline and cold fright flowed into her bloodstream. Better to face an enemy head-on than be attacked from behind.

She stopped and turned around, gripping the strap of her bag with one hand. Maybe she could use it as a weapon.

But only the shadowed, empty sidewalk met her scrutiny.

She slowly released her held breath. This was ridiculous. She would never make it on time to Dad's if she kept checking for a phantom.

She aimed forward again, determined to control her imagination and reach her car before her fingers froze. Perhaps she should speak with Treese about finding a different location for her fitness studio, one that had an adjacent parking lot.

The sight of traffic at the stoplight ahead was comforting. Even though she had to wait at the corner for the traffic to pass through, it meant people were present. A deterrent to anyone who might have nefarious intent.

As she waited, hands sheltered in her pockets, a man and woman walked up to the light on the opposite corner and also waited to cross. They'd arrived separately, so didn't seem to be together. But the presence of fellow pedestrians who appeared harmless was also a balm to her nerves.

The light changed, and Victoria crossed the street, nodding to the other pedestrians as they passed.

Only a short distance left now. She pushed a little faster as the traffic sounds faded and the number of cars on the road dwindled. She would park in the most isolated area.

*Clip, clip.*

The unmistakable sound reached her ears.

She stopped herself from swiveling her head to look. Wouldn't that only make her appear afraid? Or perhaps it would be a good thing to show she wasn't an unsuspecting victim. Yes, that sounded correct.

She kept walking but turned her head to look over her shoulder.

Something dark moved.

# CHAPTER
# ELEVEN

THE BLUR of movement happened so quickly, Victoria wasn't positive she actually saw it.

She stopped and peered into the shadows near the entrance to the building that held condominiums.

Was that the outline of...a person? Tucked in the corner by the doorway?

She didn't breathe. She couldn't be sure it was a person. It was so dark there.

But fear spiked through her.

*Lord, please keep me safe. If there is real danger, if there's someone there, please protect me. I know You can do all things in Your power.*

The prayer filtered courage through her, combating some of the fear and clearing her mind.

Should she stay facing the person, if there was one there?

Or should she make a break for her car? It was close now.

A noise broke the silence. The door started to open from the inside.

The shadow moved, darted out from behind the door as it fully opened. A person—a man, it looked like—dressed all in black, seemed to slither along the wall and quickly disappeared into another dark crevice.

Laughter yanked her attention to two well-dressed men in their twenties who emerged from the building, evidently unaware they'd spooked a lurker.

If a lurker was all he was.

Victoria tried to breathe as she hurried toward her car.

The two young men followed behind her at a normal distance, talking and laughing, like an added assurance from the Lord that she was safe now. He had answered her prayer and protected her.

*Thank you, Lord.*

But despite her gratitude and silent prayer, she felt as if she didn't breathe again until she'd driven away, leaving that section of the city and the dark phantom far behind.

By the time she drove into the gated community she'd grown up in and pulled up to her childhood home, blood was circulating through her normally, and her pulse had calmed to a healthy range. The car heater blasted physical comfort while her prayers of thanks in her conversation with God all the way there had strengthened her inwardly.

She couldn't be more grateful for His protection and presence with her this evening. She had called Treese to warn her about the phantom man in case he was still lurking in the area when she left her studio. But Treese had said she wasn't going to be leaving alone anyway, so she was fine.

Victoria indulged in an exasperated sigh at no one as she reached for her purse on the passenger seat. *Fine* being a relative term, considering Treese was apparently going to have another fling with a man she'd only just met.

But Victoria wasn't at her father's to discuss Treese. Hank was no doubt the person on the topic list in Dad's mind, and Victoria should be gearing up to address that situation and maintain peace between the two.

She checked the clock in the dash. Two minutes. Cutting it much too close.

She leaned over to look in the rearview mirror and smoothed some flyaway hairs and a loose strand that had escaped her bun. Dad would wonder about her if she appeared a mess.

She hurried to the front entrance and reached to insert her key in the lock, but the large door swung open.

Hank's tentative smile greeted her. "Hey." He opened the door the rest of the way and stepped aside to let her in.

"Hi." She closed the door behind her, then looked at her brother.

He slid his hand through his blond curls as he always did when he was nervous. "He wants to talk to you about me, doesn't he?"

"I assume so." She gently squeezed Hank's shoulder. "Don't worry. It will be fine."

"Okay." He managed another shaky smile. "Thanks, Vicki."

"I need to go in."

He nodded.

She walked briskly from the entryway into a long hallway, her boots clicking on the tiled floor. Like the sound of the man who'd followed her tonight. He must have worn dress shoes to make such a sound. Wasn't that odd for someone who—

No. She needed to focus on her father and making peace between him and Hank.

She stopped in front of the closed door to his office library on the left. She knocked.

"Enter." Her father's familiar voice reached through the heavy wood.

She opened the door and walked in. Hopefully, he wouldn't make a point of her being one minute late. She was never late.

He looked up from his massive wooden desk as she entered, his short auburn hair as neat and tidy as always, and his expression serious and observant. He never seemed to change. Except for the tiny, silver flecks of hair that caught the light, suggesting that even he was aging.

"You've had a busy day."

Her stomach clenched as she stopped in front of his desk, waiting to discover what he meant by that comment.

He looked at his wristwatch and then directed his gaze to her, his eyes angling toward her hair.

She reached up, her fingers touching a loose clump she must have missed in the darkness of the car. And he wasn't going to let the one minute of tardiness go. Not a wonderful start for Hank's sake, but there was always some critique to overcome.

"I came directly from Treese's Pilates class." Supporting Treese's business should earn her a few grace points. "I must have mussed my hair when I changed, and I didn't want to hurt her feelings by leaving early, of course."

He leaned back in his chair and pointed with his whole hand to the chair that faced the front of his desk.

She removed her coat and hung it over the back of the chair, then smoothed her skirt beneath her as she sat.

"Henry, Jr., is confused." Her father's hazel eyes, sharpened by his intensity, locked on her. "I've talked to the boy, but he's been rattled and forced off course by what happened to your sister."

Victoria nodded. She took his pause as her queue to speak. "What happened to Spring has affected all of us deeply. We all need time to process it in our different ways."

Her father arched an eyebrow. "You're not throwing away your career."

She pressed her lips together, taking a moment to consider her next words and check her approach against her model— her mother's peacemaking technique. She would show sympathy for both parties, try to help their father understand his child, but then conclude with a positive assurance that all would work out in favor of their father. "No, I'm not. But Hank hasn't done so either. He's young and hasn't yet begun his career. He feels great compassion for Spring and others in need. He'll find his way once his emotions settle down."

Her father leaned forward, planting his forearms on the desk and bringing his hands together as he stared at her. "Neurosurgeons don't make decisions based on emotion, and youth is absolutely no excuse. I never deviated. Robert never wavered from his goals, even as a child."

Victoria held back the urge to point out that Robert's goals had been his own, not his father's. Though they had, thankfully, aligned with what Dad wanted him to do—excel as a medical doctor of some kind. Robert had also set an incredibly high bar when he'd graduated high school at fifteen. It wasn't fair to hold Hank to the same standard. "We aren't all identical, so our paths may look different. But I know Hank wants to make you proud. He worked very hard to graduate a semester early from Harvard and be accepted into Johns Hopkins for next fall."

Graduating from college early may have been a mistake, given how much time Hank now had on his hands to ponder and doubt his future. But Victoria kept that observation to herself. The point was to remind Dad of Hank's accomplishments.

"He cannot end up like Spring."

They both knew her father didn't mean paralyzed from the waist down. He meant Spring's rejection of his aspirations for her, that she had become a professional cyclist and was now pursuing a teaching degree.

"I will not allow that to happen to Henry, Jr. Is that understood?" Her father pinned Victoria with the look of warning that used to send fear shooting down to her toes.

Now it only twisted her stomach and dried her mouth as she nodded. "Yes." She cleared her throat. "I don't believe there's any cause for concern. I've spoken with him, and he's no longer considering physiatry."

Her father's shoulders visibly lowered, and his glowering expression lessened a fraction. "Good."

She wouldn't mention that Hank was pondering pediatrics now. Hopefully, that was only temporary, and he would soon return to his goal of becoming the neurosurgeon their father had planned he would be since Hank was born.

"I'll continue to guide him through this time of upheaval." She infused her tone with confidence. "He'll be fine."

"He can't throw away his talent and his future. I won't let him do that."

She nodded. "I know. He won't. I'll make sure of it. He respects you too much to...." she almost said *hurt you*, but that would suggest a vulnerability her father wouldn't appreciate her assuming he had, "...disregard your advice."

"You had better be right. I've invested too much in that boy's future to watch him throw it away for nothing. He'll thank me for it in the end."

"I'm sure you're right." Victoria didn't want Hank to regret any of his decisions either. And decisions made in the midst of confusion and emotion where almost always regrettable. She had firsthand knowledge of that.

"Good. I'll trust you to take care of it then." He lowered his gaze to the thick hardcover book lying on the desk in front of him.

They were apparently done. She let out a breath slowly enough not to be heard and stood. "I wanted to confirm the time for your birthday dinner next Tuesday. Is eight o'clock the best?"

"Birthday dinner?" He didn't lift his head from the book.

And Victoria knew why. She heard it in his voice—the subtle shift she'd only learned to recognize after Mom was gone. The reason he hadn't met Victoria's gaze for months after Mom's passing.

"Yes. Eight p.m. sharp." He'd regulated his voice to his normal firm, no-nonsense tone, and he still didn't lift his gaze.

Victoria took a few steps toward the door, but something made her pause and look back.

And for a moment, she didn't see his head angled down toward the book.

She saw him as she'd come upon him sixteen years ago, sitting upright but slumped, a posture she'd never seen him in before then. She saw his vacant, lost stare across the room at nothing. And she saw what she'd heard now in his voice, at the reminder of the annual birthday dinner her mother had cooked for him every year of their marriage.

Pain. Grief. Emotions she hadn't known her father could feel until that night when their lives had changed forever. That night she'd seen, as if through the tiniest clear streak across a dirty window, what her mother must have known about the man she'd married. The man she had loved.

That he, too, was human. That he loved. And that he, perhaps more than most, needed to be loved.

Victoria didn't have her mother's infinite compassion and love, but she would keep trying to do everything Mom would've wanted for her family. "Good night, Dad. I love you." She said the words as her mother had, often and generously, though Victoria had never heard him respond in kind.

So Victoria didn't wait for a response as she left. She only hoped and prayed that she would continue the witness her mother had begun of the love of Christ in her father's life so that, someday, he might realize his need for that love and salvation.

———

There she was. The woman Cillian hadn't been able to forget in sixteen years of trying. Now that was a sight a man could get used to seeing first thing in the morning.

Cillian couldn't shake the smile that stretched his mouth as he watched Victoria, looking impossibly elegant with her upswept hair and wearing navy blue scrubs as she talked to Racquelle at the counter in the open office area. Then again, he didn't want to lose his grin or the heat that shot through him when she was near. He would never get tired of the way she drew him irresistibly to her.

And the feeling was still mutual. That had been clear yesterday when her cheeks had flushed and her eyes lit like they used to when he'd leaned in close. When he'd been tempted to kiss her, right there in front of a bunch of cops.

She hadn't moved away. Which meant she still felt something for him.

Fired by the encouragement, he sauntered toward her.

"I'm sorry you had to go through that, but it sounds like you handled it correctly." Racquelle's dark curls swung as she tilted her head to one side. "We'll have a staff meeting to cover what happened and refresh the instructions on what to do in a home visit situation like that."

Must be talking about Victoria finding Thomas Briscoe's body.

"Morning, ladies."

Racquelle gave him the bright smile he'd hoped to get from the other lady.

But Victoria's eyes widened slightly as they landed on him. And not in a good way. Like she was alarmed to see him there.

Well, setting her back on her heels could be a good thing. Maybe she'd reach out to him for balance. And realize she needed a change, especially when it came to letting her dad run her life.

Might as well push her a little more off-kilter. "Did you follow up with McCully on the murder?"

"Murder?" Racquelle's mouth dropped open. "What murder?" She jumped her gaze from Cillian to Victoria.

"Didn't you tell her?" Cillian aimed the question at Victoria.

Her eyes narrowed a tad at the corners as she met his gaze.

He barely held back the chuckle that wanted to escape.

She'd always been cute when he ruffled her feathers.

"Tell me what?" Impatience edged Racquelle's tone.

Victoria turned her attention to her boss. "I thought there were some suspicious aspects to Mr. Briscoe's death. I shared those with the police when they were asking me about him."

"Do they think it's a murder?" Racquelle tossed a glance at Cillian.

He shook his head and answered before Victoria could downplay it. "The detective on the case is being muleheaded about it. Victoria has terrific evidence that points to murder, but he won't listen. I suggested she talk to him again or go above his head."

"I can't comment on that." Racquelle gathered some papers into a folder she had lying on the counter. "What you do on your own time is your choice, of course." She looked at Victoria. "But we wouldn't want CareFull to be associated with a criminal investigation, so you'd have to be cautious with how you go about any involvement."

Victoria gave a small nod. "Of course." She watched Racquelle walk away and disappear into the hallway while Cillian watched Victoria. Her profile anyway.

Her head suddenly swung toward him. "What are you doing?" She lowered her voice to a harsh whisper. "Are you trying to get me into trouble?"

He did chuckle then. As much as she'd grown up since they were teens, she apparently still freaked out at the idea of getting in trouble more than anything else. He grinned and shook his head. "Maybe things haven't changed so much after all."

She pinched her lips together and stretched her spine to straighter than straight since she already had perfect posture. "If you didn't come here to sabotage me or my life, then you have an odd way of showing it." She spun on her heels and marched away, headed toward the hallway that led to the back of the building.

He strode after her, catching up in seconds with his longer stride. "Look, you can't blame me for talking about the murder. I figured you would've told Racquelle you thought it was a murder."

"Why would I do that?" She kept walking, her breaths becoming a little heavy as she tried to outpace him.

"Why wouldn't you?"

She threw him an exasperated glance, then stared ahead,

speed walking to the end of the hallway. She snatched a purple parka off the line of hooks on the wall next to the lockers. "I wouldn't mention that because I knew she would react exactly the way she did. That she would be afraid I'll become involved in something that will damage CareFull's reputation." She swung the jacket behind her back and reached her hand toward one sleeve.

He grabbed the jacket and held it for her to insert her arms more easily.

But she froze. Turned to stare at him like he was a snowman who'd just come to life.

"What?" He lifted the outspread coat slightly to show she should put it on.

She slowly rotated forward again and slipped her arms into the sleeves. "Thank you." Her soft words floated up to him as she moved closer to the parka...and him.

Her familiar scent tickled his nostrils. She still smelled like lilacs. Never had figured out if it was from a shampoo or perfume or was just...her.

He barely resisted the instinct to rest his hands on her shoulders as the jacket fell in place there. Taking advantage of the situation would only prove her shock right. So he hadn't been the most chivalrous guy when they'd dated before. He hadn't had anyone to teach him how or why to treat a lady that way. But she would see he had changed.

He cleared his throat and took a step back as she pivoted to him, zipping up her jacket so that it lightly skimmed the curves of her slim figure. He pulled his gaze up to her face. "Well, I only wanted to find out if there were any developments. If you talked to McCully again and got him to listen to you."

She paused. Like she was trying to decide whether or not to admit something. "Yes, I did."

Warmth pumped through him. She'd listened to him. Taken what she would think of as a big risk—daring a cop's disapproval and anger—because Cillian had persuaded her to.

"And as I predicted, he still wouldn't take the evidence seriously and became quite irritated with me." She went to the lockers, taking a key from her pocket to unlock one. "I knew I shouldn't have bothered him further." She pulled out her purse and PT bag, which probably contained essential items she didn't want to freeze if left in her car.

"What are you talking about? Of course you should have. And now you'll need to go over his head."

She slammed the door shut on the locker and swiveled her head toward him. An unusual flash lit her eyes. "No, I will not. I need to leave him to do his job, exactly as he told me to do in the first place." She pulled back the cuff of her jacket sleeve to check her watch. "And I also need to go to my first appointment." She pulled on a purple pair of thin gloves. "I hope you have a good day with whatever you're *supposed* to be doing." She threw him a glance and marched to the door.

"Hold on." He scrambled to grab his leather jacket from another hook and pushed through the door she'd let close behind her. How come she listened to everyone's orders but his?

He stuck his arms through the sleeves as he jogged after her. "Vicks, wait."

She stopped abruptly. So abruptly he nearly crashed into her. "I don't think you should call me that anymore." She didn't face him as she said it.

But she would have to if she expected to convince him she didn't want him to use the nickname she'd loved sixteen years ago. The one that had always made her smile or blush.

He stepped in front of her. "Why not?"

She lifted her gaze to his. No, she wasn't the naïve young girl anymore. She didn't shy away from eye contact now with that cute, embarrassed smile. Her hazel eyes held a grim firmness they'd never had before. And a confidence, determination, and strength that made her more beautiful than ever. But the orbs that watched him also held a wariness born of experience.

Experience with him or someone else? Either way, he didn't think he'd like the answer or what she was going to say next.

"Before you answer that," he cut in before she could speak, "we didn't really get dessert last night. How about dinner tonight?"

Her eyebrows lowered like she was getting ready to say a pretty heavy *No*.

"Or lunch or whatever kind of meal or coffee you're comfortable with." He gave her a grin. The one that used to melt her defenses.

"I still don't understand why you're here, but it's best that we see each other as little as possible."

Okay, melting was not the effect anymore. More like the opposite. He rubbed his hand along the back of his neck. "I want to tell you why I'm here. Isn't that worth getting coffee or something? I promise I won't get you into any trouble at all. It'll just be coffee."

Her gaze followed his hand as he dropped it to his side. "Why aren't you wearing gloves?"

"They're on the bike." He pointed to his motorcycle, and she swung to look.

"You're still riding a motorcycle? In the winter?"

He laughed. "Of course."

"You were driving a jeep yesterday." She brought her focus back to him, confusion shaping her features.

"And now the bike today. Want to go for a ride?"

Her eyes widened, making him laugh again.

He'd never forget the day he'd sat her on his bike and taken her for the first motorcycle ride of her life. Prim and proper Victoria had squealed for a block before she'd settled for squeezing his waist in a death grip from behind. Which hadn't bothered him one bit.

She frowned. Apparently, the memory wasn't as enjoyable for her. Or she was trying to pretend it wasn't. "I'll stay with my warm and safe car, thank you."

"Ah, yes." He looked at her gray Honda Civic. "The dependable—"

Something white on her windshield caught his eye. Not snow. Paper? He walked to her car. Sure enough, a piece of paper was folded into a square and tucked beneath the wiper blade. He pulled it out. "Don't tell me Victoria Weston got a parking ticket." He tossed her a grin.

She arched one eyebrow. "In the employee parking lot?"

"Maybe you have a secret admirer."

She blew out a sigh. "Give me that." She reached for the note.

He almost couldn't squelch the urge to hold it out of her arm's length, but that would only convince her he was still the immature kid she'd known before. He let her slip it from his hand.

A much better choice since an electric shock buzzed through him when her gloved fingers brushed his skin.

Her long eyelashes lifted as she glanced up at him. Then she dropped her attention to the paper and unfolded it.

He stepped to her side and looked at it, too, prepared to make a crack about the flyer some salesman had probably left.

But his gaze collided with cut-out letters pasted to the paper like something out of a movie.

*Leave well enough alone or you'll get hurt.*

# CHAPTER
# TWELVE

How did he do it? Victoria walked beside Cillian up the hallway at the police station, following an officer to the lieutenant's office.

Cillian still had the inexplicable ability to talk her into things, apparently, and to persuade her to change her mind. Something no one could ever do, according to her siblings.

The moment Cillian had seen the threatening note left on her windshield, he'd announced they were going to the police at once. Never mind that she had a patient appointment. Or that the detective clearly didn't want to see her again, especially regarding anything to do with Thomas.

Cillian had shot down those objections easily enough by reminding her that Thomas, her friend, had been murdered, and no one was going to be punished for that if Detective McCully was left to his own hunches. Cillian had also insisted that the threatening note should be reported, regardless, since she could be in danger.

Victoria would just as soon forget that last part of Cillian's argument. And the way his eyes had sparked with something ferocious ever since he'd read the note, as if the thought of her being in danger made him angry and protective.

Did he feel that strongly about her? Did he care for her?

What would she do if he did? She couldn't allow—

No. She wouldn't go there. Not right now. She redirected her thoughts as she and Cillian turned into another hallway, officers in uniforms and suits passing in the other direction.

She hoped Cillian was right about one thing—that going over Detective McCully's head to his lieutenant would result in Thomas's needless death being given the attention it deserved. That Thomas deserved.

But nerves fluttered in her stomach as they entered the office where a man in his fifties stood behind a desk with a stern expression.

"Lieutenant Willis, thanks for seeing us." Cillian's strong voice gave her a modicum of reassurance. Perhaps his persuasive powers would work on the lieutenant as well as they did on her.

The lieutenant jerked a nod. "Have a seat." His tone was polite, but not friendly.

Victoria couldn't blame the man. Cillian had only secured this unplanned meeting by...actually, she wasn't quite sure how he'd achieved it. He had walked up to the officer at the front desk while Victoria hung back, still debating inwardly whether or not they should go through with Cillian's plan to circumvent McCully. It would only make the detective angrier with her, which would completely destroy any hope that she could still convince him to investigate Thomas's death. She knew how to deal with people like the detective and keep the peace, if Cillian would only be patient.

But while she'd been deliberating, Cillian had apparently said something to the desk officer that unlocked an immediate meeting with Lieutenant Willis. Victoria didn't particularly want to know what he'd said or done to obtain such a quick but inhospitable meeting.

The lieutenant spoke again as soon as he sat behind his desk and Cillian and Victoria took the uncomfortable chairs facing him. "I understand you have a serious complaint about one of our staff, Detective McCully."

Oh. That was what Cillian had said.

Victoria shot him a dismayed glance, but he watched Lieutenant Willis, giving him a confident smile.

"It's only serious if he continues to ignore the evidence in a murder case. But I'm guessing you can steer him in the right direction."

The lieutenant tented his fingers above the desk. "You're talking about the death of Thomas Briscoe."

Cillian gave a controlled nod. "A clear case of murder, but McCully is determined to ignore all the evidence and proclaim it's an accidental death. I can't help but wonder why he would do that. Do you have any ideas?"

Heat crawled toward Victoria's cheeks as she fought the urge to shrink down into her seat in an effort to disappear. Was Cillian actually implying to the lieutenant's face that his detective wasn't honest? That he had improper or sinister motives in Thomas's death?

The lieutenant's mouth worked for a bit as his eyes narrowed. "I can assure you McCully is an experienced and skilled investigator. He knows how to read the evidence and not make assumptions."

"Then why is he sweeping this death under the rug as an accident? Maybe his case load is getting out of control?" Cillian lifted his hand off the skinny metal armrest of the chair that was much too tiny for his large frame. "You see what reporters or the public could make of this if it gets out, right? And from what I hear, Thomas Briscoe's death is a pretty big deal with the press."

Her insides stiffened at the implied threat. Cillian had always been forceful and resented authority. But this way of rebelling with a smile and dropping threats he seemed ready to fulfill was new.

She braced for the lieutenant to expel them from his office.

And the station. Hopefully, he wouldn't arrest them for making threats.

The lieutenant shifted his gaze from Cillian to Victoria. "You're the one with this supposed evidence?" He would have had to speak with McCully about the case to know that.

She nodded. "Yes, sir."

"Okay." He leaned forward on his elbows. "Let's hear it."

She shot Cillian a quick glance. Perhaps his approach worked better than she thought. Straightening her spine, she used the calm, polite, but confident tone that worked best with people like the lieutenant and her father as she laid out the evidence she'd shared with McCully.

Lieutenant Willis listened in silence until she described Thomas's fear of falling. He held up a hand like a stop signal. "I have to agree with McCully on this point. Mr. Briscoe's balance issues and fear of falling are further evidence of an accidental fall, especially on an icy driveway where anyone could have slipped."

"But he didn't actually have balance issues." Victoria met the lieutenant's gaze. "He only feared that he did."

"All the more reason for him to have gone out to get the mail."

"We're going to have to claim professional knowledge here, Lieutenant." Cillian glanced at Victoria before returning his focus to the older man. "Ms. Weston here has been a practicing physical therapist for years, and I'm a clinical social worker. When a patient, especially an elderly one, has fallen, they can develop fears like Briscoe's. The fear that they'll fall again can convince them that they can't trust their balance. And that fear is so strong that I promise you, that person is not going to suddenly go out into icy weather to get the mail. Especially when he knows his favorite person who collects his mail is coming that morning." Cillian smiled. "I'd be willing to give expert testimony on the stand, if you'd like."

Lieutenant Willis watched Cillian in silence for a few moments again, his expression appearing to transition between irritation and grudging respect. "All right." He shifted his gaze to encompass Victoria. "You've brought out some interesting details that could…" he lifted his hand again, "I'm only saying *could*, be relevant. I'll discuss what you've told me with Detective McCully to be sure he understood it all."

"Thank you." Victoria kept the surprise from her voice. She hadn't expected that much progress to be made from this meeting.

"But that said, I don't want civilians like yourselves interfering in police investigations or trying to play amateur detective." His stare turned stern enough to be her father's. "I expect your involvement in this to end here, is that understood?"

Her shoulders stiffened. Wonderful. They had irritated him, after all. At least his response wasn't quite as impolite as the detective's.

"Whether you like it or not, Lieutenant, she is involved." Cillian's tone hardened next to Victoria, twisting her stomach. He shouldn't challenge the lieutenant like that. He could push him too far. "And so am I. Someone left this note on her windshield this morning." Cillian leaned forward and placed the paper on the desk.

Lieutenant Willis opened the note, appearing to read the contents. He looked up, his jaw still set in the same grim expression. "This could have been left by anyone for a myriad of reasons. It could be a harmless prank, completely unrelated to what happened to Briscoe."

"Wow, really?" Cillian shook his head. "I'm beginning to feel like I'm talking to your detective, and the same suspicions are coming to my mind. I suppose there are people who want this death to have been accidental, right?"

Victoria put her hand on Cillian's arm, squeezing her fingers into the leather of his jacket and the tight muscles underneath.

But she was too late.

The lieutenant's eyebrows pulled lower, his expression

darkening as he stood. "I'm going to have to ask you both to leave now. And I suggest you steer clear of this situation and my detectives." The warning in his tone didn't need any further clarification.

Cillian rose, as well, and Victoria lifted her purse off her lap to do the same.

"You'd like that, wouldn't you?" Cillian couldn't resist taking another stab at him, apparently. "We'll be back."

Victoria grabbed his forearm and tugged him toward the door with the most normal smile for the lieutenant that she could manage. "Thank you for your time. We're sorry to have bothered you."

Cillian thankfully allowed her to pull him from the room and move quickly back up the hallway.

"We're sorry to have bothered you? Really?" Cillian's tone was more amused than irritated as he looked down at her.

"I was trying to do damage control."

"That wasn't damage. It was laying the groundwork. We've got him nervous now. He'll get on McCully and look into all the evidence again, questioning all the assumptions. You didn't need to placate him like a scared puppy."

She kept walking without looking at Cillian. "Politeness goes a long way toward keeping the peace with people like him. You should try it sometime."

"I'll stick with putting bullies in their place, thanks. I am enjoying this part, though."

What part? She glanced at him.

He grinned and sent a pointed look to her hand. Which was still holding his arm.

She yanked her hand away. She had not meant to do that.

"Feel free to grab my hand next time instead." A flirtatious tone colored his words.

The heat flooding her cheeks turned several degrees hotter. She walked faster, trying to think of a clever retort as he easily kept up.

Classical music filled the air. Her ringtone. Thank the Lord for the perfectly timed rescue.

She pulled the phone from the outer pocket of her purse and held it to her ear before checking caller ID. "Victoria Weston."

"Ms. Weston, this is Robert Neely."

Thomas's lawyer?

"I'm Thomas Briscoe's attorney, and I'm contacting you regarding his will."

Victoria barely registered that Cillian held open a door for her, which she automatically passed through. Why would Thomas's attorney be contacting her about—

"You're named as the beneficiary of his estate, including his house, property, and most of his financial assets."

She stopped walking.

"Victoria?" Cillian's tone matched the concern in his eyes, but her mind was fully occupied trying to comprehend what she'd just heard.

"I'm sorry, did you say Thomas left something to me in his will? I'm a beneficiary?"

"You are the sole beneficiary of almost the entirety of his estate, Ms. Weston."

Her knees suddenly felt weak and wobbly.

A hand closed under her elbow. Cillian.

"I understand this is a shock, Ms. Weston. But the family wanted me to move forward with the will and division of his assets as quickly as possible. So I would like to schedule a meeting with you in the next day or two, if that works for you."

She moistened her lips, trying to remember to breathe. "I…Yes. I'll need to check my schedule. Would you mind if I call you back?" The shock clouding her mind meant she was in no condition to think clearly at the moment.

"Not at all." He gave her his number, which she couldn't possibly remember in her current state. But she would count on her caller ID to return his call. "Please call soon."

"Of course. Thank you." Her voice sounded so oddly normal to her own ears. She lowered the phone.

"Victoria? What is it?" Cillian's support of her elbow seemed to be the only thing holding her up.

She looked at his dark eyes. "Thomas left me his…estate. Almost everything, according to his attorney."

Cillian's brows lifted toward his hairline. "You're kidding."

"I don't believe so. He sounded serious. He said Thomas named me as beneficiary of his house and financial assets."

"The house?"

Why did Cillian's eyes light with that expression she knew all too well? He had an idea. One that would likely lead her into trouble.

"Yes…" She let the word out cautiously.

"That means you can legally search his house now. We should go there."

"Why?"

Cillian glanced at the people moving about in the lobby. He tugged gently on her elbow, guiding her to the exit doors. "Because we clearly need more evidence to convince the lieutenant and his blind detective that Briscoe was murdered." He pushed open the glass door and pulled her along with him into the bright sunlight that failed to warm the air. "Or to convince the press, if we have to go to them."

"Cillian, no." She halted, slipping away from his loose hold. "We've done enough. I don't want to risk irritating the police any more than we already have. You do realize they can arrest people."

He laughed. "They can't arrest us if we don't do anything illegal. You just said you own the house."

"That's not exactly what I said."

"But it's the truth. All we're going to do is take a look inside and see if we can find more evidence."

"The lieutenant told us to stay out of this, and so did Detective McCully. I'm going to listen to them, as I should have done in the first place." She brushed past Cillian to head for her car two rows away in the parking lot.

"What about Thomas?" Cillian's voice and his tall frame caught up with her infuriatingly quickly. "Are you just going to forget about him?"

"Of course not." The heat of her irritation and brisk pace created a cloud in front of her mouth as she walked.

"Do you want his killer to get away with murdering him in cold blood?"

She didn't answer. Cillian already knew she didn't want that. But she also didn't want to rub the wrong people the wrong way. "It's better to be patient with people like this. I can likely convince them, in time, if we don't keep angering them."

"Time is not a luxury we have with murder. We need to act as quickly as possible before the killer or killers have a chance to cover up their tracks or disappear."

She threw him a glance. Where did he learn these things? But he wasn't wrong. At least as far as she knew.

She slowed as she passed his motorcycle parked in the stall next to her car.

"Look, I know Thomas was a friend. Someone special."

Victoria stopped by her car, reluctantly facing Cillian as his tone softened. She should duck into her car before he really turned on the charm.

"I know how much you care about people. You want justice for Thomas. I know that."

She met Cillian's intense gaze. "Of course I do."

"Then come with me to his house tonight, and let's find the evidence that will catch his killer. Let's do it for Thomas."

For Thomas. The memory of his face the last time she'd spoken with him, the uncharacteristic fear in his eyes, blocked her vision. He'd wanted her help. He had trusted her when he couldn't trust anyone else. She couldn't fail him now. She owed him that much, at least.

She took in a deep breath of cold air. "You're right. Thomas would want me to find his killer." She looked up to see Cillian's grin.

His very handsome, annoying grin.

She resisted the urge to smile in return. "But not now. I have patients to see." One of which she'd already pushed until later in the day thanks to Cillian's insistence that they immediately report the threatening note.

"Of course. So do I." His mouth straightened, an attempt to appear sober, but his eyes still twinkled with mischief.

"I can meet you there this evening."

He thumbed to his motorcycle behind him. "Sure you don't want me to pick you up on the bike?"

She narrowed her eyes at him.

The grin returned. "All right. I'll meet you there."

"Eight thirty sharp." That would give her time to feed Max at home and complete some documenting first.

"Yes, ma'am." The words and that irresistible grin sent a shiver up her spine that had nothing to do with the cold.

Why did she feel as if she'd agreed to a date with her high school crush?

She slipped behind the wheel of her car and resisted looking at Cillian as she peeled away. She would need to figure out how to deal with him, since it seemed he wasn't going away anytime soon. And since, for some reason, that idea was starting not to bother her like it should.

But one challenge at a time. Tonight, perhaps, she could help the friend who had apparently given her everything he valued in life. A life that someone had taken from him.

<h1 style="text-align:center">CHAPTER<br>THIRTEEN</h1>



Victoria angled Cillian a look as they stood in the foyer of Briscoe's mansion. "I'd rather not."

He chuckled. Couldn't help it. She was so cute when she got her nose bent out of shape. "Okay, then let's think like a detective and go over the evidence."

"I thought that's why we're here. To find more evidence."

"Right. But we should review the facts we do know so we have a better idea what to look for. Like how he was killed. You said you saw blood from a gash on the back of his head, right?"

Victoria stared at something ahead. Or at nothing.

"Vicks?"

She turned her head toward him. The light from the chandelier caught her eyes, and they were filled with sadness.

His chest squeezed. His hand went toward her arm, aching to touch her, to comfort her. She'd touched his arm at the police station for a different reason. And the contact had worked better than a defibrillator to jumpstart his heart. Their chemistry always had been off the charts.

But even though she was clearly still attracted to him, she

107

didn't want him to touch her. That was obvious. At least not yet.

So he clenched his fist at his side and cleared his tight throat instead. "Are you okay?"

"It's so strange to be here, in his house, without him." She looked up at Cillian then, unshed tears pooling in her beautiful hazel eyes.

His gut twisted. "I'm sorry, Vicks."

"I don't want his house. I want him back." Her voice squeezed with pain like it had that last time he'd talked to her sixteen years ago. When she'd called him to say goodbye.

He couldn't hug her then. Couldn't help. But maybe he could now.

A tear escaped and fell down her cheek.

That did it. "I know, Vicks. Shh…" He stepped toward her, reaching to take her into his arms.

But her eyes widened, and she stepped back, spinning away. "I'm sorry. I shouldn't have let my emotions get the better of me. I don't usually do that."

He blinked at her back, her parka shutting him out like it shut out the cold. A pang seared his chest. Man, that hurt.

"You're right. We should review the facts and determine what we're looking for." She angled halfway toward him but avoided directly meeting his gaze. "Yes, there was a cut on the back of his head. Swelling, as well, I believe. And blood. Though not as much as I would have expected for a head wound like that."

He swallowed. Steeled his jaw. "Okay. So it's likely the killer hit him with something on the head but not where you found him. Probably here, in the house. Then moved the body."

She nodded and walked toward the base of the staircase she had sat near on the bench before. "That could explain the missing rug. It was very expensive, so it could have been stolen. Or…"

"The killer could've taken it because it had blood on it."

Cillian went to join her, stopping close by her side. Maybe reminding her that she was attracted to him, too, would help break down her defenses. He'd made progress already. Persuading her to go against the orders of domineering authority figures like McCully and Willis was an almost unimaginable achievement. She was starting to trust Cillian and listen to him. Whether she liked it or not.

"Yes." She looked at him, and her head jerked up to his face as if surprised he was so close. Her cheeks flushed an encouraging shade of red. She quickly turned her head away and walked even closer to the steps.

She crouched and peered at the lower wooden steps that had a runner of carpeting colored burgundy and black in a swirling pattern. "I don't think we'll be able to see blood on this carpet."

He grinned. "Look at you. Just like a detective."

Her mouth tugged in a smile she was obviously trying to repress as she tossed him a glance. "I've watched TV shows, too."

"Have you?" He responded with a matching teasing tone. But he was a little surprised. TV used to be outlawed by her father. Thought it was a waste of time when his kids should be studying for the academic and career success he had planned for them. Maybe she had broken free of his control a little.

"I suppose the killer could have been here, possibly trying to steal the valuables." Victoria stood and peered up at the staircase. "Thomas could have heard him and come downstairs to check. And then..." Her lips pressed together.

"Yeah." Cillian let the heaviness of the situation weight his voice. She needed to see he could take things seriously. He always took victimization of the vulnerable more seriously than anything. "If it was dark, it could've been pretty easy for the killer to hide by the stairs and then hit Thomas from behind."

Victoria took in a visible breath, like gathering her courage to shake off the sadness again. "It would explain the two paintings being switched. If it was a thief, he could have taken them off the walls, intending to steal them."

"But then got interrupted, clobbered Thomas, and panicked." Cillian shook his head. "Makes sense as an unplanned murder. The robber probably hadn't killed anybody before, so he would leave the valuables behind. He wouldn't want to risk getting caught for a murder rap."

"Yes, I suppose so." Victoria crossed in front of Cillian, moving toward the back of the foyer where large, cherry wood doors stood closed.

Cillian followed her, scanning the rest of the foyer for anything he might not have seen before. "You don't sound convinced."

She opened the two doors, pushing them inward.

He followed her through.

A massive room with high ceilings and several chandeliers opened before him. Shelves of books lined almost all the walls like at a library, flanking an impressive fireplace in the farthest wall. "Wow. You must love this room. No wonder you got along so well with this guy."

She turned toward Cillian and stared at him.

"What? You didn't think I'd remember how much you love books?" His ribs pinched. Man, she really didn't give him any credit at all.

Her mouth opened like she was going to answer. Then closed.

She faced away again. Of course.

She walked toward the seating area by the fireplace where two armchairs and a velvet, antique-looking couch stood. "He was here." She gestured toward the larger armchair that also looked like an antique, though Cillian was far from an expert.

"When you saw him?"

She turned her gaze on Cillian, pain reflecting in her eyes. "When he told me he couldn't trust anyone but me." She aimed her gaze at the chair. "'You're the only one I can trust,' he said." Her voice tightened.

"So it maybe wasn't a burglar. Maybe it was premeditated."

Victoria nodded as she folded her arms across her parka. "The evidence fits that theory, as well. The rug could have been removed only because it had blood on it from the blow. The paintings could be switched because..." She tilted her head at an adorable angle as she touched a finger to her chin.

"Maybe the killer was looking for something behind the paintings." Cillian threw out the idea as soon as it came to him. "Like a safe with blackmail evidence Thomas had against him?"

"Blackmail?" She lifted her eyebrows. "I don't think Thomas would blackmail someone. Though he did say he was considering speaking with Mr. Neely about something he had 'discovered.'"

"And idea what or who that would've been about?"

"He didn't trust his niece and nephew. They weren't very convincing at playing the role of loving relatives."

Cillian nodded. "So they might've been after his money. Trying to get on his good side to be sure they were in his will. Which, ironically, you were instead." He smiled, but she didn't smile back. Too soon for jokes about her inheritance, apparently. "Okay, who else would've wanted to hurt him or kill him?"

She sighed, lowering her arms. "It's hard to imagine anyone would. But there was a strange incident that last day I saw him."

"Strange how?"

She moistened her lips. "Well, I had thought he and Clinton Glenn were friends. He's the curator of the Chicago Renaissance Art Museum, to which Thomas is a major contributor. But that day, Thomas sounded cold and angry with him."

"What did they say?"

"I don't know beyond the initial greeting. Ryan, his nephew, escorted me out just then."

"Like he didn't want you to hear what they talked about?"

"More like he wanted me out of his uncle's life. He and his sister, Brenda, often behaved that way, though Brenda covered it beneath a veneer of politeness."

Cillian nodded. "Okay, great. So we have at least three other suspects."

"Other?"

"Besides you." He grinned.

"Thank you so much." A small smile curved her mouth with the sarcastic remark, making his pulse skip a beat.

"So does anything in here look disturbed?" He pulled his gaze away to scan the immaculately organized and cleaned library. Looked like something Victoria herself would've set up and maintained.

"No." She rotated, glancing around the room. "It appears the same as when I was here two days ago. Unless..." Her gaze stopped on something near the doors, and she headed toward the bookshelves there. "Oh, my."

"What?"

"The bookends."

Cillian followed her to the shelves that lined the wall just to the right of the doors, or the left if a person were entering the room. With that many books filling the room, the whole place must be home to hundreds of bookends.

She put her hand on a shelf just above her eye level. "I only see one."

"One what?"

"Glass bookend. Thomas had a beautiful set that caught my eye once when I was browsing this section of books."

"Oh, yeah." Cillian's gaze fell on a large, ornately sculpted glass bookend.

"You're taller. Do you see the other one? Maybe on the higher shelves?"

Cillian stepped back and scanned one shelf at a time. "Nope. Some wooden and metal ones. No glass."

"He never would have gotten rid of that." Her eyebrows dipped together toward her nose.

"Maybe it broke."

She lifted her gaze to Cillian's. "Perhaps when someone used it to hit Thomas."

"Good point." He glanced toward the closest open door. "Maybe the killer hid in here when he heard Thomas come down the stairs. If it was a thief not meaning to kill anyone, he could've panicked, grabbed the glass bookend, and just stepped out and—" He stopped at the sight of Victoria's wince, her eyes sliding shut.

She'd really cared about the old guy. Good to know that hadn't changed—her caring about people. It was one of the things he loved about her. Probably one of the reasons she'd cared about Cillian so much.

He'd known even then, when they were just kids, that she saw he needed someone. That she was trying to fill the void he had from a messed-up home life and a mother who'd rejected him from day one. But it hadn't been pity. It had been real love. Love for someone who needed her. But he was pretty sure it had blossomed into something more before her dad forced her to end things.

Victoria cleared her throat. "This is good. A missing bookend is more evidence that something happened here."

He mustered a teasing smile. "See? Aren't you glad we came?"

Her mouth angled in a reluctant, adorable smile. "Let's check the other rooms on the ground floor." She exited the library and turned left. "If our theory is correct, that either a thief or another killer woke Thomas and then surprised him downstairs, that likely means he didn't make it upstairs before then."

"Or she." Cillian caught up to Victoria and walked by her side.

She shot him a surprised glance.

"If an object like a bookend or fire poker was used, a woman could've done it, too. Wouldn't take a lot of strength."

"But what about moving the body out to the end of the long driveway?" She had a point.

"How big was Thomas? I didn't get to see him when..." Best not mention the day Victoria had found him.

"Not very. Only an inch or two taller than me and slim."

"I'm guessing a woman could move him, too, if she used a tarp or something."

"Perhaps." Victoria slowed, angling toward a closed door on the right. She reached for the handle and opened it. "But I don't—" Her gasp cut off the words.

"Victoria?" Cillian stepped between her and the room she stared at as if it contained some kind of threat.

Papers scattered the floor and a desk. Books were tossed all over the room. Chairs were flipped upside down, toppled.

The room had been ransacked.

Cillian stepped inside, scanning the space. "Was this his office?"

Victoria didn't answer.

He turned to face her.

Shock paled her cheeks and widened her eyes. "This wasn't the work of a thief looking for valuables. What if Thomas was right? What if one of the people he said he couldn't trust turned on him, and—"

Something dark appeared at the corner of Cillian's eye.

It moved quickly. Slammed into Victoria, knocking her down.

A person.

"Hey!" Cillian's shout launched at the same time as his body, but the dude in dark clothes and a mask dodged the lunge and took off up the hallway. Cillian crouched by Victoria as she sat up. "Are you okay?"

"Yes." She gestured toward the hall. "Go after him."

Cillian sprinted in the direction the attacker had gone.

No one was in the hallway. The attacker had a good lead.

Cillian pushed his speed faster, reached the foyer.

Front door stood open.

He didn't slow. Kept running through the doorway, into the dark night. He pumped his arms as he dashed down the driveway, cold air filling his lungs.

Movement. By the gate.

The dark figure was climbing over it.

Cillian ran for him, but he dropped on the other side. Cillian jumped, grasping the top of the wrought iron bars. With one pull, he hefted himself up and over the top, landing on the blacktop on the other side. Paid to be taller than the bad guy.

He'd gained but still had his work cut out for him. He sprinted after the fleeing coward. His blood seethed as he remembered the way the thug had knocked down Victoria. Right there in front of Cillian.

Anger pushed him faster, following the guy's scramble up the sidewalk, then across the empty road.

The attacker must have a getaway car somewhere in the quiet, ritzy neighborhood.

But Cillian was closing in. He would catch him in a few more seconds if—

No.

The attacker reached a silver Mercedes parked along the curb by the entry into the neighborhood. He darted to the driver's door and disappeared inside.

"Hold it!" Cillian kicked into his highest gear.

The engine rumbled to life. The car took off, Cillian only feet away.

He stopped, straining to see the license plate in the darkness.

Shadows covered the numbers in the second before the car turned onto the main street.

But Cillian had seen the attacker's vehicle. Knew the make. Knew from the build and speed he was a man. And that, despite the ignorant claims of the detective and lieutenant, someone apparently had motive enough to break into the house of the dead man and search for something.

Which meant that same person also must have had a motive to murder Thomas Briscoe.

---

"Thanks for making time to see me tonight." Robert lifted the mug of coffee Victoria had given him and took a sip, his brown eyes watching her over the rim.

"Don't be silly. We both know why you wanted to come." And she was thankful he had texted her first to make sure she'd be home at nine thirty. She nearly hadn't been. Or rather, Robert might have seen Cillian following her home on his motorcycle to ensure she made it safely.

But Cillian had thankfully left immediately, allowing Victoria enough time to get her house in order and appear as if she'd been home for hours before Robert arrived, rather than only ten minutes.

Robert was going to have enough questions for her as it was.

She picked up her own mug of coffee from the kitchen counter and met his gaze. "Treese told you about my patient, didn't she?"

His eyes twinkled, and a closed-lip smile shaped his mouth between the dark mustache and wide chin strip of his carefully styled beard. "You've always known what we're thinking before we do."

She lifted her eyebrows. "I believe that's your forte, Dr. Weston."

He chuckled as he lowered the mug and leaned back against the counter opposite her in the small kitchen. "I still look around for Dad every time someone calls me that."

"That may be why I insist my patients call me Victoria." She gave him a smile.

He laughed again. "Here I was thinking I'd be your shoulder to cry on, but you seem like you're processing your patient's death perfectly fine without me."

Victoria added her other hand to her mug, letting the warmth seep into her cold fingers. "I never mind being thought of. I appreciate that you care."

"Always." His mouth settled into a more serious line. "Treese says you found his body. Thomas Briscoe?"

"How did you know that?" Victoria had intentionally not told Treese his name.

"Saw it on the news. I put two and two together. I think you mentioned once you had to go to an appointment with a patient in that neighborhood." Robert and his steel trap memory.

"You're correct, as usual. And, yes, I was the one who found him." Her mind returned to the scene. To Thomas. Lifeless.

She blinked and turned away from Robert to set her coffee on the counter. "I was supposed to see him that morning. He asked me to come since he had to cut our appointment short the day before."

Movement by the doorway caught her gaze.

Max's huge, dark head appeared.

"Hi, sweetie. You can come in."

The Leonberger stood frozen and erect, staring at Robert.

"I won't bite, buddy. I promise." Robert used a soft tone, but Max didn't budge. "I don't think he believes me." Robert switched his gaze to Victoria. "Don't know how Hank won him over."

She gave her brother a smile. "He'll get used to you someday. He warms to certain people more quickly than others."

"I'm not sure what that says about me." Robert gave her a rueful smile.

Max turned from the doorway and walked away, his toenails clipping with the thud of his giant paws as he went up the hallway and, judging from the sounds, lay on his dog bed in the living room.

"So you were there for an appointment?"

She took in a breath. Of course, Robert wouldn't let her change the subject so easily. He'd come all that way to get her to talk it through, after all.

"Yes." She pinched her lips together. "And no." She folded her arms across her sweater. "He said he wanted to talk to me. It was very strange."

"What was?" Robert's tone was so calm and gentle, she didn't even think before continuing.

"The day before, he acted so peculiar. He kept saying he couldn't trust anyone, that he only trusted me. And he said he would explain when I returned the next morning." She brought her gaze to Robert.

She knew that look. The wheels were clicking in his intelligent mind, reflected in his eyes. She had probably said too much, which often seemed to be the case around Robert. He'd definitely chosen the right profession in psychiatry.

"You think it wasn't an accident like they reported on the news." His eyebrows lowered as he watched her. "You think it was murder."

Astute, as usual. She'd always had her work cut out for her keeping ahead of Robert's deductions and cleverness when he was a child. Praise the Lord, Robert had been too focused on academic pursuits and feeding his thirst for knowledge to get into any significant trouble. "Yes."

"Have you told the police?"

"I have, and they disagree. Quite emphatically."

"Really?" His eyebrows reversed direction.

"Yes. Despite the evidence w—" she stopped herself just in time and quickly continued, "...I found. I told them all the details, but they are determined Thomas's death was accidental." She forced herself to hold Robert's gaze so as not to make another obvious blunder. She was still recovering from being knocked down by the intruder at Thomas's home. She was in no mood to explain Cillian to her younger brother at the moment.

Something flickered in Robert's eyes. He'd noticed the slip. "Well, I'm glad you told them. It's strange they wouldn't be open to considering other theories." Was he going to let it go without question? It appeared so.

She nodded, tension still pinching her chest. She shouldn't have tried to hide the *we* once she'd started to say it. Now he would make something even more significant out of her avoidance. "I think so, too. But they did say an autopsy is standard in deaths like these, so my hope is those results will prove that he was killed."

Her words bounced back at her. "Not that I want something so tragic to be true, of course. But I do want justice for Thomas if he was indeed the victim of a crime."

"I know, Vicki. You cared for him." Something about Robert's understanding tone and the reflection of sadness in his own eyes formed a lump in her throat.

"Yes." She managed to speak around the swelling. "I did." She blinked back the oncoming tears that pricked her eyes. She'd made it a point never to cry in front of the children. Not since their mother's funeral. They needed to be able to depend on her strength and fortitude, not the other way around.

"I don't mean to pry, Vicki." He paused. His tone signaled he was about to say something she wouldn't like.

She tensed. Was he going to ask who the *we* was that she had referred to and why she'd tried to hide the slip?

"But I saw this while you were making the coffee." He went toward the doorway of the kitchen and reached for something on the counter there.

Oh, no. The—

He held up the threatening note.

How had she forgotten she'd left it there?

"Is someone threatening you?"

She swallowed, staring at the paper in his raised hand. "The police believe it's a harmless prank."

"The same police who don't think Thomas Briscoe was murdered?"

She met Robert's gaze. "The same."

"Then we both know they're probably wrong." His eyes darkened. "Do you know who this is, threatening you?" A rare edge lined his tone.

"No. But you don't need to be concerned. You have your own life to focus on. Didn't you say you were having issues with Dr. Jackson?" The contentious psychiatrist who shared office space with Robert seemed a perfect way out of this conversation.

"Vicki, you don't need to always be a mom anymore. We're grown now. Grown enough that we can help you, too."

Leave it to Robert to shoot an arrow right into the heart of a matter.

But a mother's job was never done. Even if she wasn't the actual mother of her siblings, her mom would've wanted them to still have a mother's love and help into adulthood. For all of their lives, if possible.

"I appreciate that, Robert. I really do." She straightened her spine and lowered her arms. "But I'm fine and will handle this situation with the Lord's help as I always do. I don't believe I'm in any real danger, so please don't worry."

The words hitched in her mind as she said them. The sore spots on her body that would no doubt turn into bruises tomorrow suggested she might be wrong.

A man had crashed into her with a shocking force she'd never experienced before.

*Lord, please protect me as You always do. And help my faith in You to be a witness of Your power and mercy to Robert and Treese.*

*And thank You for Cillian being there tonight.*

If Cillian hadn't been with her...She didn't want to consider what else the attacker might have done.

# CHAPTER
# FOURTEEN

CILLIAN PULLED into the parking lot of Weston Neurology. No surprise the clinic Dr. Henry Weston shared with three other neurosurgeons would be solely named after him. He did likely draw the most clientele and profit to the business.

Cillian swung his jeep into a stall by the front entrance, staring at the modern one-story building without really seeing it. Hard to concentrate on the malpractice investigation when another one was heavier on his mind.

His blood still boiled when he remembered the thug slamming Victoria to the floor. What a coward, knocking a woman down on purpose to try to make his getaway.

And it had unfortunately worked. For now.

Victoria had been right when she'd stopped Cillian from going to the police about the incident.

The detective and lieutenant wouldn't have believed it and might've hassled Victoria for going to the house and sticking her nose where it didn't belong, as they saw it. He and Victoria needed more hard evidence before they approached McCully or Willis again. It would have to be really good to convince those two.

If only they'd hurry up with the autopsy results. That

would prove Victoria was right. With any luck, it might also reveal something that could lead them to the killer. Maybe the same guy Cillian had chased out of the mansion last night.

That guy was probably the one who'd left the note on Victoria's windshield. The threat.

Cillian clenched his jaw. If he ever got his hands on the—

Someone walked across his field of vision, breaking through the intensity of his thoughts. A woman, holding the hand of a boy who looked about eight years old. Hopefully, the kid wasn't the one who needed neurosurgery.

Cillian pulled in a long breath, trying to calm his system. He wasn't going to be able to charm anyone if he went in like Jack Reacher looking for revenge.

He opened the door of the jeep and got out, the crisp air like a cooling balm to the heat of his anger. He should've caught the guy. Or stopped him from hitting Victoria. The attacker must've hidden behind the door when she'd opened it. And the coward went for her instead of Cillian when his back was turned.

Cillian reached into the back seat and grabbed the bouquet in a glass vase he'd spent way too much money on. But Victoria was more than worth it. If he could free her from her dad's hold, they could finally have a future together.

He headed for the building, straightening his shoulders and trying to look cheerful.

The third malpractice plaintiff he'd looked into admitted he had simply run out of money. Didn't seem to be anything suspicious or helpful for Cillian there.

But that second lady he'd spoken with...Marsha Faint. She'd acted so scared. So strange. That was the case he needed more intel on. The one that might hide the skeleton Cillian could drag out of Henry Weston's closet to make him back off.

Nobody knew more about doctors than their nurses. If he could get one of them to talk, he might be able to find out what had happened to Marsha to make her drop the lawsuit and shut up.

He wasn't likely to run into Dr. Weston himself at the clinic, since doctors didn't usually hang out in the reception area where Cillian would be. And Victoria's old man probably wouldn't recognize Cillian even if he did see him. Cillian had been a skinny young kid with long hair the one time he'd met the famous Dr. Weston in person for like two seconds. The angry doctor had barely looked at him.

Which meant Cillian could saunter right onto Dr. Weston's home turf now.

He pulled open the glass door and quickly surveyed the small lobby.

Two receptionists worked behind a curved desk that faced the door. A couple of patients sat in chairs along one wall about fifteen feet away.

The redheaded receptionist glanced at him from behind her computer.

He donned a smile and strolled to the desk. "Good morning." He held the bouquet in front of his chest as he stopped in front of the receptionist.

Nametag said *Lydia Sommers*. The middle-aged woman shot a quick glance at her younger officemate before she smiled at Cillian. "What gorgeous flowers."

The twenty-something brunette leaned back in her chair like she was trying to see him better. "Are they from you? For somebody here?"

He recognized that light in her eyes and the way she scanned him instead of the flowers. Good. If she liked what she saw, she or Lydia would be more likely to give him the info he needed.

He gave her an angled grin. "No, they're from my grandmother."

"Your grandma?" The girl shot another conspiratorial look at the older receptionist as she stood and walked to Lydia's chair. "That's so sweet." She fastened her attention on Cillian.

He quickly checked her nametag. *Brooke Denton.*

He broadened his grin. "My grandma is very sweet." He

shifted his gaze to include Lydia. "Grandma had surgery performed by Dr. Weston three years ago in June." Which just happened to be the time when Marsha Faint had a surgery that she later sued over. "She really wants to thank the wonderful nurse who was especially kind to her."

"You mean these flowers are for the nurse?" Lydia's eyes widened.

"Yes, ma'am."

"Wow. That's very kind. Our nurses don't usually get personal thank-yous like this. Which nurse is it?"

"That's the problem." He gave a small wince. "Grandma's memory isn't quite as sharp as it used to be, and I'm afraid she can't remember the nurse's name. But she wanted to thank the nurse so badly that I offered to bring the flowers and hopefully deliver them to the correct lady. Office assistants rule the world, so I figure you two can help me out." He landed his attention on Brooke, since she continued to stare at him with a melting expression.

Her cheeks flushed as if she'd been caught. Then she touched Lydia's shoulder and looked down at her. "You can figure out who it is, right?" Brooke must be too new to accomplish the task herself.

He shifted his gaze to Lydia. "I and my grandma would be so grateful. It's been several years, but she had a lot of healing to do, and she's said every year since that she still needs to thank that special nurse. I'd like to thank her, too, at least with these flowers."

Lydia smiled and nodded. "Well, I'm sure it would've been either Hannah or Mary. They've both worked with Dr. Weston for over ten years." She glanced at the computer screen to her left. "But I'm afraid I don't have access to records that would tell me which of them saw your grandmother."

Names. That was all he needed. "That's great. I was afraid we wouldn't even get a first name. I'll ask my grandma if one of those names rings a bell. I think she'll remember. Thank you so much, Lydia. And Brooke." He aimed his smile at each of them in turn, earning another blush and eyelash flutter from the younger receptionist.

"Oh, and you two keep this for your kindness." He set the bouquet on the elevated part of the desk to the right.

"Oh, my goodness." Lydia stared at him in pleased amazement. "Thank you."

"Of course. Have a wonderful day, ladies." He gave them a nod and turned away.

Brooke's giggle reached his ears just before the door closed behind him.

He chuckled as he returned to his jeep. But his smile slid away as he sat behind the wheel and took out his phone.

Opening the Internet search bar, he pulled up Weston Neurology's website. He navigated to the *Our Staff* page and scanned the photos and names.

There. Hannah Pyle and Mary Hovde.

Perfect. With full names, he could track them down and talk to them next. If he could charm them into sharing as easily as the receptionists, he should be able to learn the truth behind what had happened to the frightened Marsha Faint.

If it was illegal or at least unethical, as he suspected, he could be very close to the leverage he needed to change Victoria's life, and his, forever.

Victoria navigated the heavy traffic on the residential street as she mentally reviewed the patient visit she had concluded a few minutes ago.

At least, reviewing and planning ahead for the visit documentation was what she should be doing. She blamed her distraction on the aches and bruises that kept her from getting comfortable in the seat and reminded her of the evening before.

The man had come at her so fast she hadn't even known what was happening. A surge of fright had hit her at the same moment he had, but she'd had no time to react or try to defend herself.

She'd never been so thankful Cillian was with her. After he had impressively chased the attacker away, he'd returned with fury simmering in his eyes. But he'd treated her with a gentleness she didn't know he had, asking if she was hurt, guiding her to the car with a strong hand of support on her back, offering to drive her home in her car and return for his motorcycle later.

He hadn't cracked a joke or blamed her for getting in the way. He'd only muttered something about teaching the coward a lesson for knocking down a woman.

The memory of Cillian's protection and sweetness sent a tingle through Victoria's torso, ending in her fluttery stomach.

But she shouldn't allow such feelings, so similar to what she'd felt for him when she was fifteen. Caring for Cillian would still bring trouble, to her family and to her. She hadn't seen or heard anything from him to indicate he had come to Christ in the sixteen years of his absence. As a new Christian herself when they'd first met, she hadn't had the knowledge or spiritual maturity to avoid a romantic relationship with him on the basis of being unequally yoked.

Now would be quite different. Not that she was even considering romantic—

The classical strains of Chopin interrupted the thoughts that were only making her more uptight than before.

She tapped the screen of her smartphone where it sat in her dashboard holder. Caller ID showed *CareFull Home Health*. "This is Victoria."

"Victoria?" Racquelle's voice came over the line. Was it Victoria's imagination, or did her boss sound stressed? "The police are here, asking for you."

Had she heard that correctly? "I'm sorry, the police are there?"

"Yes. A Detective McCully and other officers. He says he wants to talk to you immediately."

Could they have the autopsy results? Perhaps they'd found something to indicate she was right, and Detective McCully wanted to apologize in person. Not likely, given his pride, but he must at least want to share the findings with her or ask more questions about the evidence she had tried to convey before.

"Okay. Please tell them I'm on my way." Victoria ended the call with Racquelle, then contacted her next patient to let him know she would have to push his appointment due to an emergency. The police asking to see a person seemed to qualify as an emergency. It was certainly a request she couldn't deny.

As she pulled into a stall at CareFull, her gaze caught on Cillian's jeep. At least he'd driven a more sensible vehicle today. Safer, as well.

Though why his safety should concern her as much as it did, she wouldn't ponder. Nor would she allow the tickle in her belly to progress any further.

She checked her reflection in the visor mirror.

Oh, honestly. What was she doing? It didn't matter what Cillian thought of how she looked.

She smacked the visor back up to the ceiling with a little too much force and stepped out into the cold air. Briskly walking into the small lobby, she immediately spotted Detective McCully and two uniformed officers, a woman and a man.

And Cillian.

A smile upturned her lips despite her intention to appear unaffected by his presence.

But he didn't smile in return. His black eyebrows dipped low as his gaze landed on her. Perhaps the news from the autopsy had disturbed him.

She wasn't sure she was ready to hear the details herself. But if it would help find Thomas's killer, she could handle it.

She stopped several feet from Racquelle, who stood facing the detective and his colleagues. "Detective McCully. I understand you wanted to see me?"

"We got the autopsy results."

Relief eased some of the tension squeezing the tendons near her sternum. So that was why he wanted to speak with her. "Did it show evidence that someone…killed Mr. Briscoe?"

"Yes, it did." McCully's expression was as unfriendly as ever.

"How so?"

"I won't discuss the details here." He glanced at Cillian and Racquelle before returning his foreboding attention to Victoria. "I'm going to have to take you in for questioning."

The words slipped through her ears as if from somewhere far off or from a dream. She couldn't have heard him correctly.

"What?" Cillian stepped toward the detective. "You can't do that."

The detective straightened, still falling far short of Cillian's height. "I wear the badge. I can definitely do that."

"On what grounds?"

"She's a person of interest in this investigation."

A person of interest? Wasn't that what the police said on TV? This couldn't be real.

"That's crazy. You know she was the one trying to convince you from the beginning he was murdered. Why would she do that if she'd killed him?"

*If she'd killed him.* Cillian's words rang in her ears, echoing as if caught in a chamber her mind didn't want to acknowledge or absorb.

"Look, buddy, you'd better back up, or we can take you in, too. On a different charge." The detective's threatening tone and the sudden movement of the other officers pulled Victoria out of her shock.

She blinked in time to see Cillian standing in the detective's personal space with an aggressive stare.

"I'm going with her either way, buddy."

Alarm rushed through her, awakening her senses and mind at the same time. "Cillian, don't." She took hold of his arm, every muscle in it clenched and rock hard. "It's fine. Of course, I'll go with them." She dug for some semblance of a smile as she looked at the detective. "I'm relieved the truth has come out so that Thomas can have justice. And I understand you need to eliminate every possible suspect to find his killer. I want to facilitate that in any way that I can."

"You don't have to talk to them without a lawyer." Cillian's breath dropped down to brush against her neck, his deep voice edged with anger. But not at her. He aimed his fury at McCully for her sake. He wanted to protect her.

No one had ever done that—behaved as if she was worthy of protection. No one except, perhaps, Cillian. He'd proclaimed sixteen years ago that he would free her from the father he said didn't deserve her.

The unease beginning to surface in Victoria's nervous system yearned for her to slide her grip down a little farther and find a safe home in Cillian's strong hand.

But the Lord would be her strength.

The reminder that must have come from the Holy Spirit within her made her release the hold and look up at Cillian. "I don't need a lawyer. I have nothing to hide."

He glared past her at McCully. "If she's only coming in for questioning, why can't she drive herself?"

"She's a flight risk." Defiance edged McCully's response. He landed his attention on her, real anger instead of annoyance reflected in his gaze. This argument was not helping her situation. "I won't cuff you if you agree to come along peacefully."

Handcuff her? She hid a swallow and kept her features calm. "I'll come peacefully. I always cooperate with the police."

"Victoria, you don't have to go along with this. McCully here is overstepping his authority." The flash in Cillian's eyes said he still didn't intend to let her go with them.

"Cillian, it's okay. I don't mind." She gave him a small smile and tried to signal with her eyes that he should stay put.

He seemed to take the hint, clenching his hands into fists at his sides as he let the detective lead her away.

She walked from the building with the detective, her pulse accelerating with each step toward the police car that waited in the parking lot. Waited to take her away. Someone guided her into the back seat. She stared at the dirty glass barrier between her and the two officers in the front. Cold shock started to creep through her system.

The weak link in her resolve replayed her last words to Cillian with emphatic denial. This was far from okay.

# CHAPTER
# FIFTEEN

SHE WAS LOOKING at her father.

Victoria tried to picture his stern, intelligent hazel eyes instead of the brown ones that watched her across the table with a personal dislike her father never showed.

But in essence, Detective McCully was the same. He was an authority figure used to having his way. Someone who did not like to be crossed and could make a person sorry for doing so. A man who should, then, respond well to the same approach that worked with her father.

If she cooperated and did her best to show she was on his side, she should be able to keep the detective calm and bring about some semblance of peace between them.

"Did Briscoe tell you he was leaving you everything?"

She swallowed, an act that was becoming increasingly difficult since McCully had never brought her the glass of water she'd requested. How long ago was that? An hour? Two? "No, he never said anything to me about his will, an inheritance, or anything of the kind." She refrained from adding that McCully had already asked her the same question three times. That would only antagonize him further and counteract her efforts to placate him.

At least attempting to picture her father across the table distracted her from thinking about where she was. Thank the Lord, they'd put her into a room that looked more like a boardroom than the dark, cold interrogation cells one saw on TV shows.

But she was still being interrogated. McCully's belligerent questioning and accusatory tone left no doubt about that.

She, Victoria Weston, was a suspect in a murder. She had been driven to the station in a squad car and was now undergoing interrogation like a criminal.

Cillian must be laughing at her expense right now. She, the ultimate rule-follower, being detained by the police and questioned.

Perhaps one day, she would laugh about it, too. But that was impossible to imagine at the moment.

She tuned in to yet another repeat question from McCully.

"You honestly expect me to believe you didn't influence him, and you didn't even know what was in his will?"

She met his gaze steadily, as she'd been doing the entire time. "All I can do is answer your questions truthfully. Whether or not you believe the truth is up to you. We never discussed his will or an inheritance beyond what I already told you, that he referenced his niece and nephew waiting for him to die so they could collect their inheritance."

"So you're suggesting they might be the ones who bumped him off." It was an accusatory statement rather than a question.

She stifled a wince at his callous wording. "Not at all. I'm only answering your questions honestly." Though reviewing her conversations with Thomas and recounting for McCully that final day she'd seen him made her view the people in Thomas's life in a new light. Now that his death was positively an intentional killing, there had to be a killer.

Could Thomas have been correct? Would his own flesh and blood have wanted him dead and done something to bring that about?

"Look, Ms. Weston." The detective slid a hand over his mustache as he shifted in his chair. "In my experience, guilty people try to point the finger at anyone else they can to get us to look elsewhere."

She pinched her lips together and brought in a small breath through her nose. "Detective McCully, Thomas Briscoe was not only my patient, he was also a dear personal friend. His death is a tragedy, and as you witnessed when I brought this evidence to you immediately on that dreadful morning, I want to ensure that the person who ended his life is found and caught."

A smirk pushed up the detective's mustache. "Guilty people always want to appear helpful."

"I wouldn't know, Detective. But I do know that I want to cooperate and help you find Thomas's killer in whatever way I can."

"Good." An unpleasant smile revealed his uneven teeth. "Then you won't mind answering more questions."

"Of course not." She didn't blink. "I will help in whatever capacity you need. But I would also like to tell you the additional evidence I found at Thomas's house."

"You were at the house after Briscoe's death?"

"Yes. The lawyer informed me I had inherited the estate, and I went to see if more evidence of foul play could be found."

"Foul play?"

Victoria stared at him. Was the man actually going to criticize her use of formal vocabulary? It would become even more difficult to picture her father in his place if he continued that line of criticism.

"You sure you didn't want to get in to start collecting what was yours? Or maybe cover up some evidence you left behind?"

She resisted an ill-timed swallow that could make her look suspicious. She probably shouldn't have mentioned she'd returned to the house. It could sound like someone returning to the crime scene to ensure nothing incriminating could be found. She needed to forge ahead and get to the point. "I thought that as the detective investigating this murder, you would want to know that we noticed a bookend was missing and the office had been ransacked. A man—"

"A bookend?" Sardonic amusement laced his tone.

"Yes. From a valuable glass set Thomas had loved. It was near the door of the library, suggesting perhaps someone grabbed it and could have used it to attack Thomas."

McCully's mouth straightened into a more serious line. Was he finally taking her seriously? "Anything else?"

"The office was a mess. It was clearly searched by someone. And then a man ran out of the office and fled the house."

"Really?" His raised eyebrows didn't match his thoroughly skeptical tone. "Let me guess, he got away, and you can't identify him."

She paused. But she had to cooperate and answer truthfully. "That's correct. But Cillian saw the car he used for his getaway."

"Ah, Doherty. So you were there with your boyfriend." Another cynical statement worded as a rhetorical question. But he was completely incorrect, as usual.

"Cillian Doherty is not my boyfriend."

"Avoiding the question?"

She held his gaze, fighting to keep her expression open and calm, a feat that was becoming more difficult by the second. "Not at all. Merely giving you all the facts, as I'm sure you want me to. We are not dating, and, yes, he was at the house with me and can confirm everything I've shared about the intruder and the evidence we found."

"You have a lot to learn if you think that's evidence. But maybe you'll learn as we keep chatting. Now, tell me again when you befriended Briscoe and became his confidant. And how you got him to give you the security codes to his property and house."

Wonderful. Apparently, they were starting at the beginning again with the same innuendo, suggesting Victoria had conned her way into Thomas's affections for personal gain. Perhaps she should have followed Cillian's advice and called a lawyer instead of agreeing to speak with the detective.

She still could say she wanted a lawyer. She knew that much from the bit of TV and movies she had watched. But doing so would only make her appear guilty and increase the personal vendetta McCully already seemed to have against her. Men like him did not appreciate someone else being right when they were proven wrong. He must be seething over the fact that the autopsy did not prove his accidental death theory correct, despite his insistence that it would. Yet that did not excuse detaining her so long when she hadn't even been able to reschedule her appointments.

"Detective McCully," she maintained a calm, controlled tone, "I'm willing to help you however I can. But could you tell me how much longer this will take? I have two more patient appointments scheduled for this afternoon."

"Had appointments. You said you want to cooperate, right?"

She squashed the urge to narrow her eyes at his use of her own words against her. She didn't know if he had the right to hold her longer or not, but since she was claiming innocence and trying to prove it by cooperating, she had no other choice but to stay. Even if she tried to leave, he might then decide to detain her overnight or even arrest her. The thought nearly made her shudder.

Then she would have to call a lawyer. But calling a lawyer would mean calling her father. It was bad enough that she was being questioned as a suspect at a police station. Having her father find out would be far worse.

No, she would have to deal with the detective herself. By using the peacemaking skills she'd honed during sixteen years of managing the Weston family dynamics, she should be able to handle this detective. She would simply cooperate and give him what he wanted—short of a confession of guilt—until he finally, hopefully, let her go free.

---

"This is insane. You know she was the first one trying to make you people see he was murdered, right? She could sue." Cillian dropped the threats on the officer who'd been sent to the front desk at the police station when Cillian had demanded to see someone about Victoria. The guy was one of the two backup cops McCully had brought with him to drag Victoria away for questioning.

"She hasn't been arrested yet. Detective McCully is only talking to her."

That *yet* didn't help cool the hot blood rushing through Cillian's veins. "He isn't seriously going to try to hold her, is he? She's already been detained well beyond her legal rights."

"She's stated that she wants to cooperate."

*Come on, Victoria.* Frustration gripped his gut. She would play long, trying to follow all the rules like she did with her father. That wasn't exactly keeping her out of trouble this time. He glared at the cop. "I don't think she meant she wants to give up all her legal rights. What if I call her a lawyer?"

"She's agreed to be interviewed without one."

Terrific. The one time Cillian almost wished Victoria had called her father, and she apparently wouldn't. With his connections, he could get her out in two minutes flat. But she was probably afraid that would get her in more hot water with McCully. Or her father.

Cillian glanced at his watch. "Did she agree to be questioned for three hours? I don't think so."

"She hasn't been interviewed for that whole time."

"Oh, that helps a lot." Cillian laced the response with heavy sarcasm. "What were you—"

The heavy door where the officer had emerged opened.

Victoria.

Cillian's heart lurched as she walked into the lobby, followed by the female officer who'd helped take her away. He hurried to Victoria, stopping short of pulling her into his arms like he wanted to.

Strands of auburn hair had pulled free from her bun and framed her beautiful face. Her green scrubs beneath her open jacket intensified the color of her eyes. Worry and fatigue reflected in them as she met his gaze, twisting his gut.

*Oh, forget it.* He reached for her and pulled her into his arms. He had to show her it was going to be okay. To be the strong one for her so she didn't have to be strong for herself and everyone else, just for one moment.

She didn't fight it. Didn't pull away.

She actually let her cheek rest against his chest. She was letting him hold her. In public, no less.

His heart thumped harder, probably crashing into his ribs where she would feel it.

She pulled away in one graceful move, leaving his arms and heart feeling empty and lost without her.

Man, he'd missed her. But the fact she'd let him hug her showed how badly she needed support and comfort right now, even if a guy couldn't tell from her poised and composed exterior. He still needed to give her that support somehow, no matter how badly he wanted to hold her longer and much more often.

"Did they let you go?" He scanned the lobby. No sign of the officer who'd brought her out or the one Cillian had been blasting.

She nodded, giving him a glance. "My father."

"You called him?" Annoyance crept into his belly. Her daddy was the hero who got her out of trouble, once again. That would only make her depend on him all the more.

"No. I didn't want him to know." She folded her arms across her jacket and rubbed her own triceps, like she was cold. "They let me call Hank earlier to ask him to take care of Max."

"Max?" Was he a patient? Or some guy in her life Cillian didn't—

"My dog. He must have told Dad where I was." She clearly knew Cillian never would've called Henry Weston.

But Cillian's mind was stuck on the news she'd just dropped. "You have a dog?"

"Yes." Her hazel eyes connected with his. "That surprises you?"

"Yeah, it does." Her dad had never allowed pets in his home. Maybe she had learned to rebel just a little. Cillian grinned. "Let me guess, some little yappy thing?"

Her chin lifted. "Actually, he's one hundred and forty pounds and rarely barks."

Cillian stared at her. That was unexpected. But the glimmer of the strong Victoria with her new spunk filled him with relief. She was okay. "I'll have to see this dog to believe it. Let's get you home." He resisted the urge to put his arm around her and instead headed for the exit door. He'd already pushed it with that hug.

He stepped into the crisp air outside, stopping to hold the door for her.

She glanced at him as she passed through. "Thank you for the ride, but I need to go to my father's house. He texted me a few minutes ago."

Cillian let the door close and walked beside her, leading the way to his jeep parked in the lot a couple rows away. He knew why her old man would want to see her now. "You need rest, not a lecture."

Victoria paused, touching Cillian's arm through his jacket sleeve.

He stopped. Looked down at her slim hand. She kept doing that. Touching him. It was a good sign.

"Cillian." Her tone brought his gaze to hers. Emotion swirled in the hazel depths. Anxiety, urgency, and probably something she didn't know showed—a vulnerability that made him want to take her into his arms again. "Please."

He clenched his jaw. But he nodded and put his arm around her shoulders as he guided her to the jeep.

He would take her to her father. But he would not leave her there alone. Never again.

# CHAPTER
## SIXTEEN

VICTORIA'S STOMACH twisted into yet another knot as Cillian drove them up the driveway, the setting sun ducking behind her childhood home.

He switched off the engine.

But it was cold outside. Alarm flared in her mind. Wasn't he going to keep the car running for heat while he waited?

She turned her head to see him, breaking the silence they'd maintained during the drive there. "You don't need to wait for me. I'm not sure how long I'll be." She glanced away to aim her gaze at Treese's car parked by the garage. "Treese is here. She can drive me to my house later."

"I'm going in with you." Cillian's answer squeezed her lungs, nearly making her cough.

"You can't."

"You bet I can." His hard tone matched the flex of the muscle in his jaw. He turned to her, his coal eyes flashing. "You are not going to face him alone. You don't have to anymore."

Her throat shrunk even more, but this time from a ball that seemed to fill the space there. Her ribs pinched and moisture stung her eyes. The only one who had ever faced her father with her was her mother. Oh, how good Mom had been at smoothing things over with him, at shielding Victoria while still keeping the peace with Dad.

If only Victoria was half as skilled at peacemaking as her mom. If only she was half the person her mom had been.

But she did have the Lord. And if Mom was with her now, she would remind Victoria that her real strength in times of trouble came from and through Jesus Christ.

She cleared her throat but didn't look away from the intensity of Cillian's gaze. "Thank you. But seeing you would only upset him more and give me more to explain."

"Maybe it'd be good for him to know I'm back in your life."

She blinked. He made it sound as if they were dating. That would be the worst thing for her father to think was happening right now. "That would only bring up bad memories for all of us."

Cillian stared at her.

Perhaps she shouldn't have used such strong wording. She hadn't meant to hurt or insult him.

Something sparked in his eyes, the flare of heat that used to signal he was attracted to her and about to act on it. "I have a lot of good memories of that time. Of us." His voice pitched lower than usual. "Can you honestly tell me you don't?"

She tried to swallow, her throat dry. Memories she hadn't thought about for years cascaded through her mind. The powerful elation, butterflies, and wonder of her first crush. How he'd made her laugh harder and more often than she ever had. How he'd made her feel special, beautiful, wanted. The happiness she'd felt when she was with him.

Until that night.

The image of her mother, lying in the bed when Victoria had returned home, banished all the other memories from her mind.

She looked away, staring out the windshield at the darkening sky. "That last night overshadows everything else."

Tension filled the silence between them.

She should go. She reached for the door handle.

"I suppose your father still blames you for that."

She paused, then moistened her lips. "He doesn't know."

"How could he not know?" Surprise lifted Cillian's tone.

She looked at him, removing her hand from the door. "He wasn't there when I returned. When..." Her mother died. The words lodged in Victoria's heart, far from being voiced. But Cillian knew. He was the only one who really knew.

His lowered eyebrows and the gravity filling his dark orbs confirmed that knowledge, that understanding.

But she couldn't leave him thinking she had lied to her father to save herself, to cover up her disobedience and the worst mistake of her life. "I knew it would upset him more if I told him. And the children needed me so much. I needed to be trustworthy for them, to be like their mom. I had to do everything I could to minimize the trauma and pain for everyone." If she hadn't, the family would have fallen apart.

Every time she'd considered telling her father the complete truth of what had happened that night, she had realized it would only harm the family, causing pain and possibly division. Mom would not have wanted that.

It would have been one of those things, like the only B grade Victoria had ever received in school, that Mom would've said to keep between themselves to avoid upsetting Dad. Keeping the full knowledge to herself was exactly what Mom would have done and instructed Victoria to do, for the sake of peace in the family.

"That must be a lot of weight to carry by yourself." Cillian's softer tone drew her attention back to his face. Concern pulled down the corners of his mouth and furrowed his brow.

Her heart warmed behind her ribs, though it shouldn't. She couldn't rely on Cillian or let him become important to her again. That was the very mistake that had led to that awful night.

"Must be a hard burden to keep everyone else happy all the time at the expense of your own happiness."

"I don't carry it alone. God helps me to care for and serve others. And I bring my cares and burdens to Him." Precisely as she should be doing right now.

*Lord, please give me the strength to resist Cillian and face my father.* The quick, silent prayer infused her cold limbs with energy as peace started to ease the tension in her stomach.

"I had better not keep Dad waiting." She reached for the door handle again, casting a firm gaze at Cillian that she hoped would silence any further arguments. "Thank you for the ride, but I'll have Treese drive me home." She opened the door before he could contradict her again.

"I'll wait." His voice caught her as she stood.

She looked through the dimming interior at his grim, handsome face. "Thank you." She closed the door and swiveled away, pushing her bare hands into her pockets as she hurried through the cold to the house.

At least she had peacefully resolved that situation. Now for the next faceoff with a strong-willed man, one with far less understanding and much greater power.

It wasn't right. No one should have to carry their whole family starting at the age of fifteen. Especially not someone as good and kind as Victoria.

She couldn't even tell her own father about the guilt she carried. Not that she was actually guilty of anything wrong. What happened with her mom wasn't her fault. But he would never forget the phrase she'd kept repeating when she had called to say she couldn't see him anymore.

*It's all my fault. It's all my fault. I'm so sorry.*

In true Victoria fashion, she'd taken the blame when her dad was to blame, not her.

And she didn't deserve to be blamed now either. Not for

leaving her mother for barely thirty minutes that night sixteen years ago or for getting questioned by the police today. She was always bending over backwards and sacrificing everything to please a father who didn't deserve her. A man who was probably blasting her right now for something that wasn't even her fault.

Cillian couldn't let her face the bully alone. Not this time.

He would do what he should've done sixteen years ago. He left his jeep and stalked to the front door.

He reached for the handle, and it opened. Great. Victoria had left it unlocked.

He stalked into the foyer that brought back vague memories of the few times he'd been allowed inside. The times Victoria had the courage to sneak him in when her dad was away. And that one night when her mom had wanted to meet Cillian, and Victoria's dad had caught them.

The white marble floor and open space looked even colder and emptier than before. Seemed like some of the decorations Victoria's mother had put up were missing now.

"May I help you with something?" A feminine voice drew his attention to the staircase on the left.

A petite young woman with long brown hair stood on the bottom steps of the staircase by the wall, watching him. Her body skimming black dress dipped low at the neckline and cut off at her thighs, leaving little for him to imagine of her figure. If he'd wanted to. But he had an elegant woman and a much more important mission on his mind.

"Did you see where Victoria went?"

The girl left the staircase and walked toward him, her high heels or her own effort swaying her hips side to side.

He stifled an eye roll at the obvious attempt to attract him. "I'm in a hurry."

"You know Victoria?" She tilted her head as she stopped two feet in front of him and looked him up and down. The surprise in her tone matched the way she raised her eyebrows as her brown eyes lifted to his face.

"Yes. She went to talk to her father. Do you know where she is?"

The woman shrugged one bare shoulder. "I couldn't say for sure." She bit her full, lipstick lined lower lip. "I'd be happy to wait with you." The way she dragged up her mascara-loaded eyelashes was probably supposed to be attractive. But Victoria had made him immune to such artificial ploys. Who was this girl, anyway, and why was she in the Westons' house?

Oh, wow. "Are you Treese?" He stared down at her, searching for any trace of the chubby cheeked little girl who'd run around the house with her brother, Robert.

She blinked those eyelashes, but without flirtation this time. "Yes."

"I'm Cillian Doherty. Victoria's b—" He wished. If only he could call himself her boyfriend as he had the first time he'd met her siblings. "Her friend from high school."

"Oh." Treese's mouth dropped open slightly as she scanned him with a far more innocent expression, her brow furrowed as if trying to recall him.

A raised voice—a man—reached the foyer. Seemed like it came from the hallway to the right. "Is that your dad?"

"Uh-huh." She tapped her fingertip against her bottom lip as she stared at Cillian.

"Thanks." He took off in the direction of the yelling. The voice led him to a closed door. And the voice he still remembered, bursting through the heavy carved wood.

"You know better than to become personally involved with patients." Henry Weston's shout carried a domineering bite that few but the powerful could deliver. "Look what disregarding my guidance and best practices has brought about. I cannot believe you would bring shame on our family in such a way."

Anger surged through Cillian. He flung open the door, his gaze finding Victoria as she stood up from a chair facing a desk and spun toward him, her cheeks flushed and eyes wide.

But he didn't linger on her. He landed a glare on Henry Weston. The tormentor and controller of the woman he loved.

The man straightened from leaning over his desk to intimidate Victoria as much as possible.

"That's enough." Cillian stalked closer to Henry Weston, stopping at the desk to face him. He was shorter than Cillian remembered. A little older. But the same sternness defined his features. And hardness coated the eyes that were unbelievably the same color as Victoria's.

"Who are you, and what are you doing in my house?" The doctor drew himself up to his full height, still smaller than Cillian, and sharpened his stare.

"You have no business talking to Victoria like that. She doesn't deserve it."

A flicker of something lit Weston's eyes for a split-second. Recognition? His attention aimed at Victoria behind Cillian.

"Is this who I think it is?" The unleashed fury in Weston's tone warned she'd better say no.

Cillian twisted his head to see her, not wanting to turn his back to the bully.

Her widened eyes darted from her father to Cillian. The alarm in her gaze clenched Cillian's gut.

He hadn't come to make things worse. He'd come to support her. He swung his focus back to her father. Cillian would deal with this for her. "I'm Cillian Doherty, your daughter's ex-boyfriend. Remember me?" He let his own edge of fury undergird the question.

"All too well." Weston's tone cooled along with his expression. "No wonder she's in this mess." He folded his arms across his blue dress shirt and tie as he walked around the desk, staring at Victoria. "I always said the Doherty boy was trouble."

The Doherty boy. Been a while since Cillian had heard that familiar title, always said in a derisive way. Still cut into him more than it should.

"What is he doing in my house?"

"I..." Victoria shifted her gaze between them as her father faced Cillian about eight feet away. "I asked him to wait in the car."

"You drove here with him?" Weston pinned her with a searing stare as his voice raised. "You're seeing this boy again?"

"No, Dad. We're not dating." She took one step toward her father, placating him again. "He was only giving me a ride because I didn't have my car. He works at CareFull Home Health as a social worker. We're co-workers as of only a few days. That's all." And there she went, throwing Cillian under the bus again.

She glanced at Cillian for a second. "He isn't the cause of this. It's solely my doing. Cillian has only been helpful and kind."

Oh. Maybe not throwing him under the bus. Was she defending him to her father? Warmth started in his belly and surged up into his chest.

"I find that very hard to believe." Weston kept his stare on Cillian as if he was some criminal or ex-con who'd broken into his home. "Leopards don't change their spots, and this one is obviously as wild and reckless as before."

Cillian opened his mouth to answer the insult.

"I'm sorry I disappointed you." Victoria beat him to the punch, her focus transferred to her father. "I did not intend to, and I will do everything I can to fix this situation. Unfortunately, I believe Detective McCully, the man in charge of this investigation, has a personal vendetta against me."

Her father angled his head toward her. "Why would that be?"

"After I found Thomas Briscoe's body, I pointed out the evidence that indicated he was murdered. The detective insisted the death was accidental and ignored the evidence." Her voice was back to her usual controlled, smooth tone. "I left him to the case after that, but I believe his pride has been injured by the autopsy proving he was wrong. He seems to be taking that out on me."

"If that's the case, he could lose his job." Not an empty threat from someone like Henry Weston. "You will stay away from the detective and this investigation from now on, is that clear? You're not in law enforcement." Weston delivered the order to Victoria, then aimed his gaze at Cillian, his jaw tight. "I'll give you one minute to get out of my house before I call the police."

Cillian smirked. "Sure you don't want to try kicking me out your—"

"Cillian?" Victoria's grip on his arm was a lot tighter this time, her fingers digging into his skin. "Would you please drive me home?" The look of pleading and worry that defied her calm tone reached inside him to squeeze harder than her hand.

Fine. He'd go this time. But if her old man ever treated her like that again, Cillian would not let him off so easily.

"Sure." He shot her father a nonchalant glance. "Nice seeing you again. I'll be back."

Victoria pulled his arm harder than he thought she'd be able to.

He let her drag him from the room, though he watched the doctor's glare over his shoulder until they'd turned into the hallway.

She kept pulling until they'd walked through the foyer—completely ignoring her sister watching from the stairs—and out the front door into the cold darkness.

She dropped her hold and faced him on the step. "How could you do that? I asked you to wait for me out here."

"I couldn't let you face him alone. I knew he'd be berating you for something that wasn't your fault. You shouldn't just take that from him."

"He's my father, Cillian." She lifted her arms out from her sides. "I don't know how I'm going to smooth this over with him. And now he knows you're back. That I'm talking to you, driving with you." She pressed her fingers to her forehead as if Cillian's existence was giving her a headache.

A pang he hadn't felt for a long time struck him behind the ribs. Even her dad's demeaning comments hadn't given him that sting of rejection, the reduction to a worthless nuisance. The ghost of his childhood.

"Oh, you'll figure it out. You've always done whatever it takes to make him happy, no matter who gets hurt. Just so long as it isn't him, right?" Cillian spun away, marched to his jeep, and got behind the wheel. He might as well start the engine and go. She would stay and get a ride with her sister now.

But as Cillian reached for the key he'd left in the ignition, Victoria crossed in front of the jeep and walked to the passenger door.

She opened it and took her seat with the characteristic grace even the blowup with her dad couldn't shake. She didn't say a word.

Cillian kept his mouth shut and started the engine. Because even though she hadn't defended him or shaken off her father's hold, and even though she hadn't appreciated Cillian's help, she was still sitting in his jeep, choosing him as her ride home.

# CHAPTER
## SEVENTEEN

Victoria blinked at the dark ceiling above her bed. She rolled over to check the lit clock on the nightstand.

*1:12 a.m.*

She let out a small groan and returned to her back. Why couldn't she sleep? She had to get up in less than five hours to get ready for work. She wasn't even a night person.

But the logic didn't seem to make a difference to her very awake system. She felt wired, energized, as if she'd drunk caffeinated coffee too late in the evening. And yet, exhaustion weighted her limbs at the same time.

So much for getting to bed early since she didn't have much documentation—the one silver lining of missing her patient appointments due to police interrogation. Remembering that humiliating and frustrating experience, however, would not help her fall asleep.

Perhaps Mom's warm milk trick would work. Or some green tea.

Victoria pulled back the comforter and sat up, dangling her legs off the side of the bed to find her shearling slippers.

Max's dark eyes gleamed at her, catching the light from the hallway outside her partially open door.

She smiled at him where he lay in his open crate, his preferred spot even when he didn't have to be confined. "I can't sleep tonight for some reason. I'm going to get some tea. Would you like to join me?"

She stood and slipped on her robe as she went to the door.

The sound of Max rising and padding behind her drew her gaze to him.

"You're a sweetheart to accompany me. Thank you." She pushed open the door and walked through the hallway she always left illuminated while she slept. She kept the lights on in the kitchen, too, after reading home security advice to leave lights on overnight.

Now if she could only have some way to deter unhelpful thoughts from preying on her mind and keeping her awake.

*Thump.*

She whirled toward the sound, her heart leaping into her throat.

Max. The giant Leonberger had simply lain on the floor by the kitchen cabinets, which usually included a dramatic thud as he collapsed.

She pressed her hand to her chest where her heart pounded through the skin. No wonder she couldn't sleep. Her nerves were wound tighter than the snarls she used to have to untangle from Treese's long hair after every shower the girl took.

The dangers and stress of the past few days were apparently getting to Victoria more than she'd allowed herself to acknowledge.

She went to the corner cabinet and pulled out her tea kettle. It wasn't surprising she would be somewhat shaken. In the span of four days, she'd been threatened by a knife-wielding thug, found her friend and patient dead, was followed to her car, knocked down by a mysterious attacker, and questioned by the police. Oh, and someone had left a threatening note on her car. She didn't have to be weak for such a series of events to put her on her guard.

But as she filled the kettle from the faucet and set it on the stove to boil, the truth she wasn't facing broke free of the vault where she'd tried to keep it locked away.

She sighed and turned from the stove, her gaze falling on the handsome dog who watched her with his usual serious expression.

"Oh, Max." She went to him and crouched to stroke his soft ears and plant a kiss on his velvety head. "I can't fool you, can I? You know something's wrong. Somehow, I'm in trouble, even though I always try to do the right thing."

His dark eyes stared into hers, as if he understood every word.

She smoothed her fingers over his dark muzzle, then stood. "I think you could offer me very good advice if you spoke English."

But could anyone get her out of this mess?

Cillian and her father had seen each other tonight. And it had been a disaster. More so than the brief meeting they'd had sixteen years ago when Victoria and Mom had tried to introduce Cillian to her father. At least then, only her father had done the talking and Cillian had kept silent before he'd stalked off.

This time, Cillian had been far from silent. What had he been thinking, bursting into her father's house and yelling at him like that?

But she knew what he'd been thinking. He wanted to protect her. That much was clear in what he'd said before, during, and after the confrontation.

Part of her, the part that had spiked gladness through her heart when he'd flung open the office door and told her father not to speak to her that way—that part of her was grateful. No one had stood up for her against her father in such a strong and unapologetic manner. No one had stood by her so resolutely without question or compromise, without shrinking and cowing before her father.

Perhaps because of the hours of police interrogation she

had just endured, Cillian's show of protectiveness and willing-ness to fight for her had raised her up from the depths of guilt and regret that Dad's accusations had plummeted her into.

But only for a moment. Attacking Dr. Henry Weston never ended well for the person who had the nerve or lunacy to confront him. And Cillian doing so on her behalf would only mean they both would suffer greater wrath and consequences.

Her shock over what was happening—Cillian challenging her father openly to his face—had delayed her intervention for too long as the conflict escalated. But at least she'd finally found enough strength to interrupt their faceoff and bring about some semblance of peace, at least between Dad and herself. Thank the Lord that He had given her the idea to tell her father Detective McCully was carrying out a personal vendetta against her.

But she'd thought about the fallout as she had silently ridden in Cillian's jeep all the way back to her car at the office.

Thankfully, Cillian hadn't tried to follow her to her house after she'd thanked him and quickly left, seeking refuge in her own cold car.

Hank had been waiting at home with Max, and Victoria did not need another family member learning about Cillian. She'd already noted Treese staring at them from the staircase as Victoria had pulled him from the house. Treese had probably heard most of the argument in the study, and perhaps she'd seen him enter.

Victoria only hoped they hadn't spoken. What would Cillian have told Treese about their relationship? Their history?

Treese likely wouldn't recognize him, since she had only been nine or ten the last time she had seen Cillian. And he had only been to the house twice.

Unease squeezed Victoria's stomach. What Treese had heard or recalled wasn't nearly as significant as what had tran-spired with her father.

He knew now that Cillian had returned. And he clearly

thought Victoria was in a relationship with Cillian again, despite her protest.

She worked so hard to keep her father happy, to stay on his good side so she could be an advocate and go-between for her siblings. That was the only way she could keep the family together and peaceful as her mother would have wanted. Would tonight's events jeopardize that?

She would need to speak with her father again, without Cillian this time. Perhaps she could convince him that Cillian wasn't the cause of the trouble she was in, as her father had claimed.

The memory of the things Dad had said about Cillian, with him standing right there, made her wince. He'd been so rude and unkind to Cillian. But she could never tell her father that or call him out for his behavior. Direct criticism made her father angrier than anything else. He never seemed to forget or forgive anyone who dared to critique him personally.

So she had done her best to end the mischaracterization of Cillian by redirecting her father's attention to Detective McCully. And by making a quick ex—

A scream broke the silence.

Victoria's breath caught.

Not a scream. Only the tea kettle's high-pitched whistle.

Air returned to her lungs, but her pulse sprinted erratically. She pressed her hand over her racing heart. She really needed to calm down and stop overreact—

A booming bark filled the kitchen, making her flinch again.

"Max?" She glanced at the dog as he stood. "Why are you barking? It's only the tea kettle." She lifted the kettle from the stove, and the high-pitched sound rapidly faded.

Another bark jerked her head toward Max. His bark was so much louder than she remembered. He had only barked one other time in his life, probably two years ago.

He stared through the doorway to the hallway, his ears high and his stance rigid. His tail tucked between his legs.

Strange. Max was easily and often frightened, but his fear never made him bark.

Her mouth grew dry as her pulse accelerated again. "What is it, Max?"

The hallway led to the garage door. Could there be an animal or something in her garage?

The *or something* possibility gripped her mind.

She stepped out into the hallway, inching her way to the closed door that led to the garage.

A sound. Something shaking or rattling?

She froze.

Max let out another *woof* and rushed up to her, bumping his head into the backs of her knees as he stayed hidden behind her. The poor boy's tail tucked more tightly between his legs, and his ears flattened against the sides of his head.

She wasn't helping his fear level. She took in a breath and pulled her shoulders back.

*God gave us a spirit not of fear but of power and love and self-control.*

The reminder straight from Scripture pushed back her apprehension. She used to have to deal with many an unknown sound and imaginary danger when alone at night, watching the children in their big house. She could certainly face another threat—real or imaginary—with God's protection.

She glanced around for something she could use as a weapon if necessary.

The shovel she'd used to clear snow off the driveway leaned against the wall in the corner where she'd left it. Grabbing the long handle, she stepped in front of the door, inhaled through her nose, and slowly turned the knob.

She opened the door a crack and peered through.

Darkness stared back at her. If someone was in the garage, the intruder would be able to see her well with the hallway light on. She should have thought of that, but it was too late now.

She'd better even the playing field. She opened the door wide enough to reach through to the light switch on the wall outside the door.

The bulbs in the ceiling lit, instantly illuminating the single-car garage.

She scanned the small space. No noises or signs of anything amiss.

The big overhead door and the side door were closed.

Had she imagined the sound she'd heard? But what about Max? There had to be a reason he had barked.

She shifted her grip on the shovel handle, forcing a swallow down her sandpaper throat.

She should check the whole garage to be sure there was no danger. On those nights when she'd been the one her siblings had trusted and depended on, she had checked the whole mansion alone. She'd made sure they were safe, even when she'd had to check empty rooms in the big house that had once been warm and happy but seemed so cold and frightening after Mom was gone. Especially those first nights and weeks. Though they were followed by the long first months, when mothering and responsibility had filled her days and lonely isolation and regret had darkened her nights.

She was used to it now—all grown up with shoulders strengthened to endure the weight of responsibility with joy. Speaking of which...

Recognizing her own stalling, she shrugged off the hesitation and walked purposefully around her parked car. She probably should have approached the other side of it more cautiously, checking around the hood first. But she was beginning to feel rather ridiculous, carrying a shovel around her garage in her robe and pajamas at night. She only hoped the neighbors wouldn't catch a glimpse of her embarrassing behavior through the small windows halfway up the garage wall.

Nothing odd on either side of the car or behind it. She even squatted to peer under the vehicle.

Empty shadows greeted her searching gaze, thank the Lord.

Only one thing left to check—the only explanation she could think of for the sound she had heard.

She stepped to the side door and stared at the knob. The sound she'd heard had a familiarity to it. She gripped the knob and turned without unlocking it first.

Not quite the same sound. It had been more rapid.

She twisted the knob again, back and forth, quickly.

She jerked her hand back as her pulse lurched.

That was it. The same noise.

Had someone been twisting the knob from outside, trying to access her garage?

Her heart lodged in her throat. But she had to know, had to make sure she was safe, or she would never be able to sleep tonight.

She moistened her lips with her tongue. *Lord, please keep me safe or stop me if I'm being unwise.*

Rotating the small lock on the knob, she gripped the handle again and opened the door. She swung it wide, pushing it with her hand so it would hit the outside wall, ensuring no one hid behind it.

She held her breath, waiting for someone to jump in front of her.

But only cold wind greeted her, whisking inside and chilling her cheeks. Its swirling sound was all she heard, the black sky silent above the leafless trees of her neighbor's yard.

She stepped to the doorway and leaned out, checking right and left.

Nothing but the white siding of her house greeted her. That and the matching snow on the ground that had fallen earlier that day, while she'd been at the police station.

And footprints.

Her heart rate sped up again.

But of course, there would be prints. Hank had entered through the side door to feed Max for her.

His feet were larger than average, a men's sixteen shoe size. She knew, since she had been the one to buy each sequential shoe size for him as he'd grown rapidly during his teen years.

Indeed, some of the prints were massive.

But there were others. Smaller. An average men's size.

She stared at the prints as her heart bumped into her ribs.

Their direction indicated the wearer of those unfamiliar shoes had come around the front of her house and walked directly up to the side door of the garage.

And if she and Max were correct, the man had then tried to enter her house.

# CHAPTER
# EIGHTEEN

VICTORIA WENT to the counter in the kitchen and poured coffee into her thermos. Judging from the reflection she'd seen in her bathroom mirror as she prepared for work—droopy eyelids advertising her fatigue—she should allow herself a second cup of the caffeinated brew this morning. Barely shutting one's eyes all night called for extreme measures, especially to ensure she was alert enough for her patients today.

Only a few days ago, her first reaction to someone prowling around her house, trying to enter, would have been to call the police. She still almost had last night, but she lived in Gealanden, the same suburb and jurisdiction as Thomas. Detective McCully could hear of it and think she had fabricated the sounds and footprints to make herself look like a target instead of the killer he suspected she was. He could have even shown up himself if she had called.

Ironically, the incident could be connected, though she wasn't certain how. But it seemed entirely too implausible that a prowler outside her home, the threatening note, and being followed outside Treese's studio could be unrelated to Thomas's murder.

Then again, why would someone want to get into her

home? To do her harm, as unpleasant as that idea was, seemed the most likely answer. Yet she wasn't sure what the motive for an attack could be. She hadn't seen the murderer when she'd found Thomas, though she had been the one to claim there was foul play. Would the killer want to silence her because of that?

No matter. She wasn't going to stop her life out of fear. She glanced at her watch. Just enough time to put Max into his crate where he would be most comfortable while she was at work.

It would be a long day, given that she would have to fit the patients she hadn't seen yesterday into today's schedule. She trusted that Racquelle or whoever had phoned the patients to reschedule hadn't cited her police interrogation as the reason. Victoria would stop at the office before seeing her first patient to confirm what had been said.

"Time to go in your condo, Max." She called out the statement as she headed for her bedroom where he was probably lying on the floor near his crate. Or he could be in the crate already, since it made him feel safe.

The musical tones of her phone made her pause. She followed the sound back to the kitchen where she'd left the device in her purse. She pulled out the phone and checked the screen.

*CareFull Home Health.*

Odd. She wasn't running late, and it was too early for Ginny to be calling with questions. Perhaps there had been a cancellation.

She pressed the phone to her ear. "Victoria Weston."

"Victoria, good morning." Racquelle's voice came across the line, a peculiar tight tone modifying her normal pitch.

"Good morning. Is something wrong?"

"No, not wrong. But I called to convey a request from the higher-ups."

Higher-ups? Only the board members had greater

authority than Racquelle. Why would they have a request for Victoria? Unless…

Her throat pinched. They wouldn't…Would they?

"They'd like you to take some time off until things are resolved with the police."

Anxiety and the horrible feeling of guilt tangled with the frustration of injustice in her stomach. She hadn't done anything wrong, nothing to deserve a disciplinary leave. "I understand." The safe and respectful response emerged from her lips automatically, even as her mind screamed a different reaction. A defense.

She was innocent. The police had only wanted to question her. They hadn't charged her with anything or arrested her. She had a perfect record of following all regulations and serving patients without a single complaint. She was, as Racquelle had once told her, their best and most reliable PT.

But arguing wouldn't help her situation with Racquelle or the board.

"I'm sorry, Victoria. But I look forward to welcoming you back when this all blows over."

"Of course." Victoria swallowed the large lump in her throat. "Thank you."

"You take care."

"You, too."

The line clicked, and Victoria set the phone on the counter. She stared at the screen as the *Call Ended* message appeared.

She only hoped her job hadn't ended, as well. What had she gotten herself into? She wouldn't have thought Racquelle or the board members of CareFull would distance from her when she'd only been questioned. That shouldn't affect how they saw her. Many people were interviewed for murder investigations.

Though having the police come to the CareFull office and escort her away had surely not helped.

Regardless, God was in control of all these events. He had

a good purpose in everything that happened and would happen.

The reminder relieved some of the tension clenching her stomach. She took in a breath. "Okay, Lord. What do you have planned for me to do today if not help my patients?"

Sydney. Her pregnancy checkup appointment was this morning. Sydney had wanted Victoria to be there for it, but she'd had to decline due to work.

"Well, thank you, Lord. Perhaps Sydney needs me more today than my patients." Victoria crated Max as quickly as she could and left the house.

During the drive to the Life Center, the events of the past few days cycled through her mind, bringing back the unease she'd felt last night. Her gaze drifted to the rearview mirror.

Was that...a motorcycle behind her? Who drove a motorcycle in twenty-degree weather? She knew of only one person.

Cillian.

Still being protective? Or did he have a different reason for tailing her?

Warmth filled her torso as she glanced in the mirror again. She shouldn't be pleased to see him. Especially not after last night. Though her father was wrong to call Cillian trouble to his face, even if he did have the ability to lead her into making wrong choices.

That was her own weakness. One she would keep under control today, regardless of Cillian's reason for following her.

She could interact with him without letting herself be influenced and persuaded. And without letting her feelings go in the direction they seemed so inclined to.

Her resolve was fixed by the time she turned into the parking lot at Life and found a stall near the entrance.

Cillian pulled his motorcycle into the empty spot beside her.

Those butterflies that refused to give up residence in her stomach launched into flight at the sight of his tall figure, clothed in jeans and black leather jacket. He swung one long leg over the motorcycle to dismount and pulled off his helmet, running fingers through his thick black hair.

Her breathing grew shallow as her pulse skipped into an irregular beat.

He suddenly looked her way. A grin stretched his mouth, and he waved.

Her heart jolted. She jerked her head away. Why had she even been watching him? Surely she was too mature and grown now to be drawn to a man with a so-called bad boy appearance.

Of course she was. She forced a swallow down her dry throat, grabbed her purse, and exited her car with as much dignity as she could muster.

"Morning." Cillian stood on the sidewalk waiting for her, thumbs hooked in his front jeans pockets and that confident grin still in place, as if he knew how attractive he was and didn't mind using it against her.

Well, he didn't need to know it worked. "I expected you would outgrow your dirt bike and motorcycle obsession with age. And maturity." She added the last comment with an emphasis intended to suggest he hadn't matured.

"Nah. I just graduated to nicer bikes. You really should take a ride with me sometime. You'd love it."

She joined him on the sidewalk, trying to keep a safe distance between them. "You know I don't trust those things." She cast a suspicious glance at his motorcycle. "Much too dangerous."

"I remember I got you to ride with me once. It was fun." His eyes sparked, signaling what he meant.

She remembered, too. Her initial fear of falling, but then the thrill of their closeness. She'd never put her arms around a man's waist like that before, feeling his warmth, his solid torso beneath her fingers. The experience had awakened feelings—uncontrollable, intoxicating feelings—she hadn't known or imagined before meeting Cillian.

Feelings she was much better off without now. She

preferred to keep her mind sound and her heart in check, lest she do something disastrous she would regret forever. Once was quite enough.

She reached for her usual unflappable tone and expression, lifting an eyebrow. "That was summer. It's bizarre to ride a motorcycle in the winter unless it's your only mode of transportation."

"You know me. Never did like to follow the rules." Challenge lit his gaze. "Cold never bothers me anyway."

Did he intend a double meaning in that statement?

No, she would not be drawn into his games that led to him charming her into something when she knew better. "That may be, but your love of the cold doesn't explain why you were following me. And don't try to claim that you weren't."

"Wouldn't dream of it. I heard about CareFull putting you on suspension."

She hid a wince at his word choice. "It's only a temporary leave of absence."

"Sure." His mouth angled in a closed smirk. "Anyway, I was headed to your house to check on you when I saw you pull out."

"So you decided to follow me." She stared at him. He'd have to do better than that.

"Yeah. I wanted to talk to you about the plan."

"The plan?"

He nodded. "Now we'll have time to figure out who killed Briscoe before McCully thinks of a way to pin it on you."

The proposition brought the uneasiness back in full force, knotting her stomach. She certainly hoped the detective wouldn't do anything of the kind. But she couldn't interfere with his investigation any further. She would get in worse trouble than she already was. She needed time to think. "We? Don't you have to work?"

"I get vacation time with this job. I'm taking it now."

She blinked at him. "You can't do that. You just started."

He shrugged his broad shoulders. "They're desperate for

another clinical social worker. They know it and I know it. They're not going to fire me."

She shook her head, disbelief swirling in her mind. "How can you risk your job and angering management, especially so early on in your new position?"

His gaze darkened. "I don't like what they're doing to you." There it was again. The look in his eyes that said he cared for her. Quite a lot.

A shiver passed through her. It must be the temperature. She pulled her gaze from his. "Well, I am not impervious to cold, so I will be going inside."

"What are you doing here anyway?" He glanced up at the Life Pregnancy Care Center sign. "Something you're not telling me?"

Her cheeks flushed with heat. "Of course not." She spotted his teasing grin too late. She should have known he'd only said that to embarrass her. "If you must know, I volunteer here."

"Of course you do." His grin gave way to a lesser smile that matched the softening of his eyes. Was that approval that shone in his gaze?

Why that pinched her chest, she didn't need to ponder at the moment. "I'd better hurry, or I'll be late for an appointment." She headed for the front door.

"Right. Let's go." He passed her and reached the door first. He swung it open, gesturing for her to go through. He was going in with her? That was the last thing she—

"Victoria!" Sydney hauled herself out of a chair beside her brother in the lobby and hurried to Victoria, her hand on her large belly. "You made it." Her smile beamed, making Victoria very thankful the Lord had rearranged her schedule so she could be there.

"I did. I had some unexpected cancellations today." As in, the entire day's worth of clients. But Sydney didn't need to hear that saga. She had enough drama in her own life.

Victoria returned the girl's hug as best she could around the baby she was carrying.

"Yay! I'm so happy you're here." As Sydney pulled back, her gaze jumped behind Victoria. To Cillian, judging from the upward trajectory.

Wonderful. Now more people in Victoria's life would learn about him and likely arrive at mistaken assumptions. Nevertheless, she wouldn't be rude.

She angled to see Sydney and Cillian. "Sydney, I'd like you to meet Cillian Doherty, my co-worker."

He shot her a glance at the co-worker description. What did he expect her to call him?

She pressed on as if she hadn't noticed. "Cillian, this is Sydney Morris, my friend."

"Delighted to meet you, Sydney." He gave the teen a charming smile as he took her small hand in his.

Sydney giggled, her wide eyes sparkling.

It was remarkable how many women reacted to Cillian that way. No wonder he tended toward cockiness.

"Victoria's been my mentor for like six months, but she's never mentioned you." Sydney kept her attention on Cillian, her head tilted back for her to aim her mesmerized smile up at him.

"Is that so?" He sent Victoria a teasing glance as he released Sydney's hand. "I guess I'm a secret she likes to keep all to herself." He winked at the girl with that rakish grin he used to wear as a teen whenever he wasn't sulking at people.

Warren stalked toward them, a frown on his face as he scanned Cillian as if sizing him up.

"Cillian, this is Warren, Sydney's brother."

"Hi." Cillian extended his hand to the tall eighteen-year-old who was only an inch or two shorter than Cillian. "Good to meet you."

Warren didn't take Cillian's hand. He likely wasn't happy with the way Sydney was clearly charmed by Cillian. Couldn't blame Warren, given that his sister had been charmed and impregnated by an older man. It was good someone cared enough to protect Sydney.

"He's a friend of mine, Warren."

The teen's brown eyes, a duplicate of Sydney's, went to Victoria, then shifted back to Cillian. He stuck out his hand and gripped Cillian's with a nod.

Victoria glanced at the clock that hung on the wall of the lobby. "Sydney and I have an appointment. Warren, are you staying?"

He nodded. "Yeah, I'm taking her home after."

"Good. I'll see you when we're done, then." Victoria let her gaze go to Cillian. She assumed he would say goodbye or turn to leave.

"See you afterward." He was staying, too?

She bit her tongue and guided Sydney past the front desk to the exam room. The problem was, Victoria didn't know what she would have said—tell him to go or thank him for waiting. Her swelling heart was at war with her better judgment. Lord willing, the latter would win the battle by the next time she saw Cillian.

---

"Later, brother." Cillian gave Warren a fist bump dap.

"Later." The kid jerked a nod and swung away to lead his sister to the front door of the pregnancy center.

"See you soon!" Sydney turned to wave at Victoria one more time, then followed Warren.

As the door closed behind them, Cillian felt Victoria's attention on him. He looked at her out the corner of his eye. "What?"

"You seem to have bonded with Warren."

He shrugged and angled to face her. "He liked my bike when he went out to smoke."

Her slim eyebrows lifted. "What was he smoking?"

A smile tugged at Cillian's mouth. She was so adorable

sometimes. "Not everybody lives by the rules like you do, Vicks."

She folded her arms over her purple turtleneck. "Do you still smoke?"

"No." He'd quit for the sake of his health and, probably most of all, because every time he'd lit up after leaving, he saw her disapproving, wide-eyed stare in his memory. "But you know I never smoked pot or anything like that, right?"

"Yes, I know." Her hazel eyes softened as she lowered her arms. She remembered. Knew why that mattered to him. "How is your mother?"

Yeah, she knew. He looked away. "She OD'd."

Silence fell between them, the clicking of the clock filling the void in the empty lobby.

"I'm so sorry." Sadness—more than the news deserved—colored her tone. "When?"

He thought back. He'd been in California. Just had his twenty-first birthday. "Twelve years ago."

Another pause. "I'm truly sorry."

He mustered a rueful smile. "It's not a big deal. You've already done enough today to qualify for angel status, if that's what you're going for."

She tilted her head slightly. "More like Christ-likeness."

He watched her.

She didn't blush when she mentioned God or Christianity like she used to when they'd dated. She met his gaze without flinching or blinking.

"You're still into that."

"It's who I am, Whom I belong to. I'll never not be into Christ and Christianity."

"You don't need that crutch."

"I've learned not to try to navigate life on my own. His wisdom and strength are so much greater than mine."

"He's not going to get you out of being suspected for murder."

She didn't hesitate or look away. "He will if He wants to."

Cillian held her gaze. Searched her captivating eyes. She really seemed to mean all that. To believe it.

But Cillian didn't need God to tell him what he should do with his life or in any situation. His instincts and mind served him well. He'd been able to tell what needed to be done, what *should* be done to right the wrongs in this world, since he'd been a kid.

"Well, I want to get you out of this." He gave Victoria a sideways smile. "Mind if I try to help?"

She returned his amused expression with one of her own. "I suppose not, though God doesn't need your help, of course."

"If you say so." Cillian shook his head side to side. "My little pea brain says we should go to the Briscoe estate again to look for evidence. You game?" Probably poor choice of words to use with Victoria.

But she observed him for a few silent seconds. "Only if you promise I won't get knocked over this time." The twinkle in her eyes gave away the teasing as she kept a straight face.

He chuckled. "Deal." Here he'd thought Victoria couldn't get any better, but her new smart-aleck side just might make him forget to move slow in rekindling their relationship.

He distracted himself from tempting thoughts about kissing her by grabbing their coats and escorting her to her car. Though he maybe considered that option a few more times as he followed her on his bike to the Briscoe mansion.

The gate stood open when they arrived. The first sign something was off.

Victoria slowly led the way up the driveway in her Honda as Cillian drove behind her.

Four cars parked at odd angles in the paved area near the front of the house. Obvious from the models and attached scanners what they were. Unmarked police cars.

Cillian pulled his bike to a stop next to Victoria on the driver's side as she parked a short distance from the nearest cop car.

She got out, glancing at the cars and the house, then swung back to Cillian. "What do you think is going on?"

Cillian got off his bike as he scanned the house. "Maybe checking for evidence? They never did search it or process it properly when he was killed."

"We should leave." She turned to her car and reached for the door handle.

"This is your house. You have every right—"

"Ms. Weston!" The call jerked both their heads toward the mansion's front door. McCully and a couple of officers, or detectives not in uniform, poured out of the house like cockroaches.

Great.

"So nice of you to stop by." McCully's tone was oddly happy. With somebody like him, happy wasn't good.

Cillian stepped closer to Victoria as McCully trotted around her car to approach her.

The detective grinned—a more annoying expression than his usual scowl. "I guess I can tell the officer at your house he can forget it."

"There's an officer at my house?" Victoria's tone was strong and calm, despite the dread she must be feeling.

"He's been waiting for you there most of the morning."

"Why is that, Detective?" Still no sign of nerves as she held her tall, unbothered posture.

That was Cillian's girl. At least the new version of her. No hesitation or submissiveness, even if she did still go along with jerks like McCully too often in the end.

"We have a warrant to search your vehicle."

There it was. The reason for McCully's cheshire grin and the gleam in his eyes.

He spread his arms wide toward her Honda. "And here you've brought it right to us. Thanks for saving us time and resources. You are saving tax payers' dollars today, Ms. Weston."

Her lips pressed together in a thin line as if she was holding back what Cillian wanted to say to the guy.

But she handed over her keys to McCully when he asked for them and watched silently, her spine rigid and arms folded across her coat, as they searched her car.

This had to be one of McCully's stupider ideas. Like Victoria would leave something incriminating in her car if she had murdered Briscoe. She was way too smart for that.

"McCully." A guy wearing a black coat waved McCully to the back of Victoria's Honda, where he held the trunk open.

Cillian's gut clenched. They couldn't have found something.

"Ms. Weston." McCully beckoned Victoria with his fingers.

She headed toward the trunk, Cillian sticking to her side.

They rounded the rear bumper.

Cillian's gaze landed on a glass block lying in the otherwise empty trunk.

Victoria stiffened beside him with a small intake of breath.

Oh, man. It was the glass bookend. Covered with blood.

"Care to explain what this is and what it's doing in your trunk?"

She faced McCully. "The last time I saw that bookend was two months ago when Thomas showed it to me. I never put it in my trunk. Someone else had to have placed it there."

McCully glanced at the guy in brown.

The detective or whatever he was shook his head in the negative.

McCully swung his stare back to her. "There's no sign of forced entry into the trunk, Ms. Weston. Nice try. Unless you want to claim you leave your car and trunk unlocked?"

She didn't answer for a second.

*Tell him you leave it unlocked.* Cillian mentally willed her to take the easy way out. To protect herself against the cop who was clearly determined to nail her for a crime she hadn't committed.

"No. I always lock my car."

Disappointment and frustration tangled in Cillian's gut.

"Then Ms. Weston, I'm placing you under arrest for the murder of Thomas Briscoe."

Another officer appeared behind her and Cillian, pulling Victoria's hands around her body to cuff them.

"Hold on." Cillian grabbed the officer's wrist. "You can't do that."

"Take your hand off him, or I'll gladly bring you in, too." McCully leveled a threatening glare at Cillian.

"Cillian, don't." Victoria twisted her head to look at him over her shoulder. "You'll only make things worse for me."

He forced himself to drop his grip, though everything in him wanted to punch out McCully and the cop who dared to touch her. To cuff her like a criminal when she was the purest, kindest, and most harmless person he knew.

Harmless to everyone but him.

Because the look she gave him as they pulled her away seared like he was being gutted from the inside out.

They stopped her next to a black car and opened the door.

He locked eyes with her, fighting every instinct that screamed at him to grab her and never let go. To make them have to take her over his dead body.

But she was right. He could make things worse. And he couldn't save her if he was shot or locked up, too. "I'll find the truth and get you out."

"Please, be careful." Her last words floated to him on the icy wind as they lowered her into the car, and she disappeared from view.

His chest pinched. Was she worried about him? Did she care?

Or maybe she only meant she wanted him to follow the rules and be cautious like she was. Too bad, because that was not going to happen. Not when he'd just watched a power-hungry detective haul away the love of his life in handcuffs.

# CHAPTER
# NINETEEN

IT WAS ONLY TEMPORARY. She would be out soon.

Victoria tried not to look at the bars that surrounded her in the holding cell at the police station. She stood in the middle of the square cage. She couldn't sit in such a place. She wouldn't be there long enough to need to.

At least she was the only person in the damp room that housed two other cells. An unpleasant stench was her only companion. She tried not to ponder what could have created such an odor, tried not to imagine having to sleep there on the cot in the corner.

Dad would secure her release soon.

She almost hadn't phoned him. Since he'd already blamed and berated her for being questioned by the police, being arrested would bring even greater wrath upon her.

But she also knew he wouldn't waste time lecturing her or doling out consequences yet. He would wait until he secured her release. With all his faults, he always protected his children and family from physical harm or public embarrassment, at least as much as he could. He would see that she was released and well-represented, should the murder charge come to court.

The possibility swelled in her throat, thwarting her ability to breathe and remain calm.

*"I'll find the truth and get you out."* Cillian's last words to her rushed to the front of her mind. The look in his eyes as he'd said those words, a sparking blend of ferocity and passion, had comforted and frightened her at the same time.

*Lord, please don't let him do anything foolish that will get him into trouble or put him in harm's way.*

He'd already nearly gotten himself arrested trying to protect her from the police.

The situation was the ultimate irony—rebellious Cillian Doherty promising to rescue her, the rule-follower, from jail.

She always followed the rules, at least according to Cillian and her family. She certainly always tried to. Yet here she was, incarcerated.

The circumstances might make her reconsider whether obeying the rules, following directions, and submitting to those in authority was the correct choice.

But her mother had modeled those life choices. And she had thrived, beloved and respected by all, even her exacting husband, as she maintained peaceful relationships. Her friends had flocked to her, seeking counsel for their marriages and work relationships.

More importantly, Christ commanded His followers to submit to people in authority and be peacemakers. As with many of God's commands, following them did not guarantee pleasant results.

Sometimes, apparently, one could even end up behind bars.

A clang jumped her pulse.

The large, heavy door of the holding area opened, and a female officer stepped through, the same one who had searched Victoria and given her the horrid orange uniform to wear. The officer held the door open as if someone else was going to appear.

Something black and silver emerged from the doorway first. Then feet.

A wheelchair. Spring.

Victoria's heart warmed at the sight of her sister as Spring wheeled herself into the room with strong, smooth rotations.

Spring rolled past the first side of bars and rounded the corner closer to where Victoria stood. Then she effortlessly angled the chair to face Victoria through the bars.

Pride swelled in Victoria's chest. To think that only four months ago, Spring had refused to even try to push her wheelchair. And now she was poetry in motion, in every area of her life.

Spring looked at the officer, apparently waiting for her to step out of the room and let the door close behind her. The police would've thoroughly searched Spring and would be watching them on the cameras, of course. But it seemed she wanted a sense of privacy as much as Victoria did in this cold space that simultaneously felt exposed and claustrophobic.

As soon as they were alone, Spring aimed her gaze at Victoria and then the bars between them, her large brown eyes reflecting more sadness than Victoria felt herself.

"I didn't think they would allow visitors." Victoria mustered a small smile. "At least not this soon."

Spring's tongue slid over her lips to moisten them. "Dad pulled some strings."

Of course he had. "Was he able to secure my release?"

A disheartening frown shaped Spring's mouth. "He's ready to post bail just as soon as the judge okays it. But the decision won't be made until tomorrow."

Victoria's stomach twisted and her heart rate increased. She would have to stay in this place overnight. She couldn't do that.

*I can do all things through Him who strengthens me.*

The Scripture verse sprang instantly to mind—God's answer to her fear. He would get her through this, somehow.

She smoothed her features. Hopefully, she hadn't let her momentary apprehension show. Spring and her other siblings needed her to be strong, not wallowing in fear and self-pity. Oh, how she hoped this situation wouldn't shake them or unsettle them in any way. She would never forgive herself if it did.

She managed another smile. "Well, thank you for the update. I'm grateful I might be released tomorrow. Thanks for coming all this way to tell me."

"I didn't want you to be alone." Spring's gaze traveled up and away, as if surveying the room. Was she thinking of the rehab center that had been her own prison for too many months?

Sadness squeezed Victoria's ribs. "You don't have to stay if this reminds you of the rehab center."

Spring's gaze jumped to Victoria as if the statement surprised her. Did she think Victoria had forgotten or not understood how she had felt then, when Spring's paralysis was new and seemed to have destroyed her life?

"I've never given you enough credit. Or thanks." Spring's eyebrows lowered. "You've done so much for all of us. Me, especially. And I'm ashamed to say I've never thanked you for any of it."

Victoria stepped closer to the bars, closer to her sister. "There's no need to thank me."

"But I want to." Spring lifted her chin. "You stepped into Mom's shoes for me and the other kids. And you've done an amazing job."

Victoria stood silent. She'd never expected any of her siblings to recognize what she'd tried to do or thank her for the effort. She certainly didn't deserve that.

"I'm sorry that I made your job more difficult through the years. I've been so ungrateful."

"No." Victoria moved near enough to see her sister through the gap in the bars. "I need to apologize for making you feel unworthy for so many years. I failed to help you and make sure you knew you were loved and valued."

Spring shook her head. "That wasn't your fault. Dad and I always had issues, and that's the heart of it. But I was also looking in the wrong places for worth and purpose. I've found both in Jesus now."

Victoria nodded, a witness to Spring's transformation since she'd become more grounded in Christ and found her value in His love. "I'm so thankful for that."

"Me, too." Spring's expression remained serious as she watched Victoria. "And I'm thankful you were there with me at the rehab center when Luke…"

Held them hostage. Spring didn't need to finish the sentence for Victoria to know she was referring to the shooter that had held them and others at gunpoint for what had felt like an eternity.

*"She knows how to do as she's told."* The shooter's comment about Victoria echoed in her memory, as fresh and sharp as if he'd just spoken. She had done her best to cooperate, to keep the peace and keep the criminal calm—a difficult task while Spring's now-fiancé, Torin, had kept angering the shooter with his attempts to free them.

But in these four months since it was over, she continually questioned her decision to cooperate with the shooter's instructions that final time. She had thought it was the right choice, the safer choice for Spring and the other vulnerable hostages. But when she'd learned what had happened afterward…

And here Spring was, thanking her. Regret squeezed Victoria's throat. "Nonsense." She could see the moment like it was yesterday, looking over her shoulder as she'd left Spring with a killer. "I should have stayed with you. Then perhaps you wouldn't have almost been killed."

"You had to leave me to save the others. You had to take Bradley to safety, and I'm so glad you did."

It was kind of Spring to say so.

"When you left, it was like a wakeup call to me." Spring's fingers tightened on the arms of her wheelchair, and she glanced away. "I hadn't realized how badly I had been treating you until then. And how wonderful you'd been to me. Not just when I was paralyzed but my whole life, especially since Mom..." Spring landed her gaze on Victoria, her eyes glistening with moisture.

"Thank you, Victoria. Thank you for that night. I remember you woke me to tell me, just like I'd asked you to. And you held me when I cried. 'I'm here. I love you.'" Two tears escaped and trailed down Spring's cheeks. "You kept saying that over and over." She wiped the tears away with her fingers. "And I really, *really* needed to hear it."

The comforting words had come easily to Victoria that night, because her own breaking heart had yearned to hear them in her mother's voice. She had ached to feel her mother's arms around her, smoothing her forehead and telling her everything would be fine.

But there had been no comforter for her that night when her world had shattered. When she'd born the weight of her horrible mistake and the crushing pain of grief at the same time. When she'd become a mother to four children at the age of fifteen.

Encroaching tears burned as they reached her eyes. But she blinked them back, swallowing down the lump filling her throat. Spring still needed her to be strong. All of her siblings did. "I'm thankful the Lord used me, though I know I've fallen short many times through the years."

Spring shook her head as if she disagreed. "You've stepped into Mom's shoes better than anyone else could have. You were God's gift to us during that time and since." Her lips firmed into a line. "I wanted to make sure you know that." Her gaze traveled across the bars of the cell. "Though I suppose this isn't the ideal place to have a heart-to-heart." A half-smile pulled up the corners of her mouth.

Victoria grabbed at the humor for a distraction from the

heavier emotions pushing in on her. It would be easier to stay strong if she made light of the situation and stopped focusing on the past. "You must think I'll be in here for a very long time."

Spring let out a laugh. "No, no. I'm positive Dad won't let you stay here for more than one night. You should've heard how mad he was that the judge wouldn't hold your bail hearing today instead." She gave Victoria a rueful smile. "Apparently, he's the only judge in the county our dad can't get to do his bidding." Her smile faded quickly. "But you know he doesn't like anybody pushing his kids around."

Victoria nodded. "I know." And it was a good sign Spring realized that now, too. It would help Spring to mend things with their dad if she recognized he did have some positive qualities—that he did love her and all his family, in his own way.

A click and sliding sound drew their attention to the door. It opened, and the female officer stepped into the room again.

Spring shot Victoria a grim look, her brow furrowing. "I wish I could stay with you. I asked, but they wouldn't let me."

Victoria's heart warmed at the gesture. "That's very kind. Thank you." She dug up a smile. "But I don't think Torin would forgive me if I kept you in jail overnight. And I know Dad never would. I can already hear the lecture I'm going to get for dragging down the Weston name and reputation. I suppose this will make the news." She shook her head as if she wasn't concerned, though the thought of his reaction, how furious and disappointed he might be, churned her stomach with dread.

Spring cringed. "I'll try to talk him down, if I can. This isn't your fault. He should know that."

"Thank you for saying that." But Spring would be the last person to be able to smooth things over with their father. They still had their own issues to work through. "I'll try to speak with him when I'm released. Hopefully, he'll come around when he understands I'm being..." she glanced at the officer standing by the door and lowered her voice, "framed and targeted." Framed by a criminal and targeted by a police detective. Things were not looking good.

"Time's up." The officer's forceful tone nearly made Victoria flinch.

"Sorry. I guess I have to go." Spring frowned and wheeled back around the corner of the cell. She gave Victoria one more lingering look.

It was her turn to leave Victoria behind in captivity. At least she wasn't abandoning Victoria to life-threatening danger, as Victoria had done to Spring.

But although Victoria had doubts over her decision then, she had arguably done the right thing in following the shooter's orders to keep him calm, letting him believe he was in control. And she had thereby been allowed to save a paralyzed boy.

"I'll see you tomorrow." Spring's farewell drew Victoria away from the memory and her attempts at self-justification. But she would need to stay positive and optimistic to survive a night in this unnerving place.

"See you tomorrow." Victoria watched her sister wheel out of the room, the officer trailing behind her.

The door shut with a slam that rang in her ears.

Victoria was literally imprisoned. And at least for tonight, there was no way out.

---

Cillian gripped the steering wheel like it was McCully's neck as he drove his jeep to the Chicago Renaissance Art Museum.

Victoria was in jail. Right now. And it was only six fifteen. She was going to be there all night, at least according to McCully.

When Cillian had confronted the detective after hours of waiting at the station, trying to see Victoria, McCully had happily told him she couldn't possibly get out until bail was set. Which wouldn't be until tomorrow morning, at the earliest.

Cillian still couldn't believe he'd threatened McCully with calling Victoria's father. But it was all he'd been able to think of at the time. Dr. Henry Weston was good for one thing, at least—getting his way and pulling strings. Shouldn't he have been able to get her out of jail right away?

The idea of Victoria—beautiful, innocent, elegant Victoria—spending the night in a jail full of criminals made his blood boil.

She'd better be in a private cell, at least. If anybody touched one hair on her head, they'd have to answer to him. Personally.

He yanked the wheel to turn into the parking lot he'd nearly missed.

He zoomed toward the front of the museum. He couldn't just sit at his apartment while Victoria was rotting in jail.

He needed to do everything he could to get her out. And if her dad beat him to it, Cillian had to make sure she didn't get arrested again.

McCully wouldn't rest until he brought her to trial for murder. Or until she was convicted.

Not happening. Cillian needed to figure out who the real murderer was and find enough evidence to convince Lieutenant Willis, if not the bully detective. Since Victoria had told him about three suspects, Cillian knew where to start.

He would find out what kind of cars each of them drove, and one would likely be a match to the getaway car driven by the guy who'd ransacked Briscoe's home.

The curator was the easiest one to check first, since he was likely at the museum.

Which was why Cillian had driven downtown in the hope of catching him before the museum closed at eight.

Cillian slowed his jeep as he drove behind the row of parked cars closest to the museum. He studied each closely, moving slowly.

There.

A silver Mercedes was parked next to the handicapped stalls near the entrance. A sign stood in front of it.

Cillian stopped behind the car and got out to check the sign.

A reserved parking stall. For none other than Clinton Glenn.

CHAPTER
# TWENTY

W HAT WAS with the crowd of people?

Cillian kept his attention on the cluster of four adults as he crossed the street to the police station.

Two tall guys and two women, one sitting in a wheelchair, grouped in the courtyard some designer must've thought would help the police with their public image. Whoever the people were, they apparently didn't mind the cold since they were choosing to stand outside, all glancing toward the entrance as they chatted.

Wait. Wasn't that Treese?

He should've guessed, since she wore a skin-tight skirt that ended mid-way down her thighs, despite the nineteen-degree temp. At least her fur coat was thick enough to cover whatever flirty top she was probably wearing.

He'd love to hear what Victoria would say about her sister wearing such a skimpy outfit. And maybe he soon would. When he'd stopped by the station again last night, one of the cops had told him she had a bail hearing set for this morning. He'd said if she got bail, she could be out by nine.

Must be why Treese was hanging out at five minutes to nine. Were those her siblings with her?

Could be, but Cillian wouldn't wait to find out. All he wanted to do right now was see Victoria, free. He walked around the group and hurried toward the station entrance.

"Hey, Cillian!" The female shout made him stop.

He turned around to see Treese wave and smile. Now he'd have to stop by her. Couldn't be rude to Victoria's siblings. He headed back toward them, returning Treese's smile. "Hi."

"Are you here to see Victoria?" Treese's gleaming white teeth didn't stop him from noticing the glint in her eyes.

Just how much had she heard of his blowup with her dad the other night? Enough either to hear he was a bad boy, according to her old man, or get the idea he was into her sister. Good thing he didn't care who knew either.

"Yeah." He glanced at the other three, who watched him with curious stares. "I was told she could get out on bail right about now." Yep, they were definitely Westons. Robert had probably changed the least since Cillian had seen him when the kid was about twelve or something. Same dark brown hair and intelligent brown eyes, though the facial hair showed he'd matured.

The tall, skinny blond-haired guy didn't look familiar at all, but his features favored his brother with a little of Victoria thrown in. Had to be the only blond sibling in the family, the youngest, Hank.

That left Spring, next in age after Victoria, though there was a gap of like three or four years, if he remembered right. But the only one who looked like the girl he remembered was the lovely brunette who sat in the wheelchair.

Wow. That had to be rough for her and the whole family, especially Victoria.

"I remember you." The woman he was observing aimed big brown eyes up at him. "I wondered if it was you when Treese told us about a friend of Victoria's visiting the house the other night."

She put it so nicely. Like he was an old friend paying a

social call. Was that really how Treese had painted his confrontation with their dad?

Cillian's mouth twitched as he held back his amusement and nodded. "I remember you, too. Though you've grown up." He swung his glance to include the whole group. "You all have."

Robert stuck his hand out to Cillian. "I'm Robert. I remember you taught me how to make rubber band slingshots that time you were at our house." He smiled as Cillian returned the handshake. "My dad wasn't too happy with you for that."

"Neither was Mom when you broke her favorite vase shooting pebbles with that thing." Spring smiled as she shook her head at her brother.

"I'd say I'm sorry, but every man should know how to defend his family." Cillian grinned, and the siblings laughed. He transferred his gaze to Hank, who matched Cillian's height. "You're the only one I haven't really officially met yet. You were a toddler tumbling around when I saw you last. Hank, right?"

"Yeah. Henry, Jr., but don't hold that against me." Hank accepted Cillian's offered handshake with a firm grip and a smile.

Yep, Treese must've told them something about the blowup. "I won't if you don't hold whatever you heard against me."

Hank chuckled. "Deal."

"There she is!" Treese's exclamation jerked Cillian's attention to the police station entrance.

And dropped his heart into his stomach.

Victoria. She paused outside the door, her gaze seeming to find them. She wore the purple turtleneck and darker purple pants she'd been wearing when McCully had dragged her off to jail. Somehow, the clothes were as wrinkle-free as before, and she was as elegant and beautiful as ever.

"Victoria!" Hank jogged toward her.

Cillian's chest squeezed as his muscles twitched. He couldn't be jealous of someone's brother. But he was. The run to her, the hug Hank gave her—it was everything Cillian longed to do.

Though she didn't look like she needed it. Her spine was straight as ever, her posture perfect and strong as she walked with Hank toward her siblings and Cillian.

"You didn't all have to meet me here." She scanned her family with her eyebrows lowered. "You have work." Her gaze ended its survey on Cillian. Lingered there.

Then he saw it. A hint of the expression he'd seen on the faces of trauma survivors who had developed an exterior facade that usually fooled everyone. She had been bothered, shaken by spending the night in jail. But she would hide that from her family, from the world because she thought she had to.

His gut twisted. He should just pull her into his arms right there, never mind if her siblings were watching.

"We can take off for family emergencies, Vicki." Robert's reply pulled her gaze away, stopping Cillian from acting on his instincts.

*Vicki.* So somebody in her family had given her a nickname, too. Good for Robert.

"And this definitely qualifies as an emergency. I couldn't believe it when I heard."

"Yeah, of all the people to put in jail." Hank wrapped his arm around Victoria's shoulders. "Vicki? It's insane." His frown and protective body language showed how much he must care about her.

About time someone in her family appreciated her. Maybe all the siblings did, since they'd shown up there. They'd better, given all she'd done for them.

"What's that on your ankle?" Spring's strange question drew Cillian's attention to her. She was staring at…He followed the angle of her eyes…Victoria's ankle?

Victoria tugged up her left pant leg slightly.

A steady light shone, a red dot in a black device wrapped around her ankle.

"They didn't..." Cillian's shocked statement choked on a new wave of frustrated disbelief.

She met his gaze, her cheeks flushing red. Like she had something to be ashamed of. "Wearing an ankle monitor is a condition of my release. I'm not allowed to leave the greater Chicago area."

"They can't possibly think you're a flight risk?" Robert's incredulous, irritated tone was a weak echo of the raw anger that burned in Cillian's chest.

"They've gone way too far." And Cillian needed to do something about it. McCully couldn't monitor her movements and basically shackle her for doing nothing.

"This confirms it, you guys." Hank shared a look with his siblings, the set of his mouth firm.

"Confirms what?" Worry lined Victoria's forehead.

"We've all talked about it," Treese answered first, "and we've decided we need to help prove your innocence."

"No, you do not." Victoria adopted a motherly tone as she stared at her family. "You'll let the police handle this."

"The police are the ones who put you in jail." Treese tilted up her chin in the same stubborn way as Victoria.

Cillian stifled a smile. Treese probably had no idea she'd picked that up from her big sister.

"What she means to say, Vicki," Robert cast Treese a tolerant, fond gaze before swinging his focus to Victoria, "is that the police seem to need help in this particular case."

"And we are not going to sit by and let our sister be falsely accused of murder." Spring's tone was as serious as her expression.

Victoria opened her mouth, probably to protest.

But Spring spoke first. "Even if you don't think you need our help, we're not going to let you face this alone."

Victoria shut her mouth, meeting Spring's stare for a few seconds as they seemed to communicate something silently between them. "I appreciate that." She lifted her gaze to scan the others. "I don't think it's a good idea for any of you to become involved in this." She held up her hand when at least two of them started to speak. "But I'll consider it."

Though she stood as tall and undaunted as ever, apparently the leader of their family when her dad wasn't around, Cillian didn't miss the exhaustion that paled her cheeks and filled the eyes she aimed his way. His ribs squeezed tighter.

She probably hadn't closed her eyes once all night in that place. How could she? Perfect Victoria who'd followed every rule in her life in a jail cell?

It was beyond unfair. It was cruelty and injustice. If he ever saw McCully again, Cillian might do something that could get *him* arrested.

"Let's pick this up later, guys." Cillian tossed her siblings a quick glance, then stepped closer to her. Exactly where he'd wanted to be the whole time. He cupped her elbow through her coat as he bent his head slightly toward her. "I'll take you home."

"Good idea." Robert's reply drew her attention to her brother, but she didn't pull away. "Sleep will really help right now. How about you take the day to rest, and we'll meet at my house tonight at six for dinner."

"*You're* going to cook?" Treese raised a carefully plucked eyebrow.

"My favorite dish." Robert grinned. "Pizza from Renny's."

"Of course." Treese rolled her eyes as Hank and Spring laughed.

"You're welcome to come, too." Robert looked at Cillian.

Surprise filtered through him. He probably would've insisted on showing up with Victoria anyway, but to be invited by a Weston was unexpected. Apparently, Robert didn't share his father's prejudices. And neither did the others, judging from the smiles they gave him.

He glanced down at Victoria. She didn't look his way, but she leaned, just slightly, into his supportive hold. His pulse stopped altogether. "I wouldn't miss it for the world."

CHAPTER
# TWENTY-ONE

This scene was almost as surreal as spending a night in jail. It was far less unpleasant, but still hard to comprehend.

Nothing was amiss in Robert's professionally cleaned home, other than the fact that the large, modern house, decorated by interior designers in a minimalist white aesthetic of harsh lines, abstract art, and black accents, had little in common with the house's owner. His casual attire tonight—khaki shorts and a blue college sweatshirt—made the incongruity obvious. But that oddity was a familiar one.

Cillian sitting beside Victoria on Robert's white sofa with all her siblings present was much more inconceivable.

Merely being so close to Cillian was playing havoc with her senses. The spicy cologne she'd caught whiffs of when he'd first sat down kept teasing her nostrils. Thankfully, he hadn't sat improperly near to her, but she had caught Spring and Treese exchange a conspiratorial look when he'd immediately rested his arm on the back of the sofa behind her.

This wasn't good. What if their father learned Victoria was associating with Cillian outside of work?

For that matter, what if he learned she was involving all his children in the murder charge and investigation? He would be furious, and rightfully so.

"Okay, now that Robby and Hank have devoured the pizza, maybe we can get to why we're here." Treese shot a pointed glance at Hank as he transferred the last piece of meat lovers' Chicago style to his plate.

He tilted his head up to squint at Treese from his position on the floor next to her crossed legs. "What do you care? You got your quinoa salad all to yourself."

She leaned forward on the sofa cushion with a grin and tousled Hank's blond curls on top of his head. Thank goodness she kept her legs crossed. Why she'd chosen to wear that second-skin mini-skirt that revealed nearly all of her shapely legs to a family dinner was beyond Victoria.

Unless it was for Cillian's sake. Victoria's stomach tightened at the possibility. He was extremely attractive, and a confident rebel who enjoyed adventure and risk. Exactly the type of man Treese loved to seduce.

She did keep glancing his way with a sultry smile playing on her lips. As she was doing that very moment. "I want to know more of the story here with Cillian and Victoria."

Victoria tensed. Leave it to Treese to take the conversation there.

"It's hard to picture you two as high school friends. You're so...different."

"You'd be surprised." Cillian's arm shifted behind Victoria, his shoulder moving slightly closer as he turned his head to look at her. "We were very close." His tone and emphasis added meaning to the standard phrase.

She kept her focus forward, not daring to look at his face so near to hers. She'd already noticed how handsome he looked in the black turtleneck that intensified the richness of his coal eyes and dark features.

"Really?" Treese lifted one skeptical eyebrow. "Did you date?"

"No."

"Yes."

The conflicting answers came from Victoria and Cillian at the same time.

She glanced at him, instantly regretting it.

His gaze locked on hers, confusion and a hint of something that looked like hurt clouding his dark irises.

"I remember I thought you were a really cute couple. Made me want a boyfriend." Spring smiled and squeezed Torin's hand, interlocked with hers. Her fiancé had lifted her from her wheelchair to sit beside him on the sofa, between him and Treese. He returned Spring's adoring gaze.

Victoria forced a breath out through her nose, trying to ease the tension in her muscles without compromising her composure. "I only meant it was never official because..." Now she'd done it, boxing herself into a corner. She couldn't announce to her siblings that she had rebelled against their father—the very thing she and Mom had raised them never to do.

"Because I left."

Victoria jerked her gaze to Cillian.

He looked at her siblings instead of her, a nonchalant grin shaping his mouth. "Call of the wild and all that. Took me a while to settle down."

Warmth began to filter through Victoria's stomach and traveled upward as she stared at his profile. He understood her dilemma and took the blame for something she had made him do to protect her example for her siblings. He had made himself look bad for her, something the old Cillian, with all his confidence and pride, never would have done. Perhaps he had changed.

He turned his head toward her, catching her gaze with his. His eyes were full of meaning, of things she didn't have the courage to decipher at the moment.

"Well, I think we're all glad you're back." The amusement in Robert's tone made her look away from Cillian, battling to hold at bay the heat that rushed toward her cheeks. "To help us prove Vicki is innocent, of course." Robert grinned at her, his expression all too knowing. Wonderful. He likely wouldn't miss anything that was between her and Cillian, given his psychiatric training.

She might need therapy after all this. But at the moment, she needed to distract her siblings from dating speculation and put the kibosh on this whole investigation idea before it continued. "I'm grateful you all want to help. It's important that we rally around one another as a family during hard times."

"But?" Robert propped the ankle of one leg on his opposite knee, comfortably encased in the low-backed, black leather armchair. "We can all hear it coming, Vicki." His eyes twinkled with humor.

She pressed her lips together. "But none of you should become involved with a murder investigation. It could damage your reputations to be associated with it."

"That's already a risk with our sister on the news, being branded a murderer." Robert lifted his last piece of pizza off his plate and took a large bite.

She narrowed her eyes at him. "Precisely my point. You should all stay as far away from me and this case as possible until everything is resolved."

"I'm not afraid of getting my reputation a little sullied." Treese smirked.

"Is there any left to sully?" Hank grinned at the others as he asked the question.

Treese punched him in the shoulder from behind.

"Ouch, you must be working out." He rubbed his shoulder, feigning a wince.

"The point is," Victoria continued in a stern tone, "becoming involved in this carries risks. No matter how you feel about it, you all know Dad would not want any of you to get involved and would want you to distance yourselves."

"You have a valid point." Robert nodded, his expression actually befitting the gravity of this topic. "But I would argue that Dad also does not want his daughter tried for murder or convicted of murder."

"You don't think it could really go that far, do you?" Spring's eyebrows bunched as she stared at Robert.

"Someone planted evidence in Vicki's car, and the police believed it." He turned his head to the left toward Spring. "Who's to say that same individual won't manufacture more evidence?"

"How did you know about the bookend?" Victoria had been told by the lawyer her father had hired that no details about evidence had been released to the press.

"From Spring."

Victoria swung her gaze to Spring.

"I heard it from Hank."

Hank readjusted his long legs to cross pretzel-style. "I got it from Treese."

"I overheard Dad on the phone with the lawyer."

Victoria narrowed her eyes at Treese. "You overhear way too many things at that house." She barely held back a reminder of what she'd taught Treese as a child regarding the evils of eavesdropping. One more lesson Treese had disregarded, even back then, when she'd made it her business to know all her siblings' and friends' secrets.

"You'll be glad I did." Treese pushed her lips out slightly, the expression she used to adopt when she was about to dig in and refuse to obey Victoria. "Because Dad also said he'll do anything to keep this case from going to trial. So I'm with Robby. Dad would want us to help you."

Victoria opened her mouth to point out he wouldn't want that to entail his other children putting themselves in the crosshairs of a prideful detective.

A touch on her shoulder stopped her. And robbed her of breath.

Cillian's thumb gently brushed her shoulder through her sweater. Barely a whisper, but the touch still sent shivers of awareness shooting up her spine. "How about we get into what you all have in mind?" He kept his attention on the others, not looking Victoria's direction as he continued the circles with his thumb that would be comforting if his touch didn't have such an electric effect on her.

"Well," Treese didn't miss a second starting off, "I thought maybe Torin could help." She aimed her focus at the sergeant with the Chicago Police Department's Major Accident Investigations Unit. "You probably know some detectives with the police, right? Maybe you could get them to realize Victoria is innocent?"

Torin shook his head. "Sorry, but the Thomas Briscoe murder is out of my jurisdiction. I do know a couple of cops who transferred there from the CPD. I contacted them, and they shared McCully is a bit of a bulldog and even more mule when it comes to sticking with the theory he thinks is right. He'll focus on building the case that fits what his instincts are telling him, not the other way around. And he's not open to much else."

Cillian nodded, pausing his thumb's caress of Victoria's shoulder. "I can confirm that." Everyone's attention swung to him. "I took more information to him last night, and he wouldn't even consider it."

Victoria looked at Cillian with surprise. "You found something?"

He met her gaze, his handsome features so close she nearly forgot what she'd asked. "Yeah. Clinton Glenn drives a silver Mercedes, exactly the same as the getaway car of the guy we caught at Briscoe's house."

"Wait, you caught someone at Briscoe's house?" Robert planted both feet on the floor and leaned forward.

"Yep." Cillian looked across the coffee table at him. "Well, nearly caught him. He was ransacking Briscoe's office, searching for something." Cillian paused, shifting his hand to rest more fully on Victoria's far shoulder as he looked at her for a moment. "He knocked Victoria down and ran out."

Heat crawled up her neck toward her face, generating from

her heart rate's shift into overdrive, no doubt. Hopefully, none of her siblings would notice.

He shifted his protective gaze away to face the others. "I chased him, but he got into the Mercedes and drove off."

"Did you get the plates?" Torin asked the natural police officer's question.

"Too dark."

"Why are we only hearing about this now?" Spring pinned Victoria with a disapproving stare.

A ready answer eluded Victoria. She'd never been on the receiving end of a question like that from her siblings. It was something she would say to them.

She quietly cleared her throat. "I wasn't hurt. There was no reason to bother any of you with the information. You have your own lives and concerns to focus on."

"Victoria, your life is part of ours." Spring's tone carried more urgency than the minor incident warranted. "We care about what happens to you."

An awkward silence filled the room.

Victoria was supposed to care for them, not become a burden for them. She wouldn't add stress or trauma to their lives through her own difficulties, wouldn't distract them from their goals and success. And she wouldn't quit the role of being the most stable, dependable, and loving person in their lives whom they could look up to and count on, no matter what. They still needed someone to fill those shoes their mother had worn, or at least to try.

"Thank you." She gave Spring a nod. "I appreciate that."

"So like I was saying…" Cillian followed her answer quickly, as if he'd been ready to end the silence. Was he trying to help her out again?

Her chest squeezed.

"McCully refused to even consider another suspect. He's doubling down on building a case against Victoria. I don't think he'll pay attention to anything else, unless someone can show him the smoking gun."

"So you think this man you found searching Briscoe's home office is Clinton?" Robert glanced at Cillian and then Victoria.

"You know him?" Treese directed the question at Robert.

"We attend some of the same functions." Robert ran his fingers along his jawline Balbo beard.

"Ah, the parties of the wealthy and influential." Treese grinned.

Robert cast her a smile but continued. "He didn't seem like the burglar type, but people will do extreme things with the proper motivation. Any idea why he would be searching the office or want Thomas Briscoe dead?"

Victoria met Robert's gaze. "Nothing concrete. Thomas told me that I was the only one in his life he could trust. He said that, even though I asked him about Mr. Glenn, because I had thought they were friends. Then Mr. Glenn arrived to see Thomas the last day I was at the house, and Thomas sounded cold with him, almost angry."

Robert nodded. "So there was something going on between them. Let me do a little digging and maybe drop in on Clinton at the museum."

"There are probably other people who wanted him dead, right?"

Victoria landed a surprised gaze on Hank, who rested his arm across one propped-up knee.

He gave her a cute smile. "Sorry, but in murder mysteries, there are always a bunch of suspects."

Torin chuckled. "If only real-life police work was as easy as on TV."

"Okay." Hank held up a hand and grinned. "But this guy was rich and told you," he aimed his blue eyes at Victoria, "that he couldn't trust anybody. That has to mean more people could've wanted him dead."

Victoria moistened her lips. "You're right. His niece and nephew visited him frequently, but even I could tell their interest in him was inauthentic and selfish. He always said they were waiting for him to die so they could inherit his fortune."

"What are their names?" Spring accepted the glass of water Torin handed her from the end table beside him.

"The nephew is Ryan Briscoe. Brenda married and is Brenda Fellsworth now. They're siblings, the children of Thomas's deceased older sister."

"Are either of them into fitness?" Treese pushed her straight long hair behind her shoulder.

"Oh, yes. Ryan is very proud of his workout regimen." Victoria would never forget the first time they'd met, and Ryan had flirted with her, trying to impress her with his flexing muscles. Only later had he apparently decided she was a threat to his inheritance, an idea she'd thought unbelievable at the time. Evidently, he and Brenda had been smarter than Victoria had thought. And their suspicions about her and Thomas could have led to his death.

"Perfect. Know what gym he goes to?"

"I think he may have mentioned it, but I don't recall."

"No worries. Does he live in Gealanden, too?"

"Yes."

"Great. I'll find him. I know all the gym managers there."

Robert laughed. "And you've probably dated every single one."

Treese lifted one slim shoulder with a sly smile. "How else would I know them?"

"Okay, commercial break from the Treese reality show." Spring rolled her eyes before angling her head toward Victoria. "Do you know any background on Brenda?"

Victoria took a moment to think. "Well, she's very involved in raising money for charities with fundraisers. I believe she sits on a few charity boards, as well. She was often trying to impress Thomas with the money she raised or the charities she was helping."

"Oh, I know." Spring glanced at Torin with widened eyes

before sharing the same lightbulb idea look with the others. "I could approach her about the Chicago Wheels benefit."

Victoria smiled at Spring's enthusiasm. Only four months ago, Spring didn't want to get out of bed to sit in a wheelchair, and now she was volunteering with the local nonprofit to help disabled people in need.

"Okay, but what would be the purpose? The goal?" Torin took the glass Spring handed back to him. "It would take a long-term friendship and trust to get her to confess anything incriminating."

"True." She glanced at Robert across the room. "Robby could probably get them to talk more quickly with his get-people-to-tell-you-everything superpower."

Robert grinned. "About time someone recognized my superpower status." He earned chuckles from several of his siblings. "But seriously, I think all we need to do for now is establish if they have alibis for the time of the murder. Am I right about that?" He landed his attention on the only one with law enforcement experience in their midst.

Torin set the glass on the end table. "That would definitely help, and it's something the current detective on the case is apparently not looking into."

"Great. We can do that easily enough through natural conversation."

"We don't know the time of death." Victoria looked at Robert. "I found him in the morning, but he had likely been killed overnight."

"Between eleven p.m. and one a.m." Treese inserted the strangely precise information.

"How do you know that?"

She smiled at Victoria. "Your lawyer."

"Why is it everyone knows more information than I do, when I'm the one they suspect of committing the crime?"

Her siblings laughed, and Cillian chuckled beside her.

"That wasn't actually meant to be a joke."

"Sorry, sis." Hank sent her a loving grin. "You just aren't a very good criminal."

A smile tugged at her mouth. "Thank you."

"Though I can't get directly involved in this case," Torin wrapped his arm around Spring's shoulders from behind as he addressed the group, "I can run background checks on all the suspects."

"That'd be great." Cillian looked at the sergeant. "Can you check out the staff, too?"

"The staff?" Victoria hadn't considered them suspects.

Cillian turned his head toward her, accelerating her pulse from the nearness of his dark eyes. "Yeah. He had a cook or something, right?"

"Mrs. Kline was his housekeeper and cook, yes."

"Any other staff?" Torin lowered his arm to pull the miniature notepad from his pocket that he had used when he had first interviewed Spring at the rehab center.

"The groundskeeper, Ned Parker." Victoria tried to imagine either of them wanting to harm Thomas. She couldn't. "They've both worked for Thomas for decades. I believe Mrs. Kline was with him thirty years, at least. I can't believe they would want to hurt him."

Torin met her gaze with a grim one. "Sadly, I've learned you can never really know what people are capable of. Like Robert said, the right motivation can turn anyone into a criminal. Even into a killer."

Exactly as he, Spring, and Victoria had experienced firsthand four months ago.

Victoria nodded. "You're right, of course."

Cillian squeezed her shoulders, his arm making full contact. "Glad you said that."

She could hardly pay attention to his words or his grin as her senses flew into overdrive at the touch of his muscled arm, a tender embrace around her.

"I'm thinking you and I can talk to the housekeeper. Try to feel out what she knows and check for an alibi."

Victoria rotated her head away. She couldn't articulate her instinctive dislike of trying to trick Mrs. Kline while electricity sparked through her limbs and pumped her heart at an alarming rate.

Honestly. She was a grown woman, not an inexperienced girl of fifteen. She would not be swept away by emotion and hormones into mindless foolishness again.

If only his arm around her shoulders didn't feel so strengthening, so comforting, giving her support she didn't know she needed.

What if God had sent Cillian into her life again for such a time as this to help her, not to be a hindrance or temptation?

The possibility shifted something within her, as if a door had swung open, allowing tension and stress to escape as calm and optimism took their place.

So she found her voice and met Cillian's gaze. "Yes, let's do that."

How much more God wanted them to do together now and in the future was a question she would have to give serious consideration. After she was no longer the number one suspect in her friend's murder.

# CHAPTER
# TWENTY-TWO

"ANOTHER COOKIE?" Judy Kline lifted the plate of homemade chocolate chip cookies and held it out toward Cillian across the table in her modest, old-fashioned dining room that was open to the kitchen. "You look like a young man who needs more to eat. Not enough meat on your bones, my mother would say."

He grinned. "Well, I never turn down cookies as good as these. Thank you." He took a third cookie and bit into the delicious softness. Probably the best chocolate chip cookies he'd ever had.

"I'll pass, thank you." Victoria, sitting in the chair next to Cillian, held up a hand with a smile. "They really are delicious. I can see why Thomas hired you as his cook and housekeeper. The house was always immaculate."

Judy jerked a nod as she set the plate down in the middle of the table. Her lips pressed together with the emotion she'd obviously been trying to hold back since they'd started talking about her boss.

"I had the feeling you two were friends, as well. I thought, perhaps, working for him wasn't only a job for you."

Judy's gaze jumped to Victoria across the table. "We were

family in a way. I worked for him for forty years." Judging from her graying hair, she must have started the job when she was about thirty. "My family are all gone. Have been for some time. His, too."

Cillian swallowed the bite of cookie. "Except for his niece and nephew."

Judy's green eyes sharpened. "Those two hardly count as family. Circling vultures was more like it."

He tried to hold back a laugh as he shot a glance at Victoria.

She kept a perfectly proper expression, of course, as she watched Judy. "I hate to consider it, but do you believe they could have hurt Thomas?"

"You mean kill him?" Judy's hand went to her coffee mug on the table in front of her. "Absolutely." The confidence in her tone and gaze would be perfect on a witness stand if it came to that.

"Do you think they did kill him? Or one of them did it alone?" Cillian took another bite of the fabulous dessert.

"I don't know for sure. They weren't supposed to have the code to unlock the house, but that Brenda was such a snooper. I think she had found it someplace Thomas must have kept it written down."

"What makes you say that?" Victoria lifted her mug and took a sip of the tea Judy had given her.

"She was in the house one morning before I arrived. Thomas didn't let her in, but he found her in his office. He thought I must have been there and let her in."

"She was in his office?" Victoria set down the mug.

"Yes. Probably snooping."

Victoria glanced at Cillian.

Thinking the same thing he was, no doubt. The guy who'd knocked her down had been in the office, too. Could he have been the nephew, Ryan, instead of Clinton Glenn? He could've been looking for whatever the niece thought was in the office. Maybe a copy of the will?

Since Judy was turning out to be such wealth of information, he should probably see what she thought of the man who was Cillian's prime suspect at the moment. "What about Clinton Glenn, the museum curator?"

"Oh, Mr. Glenn." She frowned as her eyebrows lowered. "That's a sad situation."

Cillian's instincts fired. Not the answer he'd expected but an intriguing one. He opened his mouth to prompt her to say more, but she continued on her own.

"He and Mr. Briscoe were good friends for nearly ten years, you know." She directed her gaze at Victoria.

"Yes, I thought they were." Victoria was really good at this interview thing. She sounded empathetic when she should, calm and trustworthy with perfect timing. Mostly, she listened instead of speaking. No wonder Judy had been so willing to talk to them without hesitation when they'd shown up unannounced at her front door, even on a Sunday afternoon. And Victoria had been so worried the woman wouldn't talk to her because of the murder charges.

"That all changed when Mr. Briscoe discovered something that Mr. Glenn had done. Something very bad."

Cillian quickly swallowed the last of the cookie. "What was it?"

"I don't know."

Disappointment sagged in Cillian's chest, and he reached for the glass of milk to wash down the cookie.

"I wish I had asked more now, but I never pried into Mr. Briscoe's affairs. We respected each other's privacy."

"You knew Mr. Briscoe better than anyone, I would guess." Victoria's eyebrows dipped in an earnest expression. "You must have had an inkling as to what happened, perhaps the nature of what Mr. Glenn had done."

Judy nodded. "I got the sense it was a betrayal of some kind. It was personal for Mr. Briscoe. Very personal. He wasn't only angry with Mr. Glenn, he was disappointed. Maybe a little hurt."

"Do you know of anything they were involved in together?" Cillian lowered the glass to the table. "Something that would have put Glenn in a position to betray Thomas?"

Judy looked at him for a few beats before she responded. "Well, Thomas was a major supporter of the museum. Financially, I mean. And he donated many of the best pieces from his art collection to the museum so they could be enjoyed by others." She directed her gaze to Victoria with a smile. "You know how generous he was that way. He always thought his money should be used for good, not just for himself."

Victoria returned the smile. "Yes, I know. It was one of the many things I admired about him."

"It's why he liked you, too. After your appointments, he'd often say to me, 'that Victoria has a good heart and a sharp mind.'" Judy's eyes glistened with moisture. "Your visits were the highlight of his life this last year."

A slight sniff drew Cillian's attention to Victoria.

No tears moistened her cheeks, but she rubbed her lips together like she was trying to hold back emotion. "Thank you for telling me that. Seeing him was always the best part of my day, too."

Judy nodded as a tear escaped. She brushed it away with the backs of her fingers. "Would you look at me, getting all blubbery. Mr. Briscoe wouldn't believe it." She mustered a watery smile. "I'd better let you two youngsters go before I make more of a fool of myself." She pushed out her chair and got to her feet.

Cillian and Victoria stood, too, and Victoria rounded the table to Judy.

She put her hand on the older woman's arm. "Loving someone is never foolish. I know if Thomas were here, he would be grateful you cared enough to shed your tears for him."

"You, too, sweet thing." Judy patted Victoria's wrist. "He was right to trust you. You're one of the few good ones, these days."

"I thank the Lord for that. I wouldn't be anything good without His work in my life." Leave it to Victoria to insert a mini sermon into the conversation. Wasn't enough she'd already been to church today, insisting she and Cillian had to wait until she was done with that before they could visit the housekeeper.

But Judy didn't seem to mind. She just nodded and smiled. "I know what you mean."

The two women shared a look that seemed secretive or conspiratorial. Like they knew something Cillian didn't.

He cleared his throat. "We'll get out of your way now, Mrs. Kline. Thanks for talking to us without any warning. We'll see ourselves out." He stepped behind Victoria to her other side and put his hand lightly on her back as he spoke.

She threw him a glance, her eyes widened.

He hadn't actually meant to take advantage or consciously thought about touching her. He'd done it without thinking. Naturally, like he'd been doing it for years. Like they were a couple.

He dropped his hand away as he let her walk in front of him through the kitchen, the hallway, and out the door into the sunny winter day.

Victoria paused on the front step and turned toward Judy, so he did the same. "Thank you so much for your time. You've been very helpful, and you're so kind to invite me into your home despite…the situation."

"Oh, my dear." The older woman gave Victoria a firm stare. "Mr. Briscoe would be angrier than a hornet's nest if he knew they suspected you of having anything to do with his death. I don't know what the police are doing these days. Such a waste of taxpayers' money. You are as honest and trustworthy as the winter is cold. Anyone can see that just to look at you."

"Thank you, Mrs. Kline." Victoria barely fit in her response before Judy continued.

"And I have to say," the woman's expression lightened as she lifted her gaze to Cillian, "you two make a darling couple."

He grinned. The woman had terrific instincts.

Judy returned her focus to Victoria. "Mr. Briscoe would have been glad to meet your handsome young man."

"Oh, he's not—"

*Pop-pop-pop.*

The explosive sound that cut off Victoria's words instantly retrieved Cillian's childhood memories of a rough neighborhood.

Gunshots.

# CHAPTER
# TWENTY-THREE

"ARE YOU OKAY?" Cillian's deep voice reached for Victoria, dispersing the fog that seemed to have descended on her mind.

Gunfire. She had hoped never to hear that sound again. Once in a lifetime was quite enough.

"Victoria?"

She blinked and turned her head to look upward.

Cillian's handsome features greeted her, his coal eyes a stormy sea of emotion. Concern, anger...

"Is he gone?" Somehow the assumption that a person who shot at people from a moving car was male seemed logically sound.

Cillian twisted his head toward the street. "Yeah." He placed his hands on either side of her and lifted himself up. Surprising he'd been so careful not to actually touch her with his body when he'd shielded her.

Victoria had always known he was protective and courageous. But she'd never thought she would be in such great need of those qualities as she had been during the last few seconds. Or minutes, according to how it had felt.

He had probably saved her life. And the life of poor Mrs. Kline.

He helped the older woman to her feet as Victoria sat up, her gaze staying on the hero who had protected them both. The position of his body on Victoria at the front of the step would have also blocked any shots from hitting Mrs. Kline behind them unless the bullets traveled through Cillian first.

The thought sent a shudder through Victoria. He could have been killed.

"Are you cold?" He suddenly appeared in front of her, extending his hand toward her.

She placed her hand in his and was instantly enveloped in the warmth of his large, strong grip. Sparks emanated from the heat of the connection as he pulled her to standing, less than a foot from his chest. She tilted her head up to meet his gaze.

The same electricity and emotional vortex that she seemed to have fallen into reflected in his eyes.

"Oh, my siding." Dismay squeezed Mrs. Kline's voice.

How had Victoria forgotten she was there? Perhaps watching them. Heat flushed her cheeks as she pulled her hand from Cillian's and stepped away.

But Mrs. Kline stared at her house where bullet-holes made the blue siding resemble splintered Swiss cheese. "This will cost a pretty penny to repair."

The woman was remarkably resilient. She had been shot at, and all she was concerned about was her home repair. No wonder Thomas had liked her so well. He'd always said she was the most practical person he knew.

Victoria glanced at Cillian. "I suppose we should call the police." For the first time, she understood the way Cillian had avoided policemen when they were dating as teens. If one had been in trouble, or cared about those who were, certain police personnel didn't seem like one's friends.

"Could help, in this case." He pulled his phone from his

back jeans pocket but then met her gaze, waiting. For her approval?

She moistened her lips, trying to ignore the nerves that jumbled in her stomach. Somehow facing bullets had made her less apprehensive than the idea of facing McCully again. Likely because he could put her behind bars for a second time. But she nodded. "Go ahead."

Ten minutes later, when Detective McCully emerged from his unmarked car on the street by Mrs. Kline's house, Victoria was questioning her agreement that they should call the police.

Mrs. Kline's short driveway was already filled with the two squad cars that had responded to their emergency call. At least the officer who had called in McCully had warned Victoria he was going to do so, once the officer had learned who she was.

The incident had to be connected to the murder of Thomas. It was a good thing McCully had been called. Perhaps he wouldn't see her as the culprit now that someone had shot at her.

Victoria cycled through the hopeful thoughts in her head as McCully stalked up the driveway, stopping in front of her and Cillian where they stood by the first squad car.

"You sure seem to be in the middle of a lot of crimes, Ms. Weston." His smirk didn't distract her from the suspicion that hid behind a thin veneer of amusement in his eyes. "Guess I should've just sent a unit out as soon as your monitor showed you'd left Gealanden and gone to Feldon."

Victoria hid the shudder that traveled through her. What a horrifying invasion of privacy to have her every move watched by someone, especially someone like Detective McCully.

"Got it backwards, as usual, McCully. Someone is putting her in the middle of these crimes." Cillian's tone held challenge. "And this time, it nearly killed her."

McCully lifted his attention to Cillian, and the two men locked stares in what appeared to be a silent battle of wills.

"Detective McCully." One of the two responding officers walked to them from the house. "We need you to take a look at this."

"Right."

Victoria stepped aside as McCully passed them to join the officers on the front porch.

"That guy might be the sorriest excuse for a detective I've ever seen." Cillian's voice dropped to Victoria, low and frustrated. "And I've seen some doozies."

She folded her arms across her buttoned coat as a shiver tracked through her. Being out in the cold this long was not helping her nerves or composure. "I know." She turned her head to Cillian as they both stood facing the officers investigating the evidence on the porch. "But please let me deal with him. I know how to handle people like him."

"So do I." Cillian's tone said he still had confrontation or intimidation in mind.

She sighed. She hated to go there, but... "I grew up with a forceful man used to getting his way, remember?" She angled another look at Cillian. She didn't want to speak negatively about her father with him, but this approach was the only one she could think of to get him to follow her request. She did not want to end up in jail again, thanks to Cillian's well-meaning defense of her innocence. "I think I can claim the most long-term experience."

His eyebrows raised. The corner of his mouth twitched. "You win."

"Thank you."

Detective McCully started down the steps toward them.

"I'll hold you to that." She sent Cillian a warning glance she hoped would remind him to behave.

McCully stopped in front of them and crossed his arms over his chest. "Looks like somebody really did take a shot at you."

"A shot? It was a lot more than—"

Victoria grabbed Cillian's wrist to silence him. So much for his agreement to let her handle the detective. And how was his skin so warm in this cold?

She forced herself to focus on McCully and keep her expression neutral. "Yes, sadly, someone did. We're concerned it might be someone who wants to silence me and keep me from discovering who the killer is."

"Is that what you were doing here today? Interviewing your suspects to solve the mystery?" The detective's mocking tone warned her to keep silent. He lowered his hands to his hips. "This isn't some book or TV show. And if you were doing that, you could be charged with interfering in a police investigation."

Victoria hid the inner flinch at his threat. He would no doubt love to arrest her again and keep her imprisoned even longer than that one agonizing night.

Cillian rotated his wrist in her grip and, suddenly, he was holding her hand in his, hanging low at their sides.

She should pull away. What if the detective saw?

But she didn't pull away. She couldn't. Because the sheltering, strengthening contact sent courage spiraling through her.

She didn't look at Cillian but kept her hand in his as she met McCully's hostile gaze. "Mrs. Kline and I know each other from working for Mr. Briscoe. We were sharing memories of our time there." Completely true. Those memories just happened to be helpful for determining who had motive and means to kill Thomas. "Surely you see, Detective, that someone else, a violent person, is trying to keep some information from coming out regarding the murder?"

"Could be." McCully smoothed his mustache with his fingers. "Could be you hired the shooter to divert suspicion away from yourself."

A grunt rumbled in Cillian's throat.

Victoria squeezed his hand, hoping that would stop him from confronting the detective again. "I would never put Mrs. Kline or..." What should she call Cillian? A friend? She quickly reworded. "...Any person in harm's way, even if I do hope to prove my innocence to you."

"Seems like you need to look at the evidence a bit longer, Detective." Cillian spoke before she could stop him. But at least his tone was controlled, albeit something akin to a leash on a tiger. "We'll leave you to it." He tugged gently on Victoria's hand to turn her away, letting go to lightly touch her back as he guided her down the driveway. At least that would prevent the detective from seeing they had held hands.

Victoria looked over her shoulder at McCully.

His eyes narrowed as he watched them, but he didn't say a word.

"Just keep going." Cillian moved to her side, and they continued to walk down the driveway to the vehicles they had parked along the street when they'd first arrived. "He can't hold us for anything."

She sighed. "I had hoped this would at least show him I'm innocent."

"Yeah. So much for the smoking gun changing his mind." Cillian gave her a rueful smile as they stopped in front of her car.

"I wonder—"

Chopin's music interrupted her reply. She dug in her pocket for her phone and pulled it out.

"That ringtone is so you." Cillian grinned.

She gave him a half smile, then looked at the screen. "It's an unknown number."

"Better take it. Might be a tip or something. Or Briscoe's lawyer."

It was true, Victoria hadn't added him to her contacts yet, though she had called him back to set up a meeting to go over the terms of her inheritance this coming week.

At least she didn't have to remove her gloves to answer the call. She used the touchscreen finger, then pressed the phone to her ear. "Victoria Weston."

"Hello, Ms. Weston." The female voice was familiar. But not in a good way. Brenda Fellsworth.

"This is Thomas Briscoe's niece."

"Mrs. Fellsworth, yes. I'm sorry for your loss."

"Are you?" Gone was the faux politeness Brenda had adopted with Victoria before. Now sarcasm and destain dripped from her tone. "My loss is your gain, it seems."

"Mrs. Fellsworth, I—"

"Save it for court, Ms. Weston."

Court?

"I'm calling to tell you to stay away from my uncle's estate. Don't touch the money, the house, anything that is rightfully ours."

"Mrs. Fellsworth, Thomas did will his—"

"That's preposterous. Clearly, he was out of his mind, and you took advantage of him. Our lawyers are securing an injunction right now. You can't touch any of it, and we're taking you to court."

"But—"

The line went silent. Brenda had ended the call.

"That was the niece?" Cillian's eyebrows pressed together as he watched her. "She threatened you?"

Victoria slid the phone into her coat pocket and gripped the shoulder strap of her purse. "She says she and her brother are going to take me to court, and in the meantime, they're securing an injunction that will prevent me from accessing Thomas's house or money. Not that I have any desire to touch his money anyway."

"So they don't have the injunction yet."

She looked up at him. That tone made her uneasy, as did the glint in his eyes. "Why does that matter?"

"Because we can still go to the house right now."

"Why would we do that?"

"This Brenda and her brother clearly don't want you there, which must mean there's something they don't want you to find. Maybe her brother is the one I chased away that night when the office was ransacked. I need to check what kind of car he drives."

Victoria blinked. "But we can't."

"Why not?"

"First, lawyers are getting an injunction to prevent me from doing so and second, which is actually the first consideration," she glanced back toward the house as she lowered her voice, "Detective McCully threatened to arrest us for interfering in a police investigation."

Cillian followed the direction of her gaze, then brought his focus back to her. "In case you've forgotten, the detective is going to lock you up for murder if we don't find out who really killed Thomas. He's building a case against you, Vicks. He's not looking at anyone else. And he won't unless we force him to."

She pressed her lips together. Could Cillian be right? But even if he was, the risk that McCully would arrest her for interference was also a genuine concern. She was caught between a rock and a hard place.

"You may be willing to trust the detective to figure out you're innocent." Cillian's grim tone pulled her back to his hard expression. "But I won't take that chance. I will not let him lock you up again." The fierce protectiveness in his dark eyes made the words seem like a promise.

Her heart squeezed behind her ribs. She could only nod, her throat too tight for speaking.

He touched her shoulder, giving her a gentle squeeze through her coat. "I'll meet you there." He turned away and headed for his jeep on the other side of the driveway.

She watched longer than she should have. Especially since McCully could be observing her.

She threw a glance at the house as she rounded her car to the driver's side.

McCully seemed busy with the officers, examining the porch and steps.

She managed to start her car with numb fingers and drove,

following Cillian to Thomas's house about twenty minutes away.

She tried not to heed the discomfort as the heater began to return warmth to her fingers. And she tried to ignore her thoughts, the way they turned constantly toward Cillian. To the support he'd given her with McCully by his protectiveness and, then, through his hand holding hers.

It had felt more natural now than when she'd been a teen girl. Then, she'd been so overwhelmed with all her senses firing at his touch, so concerned that she wasn't experienced enough for a boy like him. The first time he'd held her hand, she had been sure she wasn't putting her fingers in the right place, and her hands were probably too cold or clammy. His touch had felt incredible, like nothing she'd ever experienced, but overwhelming and uncomfortable at the same time.

When he'd taken her hand now in front of the detective, it was as natural as if they'd been holding hands for the sixteen years they'd been apart. It was as if they were a team, facing life together and strengthening each other with understanding, compassion, and the courage that comes from knowing one is not alone. The butterflies that had tickled her belly proved the attraction hadn't dimmed, but there was also a connection that felt so much deeper.

A rap on her window made her jump.

Cillian leaned down and waved at her through the glass.

She peered out the windshield at the sunlit mansion. When had she stopped her car in Thomas's driveway? Hopefully, her autopilot brain was a skilled driver.

She unlocked the door and exited her car, scanning the empty curves of the driveway. "Looks like we're the only ones here this time."

"Good. We can really go over the place." Cillian fell in step beside her, clearly slowing his stride so as not to outpace her. Though his barely restrained eagerness showed in his energetic movements.

"Why don't we split up inside so we can cover ground more quickly?"

He glanced at her. "Good idea."

Relief released a smidgen of the tension balling her stomach. She needed time and space away from him. He was muddying her thoughts, and her feelings, far too much.

As soon as they entered the foyer, she pointed toward the hallway. "Why don't you take the office and the other rooms down that hallway?" She would just as soon not relive the experience they'd had there. "I'll go to the second floor and look at the bedrooms."

"Sounds like a plan. Meet you back here." Cillian smiled like a boy about to play hooky before he spun away and strode quickly up the hall.

She shook her head, a smile finding her lips, too, as she took the staircase that curved along the wall.

Cillian was still incorrigible when it came to bending rules or adventuring. Though he would likely say this didn't qualify as an adventure.

At the top of the stairs, she looked to the left and then right along the carpeted balcony. Two doors lined the wall around the bend to the left and four to her right, two of those located beyond the second staircase.

Thomas's bedroom was the second door to her right, but she didn't know what the other rooms were.

She would start with the room where she had first met Thomas.

Vibrantly patterned antique Indian carpet cushioned her steps as she walked to his bedroom along the balcony.

She paused by the closed door and took in a long breath. Then she reached for the knob and opened the door.

*"You're not what I expected for a physical therapist. I suppose I'll see you one more time."*

Thomas's voice sounded in her memory at the same time she saw him propped up in his bed, the ornate bedspread covering his legs.

She blinked, and the memory vanished from her vision, hot tears filling her eyes instead.

Perhaps she shouldn't have come to his room, the location of those first visits when he was recovering from surgery, where they'd started to become friends.

But if his office was a target for someone looking for information or evidence Thomas may have had, his bedroom was an equally possible hiding place.

She straightened her shoulders and stepped inside. Tabling her memories, she tried to remain objective and detached, while still accessing what she knew about Thomas.

Where would he have hidden something important in his room? Something he hadn't wanted his family or even Mrs. Kline to discover. Perhaps the armoire?

She crossed the room to the beautiful, antique armoire made of dark wood carved with an elegant design. The doors squeaked slightly as she pulled them open.

Clothing greeted her—shirts and sweaters on hangers, sorted by color, all infused with his familiar scent.

Moisture pooled in her eyes again.

She reached for the wool, burgundy sweater, running her fingers over the fabric.

His favorite sweater—the one she'd always complimented him on when he'd worn it, since it had suited his skin tone so well.

She sniffed. She wasn't here to walk down memory lane. And it wouldn't do for Cillian to come upstairs and find her weeping.

She scanned the armoire. Nothing appeared out of place. Shifting the clothing to one side, she ran her fingers along the back wall that was too dark to thoroughly inspect.

No bumps or hidden wires met her touch.

She conducted the same tactile search along the bottom of the interior.

Apparently, hidden compartments weren't as common in

real life as in the murder mysteries she'd read since she was a teenager. She had told Cillian she watched them on TV, but she had only seen a few such programs. She still preferred books to TV but telling him that would have only encouraged him to think she was controlled by her father's preferences.

The armoire was not proving helpful. Perhaps the dresser drawers would hide something?

She closed the left door.

"What are you doing here?" Ryan Briscoe glared at her, standing exactly where the door had been. Much too close.

Her heart stopped, then took off at superspeed. "I could ask you the same question." She lifted her chin.

She should have said something calmer and less confrontational. Cillian might be having a negative effect on her.

Anger lit Ryan's eyes, and his fists flexed at his side.

But letting him see fear would only make him more aggressive.

"You have no right to be here. This is our house. It rightfully belongs to us."

Victoria tried to pull in enough oxygen through her nose to calm her system and help her think of the best response. "I suppose that will be for the courts to decide."

His nostrils flared as he took a step closer. "Oh, it's already decided. You aren't welcome here."

She needed to deescalate this situation. Now. "I understand you're upset. You've lost your uncle, and I'm sorry for that." She stepped around him, headed for the door.

He grabbed her from behind, gripping her upper arms.

She gasped and tried to pull away.

He slammed her shoulder into the wall.

She spun toward him, but he pinned her back against the wall, pushing her hard into the wood paneling.

"You can't do this. I won't let you do this." Spit flew from his mouth as he leaned in, his hands grinding her into the wall with a strength she couldn't resist.

She forced herself to meet his gaze. Fear bolted through her at what she saw.

His eyes held the hatred of a killer.

# CHAPTER
# TWENTY-FOUR

"PLEASE, YOU'RE HURTING ME." Victoria's words hit Cillian's ears as he reached the top of the staircase.

Alarm spiked through him, and he sprinted toward her voice, the only open door on the balcony. Who could be in the house, hurting her?

He shot through the doorway.

A man pinned Victoria against the wall.

"Get your hands off her!" Cillian lunged at the thug. Ripped him away from Victoria. Landed a punch on his face.

The blond-haired guy stumbled backward, his hand going briefly to his nose. He made a fist and rushed at Cillian.

Cillian ducked under the guy's wide swing and grabbed his waist, lifting him backward with a grunt and thrusting him to the floor.

The guy blinked up from the ground.

Cillian bent over and lifted the bully by the front of his jacket, fury and adrenaline streaking through his veins. "Don't you even think of roughing up a woman again. Especially that woman." He released his hold, letting the guy drop.

His head hit the floor as he fell. He groaned.

"Cillian, stop. I'm all right." Victoria's hand on his arm

stopped him from giving in to the desire to punch the guy again, just to be sure he got the message.

But the thug used that moment to scramble away, getting to his feet.

"Stay back." Cillian pushed Victoria behind him as he stepped toward the man.

He dodged Cillian's reach and sprinted for the door.

Cillian started after him.

"No!" Victoria's call stopped him. "Cillian, don't go."

She could be hurt. Needed his help.

He turned toward her then, the beautiful, heartbreaking woman he'd do anything to protect.

Strands of her hair had come loose from her bun, falling to frame her gorgeous face. He stepped close to her and touched a silky clump, slipping it behind her ear. He let his knuckles brush her cheek.

She sucked in a quick breath at his touch, making his heart thud into his ribs.

"I heard you say he was hurting you. Are you sure you're okay?"

"I was only trying to get him to let me go." But her hand went to her left shoulder to rub it.

He had hurt her. If he hadn't gotten away, Cillian would gladly pummel him some more. But Victoria needed him right now. She wouldn't say it, but she didn't have to. An emotion he rarely saw in her eyes colored the hazel orbs. Fear.

His throat tightened. He should've stayed with her in the house, not agreed to split up. "Do you know who he was? Where he came from?"

"Ryan Briscoe, Thomas's nephew. He must have entered the house after we did. Or he was already in one of the other rooms and heard us." She crossed her arms and rubbed her hands along the sleeves of her coat. Another sign of fright he hadn't seen her show before.

That jerk had really scared her.

"I'm sorry." Cillian rested his hand on her shoulder, lightly so as not to irritate any bruises there. "I shouldn't have left you alone."

She lifted her chin. "Nonsense. I suggested we split up."

There she was. The strong, no-nonsense Victoria he loved.

"But thank you." She moistened her lips and glanced away before returning her gaze to his. "I don't know what he might have done if…" Her voice pinched as if she was about to cry.

Cillian's gut twisted. He pulled her into his arms.

She allowed it, her cheek pressing against his chest as she squeezed his triceps in one hand with a death grip that revealed more than anything.

His heart cracked a little. He tucked her in closer, cinched his arms tighter, wanting her to feel safe. "It's okay. I've got you."

She let him hold her, her grip on his arm relaxing with her whole body as she slowly melted against him.

Then, too soon, she pulled away. Her eyelashes lifted to reveal those hazel beauties, filled with something new.

Maybe, he could imagine, it was actually something old—something like the adoration and longing she used to feel for him. The affection. The love.

But no, that wasn't it. This was deeper, something more grown-up and solid. Trust?

He wouldn't know unless he asked or she told him. But if she was starting to trust him, to care for him again, he wouldn't ruin it by being nosy and scaring her off.

He cleared his throat. "Do you want to leave? I can drive you home and come back for your car later."

"No." Her jaw tightened. "We need to find what Ryan was after, what he was afraid I might discover here."

Seemed Ryan's attack had backfired. Cillian smiled. That was his Victoria. "Let's do it. I found a bunch of papers in a hidden compartment behind a bookshelf in the library."

"Really?" She stared at him.

"Yep."

"It seems they don't only exist in stories after all."

Cillian chuckled. "I guess not. I was coming to ask if you want to sift through them with me."

Her mouth curved in a closed smile that made his pulse skitter. "I'd like nothing better."

He stuck close to her as they went downstairs and to the library, but she was rebounding fast. Her walk and posture were as graceful and perfect as always.

They spread out the papers on the desk in the corner of the library and pored over them for what felt like an hour. Cillian never had liked paperwork or research.

"Did you see this?" Victoria lifted a sheet of paper in her hand.

Cillian stopped himself from pointing out he couldn't possibly have seen anything in her section of papers when he'd been busy looking through his. "What is it?"

"Documents, receipts, certificates of authenticity." Her brow furrowed adorably as she peered down at the papers she lined up in a row on the desk.

Cillian moved closer beside her and scanned the information.

Images of paintings with estimated values printed beneath them. Authenticity reports.

Wait. "This one verifies the authenticity of this painting." He put his finger on the document. "But this report," he pointed to the paper directly in front of her, "says the same painting is a fake?"

She shook her head. "It's not the same one." She sifted through papers and pulled out another sheet. "This documents Thomas's donation to the museum for both of those paintings and the dates they were authenticated prior to his donation." She set the paper in front of Cillian, and his gaze fell on the date.

"You're right. The authentication that says the painting is fake was done after it was donated to the museum." He lifted his gaze, colliding with Victoria's hazel eyes.

"Clinton Glenn substituted fake paintings for Thomas's real ones after they were donated. And Thomas had proof."

"Wow. Glenn's a thief. He must've sold them on the black market. Or is going to when he thinks he can get away with it."

Lines crossed Victoria's forehead. "So then Glenn would be the one who searched Thomas's office and knocked me down?"

"Looks that way. Though there must be a reason Ryan was so mad to find you here and his sister threatened you to stay away from the house." Cillian rested his hands on his hips. "We should probably keep searching in case there's something else to find."

She checked her wristwatch. "I'm late for Max's lunch. I need to go."

"I'll go with you."

She quirked one eyebrow as she picked up her purse from the desk. "To my house?"

"I think it's about time I meet the rest of your family."

A smile shaped her mouth. "How can I say 'no' to that?"

His pulse took off at a record-breaking sprint. Maybe he was getting somewhere with Victoria Weston after all.

She was starting to let him back into her life, starting to flex and change in good ways. And, maybe, she was starting to love him again.

———

Victoria's living room had never felt so tiny. She walked to the coffee table in front of the sofa and set down the tray, her cheeks warming as she felt Cillian's gaze on her.

He sat on her small sofa, his long legs and large frame taking up an inordinate amount of space. In reality, his mere presence, his intense observation, and the electricity that seemed to surge every time she came within a foot of him, were likely the reason her house seemed to have shrunk even smaller than its usual size.

"How do you take your coffee?" She reached for the navy blue mug she'd chosen for him and filled it with the steaming brew.

"Black, thanks." Amusement colored his tone.

She dared a glance as she lifted the mug from the tray and handed it to him.

His fingers brushed hers on the handle.

A shock blazed up her arm.

And the same spark flickered in his eyes.

She tried to breathe through her nose as she looked down at the other mug on the tray and added a spoon of sugar. She backed away and sat in the armchair a safe distance away from him.

Poor Max sat in the corner there anyway, and she needed to comfort him with her presence. The dog stared at Cillian with his steady, piercing gaze, his ears perked and body tense.

She rested her hand on his velvety head. "It's okay, Max."

"He's not the friendly type, I see." Cillian returned the dog's observation as he rested one ankle on his knee in Robert's favorite relaxed pose.

"He used to be. He started to become fearful of strangers when he was six months old. I still don't know why."

"Does he ever warm up to new people?"

"It helps if they don't stare at him."

Cillian's gaze switched to her, and he smiled. "Got it. I'll pretend he isn't there."

"He can get used to some people with patience and time."

"I can be patient."

She quirked an eyebrow at him as she lifted the mug to her lips. "That would be the first time."

Cillian grinned. "Maybe I'm learning. And maybe it's worth waiting for." The shift and suggestion in his tone said he was no longer referring only to Max.

A blush surged to her cheeks again. She took an urgent, long sip of coffee.

"Awesome dog, though. He's huge."

She grasped the subject change. "Thank you. I think he's wonderful."

"At least his size should help scare away anyone with ideas."

"So you didn't have to follow me home." She gave him a teasing smile.

"I don't know." He met her gaze with a daring twinkle in his eyes. "My bark might be as impressive as his. I know my bite is."

"Well, he's never bitten anyone, and he rarely barks, so you might have something there."

"He doesn't bark?"

She shook her head. "Hardly ever. I'd only heard him bark once in his life until three nights ago."

Cillian's brows dipped low over his eyes.

Oh, goodness. What had she stepped into now?

"What happened three nights ago?" The sudden tension in his tone signaled his protective instincts had been triggered, though his restful posture didn't change. He would never accept anything but the whole story now.

She swallowed. "He seemed to hear something outside."

Cillian dropped his foot to the ground and leaned forward. "Someone was outside your house?"

"I didn't know that at the time."

"But you do now?" A sharp edge of what seemed to be anger cut his tone.

She moistened her lips. "I went to the garage where Max seemed to think there was a problem. I had heard something that sounded like a jiggling noise." She took in a breath.

Cillian would not like this next part. But his stare locked on her with an intensity that meant she didn't dare try to soften or hide anything.

"I thought it might have been the doorknob, so I checked

it. It was still locked, but I looked outside. And I saw foot-prints in the snow that weren't there before."

"Footprints?" He abruptly stood. "And you're just telling me this now?" Yes, that was anger in his voice.

She stood, too, setting her mug on the coffee table before tilting up her chin and meeting his gaze. "I knew if I told you, you would've overreacted and camped out on my couch or insisted we tell McCully about this, even though he obviously wouldn't have believed me or done anything about it." She glanced at Max behind her.

He'd moved to standing, his tail tucked as he stared at Cillian.

"And would you please calm down? You're scaring Max."

Cillian's focus jumped to Max, then away. He blew out a breath and pushed his fingers through his hair. "I just can't believe you didn't tell me." He shook his head, then froze. "Wait, what if that's when the killer put the bookend in your car?"

"I keep my car in the garage. And it was still locked."

"Well," Cillian lifted his hand into the air, "you can't be alone until we find the killer. That's obvious."

"Only to you." She delivered the rebuttal with the incredulity his statement deserved.

"Come on, Vicks."

"Don't 'Vicks' me." She plunked her mug on the tray and snatched it up from the table, marching to the kitchen where they at least wouldn't frighten Max.

Cillian's heavy steps followed her, as she'd anticipated. "Vicks, would you please listen?"

That nickname, the way he said it with tenderness even though they were arguing, snuck past her raised defenses and rendered them useless.

She turned toward him, folding her arms across her cardigan to keep something between them.

But he stepped close, so close that he easily touched her upper arms, resting his warm hands there. "You were just shot at and physically attacked today. It could've been a whole lot worse if I hadn't been there."

She looked away. As if she needed a reminder of the frightening experience.

"You know I would never forgive myself if I let anyone hurt you." His tone, so heavy and sincere, drew her gaze to his.

A mixture of sadness and worry reflected in his eyes, undergirded by something stronger in the depths of those coal embers. How much did he care for her? Did he...love her?

He couldn't. She couldn't return that. She could care about him as a friend, but she couldn't love him. A high school crush in the past was one thing. An adult's love, given wholly and freely was another. Both her God and her father would not approve, for very different reasons.

"How about we bring it up at the meeting tonight and see what your family thinks?"

She blinked, slowly finding her voice in the dryness of her throat. "Meeting?"

He lowered his hands and stepped back. "The investigation meeting tonight at Spring's condo. We're supposed to meet your brothers and sisters and compare notes on what we've found."

"They told you about a meeting and didn't tell me?"

His mouth angled in a grin. "I'm guessing you just didn't see the text yet."

"Oh. I haven't checked my phone since this morning."

"It's at six." His teasing grin broadened. "Want to go together?"

"No, thank you. I'm perfectly capable of driving myself."

"Got it. Mind if I take a picture of Max before I go?" Cillian pulled his phone from his back pocket.

"Whatever for?"

He chuckled. "For JaKobe, a kid I helped in Philly. He's crazy about dogs, but his foster family doesn't have any. I'll text it to him."

"You stay in touch with a boy you helped as a social worker?"

"Sure. I give all the kids my contact info, so they'll know they aren't alone. I never want them to feel helpless or trapped."

"Like you did." The memory of the sullen, angry young man he'd been in high school sharpened in her mind as if it had been only yesterday. She hadn't understood, until he'd started to open up to her, sharing hints of his dreadful home life in bits and pieces, usually as a joke so he could maintain his tough appearance. But she'd known better, even then. She'd seen the pain he tried to hide. And his need for love and acceptance—the need she knew so well.

"I got out." The tough, young Cillian could have given that answer. He was still trying to keep up his macho facade. But it couldn't hold up. Not with the evidence of what he was doing for those children he'd helped. His compassion was obvious.

"And you're helping others do the same."

"Like you're doing for Sydney." His eyes warmed as he watched her. "It's awesome you're helping her out."

"You're one to talk, Mister Mentor-of-the-Year." She smiled.

"I guess I was right. We do have some stuff in common after all." He winked.

Her heart performed a cartwheel she'd never been able to achieve as a girl. She had better start praying that the Lord would keep her from succumbing any further to Cillian's charm. Because his effect on her seemed to be increasing by the day, and it was beginning to appear she may be in danger of falling for him all over again.

# CHAPTER
# TWENTY-FIVE

"NO, NO, NO!" Treese scooted to the farthest edge of the ottoman she sat on, looking like she would fall off as she interrupted Robert. "It's gotta be the nephew."

Cillian chuckled as he carried his soda can and a mug of tea to the chairs where he and Victoria were sitting together on the opposite side of the small living room. Treese sure got passionate about debating her brother.

"One at a time, Patricia." Victoria raised her eyebrows at her youngest sister, then accepted the mug from Cillian as he sat on the chair beside her.

Robert grinned. "It's okay, Vicki. If she wants to parade her false theory out in public, I won't stop her."

Treese stuck out her tongue at her brother.

"Oh, please." Spring rolled her eyes as she wheeled into her living room and set a refilled bowl of tortilla chips on the coffee table that was surrounded by a white and blue patterned sofa, two armchairs, and the wooden chairs they'd pulled from her dining room, so everyone had a seat. "We do have some non-Westons here, so let's try to act our age for once." She aimed a pointed look at Robert and Treese.

"Oh, we are." Robert's tone stayed teasing as he answered her. "It'll be years until we're as old as you and Vicki."

Hank guffawed as Treese and Robert laughed. Spring and Torin laughed, too, along with Cillian.

Victoria shook her head slowly back and forth, but the set of her mouth was soft, and fondness lit her eyes as she watched her siblings. "Treese, you were saying you believe Ryan might be the killer."

"No might about it." Treese uncrossed and then crossed her legs, once again wearing a tight, super-short skirt. Did she ever wear anything else? The rest of her family members were more comfortably dressed in jeans or even sweatpants, in Robert's case. Though Victoria never dressed down that much, of course. She wore her usual dress pants and a green cardigan that highlighted the color of her eyes.

"I talked to the staff at the gym and some of the regulars there." Treese extended her hand in a sweeping motion. "*All* of them said he has a terrible temper. Really combustible over the slightest things. And he's been worse lately, they said. Since his uncle's death."

"You didn't talk to him, did you?" Victoria's tone held concern.

What an awesome big sister she was. She hadn't even mentioned what Ryan had done to her that day, but she was all over the possibility that her little sister could've been hurt.

"Sure, I did." Treese smirked. "And I can tell you he's a total cheater. Definitely not faithful to his wife, and I wasn't even trying."

"My check on him showed he's separated." Torin emerged from the kitchen, carrying a glass of water that he handed to Spring. "They're in the process of getting a divorce."

Treese snorted. "Big surprise there."

"What is surprising is he doesn't have any assault charges, despite his temper. At least none that stuck. A few calls to the police, but no one would press charges in the end."

"Do you think he paid them off?" Cillian aimed his question at Torin, then took a sip of soda.

"Possibly. Turns out he and his sister had trust funds from their uncle, set up for them when they were kids."

"That's right." Victoria nodded. "I recall Thomas spoke about that once, saying he'd already given them far more money than they deserved. He also said they had depleted the funds, and that was their fault."

"So Ryan is violent and desperate for more money." Cillian crossed his arms over his chest, holding the soda in one hand. "Seems more than capable of having knocked off his uncle. And he doesn't want us to find something, maybe the evidence that he killed Thomas."

"What do you mean?" Robert angled his head toward Cillian from his seat on one end of the sofa across from Cillian and Victoria.

"He threatened Victoria today." Cillian felt, rather than saw, Victoria swing her head toward him. Man, he wished they'd gotten the sofa before Robert and Hank took it. He would put his arm around her now, try to remind her through his touch that he was on her side. That she could trust him. But their chairs were too far away to make the move casual and natural. "He tried to rough her up."

"What?" Hank jumped to his feet. "Vicki? Are you okay?" His blue eyes sharpened with the concern that shaped his features.

"Yes, Hank, I'm fine." Her tone was calm and firm. "He did surprise me and told me he wouldn't let me 'do this.'" She made air quotes with her fingers. "I'm not certain precisely what he meant. But he was extremely angry and intimidating." She paused.

A tense silence filled the room as all her siblings stared at her.

"I'm thankful Cillian was there." If she'd reached over and knocked him off his chair, she couldn't have surprised him more. Had she just given him credit for protecting her in front of her whole family? Well, the part of her family that counted.

Amazement and pride ballooned in his chest, threatening to pop his ribs. Wow. Now he really wished they were sharing the sofa. Maybe he could subtly scoot his chair closer to hers.

"Thanks, man." Hank gave Cillian a nod.

Cillian returned the short dip of his head.

"Glad you were there." Robert looked from Cillian to Victoria and back again. He was noticing more than he said. But his words and expression didn't show any disapproval.

"Well, I think that settles it. Ryan is the killer." Treese stood and reached for the bowl of baby carrots on the coffee table. "Now how do we prove it?"

"You might as well keep those." Robert gave the carrots a pointed look. "You're the only one who likes them, and you'll need something to fortify your strength as I debunk your theory."

She wrinkled her nose at him as she lifted a carrot to her mouth. "It'll be amusing to watch you try." She crunched the carrot with intentional volume as she smiled around it.

"Now that the amateurs have had their say," Robert teased Treese with another grin, "allow the professionals to unpack this for you."

"Oh-ho..." His siblings laughed and kibitzed about the "Great Psychiatrist in their midst."

Cillian laughed along with Torin, and they exchanged a glance—the two non-Westons being allowed to observe the family. The Weston siblings together were something else. All intelligent and opinionated, they still managed to stay friendly, their ribbing revealing an affection they didn't need to voice.

Robert met the teasing with an even wider grin and a patronizing wave. "You mock now, but you will be speechless by the time I'm done."

"Can somebody wake me when that happens?" Hank slumped into the sofa and dramatically laid his head on the cushion behind him, closing his eyes.

"Hilarious." Robert got to his feet, wiping chip crumbs off his sweats before looking upon his audience like a magician about to perform a trick. "I agree that Ryan seems like the obvious suspect."

"But it's never the obvious suspect, right?" Spring lifted her finger in the air as she grinned at him.

Torin looked at her and opened his mouth like he was about to say something.

"Oh, I know, honey." She glanced up at her fiancé as if she'd read his thoughts. "It's not like that in real-life police work."

"Don't worry." Robert nodded toward Torin. "In honor of the actual police investigator with us tonight, I will not build my case on what I've seen on TV or read in fiction."

"Thank you." Torin played along, pressing his palm to his chest as if the gesture was deeply meaningful.

"Okay, trying to be serious here." Robert pulled the corners of his mouth down. "I think we should take a closer look at Clinton Glenn. Given what Cillian and Victoria shared about the housekeeper, I agree she isn't the murderer, and the groundskeeper was with his family at home at the time of death. But the evidence Cillian and Victoria found gives Glenn a powerful motive to kill Thomas."

"Because Thomas found out he had stolen his paintings to sell them on the black market."

"Exactly." Robert pointed to Spring like she was a student who'd gotten the right answer. "He's guilty of theft, fraud, and forgery—or at least hiring someone to produce fake paintings." He sent Torin a glance. "I'll leave that to the legal expert among us. But the point is, we can't ignore his very powerful motive."

"But Ryan and Brenda have strong motives, too." Hank pushed a hand through his blond hair. "Greed."

"True. But you said," Robert pointed at Cillian, "Glenn's car matched the one you chased away from Thomas's estate. And Glenn would definitely have reason to ransack the office, looking for the evidence Thomas had against him. Even with Thomas dead, there's a risk that evidence could be found, and Glenn would still be in serious trouble."

"You're right." Torin nodded. "He has a lot to lose—his job, reputation, and money. Not to mention getting jail time. I ran a background check on him, and his record is clean. But that could only mean this is the first time he's dipped his toes in crime, or he's been careful enough to never get caught."

Torin looked at Cillian and Victoria. "I'd go ahead and take the evidence you found, or that Thomas found, to the police. It sounds solid. Even McCully should be willing to consider Glenn is involved in fraud, if nothing else."

"I doubt it." Victoria's lips pinched at the corners. "I would never have believed a police officer could be so biased against someone, but I have to admit Detective McCully seems determined to pin this murder on me."

"We could go to Willis with it." Cillian angled toward her.

"Going above his head again would only anger him more."

Cillian opened his mouth to argue, then stopped.

Worry hovered in her eyes. She wouldn't want to risk it.

But that didn't mean he shouldn't. If it was done the right way, this could get her off the hook.

"Let's not get distracted by focusing on the wrong guy." Treese held up a hand like she wanted everyone's attention. "What about Ryan's temper? He attacked our sister. He totally would've conked Thomas on the head and killed him without a thought." Treese extended a hand toward Victoria as if her presence proved the point.

"That's the thing that makes me think it wasn't Ryan." Lines creased Robert's forehead. "He's an aggressive man, someone who gets in the face of anyone he feels threatened by and anyone who disagrees with him. If he'd somehow learned Thomas had chosen to leave his fortune to Victoria, Ryan would have confronted him. He wouldn't have snuck around and surprised Thomas from behind. He would have faced him and attacked him head-on."

"That does sound accurate." Victoria moved her gaze to include everyone. "All of my interactions with him never led me to conclude he was calculating or strategic. He was emotional. If he was happy or flirtatious, you were fine. If he had a problem with you...well, he made that very clear and didn't hold back."

Ryan had flirted with Victoria? Irritation crawled upward through Cillian's torso. Of course he had. She was gorgeous. But there was no way she would've responded or fallen for a guy like that. She was much too sensible. An advantage, in this case.

"Clinton Glenn, on the other hand," Robert lifted his index finger straight up, "seems to be exactly the sort of person who would ambush Thomas from behind. The crimes we know he's guilty of already involve deception, manipulation, and self-preservation. They also indicate he has a calculating, strategic mind that would enable him to think of moving Thomas's body outside to the mailbox to make his death look like an accident."

"But what if Ryan teamed up with Brenda, and she convinced him it was better to make it look like an accident, so they wouldn't be blamed?" Spring glanced at Torin beside her.

"Could be." He smiled slightly as he looked down at her, almost like he couldn't help himself. Couldn't be more obvious he and Spring were a couple in love. "But they would normally be the first suspects in any case since they stood to inherit. Or at least thought they did."

"And that leads me to two more reasons I don't think they did it." Robert walked to the coffee table and bent to grab a handful of chips. "One, it's clear they did think they were going to inherit. That's why they were hanging around all the time and acting friendly with Thomas. And two," he held up a chip in the air, "if they did find out Victoria was the heir that last day before Thomas was killed, they wouldn't have motive to kill him. They would have wanted to kill him *before* he changed his will. And if they missed that opportunity, their next strategy would be to change his mind. Killing him only means cementing his new will and spending a fortune trying to combat it in court." He popped the chip into his mouth.

"Okay, I'm convinced." Hank stretched his legs out in front of him, swinging them to the side to bypass the end of the coffee table.

"But maybe Brenda is some kind of criminal mastermind." Treese folded her arms over her low-cut V-neck sweater. "We haven't talked about her yet."

Robert grinned. "Can't stand that I'm right, can you?" He crunched another chip.

Treese rolled her eyes.

"I wasn't able to talk to Brenda yet." Spring accepted the small plate of chips and salsa Torin brought her from the table. "I have an appointment to see her next week for a fundraising meeting."

Torin grabbed a chip for himself off Spring's plate on her lap. "Brenda's background check was clean."

"But she did threaten Victoria on the phone." Cillian thumbed toward Victoria.

"She did what?" Spring visibly swallowed down her chips, her eyes widening. "You guys, you have to tell us these things."

Cillian liked the sound of that, Spring grouping him with Victoria. He squashed the smile that wanted to reach his face.

Victoria shot him a glance that did not share his pleasure. Kind of the opposite, actually. "It wasn't a serious threat. Nothing like Ryan. She called me to inform me they were having their lawyers file an injunction that would prevent me from using the assets Thomas left me."

Cillian reached across the space between them and gripped the nearest wooden spindle in the back of her chair as he shifted toward her. "It was a little more than that. She ordered you not to go to the house."

"Yes, but it wasn't a physical threat." She met his challenge with that adorable chin tilt.

"What aren't you two telling us?" Robert's question jerked Cillian's attention to him. Was he talking about their relationship? The fact that Cillian loved Victoria and hoped she loved him back?

Robert moved his focus from Cillian to Victoria. "Is there another threat or attack you may have forgotten to mention?"

Oh. Not their relationship. Now that Robert mentioned it, Cillian had been surprised Victoria hadn't mentioned the drive-by shooting when she'd told everyone about their visit with Judy Kline.

She pressed her lips together now, looking like she wasn't going to say anything. Wow, she really did not want her siblings worrying about her. Why, Cillian couldn't quite figure out.

"Come on, sis." Hank sent her a small smile across the room. "You know he'll keep using his superpower on you if you don't fess up."

She looked up at the ceiling, then let out a sigh. "Oh, very well. When we were in front of Mrs. Kline's house, someone drove by and shot at us."

"Victoria!" Spring's shocked exclamation stung Cillian's ears. "You can't hide someone trying to kill you from us. We're your family."

"We were fine. Cillian made sure Mrs. Kline and I ducked in time." Victoria's gaze found him. "He protected us very efficiently." Something warm lit her hazel eyes, accelerating his pulse.

"Did you see the car or the driver?" Torin didn't waste any time getting to the helpful points.

"Not the driver, unfortunately." Cillian looked at Torin. "But I caught a glimpse of the truck as it drove off."

"Truck?"

Cillian nodded. "Black pickup. I think it was a Ford, but I can't swear to it."

"So that wasn't the curator?" Treese's tone didn't hold any triumph this time, and her eyebrows lowered with what looked like concern.

"I'll see if he has a pickup registered under his name as well as the silver Mercedes." Torin took out the notepad he seemed to carry with him at all times, and Spring handed him a pen. "I'll also run down the vehicles owned by Ryan and Brenda. Maybe we'll find a match." He glanced up. "Did the responding officers find any evidence to ID the shooter?"

Cillian lifted his shoulders. "Well, considering McCully showed up when they were investigating, I don't think we'll ever know."

"That snooty detective?" Treese paused with a carrot halfway between the bowl and her mouth. "Didn't that make him see Victoria isn't guilty?"

"One would have thought so." Victoria answered in her calm tone. How she didn't sound the least bit frustrated was beyond Cillian. "But he hypothesized Cillian and I may have hired the shooter to make me appear innocent."

Her siblings scoffed and voiced their frustration while Cillian smiled at Victoria. There it was again, pairing him with her. Did she notice they were sounding like a couple?

She didn't look his way, but a hint of pink colored her cheek in profile.

"This has gone too far." Treese set the bowl beside her on the ottoman. "Dad would be furious if he knew the police were letting you be in danger."

Victoria stiffened. "No one will tell him about this, is that clear?" She held up a finger as she stared at her siblings. "He doesn't need to know at this point, and his interference would only make things more difficult for me with the police. He won't be told unless he asks or a situation arises in which it's necessary to inform him. Understood?"

Her siblings slowly nodded, reluctantly but like they didn't dare cross her. Pretty obvious how they'd turned out so well.

Victoria had been a strong leader for them and still was when needed.

"There's one thing we need to take care of ourselves then."

All eyes swung to Robert as he dusted chip crumbs off his hands.

"Vicki shouldn't be alone until we figure out who the killer is, especially at night."

Cillian lifted his fist in triumph. "Thank you. I've been trying to convince your sister of that. Now maybe she'll listen."

Robert exchanged a smile and glances with his siblings.

"That's ridiculous." The rigidity seemed to fade from Victoria's posture and voice, despite her protest. Seemed like there was more room to negotiate on this one than her stance about her father. "I will not have you disrupting your lives for some ill-conceived notion that I'm unable to take care of myself."

"Then I'll do it." Cillian leaned forward to catch her attention. "I'm already planning to stay with you until this is over."

The siblings' attention latched onto him. Some with eyes widened.

"On the sofa." Cillian gave them a *Duh* look even as a grin sneaked through.

Victoria turned her head toward him, pinning him with a disapproving stare.

"Or in my jeep."

"Great." Robert jumped in before Victoria could respond. "But you can't cover every night. Hank and I will take shifts."

Victoria opened her mouth, likely to protest.

A musical tone stopped her.

"Excuse me." She narrowed her eyes at Robert before she reached for her purse on the floor and pulled out the phone. "It's Sydney. I need to take this." She stood and walked to the dining table as she answered.

"Sydney?" Treese lifted her eyebrows.

"A teen girl she mentors at the pregnancy center." Satisfaction filled Cillian's chest as he answered. He could get used to this, knowing Victoria even better than her siblings. Or at least some of them.

"I need to go." Victoria hurried toward the group as she lowered her phone.

Cillian's pulse picked up speed at the hint of urgency in her tone and the worried set of her mouth. "What is it?"

"Sydney's mother finally evicted her." Victoria glanced at her family. "The pregnant teen I've been helping. Her mother was threatening to banish her from their home for some time. I'd hoped she wouldn't go through with it." Victoria landed her focus on Cillian as she lifted her purse. "But she did, and Sydney needs to stay at my house. She has to move her belongings right now."

Cillian got to his feet. "I'll help."

Victoria gave him a quick nod.

He had to hold back a pleased smile. She wanted him to come.

If things kept coming along this well, it was looking like she would want him to be by her side for more than helping Sydney move.

Looked like he might not need to use the leverage against her father after all. The future he dreamed of with Victoria might soon be theirs. Now all Cillian needed to do was keep her alive and out of jail.

# CHAPTER
# TWENTY-SIX

"HE'S THE BIGGEST, most beautiful dog I've ever seen." Sydney smiled up at Victoria from the floor in the living room where the very expectant teen sat next to Max. "I love him."

Victoria smiled in return. "It seems the feeling is mutual."

The Leonberger swished his tail as he stood by the girl, his giant head inches from her face as he soaked up the petting she gave him. Thank the Lord, Max wasn't showing his usual fear of strangers with Sydney. He'd been cautious when she'd initially entered Victoria's home, but once Sydney had set down her purse and suitcase, he'd followed her around as she toured the house. Within about fifteen minutes, he had warmed up to her completely, abandoning his wariness to even let her pet him.

What an extra blessing from the Lord. Now Victoria wouldn't have to worry about Max while Sydney was their houseguest. But even so, Sydney living with her couldn't be a permanent solution. At least not the best one for the teen and her child.

Victoria sat on the edge of the armchair near where Sydney relaxed on the floor. "I'm so glad you can stay with me for a while."

"Oh, me, too. This is going to be so much fun." The girl grinned as she continued to pet Max.

"I hope so." Victoria hesitated. It wouldn't be good to bring down Sydney's spirits or add stress, especially when she was so close to giving birth. But at the same time, she knew Sydney. The teen didn't like to look ahead or plan for the future. She needed to be nudged and encouraged to do so. And whether anyone liked it or not, she was going to need to grow up quickly because of her situation.

"The last time we spoke, you said the father of your little girl wasn't answering your texts. Have you heard from him since then?"

Sydney slowed her strokes on Max, her mouth pulling into a frown. "No. It's weird. He used to text a lot." Apprehension colored her tone.

"I'm sorry to hear that. This is such a hard time for him to leave you to handle things alone."

"He hasn't left me." Sydney lowered her hands to her lap as she turned her head toward Victoria. "I mean, we've never really lived together or anything anyway, but I know he still loves me. He's probably just busy. He's like a super successful guy."

"Do you know what he does for a living?"

Sydney shook her head. "No. We never really talked about stuff like that."

"What did you talk about?"

She lifted one small shoulder under her cotton sweater. "How pretty he thinks I am. How much he loves me. That he's gonna marry me as long as I…"

"As long as you what, Sydney?"

"If I'd keep…you know." Her gaze slid away from Victoria. "Keep being his girlfriend. Not tell anybody."

A slow burn of righteous anger simmered in Victoria's torso. The man had no right to use and manipulate this child that way. And then to leave her alone to have their baby without support or taking responsibility. What a despicable human being.

Victoria moistened her lips. "Sydney, what he did was very wrong. He should never have asked you to be intimate with him. No man should without first marrying you."

The teen's focus dropped to her hands, resting on the legs stretched out in front of her.

Max slid down to the floor and lay beside her.

A small smile tilted her mouth as she put her hand on his massive head.

"If this man truly loves you, then he'll want to take care of you and the baby."

"He does." Sydney's gaze lifted. "I know he loves me."

"All right. Then let's tell him what happened to you. Let's tell him you need his help, now that your mother won't let you live in her home anymore."

The girl's eyebrows drew together. "I already texted him. He didn't answer."

Victoria held back the urge to tell Sydney that proved the man didn't love her. But that wouldn't help. "You're welcome to stay with me as long as you need to. You and the baby. But I want the best for you and your daughter, and it's usually best for every child to have a father. For you to have a husband, and a man who will love you and care for you and your little girl."

"I thought he didn't like strangers." Cillian's voice made Victoria jump inwardly. He approached her from behind, stopping to stand next to her as his gaze aimed at Sydney cuddling with Max.

Had Cillian been listening to her conversation with Sydney? Victoria tabled the question to answer him in a casual tone she hoped would keep Sydney comfortable and willing to talk. "He doesn't typically." Victoria tipped up her head to see Cillian. "Spring is the only person who didn't need to win his favor, even though she didn't meet him as a puppy like Hank.

Max felt comfortable with her almost immediately. Perhaps he likes petite females."

"The game is rigged." Cillian's tone was heavy with faux pouting.

Victoria lifted her eyebrows in challenge. "If it was easy, it wouldn't be worth it."

His mouth slid into a grin as that spark of heat lit his eyes. "Got that right."

Her throat dried rapidly. They apparently weren't discussing Max any longer. "Shouldn't you be helping Warren bring in the boxes?"

"We're done." Cillian shifted his body to look behind them. "Right, pal?"

Victoria hadn't seen Warren standing in the doorway of the living room, hands stuffed in the pockets of his low-slung jeans.

He gave a single nod.

"Sydney," Cillian lowered his large frame to sit on the coffee table, facing the teen, "I can tell you as a man that Victoria is one hundred percent right. If the guy who fathered your child really loves you, he's going to want to take care of you and your baby."

Sydney's eyes widened slightly as she watched him, but she didn't look alarmed.

Poor Max sat up and stared at Cillian. His proximity, though not very close, was apparently enough to make the dog nervous.

"I'm also a social worker, and I can tell you love your baby. Am I right about that?"

Sydney nodded. "Yes. I really love her."

"I knew it. I can always tell." He kept his mouth in a serious line as he watched the girl. "And that's why, as a professional with years of experience working with kids in the system, I'm going to be completely honest with you. Is that okay?"

She nodded again, though uncertainty tightened her mouth. "Yeah."

He rested his large hands on his denim-clad thighs. "You're a mom now. And you need to know the best situation for your daughter is to have her father be in her life. Kids with a mom and dad in the home do so much better and are way less likely to need my help as a social worker. Does that make sense?"

"I guess so."

"That's why Victoria," he extended his hand out from his side, gesturing toward Victoria, "wants to know who the father of your baby is. It's not to ruin anything, and we won't go blabbing it all over. But we want to know so we can make sure he's aware he has a little girl, and we can make sure he knows about your situation." Cillian glanced at Victoria, his expression seeming to indicate she should join in.

"Cillian's right, Sydney. We only want to help, and I believe this is the best way we can right now. If he's as good a man as you say he is, and he loves you, then he will jump at the chance to support you and your daughter."

Sydney bit her lower lip.

"Do you trust me, Sydney?" Victoria locked her gaze on the girl's.

She nodded.

"Then please tell us his name."

Her lids lowered again, hiding her eyes. "I…can't."

Disappointment pooled in Victoria's stomach.

The girl looked up, sadness in her eyes. "I'm so sorry, Victoria. But I can't squeal on him. I don't want to get him in trouble or anything." Her gaze went to Cillian as if he might be the cause of that trouble.

He smiled.

Not the expression Victoria had expected.

"Well, I don't know about Victoria, but with everything going on with this murder investigation, I already have enough trouble to deal with right now. Running down a delinquent boyfriend isn't top of my list." He chuckled, sending Victoria a glance.

He was very convincing with his misdirection. And perhaps his tactic was the right one. They'd hit a wall with Sydney but had also given her much to consider. Perhaps she would soften her stance, in time.

"Oh, I forgot about that." Sydney looked at Victoria. "I saw it on the news. Kathleen and I both agree you couldn't have killed someone. I mean, anyone who knows you would know that's nuts."

Good to know the Life Pregnancy Care Center founder wasn't doubting Victoria's character, though she'd already deduced that when Kathleen hadn't brought up Victoria's arrest.

"I can't believe they actually put you in jail." Sydney pressed her fingers to her bottom lip. "What was it like?"

"Terrifying." At least Victoria's wretched experience gave her an opportunity to scare Sydney away from doing anything that would lead to legal trouble. "It is not a place you want to be."

"That's for sure. But I heard on the news you're their number-one suspect."

"Not for long." Cillian jumped in before Victoria could reply. "We're not going to give up like the killer wants. We're going to clear her name, no matter what it takes."

"Hey, Syd." Warren's quiet voice drew their attention to where he stood just inside the doorway. "I've gotta run."

"Aww, not yet." She shifted up to her knees, her hand going to Max's neck. "Victoria wouldn't mind if you stayed and hung out, would you, Victoria?"

"Of course not." Victoria smiled at the young man. "Let me put together some sandwiches. I know it's late, but you must have worked up an appetite with all that lifting." Surprising how many belongings a low-income teenager could have. Sydney had arrived with many more boxes and suitcases than Victoria had imagined. She didn't look forward to seeing how congested the guest room must be now with towers of boxes.

Warren rubbed the back of his hand across his mouth. "I gotta work the late shift tonight. Thanks, anyway."

Cillian got to his feet. "I should head out, too."

Victoria narrowed her eyes at him. He wasn't heading out far, if he still intended to camp in his car outside her house.

He pulled something from his pocket and went to Sydney, extending the object to her.

She took it in her fingers. A business card?

"That has my phone number, and I've written my address on the back. If you ever need help, and you can't reach Victoria or someone at the pregnancy center, you give me a call."

Victoria's chest warmed. Cillian may be a bit sly and too clever for anyone's good at times, but sometime in the past sixteen years, he had developed a soft heart for people in need.

That new characteristic might be the most attractive thing about him. It could also be the way, if she wasn't on her guard, he could skirt around her defenses and better judgment, and persuade her to fall for him once again.

---

Cillian shifted into a higher gear, lowering his posture on the bike to lessen the wind noise that increased with his speed.

The wind's chill cut through his glove and jacket, waking him up more effectively than a splash of cold water in the face. The gray morning and lack of sleep couldn't dim his optimism. Today could be the day he would get the cops off Victoria's back.

He checked over his shoulder before changing lanes to move around slower traffic on the freeway.

The photos of the papers he and Victoria had found at Thomas's mansion were stowed on Cillian's smartphone.

He'd be able to show them to Lieutenant Willis, and this could all be over. If Willis had half a brain.

After Torin's endorsement of the validity of the evidence from a cop's point of view, Cillian would've taken what they'd found to Willis right away last night. But when Robert relieved him to take the second half of the watch on Victoria's house, Cillian had called the station and learned Willis wouldn't be on duty until morning.

After four hours of sleep and a shower, Cillian hopped on his bike, choosing the exhilaration of the open-air ride to be sure he was fully awake when he talked to the lieutenant.

At least he wasn't nearly as stubborn and set against Victoria as—

The bike wobbled under Cillian, the handlebars tugging loose from his light grip.

The front wheel.

He stared down at it, but the wobble stopped, smoothing out as he continued to ride.

Weird. Maybe he'd hit a patch of ice he hadn't noticed. Too deep in thought.

The lighting was pretty flat today through his tinted visor. Could be he'd missed—

The bike shifted. Off-balance.

He pressed the rear brake slightly, checking the mirror to see if anyone was tailing him.

An SUV was coming up fast.

He switched to the middle lane.

The bike wobbled more, handlebars dodging his hold. Definitely the front tire. Couldn't use the front brake or he'd make it worse.

He tried the rear brake again.

Not enough to calm the wobble. He'd try rolling off the throttle.

The bike slowed as he eased off, but the jerking increased.

Cillian pulled into the far-right lane, slowing gradually as the shaking started to go crazy.

The death wobble.

He was still going too fast. Couldn't stop.

He looked down at the front tire.

Oh, man.

It was coming off.

If he was going down, he'd make sure he didn't take anybody with him. He angled toward the shoulder, hitting the rear brake.

The tire separated, bike tipped forward.

He jumped for the ditch past the shoulder. Hit the ground, rolled, tucking in his arms and knees.

Snow and brown reeds created a white and brown blur in front of his eyes as he tumbled down the incline.

Then he stopped, arms and legs spread out.

Whoa. Now that was a rush.

A laugh bubbled up in his throat. He stayed lying there for another second or two, catching his breath as his heart rate calmed. Then he slowly sat up and turned to get to his hands and knees.

Pain shot through his leg.

No wonder. The denim was shredded over his thigh and knee, his skin peeled and spotted with blood beneath.

If that was the worst of the damage, he'd consider himself lucky. That tire had looked like it was coming right off the bike.

He pushed to his feet, stifling a wince as his hip twinged. Must've hurt something a little deeper than skin level, too.

He ignored the discomfort and trudged up the incline out of the ditch. Lucky for him it was lined with several inches of snow mingled with the dead weeds. Provided a nice cushion for a sudden tumble.

As he reached the shoulder by the freeway, his gaze fell on his bike.

An oath spilled from his mouth.

The front forks and axle were twisted and smashed.

Nothing a good repair shop couldn't fix, but it would cost a pretty penny.

Where was the tire? He stepped back to the ditch and looked down. There. The tire lay at the bottom of the incline on the snow.

Anger simmered as he limped closer to his bike, ignoring the traffic that sped by him. With how badly damaged the bike was, it'd be impossible to prove now, but there was no doubt in his mind—someone had tampered with his bike.

He kept his bike in good condition. And he knew how to handle the standard issues that could cause a front wheel wobble like that. None of the usual fixes had worked. Because the whole tire was suddenly loose.

Someone had to have rigged that. Probably loosened the bolts just enough so he wouldn't notice a problem until he'd been riding for fifteen minutes on the freeway.

This wasn't just a prank. Somebody wanted to kill him.

And if they wanted to kill him, they probably wanted to do the same to Victoria.

The anger burst into an all-out flame in his chest as he ripped off his glove and unzipped the front jacket pocket where he'd stashed his phone. Good thing he hadn't landed on his belly. He needed the phone to make three important calls. Victoria, tow truck, and then a rideshare so he could get the evidence against Clinton Glenn to the lieutenant.

If Glenn had sabotaged Cillian's bike to keep him quiet, he was going to learn the hard way that Cillian wasn't so easy to stop.

# CHAPTER
## TWENTY-SEVEN

Victoria glanced at the time on her cell phone, then verified the time was correct with the clock on the wall in the lobby at Life Center. Nearly thirty minutes since Cillian had called, telling her to wait there with Sydney until he arrived. He'd said he would explain when he saw her.

Victoria would have asked questions, but the tension and urgency in his voice had given her enough of a reason to wait. Something was wrong. Very wrong, judging from the edge of anger and that protectiveness she'd come to recognize.

Was he in trouble? Had something happened since he'd phoned? Thirty minutes seemed a long time for him to take to get there, given the apparent serious nature of whatever had occurred.

She drew in a breath, trying to relax her tense muscles. Obsessing over the questions when she had no answers would do her no good. And neither would sitting in the uncomfortable chair that was doing her posture no favors.

She rose and walked across the empty room, her gaze dropping to her phone as she paused near the potted fern in the corner. Her thumb moved to the text messaging app and tapped. As if she needed another obsession to replace the first.

But no new messages awaited her. She opened the thread of texts with her father.

*I plan to arrive at 6:00 Tuesday night to prepare your birthday dinner. Does that sound correct, or would you like me there earlier?*

The text she had sent yesterday morning stared up at her. With no response.

Dad never waited that long to answer a text. Not a word since her arrest meant one thing—he was giving her the silent treatment. Far worse than an in-person lecture. He must be so disappointed in her, so ashamed.

She pressed her lips together and looked up, her gaze hitting the poster on the wall with the large image of a six-week-old baby in the womb. The baby was so dependent on her mother, on her parents for safety, love, and life itself.

Strange how that dynamic seemed to continue throughout all stages, taking on different forms and degrees as the children and parents aged.

"Is he here yet?"

Victoria turned toward Sydney as the girl returned from visiting the restroom. "No, not yet." She glanced toward the front door.

Nothing but the gray light of the winter day greeted her study beyond the glass.

"Oh. My man is usually late, too." The girl smiled as she plunked herself down into a chair. "Doesn't mean he doesn't love you."

Dismay tightened Victoria's stomach, but her pulse skipped with something like pleasure at the same time. "Cillian doesn't—" Could she honestly say he didn't love her? He'd told her he did when they were teenagers. And he showed signs that, perhaps, he still did. She tried again. "Cillian isn't my—"

"Isn't your what?"

Cillian.

She whirled toward his deep voice, catching sight of his handsome grin as he let the door close, finally triggering the bell that signaled entry. Heat flushed her face. But she lifted her chin and met those coal-black eyes. "It's about time you arrived. We've been waiting for over thirty minutes."

"Yeah, I had a few errands to run." He walked toward her and Sydney. Or rather, limped.

The irregularity appeared to be originating from his right hip. "What happened?" She lowered her gaze farther down.

His right pant leg was tattered and ripped, exposing bloodied skin on his thigh and knee.

"Cillian?" Alarm pinched her chest. "Are you all right?"

"If I say 'no,' will you give me free PT?" He winked.

She gave his arm a swat.

"Ouch." He rubbed the arm as if that was the worst injury he'd received.

"If you don't tell me what happened in the next two seconds, I'm going to go straight home with Sydney like I should have done a half hour ago."

"Okay." He glanced around the empty lobby.

Victoria followed his scan. "Everyone's in the back at another prenatal class like the one Sydney just attended."

"Yeah, they hold them at different times so there's room for everybody." Sydney looked Cillian up and down. "Did somebody beat you up?"

"Yeah, you should see the other guy." He gave her a half-hearted grin, then landed his focus on Victoria. "Somebody sabotaged my bike."

"Your motorcycle?" She sucked in a quick breath. "Did you crash?"

"Pretty much. He loosened the bolts just enough so the tire would come off after riding for a while."

"Who would do that?" Sydney's question barely reached Victoria's ears as she stared at Cillian, her heart pounding.

He could've been killed. Cillian could have died. Because of her and this quest to prove her innocence.

"That's enough."

Cillian's eyebrows lowered. "What?"

"I said that's enough. We have to stop." Victoria folded her arms across her sweater. "We need to stop investigating and trying to find the killer. This has become far too dangerous."

"Vicks, it's okay." He stepped closer to her and rested his hand on her arm.

She pulled away, lifting her hands in the air. "No, it is most certainly not okay, Cillian. You were almost killed. I cannot be responsible for you getting hurt."

"You aren't responsible for this, Vicks. Thomas's killer is. And this is great. It means we're on the right track. We're getting really close, and—"

"Cillian, no." Exasperation pinched her tone, but she couldn't help it. He was the most maddening man she'd ever known. "This isn't some thrill-seeking adventure where only you are involved. You need to think, to consider how your actions will affect others."

"That's why I told you to wait for me, and I came here as soon as I showed the lieutenant our evidence against Glenn. He finally listened, by the way. He might actually follow up this time or make McCully do it."

"Cillian, you aren't listening."

"I am listening. I'm going to make sure you're safe until this guy is locked up, so you don't have to worry about a thing."

"Not worry? When you walk in here looking like you've been hit by a truck? When I might never have seen you—" Emotion choked the words. She turned away, blinking hard to banish the tears that suddenly sprang to her eyes.

"Vicks." Warm pressure touched her shoulder, his large hand comforting and strong. His masculine scent mingled with cologne wrapped around her, luring her to turn into him and lose herself in his arms.

*Oh, Lord, I can't love him. I can't. Please help me. He doesn't believe in You. He was never right for me, regardless, or for my family.*

"I'm okay, really." Cillian's voice was thick and deeper than normal.

She closed her eyes. She'd given too much away. Given him hope she never should have.

She stiffened her spine and took a step forward, slipping out from under his hand as she swiveled toward him. She pressed her lips together and met his gaze.

His dark irises gleamed, simmering with intensity and passion she somehow had to ignore.

"This is exactly why we shouldn't be involved in police investigations. They're equipped to handle danger, and murderers aren't going to attack them to keep them silent. From now on, we leave this to the professionals." She walked around him and went to the coat rack near the door. She snatched her coat and Sydney's, turning with the girl's outstretched for her to take.

Sydney hurried over, her widened eyes as she took her coat giving Victoria a guilty twinge. The teen experienced enough drama at home. Victoria and Cillian didn't need to be another example of adults arguing.

Victoria reached for her calm and normal tone as she threw a glance at him. "I assume you must have taken a rideshare or taxi here. If you would like a lift to your—wherever you're living right now—I would be willing to drive you."

"Very kind of you." His sarcastic tone sparked her defenses.

She faced him head-on, letting her silence speak for her. She'd made her decision about the investigating. They were done.

"But I'll take a ride to your house." His mouth twitched at the corner. He was amused?

Well, that was a better reaction than anger in front of Sydney.

Victoria swallowed her pride and tried to keep a pleasant inflection as she responded. "My house?"

"I promised to keep you safe." He suddenly closed the distance between them and grabbed her coat from her hands. "That's what I'm going to do." His firm tone matched the hard glint in his eyes as he opened the coat and held it up, apparently intending to assist her like a gentleman. Whether she wanted him to or not.

Heaven help her, but her cartwheeling, foolish pulse said she did want him to. Far too much.

---

Amusement tugged at Cillian's mouth as he rode in the front passenger seat of Victoria's Honda.

She sat ramrod straight behind the wheel, keeping her eyes on the road while she drove. She hadn't looked his way once or said a word since they'd left the pregnancy center.

She obviously thought she'd won that argument, but judging from her defensive demeanor, she knew her supposed win was shaky.

Weird not driving. The last time Cillian had been a passenger in a vehicle was in a taxi in Seattle. He hadn't liked it then either.

At least Victoria was a decent driver. Too cautious but smooth, as long as nothing happened to throw her off. Kind of the way she handled life.

"New plan."

Her fingers clenched the wheel at the sound of his voice. Yep. She'd been waiting for him to challenge her again.

"Since Clinton Glenn has decided to play rough, we have to beat him at his own game."

"You want to…" she shot a glance at the rearview mirror, probably checking on Sydney, then lowered her voice, "… sabotage his vehicle?"

Cillian chuckled. "Not a bad idea, but no. I think we should sit on him, follow him everywhere he goes so there's no opportunity for him to try to attack us or kill us."

Victoria looked at the mirror again.

"She's fine." He twisted to see Sydney in the back seat.

The girl stared at her smartphone as she had been doing since they'd gotten in the car.

"Still busy with her phone."

Sydney giggled at something, driving home his point.

It was obvious Victoria hadn't liked that the teen had witnessed their argument at the pregnancy center. He was pretty sure Sydney had seen much worse. Probably good for her to see how people who actually cared about each other could still disagree but keep the gloves on.

He straightened, watching out the windshield as Victoria turned onto her street. "Since neither of us has to work, we can cover watching him most of the day. And then between me, Robert, and Hank—and maybe Torin—we should be able to cover the nights while still watching your place."

"No. I won't allow that."

He raised his eyebrows at her motherly, don't-mess-with-me-tone. "You know that won't really work on me, right?"

She gave him a brief glance, then braked to swing the car into the driveway. "I suppose not."

"It's a great idea and the only foolproof way to be sure you don't get hurt."

"What about you?" She pressed the garage remote on the visor, and the big garage door lifted.

"It's the best way to be sure he doesn't do anything to me, too." Cillian leaned toward her a little, moving his arm to rest on the console between them. "And I'm loving this concern about me, by the way. Didn't know you cared."

Her head jerked toward him at that, her hazel eyes lit with the spunk he loved. And something else that confirmed his teasing was on point with the truth.

His pulse spiked faster. He winked.

She looked away, stopped the car, and shifted into park before killing the engine. A reddish hue colored her cheek in profile.

He grinned.

"For your information," she shifted toward him, her

eyebrows in a stern dip, "I'm concerned for everyone's safety in this situation."

"Mind if I go in now?" Sydney leaned forward, her head by the gap between the front seats.

Victoria twisted to see the teen. "That's fine. But leave Max in my room. I'll get him out."

"Right." Sydney scooted out the back and headed for the door that connected to the house.

Victoria let out a sigh as her hand went to the door handle. "I need to let Max out of his crate."

"Sure." Cillian got out on his side of the car, scanning the garage as he should've before they'd driven in. Just in case someone had paid her house a visit while they'd been gone. "Wow. This has to be the cleanest garage I've ever seen." Most of the neatly organized yard tools hanging on the walls didn't look like they'd ever been used.

He rounded the hood to meet Victoria at the door to the house as she pulled it open. He gripped the edge, holding the door for her. "Allow me."

Her hazel eyes met his briefly. A hint of pleasure lit the confusion there before she looked away and walked inside. "Thank you."

"Besides keeping us all safe, the other advantage to sticking to this guy is he might do something incriminating, and we'd be in the perfect position to get more evidence against him." Cillian closed and locked the door behind him before facing Victoria.

A very stern Victoria who stood with her arms folded over her coat as she stared at him. "That's exactly what I said we can't do anymore. This interference in the investigation has caused too much trouble already. We're putting ourselves, and possibly others, in danger."

He lifted his hands up, palms out toward her. "I'm not saying we investigate. I'm saying we follow the guy around so he can't try anything again. It's a surefire way to keep him from hurting you or anyone else until the *police* investigate what I gave them and pick him up."

"But if he sees you following him, he's apt to feel cornered. He could attack you even more aggressively."

Cillian grinned. "You really are worried about me, aren't you?" He stepped toward her.

She held up her finger between them. "Cillian, this is serious. He could also tell the police we're stalking him. That *I'm* stalking him. McCully wouldn't hesitate to say that's violating the terms of my bail and arrest me again."

"That's not going to happen. Glenn wouldn't take the risk of talking to the cops when he's a killer."

She rolled her eyes and turned away, walking through the short hallway that led to her kitchen. She set her purse on the counter just inside and spun to face Cillian.

He stopped short of bumping into her. Not that he'd mind getting that close, but it probably wouldn't help him win the argument.

"I think it's best if I drive you home now. That way, you can do as you please, which I know you're going to do anyway. But it needn't involve me." She glanced at her wristwatch. "I have an appointment anyway with the defense attorney my father hired."

"Oh, I'll go with you."

"No, thank you." Her chin lifted. "I'll be going alone."

"Don't you think it'd be—"

A scream rent the air.

Victoria stared at Cillian for a split second.

Sydney.

"The restroom." Victoria pointed past Cillian.

He took off, dashing through the living room into the hallway that led to the bathroom. "Sydney?"

She didn't answer his shout.

But his gaze landed on the teen just then.

She backed into the hall, facing the bathroom doorway with her hands clasped together under her chin.

"Sydney, are you okay?"

She turned her head toward him, eyes wide, mouth slightly open.

"What happened?"

She pointed weakly at the bathroom.

"Sydney? Are you all right?" Victoria's voice signaled she was behind Cillian.

"Stay back." He looked through the open doorway into the small, narrow bathroom.

The ivory tiles and walls looked clean, normal. Untouched.

He stepped inside. His scanning gaze hit the mirror above the sink.

Words streaked the glass, scrawled in red.

*You will be next.*

# CHAPTER
# TWENTY-EIGHT

VICTORIA FOLLOWED Cillian into the restroom, her gaze aiming in the direction of his.

*You will be next.*

Someone had written a threat on her mirror? In her house?

"Call the police." He cupped her shoulders as he moved behind her to leave the bathroom. "I'm going to check the house."

"Be careful." The words nearly stuck in her shrinking throat as she yanked her gaze from the unnerving message—evidence someone had been in her home. And perhaps still was.

The possibility spurred her mind out of shock and into action. Her phone. It was in her purse in the kitchen.

She hurried into the hallway and grabbed Sydney's arm. "Come with me."

The girl moved with her. "Who—" Sydney's voice choked on what sounded like fear.

Adrenaline pumped through Victoria, keeping her gaze sharper than normal and nerves standing on end. She listened for strange noises as she walked, keeping her gaze ahead.

She turned into the kitchen, quickly checking the room.

No one lurked there.

But she didn't breathe normally. Not yet. She dug in the pocket of her purse.

"Who would do something like that? Write that…" Sydney stumbled into the center of the kitchen, wild eyes landing on Victoria.

"I don't know." Victoria pressed the emergency call button for 911, then pressed the phone to her ear.

"9-1-1, what is your emergency?"

This scenario shouldn't be so familiar. It could even be the same operator from the day Victoria had discovered Thomas, dead.

She pushed aside the crippling memory and told the operator about the evidence of an intruder in her home, adding she didn't know yet if the intruder was still there.

Satisfied that the operator had officers on the way, Victoria ended the call.

She went to Sydney and gently ran her hands along the girl's upper arms. "I'm sorry you had to see that. Are you all right?"

"Yeah, I guess." Normal color had returned to Sydney's cheeks, and her breathing appeared more regulated again.

*Thank you, Lord.*

At least the incident hadn't caused premature labor. Victoria would never forgive herself if she brought danger upon this young mother.

"What does it mean?" Sydney looked up at her. "'You'll be next.' Next for what?"

Next to be murdered. Victoria kept the thought to herself and mustered a smile. "I'm not entirely sure. Bad people say very unkind things sometimes." She glanced over her shoulder to the other doorway into the kitchen. Shouldn't Cillian have completed his search of the house by now?

Unless something had happened to him. Her chest squeezed. "I'd better check on Cillian."

Though she shouldn't leave Sydney alone.

Max. The thought came to her on a wave of fear. She'd assumed he was safe in his crate in her bedroom. But what if—

"Stay with me." She hurried out of the kitchen, glancing back to make sure Sydney was following.

They returned to the hallway. Victoria glanced into the bathroom but kept going to the end.

Her bedroom door stood open.

Her breath stopped. She always closed it when she left.

She stepped closer and looked in.

Max stared at her from the crate by the far wall, watching her with his alert expression, mouth closed and ears lifted.

She scanned the room. Her bed was still made, and everything appeared to be as she'd left it.

Heavy footsteps made her jerk back out of the room.

Cillian stalked toward them up the hallway.

Relief brought air to her lungs even as her pulse raced at the sight of him. He was all right. "Did you check in here?"

"Yep. First thing." He slowed as he reached Sydney. "Wanted to make sure Max was okay."

Victoria's heart pinched. She met his sincere, protective gaze. "Thank you."

"I didn't see anything to suggest anybody went in there. And even though Max is afraid of everyone, an intruder would likely take one look at him and decide not to mess with any dog that huge." The hint of a smile angled Cillian's lips.

"I hope you're right." It would be much longer before Victoria would feel like smiling. Someone had compromised the safety of her home and endangered those she cared about. "Did you see evidence of the intruder anywhere else?"

"He got in through the rear. The window by your back door was broken."

"He broke my window?"

"Yep. Ever think of getting a security system installed?"

"Do you know how expensive those are?"

He grinned. Probably thinking of how incongruous it was

for a Weston to say such a thing. But she had stopped living on her father's money when she'd moved out of his house years ago.

She sighed. "Perhaps I should look into it. But first," she turned toward Sydney in the narrow hallway, "I need to find a different place for you to stay."

"You're kicking me out?" The girl's eyes grew as large as when she'd seen the threat on the mirror.

"No, sweetie. I'm not kicking you out. But it isn't safe for you to stay with me right now. I can't bear to think of what could've happened to you if you'd been here alone when the intruder—"

"I don't think there's danger of that."

Victoria aimed an irritated gaze at Cillian. "How can you say that? He accessed my house to threaten me."

"Not while anyone was here. Think about it. Glenn is doing everything so far when nobody can see him up close or ID him. I don't think he would've broken into your home if anyone had been here."

Cillian's reasoning made sense. But Victoria wasn't about to tell him that. His head was far too oversized as it was. "It would still be irresponsible to allow Sydney and her baby to stay here when I know my house isn't safe. And when I'm apparently a target of someone with evil intentions. It's far too dangerous."

"But you can't send me away!" The agony that twisted Sydney's voice jumped Victoria's attention to her. Tears ran down the girl's cheeks.

"Sydney, I—"

"You have to let me stay here. Please." She grabbed Victoria's hands, squeezing them hard. "I never told you this, but I've been having bad dreams. Nightmares, I guess. And what Kathleen says are panic attacks."

Concern twisted Victoria's stomach. "Sydney, I'm sorry. I had no idea."

"I know, because I try to stay positive. But I'm not always

so sure L—" Sydney clamped her mouth shut. Had she been about to say the name of her boyfriend? "I'm not always sure he's going to come for me like he promised. And if he doesn't, I could end up on the street, and…" Her terrified gaze aimed at Cillian, then swung back to Victoria as she gripped her hands even harder. "And child services would take my little girl away." Sydney's breathing grew shallow and quick as she continued. "And then I won't—"

"Okay, Sydney, please." Victoria tried to interrupt her spiral with a gentle return squeeze on the girl's hands. "I want you to slow down and take a few breaths for me, okay?" She locked her gaze on Sydney's, infusing her voice with calm confidence. "None of that is going to happen. I will not let you be alone, and I and Kathleen will help you with your baby, okay?"

The teen nodded, her nostrils still flaring.

"Breathe, sweetie. One deep breath." Victoria took in a long breath herself.

Sydney mimicked her.

"Good, one, two, three, and now exhale." Victoria started exhaling first, and Sydney followed suit. "One, two, three."

The girl's death grip on Victoria's hands loosened as she breathed.

"There. Isn't that better?"

Sydney nodded, the size of her eyes decreasing to normal as her body relaxed. "This is what I was trying to say."

Victoria looked at her, uncertain what the girl meant.

"Being around you is the only time I feel calmer. You're like so chill, it helps me feel better. I feel safe with you. It's not like that anywhere else."

Surprise filtered through Victoria, and she glanced at Cillian.

A warm smile rested on his closed lips.

In a way, she shouldn't be surprised. "That's not me, Sydney. That's Jesus. The Bible says those who belong to Christ carry His aroma."

"Aroma?" Sydney's eyebrows drew together.

"His scent. You're sensing His peace and the safety He offers through me. I'm safe because He saved me from something even worse than an intruder. He saved me from eternal condemnation, the punishment I deserve for my sins."

A knowing quirk of the mouth replaced Sydney's confused expression. "Kathleen talks like that, too. But you and her haven't done anything bad."

"Of course we have. Every human being has sinned, many times over, and we all deserve death, suffering, and separation from God for those sins."

A sound reached Victoria's ears. Sirens?

"Sounds like the police are here." Cillian turned away and marched up the hallway.

Too bad Victoria hadn't looked at him while she was speaking to see his reaction. She'd shared the Gospel with him once when they'd been dating. But very poorly. She'd only been a Christian for one month when he'd first asked her out, which was her excuse for not realizing she shouldn't have dated an unbeliever. Her mother, the one who had led Victoria to Christ, had been too ill at the time, or perhaps too eager to see her daughter happy, to warn Victoria.

"So can I stay with you longer?" Sydney seemed glad to ignore the message Victoria had tried to convey, as well.

Victoria held back a sigh. All in God's timing. "Yes, you can stay."

Sydney squealed and let go of Victoria's hands to clap hers together. "Thank you, thank you, thank you!"

"But I don't think you should be alone." And she needed more than company. She might need specialized help. Perhaps Victoria should ask Robert if he could meet with Sydney. Panic attacks indicated an extreme level of anxiety. Especially with a baby on the way and the need to minimize stress, Sydney could benefit from talking to a psychiatrist.

"Aren't you going to be here?"

"I have a meeting I need to go to this afternoon." Victoria checked her watch. The meeting with the attorney was in only one hour. She'd need to leave in thirty minutes to allow for traffic.

"Maybe Cillian can stay with me." Sydney smiled, a joyful light in her eyes now. "Or Warren. Oh, but he's working."

Cillian would be a respectful and safe guardian for Sydney, but the pregnancy center guidelines would not approve of her leaving Sydney alone with any unrelated male, for the safety of both parties.

She needed an available female. Spring would be at classes today. But... "Treese."

"Huh?"

"My sister, Patricia. I think she usually has Monday afternoons off. I'll text her."

Male voices entering the house by the back door paused the thought.

"After we speak with the police."

Poor Max would have to wait a bit longer to get out of his crate. Though he wouldn't want to until all visitors were gone, regardless.

As Victoria walked through the hallway and toward the voices, she sympathized with Max. If only she could hide in a safe room until it was all over, too. Lord willing, no one had called Detective McCully.

Although given the break-in and the menacing threat scrawled on her mirror, she apparently had far worse things to fear.

---

"Thank you for taking my case." Victoria sat as straight and stiff as a pole in the leather chair next to Cillian's in the attorney's impressive corner office.

The middle-aged Craig Lymp relaxed behind his big desk in a chair sized for his large body. "Of course. I'd do anything for your father." He smiled, but there was something slick about the expression.

Reminded Cillian of a guy he'd met in Dallas who'd tried to separate Cillian from his bike with a knife. Why that particular association jumped to mind, Cillian couldn't say. But his instincts were never wrong.

The lawyer rested his fingers on some papers in an open file on the desk in front of him. "I've looked over your case, and I think we can get a very good plea deal."

"A plea deal?" Victoria's tone lifted with surprise. Apparently, she hadn't picked up on the vibes this guy was giving off. "Wouldn't that involve pleading guilty to the crime?"

Lymp raised his gaze from the papers to her. "Well, yes."

"But I didn't murder Thomas Briscoe."

The attorney pushed out his thick lips as he stared at her. "I see." He brought his hands up in front of himself and slowly rubbed his palms together. "The evidence that you did is very convincing."

"Now hold on." Cillian leaned forward. "Weren't you hired to be her defense attorney? Not the prosecutor?"

"Yes, of course." That weak smile curved Lymp's mouth again. "And as such, I must give her the best counsel possible."

"Gentlemen, I am right here." Victoria sent a glare in Cillian's direction before returning her attention to the lawyer. "I'll thank you not to discuss me as if I'm not here. But Mr. Doherty's question is valid. You do sound like you believe the prosecutor's manufactured case against me rather than the truth I'm telling you."

"Evidence is how we know the truth, Ms. Weston."

"Not in this case, apparently." She delivered the comeback without hesitation, though she kept her tone free of irritation or fight. "I did not kill my friend, Thomas Briscoe. And we've found evidence to suggest who did actually murder him. We've been targeted by that person because we know what he did."

"Really?" Lymp tented his fingers near his double chin. "Have you shared this evidence with the police?"

"Yes." She looked at Cillian.

He took the signal and faced Lymp. "I delivered the evidence to Lieutenant Willis this morning myself. He's going to follow up on the information." Hopefully. At least that was what Willis had said.

"Good. But if your 'evidence,'" Lymp curved his fingers for air quotes, "doesn't hold up, then we need to deal with the situation at hand, whether or not it aligns with what we'd prefer it to be."

"Meaning?"

Victoria threw Cillian an annoyed glance, but he couldn't help it. This attorney was getting very irritating, very fast.

"Meaning," Lymp shifted his gaze from Cillian to Victoria, "the case the DA has built against you is so strong, we couldn't prove otherwise, and if we went with a plea of 'innocent,' we would lose."

"That's crazy." Cillian pushed to his feet, glaring down at the sorry excuse for a defense attorney. "Your job is to defend her and defend the truth. Not to roll over and play dead so you can keep your winning record in court."

"Cillian." Victoria's eyes flashed. "Sit down." Apparently, she didn't mind losing her temper with him. But she was all sweet and patient with every bully in her life.

"We need to leave." He held his ground. "This guy is not going to defend you."

She swung her head toward Lymp. "I don't believe my father would have hired you if you weren't good at your job, Mr. Lymp."

The simpering compliment in that gentle tone crawled under Cillian's skin. How could she placate someone who'd just called her a liar and murderer to her face?

"Perhaps this is simply a misunderstanding." She moved her hands to grip the top of her purse on her lap, the only sign Cillian could detect that she might be having to restrain some frustration. "I assure you, I'm innocent of all the charges against me. Since that is the case, why would you suggest I plead guilty?"

"Because we can't win otherwise." Lymp held up a thick hand to stop a response from Cillian, though he hadn't launched one yet. "And that has nothing to do with maintaining my record, though it is perfect." He threw Cillian a taunting glance.

Anger spiked through Cillian, and he clenched his fist at his side. Maybe if he let Lymp keep talking, Victoria would see what Cillian did.

"It has everything to do with getting you the best deal. If we try to say you're innocent, and we lose, you could get up to life in prison." He paused, probably hoping to scare Victoria by letting it sink in.

Cillian switched his gaze to her.

She still sat tall and straight, no paling or signs of fright. Hopefully, that meant the attorney's tactics weren't working.

"But if we go for a plea bargain, I'm confident I could get you a very good deal." Lymp smiled as if he'd just won the argument.

"We're not interested." The response burst from Cillian's mouth. He couldn't stand it any longer.

"I'll make that decision." Victoria shot him another glare, then stood, facing Lymp. "But it does seem as though I'll need to return at a different time, alone."

Really? Cillian bit his tongue to keep from voicing the frustrated response. She was too dug in for him to get anywhere, at least in front of the lawyer.

"I'll consider what you've said and set up a meeting for a different day. Thank you for your time." Her elegance and poise as she turned away and left the office was something to behold, even if Cillian was irritated enough with her to glare at the back of her head as he followed.

He stretched his stride to reach her side in the hallway as

they headed for the lobby of the large firm's office building. "You'll need to come back alone? Really?"

She quirked an eyebrow at him. "You were not behaving."

"*I* wasn't behaving? What do you call what he was doing?" Cillian flung his hands out in the air. "You know he accused you of murder and lying, right?"

"Not in so many words. But, yes, I am perceptive enough to understand what he was implying, thank you."

"Okay, so then I assume you also realize you need a lawyer who believes you're innocent."

She didn't respond as they passed the third-floor receptionist and stopped by the elevators.

He punched the down arrow button before she could, trying to catch her gaze. "You do know that, right?" He faced her directly, his back to the elevators.

She finally looked at him. "I'm not going to dismiss the lawyer my father hired who is also his good friend."

A ding sounded, and she stepped around Cillian.

So that was it. Daddy pulling the strings once again. A tennis ball's worth of frustration clogged Cillian's throat as he joined her in the thankfully empty elevator where she was pressing the button for the first floor.

"So that's it? You'll lie, say you're guilty, and go to prison to avoid crossing your dad?"

"Of course not." She flung an exasperated glare at him.

"Then what?"

"I'm simply saying I won't defy my father that way. I'm already in hot water with him right now. He won't answer my texts or my voicemails." Her voice pinched. "Firing his lawyer friend would be like a slap in the face."

"So what?" Cillian didn't try to hold back his disbelief and anger. "That's what he deserves for hiring a lawyer like that."

She shifted toward Cillian and stared at him, her eyebrows clustered. As if he'd said something to hurt her. But he was only talking about her dad. "You would like that, wouldn't you? To hurt him?"

The elevator doors opened, and she broke her stare, stalking away at a fast clip.

Cillian hurried to catch up, but he held his tongue. She was apparently still more loyal to her dad than he'd thought. At least when it came to this situation. That didn't have to mean she was still as much of her father's puppet as she was before. She'd been going against his rules and what he would want more and more recently, often in favor of Cillian. He'd been able to persuade her to do a lot of things her dad would disapprove of in the last few days.

Cillian just needed to be patient and not get ahead of himself. After she calmed down, he could get her to see things clearly again. And to want what was best for her instead of worrying about pleasing her dad.

He just needed to remind her of what she could have if she were free of her dad's control. The life they could've had and could still have now if she followed her own desires instead of her father's.

A plan started to take shape in Cillian's mind. Some time to relax and de-stress away from the pressure of her responsibilities and the danger could be just the thing. Throw in a walk down memory lane, and Victoria would see what she was missing.

And maybe, she'd agree with Cillian that they should make up for lost time and go after the future they wanted, together.

# CHAPTER
# TWENTY-NINE

"IS HERE ALL RIGHT?" Victoria angled her car toward the curb in front of the apartment building Cillian had given her directions to as she drove.

"Let's go around the corner here to the garage."

"Very well." Fatigue weighted her shoulders as she turned onto the cross street. There was nothing more exhausting than conflict. And death threats, apparently.

"Right here." He pointed at the short driveway behind the building.

Victoria turned the wheel and drove up to the closed overhead door.

It lifted, slowly opening.

She glanced at Cillian.

He held a remote opener in his hand. He glanced at her, catching her observation of him. "I grabbed it from my bike before the tow."

She lifted an eyebrow. "It didn't fall off in the accident?"

"I have a locked compartment. It was in there."

"I see. Well, have a good evening."

"Trying to get rid of me already?" He grinned.

She didn't respond.

"Just kidding." His lips straightened into a line. "About what happened earlier...what I said." He looked away and pushed his fingers through his hair. "You deserve a lawyer who knows you're innocent and will fight to prove it."

He swung his gaze back to her. "I only want to protect you." His eyes sparked. "You know that, right?"

Her irritation, already lessening during the drive there, dissipated completely. She'd known he had her best interests at heart at the lawyer's office, too. But she was caught in a difficult situation Cillian couldn't understand. He'd never known his father. He didn't know the desire to please one's father out of love and respect. And that wasn't his fault. "Yes. I know."

The tension at the corners of his mouth eased. "Could you pull into the garage? You might be able to help me look for something."

"All right." She pressed the gas slightly and drove down the incline into the underground garage. She turned left to follow the space between the stalls that lined opposite walls of the long structure. "Isn't that your jeep?"

"Yep."

She slowed to a stop behind the car parked next to his jeep. "What do you want me to help you find?"

"I was thinking, there's no way Glenn could've known for sure I'd drive my bike today instead of the jeep."

"True. Anyone rational would assume only an insane person would ride a motorcycle in freezing temperatures."

He chuckled. "There's that biting wit I love. Thought you'd lost it at the lawyer's office."

Her pulse beat erratically, skipping and hopping at an alarming rate.

All because he'd said the word, *love*. He probably hadn't even meant it in the way her emotions wanted to interpret his usage.

She wouldn't let him see her reaction. "You mean the

attorney's office where you walked in looking like you'd been literally dragged in off the street?" She pointedly scanned his tattered jeans. "You could have at least washed off the blood. It's no wonder he thought I was a murderer."

Cillian grinned. "Hey, you were the one who wanted to be on time."

"And I suppose that's why you'd like me to test drive your jeep? I assume you're getting to the point where you're going to say Clinton Glenn sabotaged that, as well."

"Very astute. But, no, I wouldn't dream of having you test drive it." His mouth twitched as if he was barely holding back a laugh. "I thought you could help me look it over and see if we can figure out what he did to it."

"You do realize I know next to nothing about vehicles of any kind, other than how to drive them."

"Ah, well." He opened the passenger door. "Then I guess you can wait safely in your car while I check it out."

"A sound plan." She looked toward the jeep as he started to leave the car.

Something dark stained the floor beneath the jeep. "Cillian."

"Yeah?" He turned back, bending to see her as he held the door open.

"There's something under the jeep."

He left the passenger door open and headed to his vehicle, crouching to see underneath. Then he lay on the ground and reached below the jeep, directly above the stain she'd spotted. Was it a puddle of some liquid?

He quickly pulled back, got to his feet, and stalked to her car. He leaned in to meet her gaze. "He cut the brake lines. Drained the fluid."

Her breath caught. It wasn't really a surprise. But something about seeing it, being close to it, made this sabotage even more real than Cillian's accident. These weren't simply acts of sabotage. They were attempts on Cillian's life. And he could've been killed by either one.

The thought turned her mouth to sandpaper. She had pushed it aside for a bit, able to do so thanks to the distraction of the attorney and the argument with Cillian. Anger and other emotions were a useful means of forgetting the more frightening, painful realities.

"There's a guest stall at the end of the garage." Cillian pointed beyond the elevator that marked the halfway point of the garage. "Why don't you park there and come on up to my apartment while we wait for the tow truck to get here?"

He was asking her up to his apartment?

Heat flushed through her. "I should get back to Sydney."

"Treese is with her." A knowing glint shone in his dark eyes. "Besides, we need to plan our next move."

"We can do that here."

"Only if you want to keep holding up my neighbor." He waved to someone behind her car.

She twisted to see a black SUV waiting for her to move. "Why didn't you say something?" And how had she not heard another person drive in? Those eyes and Cillian's unnerving proposal must have distracted her.

"I just did."

She rolled her eyes. "Close the door."

He laughed as he shut the door and stepped back.

She drove ahead, found the empty stall marked for guests, and parked. She might as well go up to his apartment. If they must talk, she would rather do it there than in a garage. And there had been nothing romantic about his invitation. Exhaustion must be the reason she had added the romantic interpretation to his casual and practical suggestion to move their conversation to his apartment.

*Practical* was her middle name. She held on to efficiency as her goal, along with dissuading Cillian to stalk the curator, as she rode the elevator to the third floor with him and followed him to his apartment.

The modest apartment was furnished with simple, casual pieces in plain beige and brown colors. Not the furniture she would have expected Cillian to pick. No boxes or clutter evidenced he'd recently moved. The apartment must have come furnished.

Though that wouldn't explain the lack of boxes or items. Perhaps he was a better organizer than she thought and had finished moving everything in quickly.

He stepped toward her inside the door.

Her pulse spiked.

"Take your coat?"

"Oh." She breathed again. "Thank you." She slipped off her coat quickly enough that he didn't try to help, her heart rate still matching the erratic dance of her nerves.

"Want some tea?" He hung her coat on a hook mounted on the wall. "I have your favorite, chamomile."

Warmth touched her cheeks. He'd remembered. "Yes, thank you."

"Have a seat anywhere." He took off his jacket and hung it up before walking into the kitchen that was open to the dining and living room areas.

She turned away and looked at the loveseat and armchairs. Her stomach knotted. What was she doing, spending time alone with Cillian? It was one thing to do so when they were working to prove her innocence or when they were dodging danger.

But this was different. It felt like two people exploring a relationship. Dating. It would be wrong to give the impression she was open to that.

She spun back and walked to the near side of the counter that bordered the kitchen. "I really should go."

He shot her a surprised glance, tea kettle in his hand.

"I don't feel right imposing on Treese to stay with Sydney longer than necessary." That was the truth, even if it wasn't the entire reason she wanted to leave. "But will you promise me you won't follow Clinton Glenn? You can't follow him now anyway, since you don't have a car."

"About that…" Cillian set the kettle on the counter between them. "I'll need to borrow your car."

"What?"

"Or I could get a rental. But it'd be cheaper to use yours, and I don't think I'll need it for long."

"Is that your way of ensuring I won't go anywhere without you?"

"Totally." He squeezed his lips together and nodded with an attempt at innocent eyes.

She fought against the smile that wanted to come in response to his adorable expression. The man was incorrigible. "If I promise not to drive anywhere without you, will you drop this idea to tail Clinton Glenn?"

"Nope."

"Cillian." She folded her arms across her sweater.

"Victoria."

She narrowed her eyes.

He chuckled. "Okay, but I'm serious." He made an effort to sober his expression. "And you'd see I'm right if you'd think about it for a second. I'm worried about you and Sydney, too. You're right she's in danger as long as you are. But she obviously won't leave you, which I don't blame her for, by the way."

His mouth quirked at one side. "You do have a calming effect about you. At least when you're not mad like right now."

She took in a long breath through her nose as she gave him a sidelong look. It was obvious what he was doing, trying to charm her into relaxing and persuade her to agree with him. But it was working anyway. "I'm listening."

"All I'm saying is that you and I both know Glenn is going to keep after us until the police arrest him. It's obvious he thinks if he silences us, we won't keep pushing this and making the police take him seriously as a suspect. So we're in danger until the police get him." Cillian planted his hands on the counter and leaned forward. "I think the lieutenant is taking Glenn seriously, so it shouldn't be too long before they bring him in. But until then, it's up to me to keep you safe."

"And what about you?"

He blinked at her. "What about me?"

"Who will keep you safe?"

His eyebrows dipped, and he tilted his head, staring at her.

She lowered her arms. "If you follow Glenn around, he could become aggressive, as I said. He could change his modus operandi and decide to confront you to your face."

A slow smile curved Cillian's lips. "You *are* worried about me."

She forced a swallow down her tightening throat. "Yes. Of course, I am."

He walked around the counter and, before she could think or react, he stood in front of her with nothing between them. "Do you remember what you used to like about me?"

The question startled her, pounded her heart against her ribs.

His gaze held her captive. "'Cause I remember what I loved about you. We had a lot of fun together. Remember that?" He took a step closer, narrowing the gap between them.

She couldn't answer if she'd wanted to.

He was so close, those magnetic eyes holding her. "You showed me life could be good. That it could be beautiful when you were with me. You made me better, Vicks. And you made me want to be better." His fingers brushed her hands where they dangled at her sides.

The touch woke her from his spell.

She stepped back. Managed to swallow. "That wasn't me. It was Christ."

"Ah, right." Cillian's lips curled into what looked like a sardonic smile. "The aroma."

"Exactly."

He turned away, his back angling toward her like a door about to be shut in her face. Though she was the one who'd pulled away.

"You could have it, too, Cillian."

He paused and pivoted partway toward her. "Have what?"

"Christ in you, changing who you are. If you truly want to be better, you could ask Jesus to save you, and He will make you a better man, a better person than you could imagine." A sense of urgency rose inside her as she spoke. Cillian seemed to be listening. "He'll guide you through life and help you to know the best way to live. He'll give you hope for the future."

"I'm not a confused kid anymore, Vicks. I know how I want to live." Cillian's mouth softened into a wistful curve. He reached toward her face.

Her breath caught.

He brushed back some loose tendrils of hair that must have escaped her bun, his warm fingertips grazing her ears, sending shivers of awareness down her spine. "And I have a lot of hope for our future."

---

*Hope for our future.*

Cillian's words replayed in an almost constant cycle in Victoria's mind as Sydney rapidly told her about everything that had happened that day. Victoria should be paying more attention to the teen, but her mind wouldn't let go of Cillian's statement. He clearly had some hope that they, Cillian and Victoria, were going to have a future together.

She'd left after that without saying more, other than agreeing to his plan to watch Clinton Glenn constantly until he was in police custody. How could she say no when Cillian wanted to do so to protect her? And Sydney, of course.

"Victoria?" The girl's voice broke through her thoughts.

"I'm sorry, Sydney." She looked at the teen where she sat on the floor next to Max, the Leonberger soaking up her attention as if he'd never received anything so wonderful in his life. "I'm a little tired this evening. Did you ask me something?"

"Yeah. I think you must've missed what I said about Treese. I wondered why you didn't get mad."

Tension crept into Victoria's chest. "Mad? Why would I get mad?"

"She told me keeping my baby was a bad idea."

Victoria shifted to the edge of the armchair cushion. "She what?"

"She said it's going to ruin my life, and abortion would be nicer for me and the baby."

Victoria forced herself to breathe through her nose before she spoke again. There was no point in taking her anger out on Sydney. The poor teen was a victim of Victoria's lack of judgment in asking Treese to stay with her.

Good grief. Victoria had known her sister had bought into much of the secular world's thinking, but abortion? And to tell a teenage girl to murder her own baby? In Victoria's home, no less. "I'm so sorry, Sydney. I had no idea she would say those things to you. I didn't even know she was so confused and believed such lies. You know they're lies, right?"

"Oh, yeah." Sydney pulled her hand away from Max's head to wave away the suggestion. "I'm still keeping my baby. She's as much a person as you and me. I think I knew that before, even when I thought about getting an abortion. But once I saw her in the ultrasound…" Sydney's gaze took on a distant look, like she was remembering the moment. A smile curved her lips. "Well, I guess I fell in love." She rested her hand on her round belly. "This is my baby girl, and nobody's going to hurt her."

*Thank you, Lord.* The transformation in Sydney was amazing, from the girl who'd visited Life Center to learn more about getting an abortion to this young mother bear, ready to defend her unborn child.

"Plus, I know her daddy will love her, too. I told Treese how he's going to marry me, and my baby will have a dad. She didn't believe me, but it's true. It's the reason I fell in love with him. 'Cause at home, well…" Sydney lowered her upper body to rest her head on Max's side. "You know what it's like. My mom never really loved me. And my dad left when I was like two."

Victoria's heart squeezed at the effort Sydney put forth to sound nonchalant. But her pain couldn't be disguised. No wonder the girl had been vulnerable to an unscrupulous man, ready to prey upon her void, the desperate desire to be loved.

"But my guy, he was the first person who ever really loved me, you know?" Sydney's fingers trailed through Max's long fur as the dog patiently served as her pillow and comforter. "That's why I can't tell anybody who he is. It would be like betraying him. But he really loves me, so he'll text me back. He's probably just waiting until our baby's born. I bet he's gonna surprise me, maybe at the hospital. He likes to surprise me with gifts and things. Like roses and chocolate..."

Sydney's voice smoothed and grew quieter as she continued to list the alleged proofs that the man loved her. It was as if the girl was repeating a list she must have reviewed many times in order to comfort herself.

But what would she do when he never did contact her again? When he never acknowledged his child or Sydney and never offered her the support and happy ending she expected? She was putting far too much hope in the mysterious man who had likely used her without ever intending to commit to her in any way.

When she finally had to face the fact that he had rejected her, that he didn't love her, it could destroy her. And then she would have a baby she was supposed to raise, another young life to be damaged by the fallout.

She needed more help than Victoria could give her. Sydney most needed the Lord—the healing and strength only He could provide. But in the meantime, perhaps Robert could help.

He should be outside Victoria's house right now. He was taking the first half of the night watching Victoria's house while Cillian shadowed Clinton Glenn.

Victoria waited until Sydney's self-talk lulled her to sleep, her head resting on Max's large belly as it rose and fell with his even breaths. Then Victoria quietly snuck out of the house, not bothering to grab her coat for the quick jog across the empty street to Robert's parked car.

The sound of the door's unlocking signaled he'd seen her coming.

She bent to wave at him before she opened the passenger door and slipped inside the warm car. "At least you weren't sleeping."

He grinned at her. "Now what kind of guardian would I be if I slept on the job?" He lifted a silver thermos. "I brought lots of coffee." Lowering the drink, he adopted a faux serious expression. "Besides, I honestly think your boyfriend would beat me up if I let anything happen to you."

"Wh—" Shock and dismay froze her voice.

Robert laughed. "I don't think I've ever seen you speechless before. Or with your mouth gaping open."

She shut it at once. "I've never heard anything so grossly inaccurate and entirely inappropriate until now."

"I'll bet." His twinkling eyes said he didn't buy it.

"I trust you only said that to get a rise out of me. You know we are not dating or in a romantic relationship of any kind."

He dipped his head toward her with a raised eyebrow. "Does Cillian know that?"

She scrambled for an evasive, yet honest answer but couldn't find one in her flustered thoughts. In any case, nothing would be able to convince her psychiatrist brother that he'd misinterpreted Cillian's attitude toward her. "As fun as this late-night banter is, I braved the cold to speak with you about Sydney."

"Okay. Subject change accepted." He nodded and placed the thermos in his cup holder. "What about Sydney?"

"Did you notice anything concerning when you met her tonight?"

"Vicki, I only talked to her for two minutes at most."

"I know, but you're a professional. I'd like your opinion."

"Okay." He looked out the windshield at the still night. "Well, she's young to be an unwed mother. Her maturity and emotional development seem to be a little shy of her age, suggesting some trauma in her life. Which, given her situation, wouldn't be surprising. She seems to trust you a lot and doesn't show fear of men or strangers." He glanced at Victoria. "Is that what you wanted to know?"

"Somewhat. I'm concerned she's developed too much of a dependency on the man who fathered her child."

"Ah. The AWOL dad."

"She's convinced he loves her because he told her so, and he apparently promised to marry her, as well."

Robert winced. "Poor kid. Do you know who he is?"

"No. That's another problem. He made her promise not to tell anyone his identity."

"Probably married."

Victoria nodded. "That's what I'm afraid of."

"He'll never show up, if that's the case. Especially now that there's a child involved."

"Exactly. But Sydney is anchoring all her hopes on the belief that he will appear and marry her and love her. She thinks he'll support her and the baby as a happy family."

"Oh, man."

Victoria shifted to face Robert. "I'm worried that when she has the baby, and he doesn't materialize, she'll finally realize he doesn't love her and that he lied to her. She's had so much rejection in her life, I'm afraid it might demoralize her so much that she won't be able to care for herself and the baby."

"It's a realistic possibility, unfortunately." Robert's grave expression mirrored what Victoria was feeling. "Want me to talk to her?"

"Would you?"

"Sure. After all, that's why you came out here, right?" He grinned.

"Yes, know-it-all." Victoria almost wished Treese was there to give him a swat. The thought of her youngest sister brought a frown. "Did you know Treese tried to convince Sydney to have an abortion?"

He looked out the windshield again.

"You're not surprised."

"She's not you, Vicki. People do have different opinions on the issue of abortion, you know."

Victoria bit back the urge to ask what his opinion was. She'd faced enough bad news and unpleasant surprises today. She wouldn't risk more. At least she'd secured help for Sydney. "Well, I trust you won't try to convince Sydney to kill her child."

He gave her a patient smile. "No, I can promise you I won't do that. But you do know I won't be able to tell you anything she shares with me in our session, right? She'll be a pro bono client with all the same rights to privacy as my other clients."

"Of course." Victoria nodded.

"Even if she tells me the name of her child's father."

"I understand. But you can advise her to tell me who he is to help her break free from her dependency on him."

Robert lifted his eyebrows. "Have you developed a devious streak?"

"Perhaps I've always had one." She smiled.

"I think you'd better stop hanging out with that boyfriend of yours. Or maybe it's being a murder suspect that's loosened you up."

"Oh, honestly." She opened the passenger door with a shake of the head. "Good night, Robert."

"Night, Vicki."

She chuckled as she shut the passenger door and glanced both ways before starting across the street.

The cold wind flowed through her sweater, and she folded her arms to try to retain some war—

A squeal cut through the silence.

Her head jerked toward the sound as she stopped.
Headlights beamed at her.
The roar of an engine.
"Vicki!" Robert, shouting.
A car barreled at her.
She dove for the curb.

# CHAPTER
## THIRTY

ROBERT ANSWERED the front door instead of Victoria. Was she that badly hurt?

The thought cinched Cillian's ribs even tighter than the crushing squeeze they'd been under since he'd read Robert's brief text. "Where is she?"

"Living room." Robert stepped aside and pointed up the hallway.

Cillian bolted past, bypassing the kitchen to directly access the living room.

"Victoria!" Her name shot from his lips louder than he intended, carried by the force of his worry.

"Keep your voice down. Sydney's sleeping." Victoria sat on the sofa in dim lighting, leaning back against the cushions. He'd never seen her have anything less than perfectly straight posture. She must be badly hurt.

"And you're scaring Max." She was giving orders, though. That had to be a good sign.

Was Max even around? Oh, there. The large dog watched Cillian, standing alert by the armchair.

Cillian strode to the sofa, staring down at Victoria. "You were hit by a car? Are you hurt?"

She let out a sigh and sat upright, slowly, as if it hurt. "I knew I shouldn't have let Robert send you that text. What did he tell you?"

"That somebody tried to run you over in front of your house." Fury burned through Cillian's insides. If he ever got his hands on whoever tried to kill her, he'd—

"Not in those exact words, but close." Robert's light-hearted tone grated on Cillian's nerves as the guy walked into the living room and pushed his hands into the pockets of his jeans. "I did not say you were hit by a car." He gave Victoria a smile that was way too amused for Cillian's taste. Didn't the guy care that his sister had nearly gotten killed?

Wait. Was that a bandage on Victoria's forehead? Cillian bent over her and touched the edge of the beige-colored bandage. "You *are* hurt. How bad is it?"

She pulled her head away. "Not severe enough for stitches."

He straightened. "How'd it happen if you weren't hit?"

"I dove to avoid being struck, and my head scraped the icy snow along the curb."

"It was really something. Here we'd always thought Victoria wasn't athletic." Robert's teasing prompted her to level her brother with a narrowed-eye stare.

Okay, that was a little funny. Cillian held back the smile that wanted to come. "We should get it checked out. And you might be hurt elsewhere, too." He pulled his phone out of his back pocket.

"Don't you dare call the police or EMTs." Her warning tone stopped him. "I'm a medical professional trained in wound care. I know I don't need additional treatment."

"What about the scrape on your arm? And you were limping at first."

She glared at Robert.

"You have more injuries?" The anger resurged, heating Cillian's insides. "I can't believe this. Whoever did this is going to pay, I promise you that."

"Cillian, no." She brought her beautiful eyes up to his face. "Don't take matters into your own hands or seek revenge."

"You don't think Clinton Glenn did this?" Robert stepped closer to them, looking at Cillian.

"He couldn't have." Cillian nearly gagged on the admission. If it was him, Cillian could go back to his house and settle this right now. "I was watching him the whole night, right up until you texted. He was still at home then, with all the lights on. I don't think he'd gone to bed, but he didn't leave either. I was watching the driveway the entire time."

"Then I really wish I'd seen the license plate." Robert's eyebrows dipped. "It was too dark."

"What kind of car was it?"

"Kind of a nondescript, dark sedan. Hard to tell at night what color, but I think burgundy or brown."

"Great. That doesn't match the shooter outside Judy's or Glenn's ride."

"So we were mistaken about Clinton Glenn killing Thomas? And trying to kill you?" Victoria pressed her fingers to her forehead as she squinted up at Cillian.

She was in pain. He could tell. Maybe a headache?

But she was still thinking about him, not herself. She cared more about somebody trying to kill him than the fact that someone had just tried to run her over.

His heart swelled behind his ribs. This woman was really something.

He sat on the sofa beside her, careful not to move the cushions too much. "Does your head hurt?"

She lowered her hand to her lap, blinking at him.

Why would she be surprised he'd care? That he would notice when she was hurt?

"A little, yes. I already took some medication. It should take effect soon."

He reached behind her and touched her slim shoulders.

They were wound as tight as a rope.

He gently began to massage one shoulder at a time with his fingers.

Her eyes slid shut.

His pulse pounded harder.

"Would you two like a little privacy?"

Her eyelids flew open at Robert's question.

And Cillian shot him a glare. But he kept up the massage anyway, moving his hand to Victoria's neck. Not going to let her annoying kid brother get in the way of that.

Robert grinned. "Now that the mood's ruined, maybe we can get back to the mystery?"

"You're enjoying this entirely too much, Robert." Victoria adopted a tone she must have used on her brother when she was being his mom. "This isn't a fictional mystery, you know."

"I know, Vicki. But real-life puzzles can still be fun." He switched his gaze to Cillian. "Are you positive Glenn couldn't have gotten past you?"

"Yes." He thought back to his stakeout by Glenn's very large home. Cillian had parked close to the front gate. A wrought-iron fence enclosed the entire property. Inside the gate was a large, circular driveway where Glenn had pulled his Mercedes into a multi-car garage. The lights had turned on in the house when he'd entered, and he hadn't left again. "I had eyes on the driveway and the house at all times. At least... from the front."

"Maybe there's another way out." Robert voiced Cillian's thoughts as they hit him. "Vicki, can I use your computer?" He looked down at the closed notebook computer on the coffee table in front of the sofa.

"Yes."

Robert slid the computer to the far side of the table and plopped down on the floor, sitting cross-legged as he tapped some keys. "What's the address?" He glanced up at Cillian.

"4129 Lilly Way."

Robert typed in the address. "Got it." He peered at the

screen. "Well, that's interesting. I don't think we need to discard Glenn as a suspect after all."

"What did you find?" Victoria leaned forward, and Cillian let his hand fall away.

Robert swiveled the computer toward them.

An aerial GPS view of Glenn's property filled the screen, showing the front driveway, and behind the house...

"There's a second driveway." The disbelief that lifted Victoria's tone was a far cry from Cillian's reaction.

Glenn had just tried to kill Victoria. He'd have to answer for that. To Cillian.

---

Victoria could feel the barely bridled fury rolling off Cillian in the passenger seat beside her. It was amazing he wasn't fogging the window with so much heat counteracting the cold morning temperatures outside.

Perhaps she shouldn't have agreed to drive him to the shop that apparently had his motorcycle repaired and ready for him to pick up. Now he would have transportation of his own and the means to confront Clinton Glenn, alone.

"I wish you wouldn't do this."

"What?" Cillian glanced her way. "Pick up my bike? I thought you'd be tired of chauffeuring me around."

He was failing at his attempt to sound casual or teasing. Even his tone gave away the tension building inside him, causing him to tap his fingers on his bouncing knee.

"That's it." He pointed at the upcoming entrance marked by the sign, *Specialty Auto Repair*.

Against her better judgment, she pulled into the small parking lot and slowly chose a stall.

"Thanks." He released his seatbelt and instantly reached for the door handle.

"Cillian, wait." She touched his left hand.

That stopped him. His gaze fell on her fingers making contact with his hand, and he settled back into the seat.

"I told you last night, I don't want you doing anything rash."

"It's not rash. I've been thinking about it all night."

"That's not funny." And even he didn't look the slightest bit amused. "You know what I mean. If you turn to violence, you'll only get yourself into trouble with the police, which won't help me or anyone."

"I can't let him think he can hurt you, Vicks." Cillian's gaze locked on hers, his dark orbs sparking. "He's not going to do that again."

Her heart squeezed. Cillian was doing this for her. He was angry for her sake.

She let her fingers linger on his hand when she should pull away. Few people, maybe no other person, cared about her quite that much. She couldn't help but be grateful.

"Thank you. It means..." She moistened her lips. She needed to be careful not to give him the wrong impression with her gratitude. "I'm grateful that you want to help me through this difficult situation, and that you're willing to put yourself in harm's way to do that."

"How could I not?" His response nearly cut hers short as it spewed out with intense energy. He put his other hand on top of hers, holding her there. "If anything ever happened to you, Vicks..." The glint of pain in his eyes and the pinch of his features finished the sentence.

Her chest rose and fell with deep breaths as she stared into those eyes, unable to look away. Butterflies fluttered in her stomach. Her pulse raced.

He leaned toward her, slowly inching closer as he kept his hand between hers. His gaze lowered to—

A loud rumble made her jump, pulling her hand free.

She looked out the windshield.

A heavyset man in coveralls spoke with another man by a

large motorcycle that made the offending noise. Or the welcome one.

Unless she was very much mistaken, Cillian had been about to kiss her.

And she had been going to let him.

# CHAPTER
# THIRTY-ONE

CILLIAN SLOWED his bike to a stop at the back door of the Chicago Renaissance Art Museum and took off his helmet.

Looked like no one was outside in the small lot for employees. Perfect timing to send a message.

He planted his feet on the ground on either side of the bike and rolled the throttle.

The engine revved nice and loud, the sound carrying far beyond the parking lot.

He rolled the throttle a few more times. Waited. Eyes on the solid back door.

Glenn must be busy.

Cillian revved the engine again. And again.

The door cracked open.

A brown-haired head appeared.

Cillian rolled the throttle one more time.

The guy stepped out onto the concrete walk behind the building. Clinton Glenn.

"Hey, Clinton." Cillian gave him an unfriendly grin. "Surprised to see me?"

The curator's eyebrows lowered as he stared at Cillian.

"Or maybe you're more surprised to see my bike." Cillian

leaned back on the seat and swept his hands down to include the bike and himself. "We're both still alive, no thanks to you. Guess you didn't fix my bike or my jeep as well as you thought, huh?"

"Who are you?"

"What is it they always say in the movies?" Cillian swung a leg over the bike to dismount and started toward the curator. "Oh, yeah. I'm your worst nightmare."

"Now hold on." Glenn moved back toward the door. "I don't know who you are, and I have no idea what you're talking about."

Cillian paused. Wouldn't do any good to scare him into the building too soon. "You sure about that, Glenn? Then I suppose you don't know anything about the fraud and theft either, right? Those paintings you had forged so you could sell Briscoe's real ones on the black market."

Glenn paled, his eyes widening.

Cillian grinned for real this time. "Oh, yeah. We know all about those. We found Briscoe's evidence. You know, the stuff you were looking for when you pushed Victoria down and made me chase you to your car. Briscoe did a good job collecting all that. Very thorough." He crossed his arms over his jacket. "I handed it all over to the cops yesterday. Same morning you tried to kill me."

"I...I don't know what you're talking about." Glenn swiveled toward the door, fumbling to find the knob.

"Hold it, Glenn." Cillian stalked toward him, stopping when the curator faced him again. "Just one last thing. While you're waiting for the cops to come get you for the fraud—oh, and for murdering Briscoe—don't even think of trying to hurt Victoria Weston again."

Cillian swapped his fake casual tone for a growl and pinned Glenn with a full-on glare. "If you do, you'll have to go through me." He moved toward the curator.

Glenn spun away and yanked open the door, running inside as fast as he could.

No surprise. With any luck, the information Cillian had just shared would make the curator keep on running. Right into a jail cell.

---

A rap on the door jerked Victoria's attention away from the notebook computer on her bedspread. She rose and went to her bedroom door, pulling it open. "How did it go?"

Robert smiled, but the curve of his mouth quickly fell into a frown, as if losing the battle with the heaviness that furrowed his brow. "Can I come in?"

"Of course." She backed away from the door and went to the edge of her bed to sit.

He scanned her room. "Your room is as ridiculously clean as it was at home."

"Thank you." She forced herself to wait to ask the questions she wanted to until he sat in the wingback chair in the corner.

He was clearly trying to stall or avoid something with humor.

She would give him a moment, though she'd been waiting an hour to hear how his session with Sydney had gone. "And thank you for agreeing to see Sydney this afternoon. I didn't expect you to fit her in so soon."

"We had that cancellation."

Victoria nodded. Robert had already explained that when he had texted earlier. He'd also shared that he would come to Victoria's house for the session since Sydney would be more likely to open up in a familiar, comfortable environment. "Did it help, holding the session in my living room instead of at your office?"

He met her gaze. "Yeah. And Max was a big help, too. If he wasn't so afraid of people, I'd want to borrow him as a therapy dog."

"I'll tell him you said that." Victoria gave Robert a small

smile. Then waited another few seconds for him to elaborate. Unless he wasn't going to share anything. "I know you can't divulge specifics. I would just like to know if the session was helpful for Sydney."

He nodded. "I believe it was. It's a pretty disturbing situation."

Her stomach twisted a little. She knew Sydney's situation was difficult, but something about hearing a professional confirm the knowledge was disheartening.

"We made real progress today, though. She really opened up, and we were able to process some things." He smiled. "She gave me permission to tell you that."

"I see. Did she..." Victoria thought carefully about how to word her question. She didn't want to put him in a difficult position. "Did she reveal anything that I had mentioned I would like to know?"

He looked off to the side. "I already said I wouldn't be able to tell you that."

But he just did, though without a name. At least she had told someone the identity of her baby's father. If only Robert could share it.

"I do think she'll tell you when she's ready."

"Really?" Hope rose in Victoria's chest.

"Definitely." The confidence in his tone either came from his professional assessment or, perhaps more likely, from some indication on Sydney's part.

"I hope that's soon. Did she seem shaken at all about Treese's advice that she get an abortion?"

"I know she'd tell you herself that she's not going to get an abortion. She's solid on that, which is amazing given her mother's pressure. I know you're already aware of that situation. It helps that she has such a supportive brother."

"Yes, Warren has been a great help to her. He drives her to—"

A knock. The front door?

"I can get it!" Sydney's eager shout carried from the living room.

"That's okay, Sydney. I'll answer it." Victoria threw Robert a quizzical glance as she stood and went to the hallway.

"Are you expecting someone?" His question caught her from behind as he followed her to the front door.

"No. But it's the middle of the afternoon. And Cillian was going to…talk to Glenn."

The knock came harder.

She flinched inwardly as she turned into the short entryway. But an attacker wouldn't knock.

"Why don't you let me answer it?"

She paused a few feet from the door. "Go ahead." She sidestepped out of Robert's way as he went to the door.

"Victoria?" The masculine voice was muffled through the door. "It's me."

Robert opened the door, and tall, dark, and handsome Cillian landed his gaze on Victoria.

Her pulse performed a cartwheel worthy of an Olympic gymnast.

"I was afraid you'd decided not to let me in." Cillian grinned.

She arched an eyebrow, restraining the smile that wanted to answer his. "Why would I do that?"

"Because I confronted Glenn."

"You did?" Robert stepped back to let Cillian enter, carrying cold air in with him.

"Yep." Cillian turned away and closed the door behind him, then spun toward them. "Called him out on trying to kill me and you," Cillian swung his focus to Victoria, then bounced it back to Robert, "and told him all about the evidence we have against him, courtesy of Thomas Briscoe."

Robert looked at Victoria. "And you didn't want him to do that?"

She pinched her lips together. "I was concerned about how Glenn might react. And now we've tipped our hand."

"Exactly." Cillian nodded, eagerness in his eyes. "He's so cornered now, I'm sure he's going to act."

Robert lifted a hand, his finger slightly raised. "But his action could be to try to kill Victoria in an even more aggressive and undisguised way—one that wouldn't miss or that would be hard to defend against. Now you two aren't only troublemakers who are prompting the police to investigate everyone. You're the people who hold the evidence that could convict him."

"I don't think he'll do that." Cillian answered Robert's objection with an equally calm and civil tone, mutual respect evident between them. "I told him we already gave the evidence to the police. But you're right, we can't be sure." He switched his gaze to Victoria. "That's why you're coming with me to tail Glenn."

"I beg your pardon?"

A smile twitched Cillian's mouth at her response. "I need to borrow your car again anyway. My bike is too easily seen."

"And you're going to leave your motorcycle parked in my driveway?"

The smile broke through, likely a reaction to her slightly horrified tone. She didn't want to consider what the neighbors would think if they saw she suddenly had a motorcycle in her driveway. They were probably already becoming curious about all the comings and goings at her house recently. But the motorcycle staying at all hours might make them think, heaven forbid, that she was having a fling with a bike-riding boyfriend.

"No worries, Vicks. I had a rideshare drop me off."

Which also meant she'd be forced to loan him her car. She narrowed her eyes.

"Well," Robert pointedly looked at his watch, "I've gotta get back to the office. You two kids have fun." He winked at Victoria.

As he stepped past Cillian to reach the door, he fist-bumped Cillian's shoulder. "Good luck, man."

Wonderful. Now even Robert had been charmed by Cillian and was on his side. She took in a resigned breath as Cillian shut the door behind Robert. "Fine. You may borrow my car, as long as you don't do anything reckless while driving it."

"No promises." Cillian grinned. "But you're going to be there anyway, so you can keep an eye on my driving at all times."

"I'm not going to participate in something I think is a dangerous and foolish scheme." She folded her arms across her sweater. "And my father's birthday dinner is this evening. I cannot risk being late."

His smile faded at the mention of her dad. "What time?"

"The dinner is at eight, but I must arrive by no later than six to prepare the meal."

"Mushroom pappardelle and veal?"

She stared at him. That was right, they had just begun dating before her father's birthday dinner that year. The last one her mother had been able to host. "Yes."

"Figured you would've kept it the same for him." For once, no antagonism or bitterness showed in Cillian's eyes. Instead, they held a softness. Something that looked like compassion and possibly approval. Certainly not for her father. But, perhaps, for her. "Don't worry, Vicks. I'll get you to the ball on time. I promise."

He stepped closer and lightly touched her arm. "But in the meantime, I'd feel a lot better if you'd ride along with me so I can guarantee you won't get hurt." The warmth of his fingers on her arm and his gentle tone started to melt her resistance.

"We really should let the police handle this." Her objection lacked the usual conviction in her tone. "We're in enough trouble as it is. Or at least, I am."

"We're going to get out of trouble, Vicks." He squeezed her elbow slightly. "I can feel it. We're going to get this guy, and then you'll be safe and off the cops' suspect list."

She nodded. Why had she even bothered trying to resist?

He'd probably known she would give in, evidenced by the fact he'd let the rideshare leave him there.

But Cillian smiled. And as she saw the happiness in his eyes, the remnant of her pride disappeared.

Perhaps he was right. Perhaps this very day she would be cleared, Thomas's killer would be arrested, and the nightmare would end.

# CHAPTER
# THIRTY-TWO

"I can't wait much longer." Victoria checked her watch for the twentieth time since they'd parked on the street to watch Glenn at his house.

"You still have like four hours." Cillian gestured to the dashboard clock.

She pinned him with her don't-be-annoying stare. "With the blizzard coming, I need to be sure to allow enough time to get there before the snow starts."

"Wait, there's a blizzard coming?"

"Don't you watch the news? They're all talking about the storm front moving in. It's supposed to be quite serious."

"Never did have much use for tracking the weather." Cillian lifted his thermos of lukewarm coffee from the drink holder. "It is what it is. But why are you still holding the dinner if there's a blizzard coming?"

"Father's birthday dinner has never been canceled, at least not in my lifetime."

"Of course it hasn't." Cillian rolled his eyes. "That doesn't mean you have to get there four hours early, does it?"

"I need to navigate traffic to go home and change, and then take the ingredients for the meal to my father's house and prepare it." She turned her head toward the windshield as her tone changed, like she was talking to herself. "I need to make sure Treese's decorations are acceptable and appropriate. I probably should have done that yesterday. And I hope she remembered the Caesar salad."

"I forgot you guys get gussied up for this big event. Did you buy a new dress for it? I'd love to see." Cillian grinned, letting his male interest show.

"It's an old dress, actually." Her disapproving expression said she couldn't care less if he was interested, but the color that infused her cheeks told another story.

"Still want to see it."

Her eyebrow arched. "Well, you're not going to, and we'd better head out now." She ducked slightly to see past him out the driver's side window. "He's apparently staying indoors the rest of the day."

Cillian shook his head. "No, he's up to something. He left work at one. He usually leaves at five or six. And he drove around to the back of his own house to park here instead of in the garage. He's going to make a move, and he doesn't want the police to see it."

"You could be right. But I can't stay the rest of the—"

"Hold it. We've got action."

The back door opened, and Clinton Glenn stepped outside, wheeling a suitcase behind him. Another large bag was slung over his shoulder.

"He's running."

"It does appear that way, but..." Her voice came from close to Cillian's shoulder. She must be leaning forward to see out his window better.

He forced himself to focus on the fleeing suspect and ignore the temptation to turn his face toward Victoria and—

Glenn put his luggage into the trunk of his Mercedes. He glanced around, like he was checking to see if he was being watched.

Didn't seem to notice them parked under a large tree on the opposite side of the street.

Glenn hurried to the driver's door and ducked into the car. He started the engine and pulled out of the driveway, swinging onto the road fast.

"Here we go. Better call the police." Cillian shifted into drive and started after the curator, resisting the urge to match his speed and get too close.

"Are you sure?"

He glanced at Victoria.

Concern dipped her eyebrows.

"Ask for Lieutenant Willis. Tell him you're with me and about everything we just saw. He's had a chance to review the evidence on Glenn now. I don't think he'll suspect you of anything for tipping him off that the suspect is running."

"But we don't know he's running." Hesitation colored her tone.

"He has luggage, Vicks. He's at least going away on a trip. But after what I said to him, we both know he's running from the cops and maybe us."

She let out a sigh.

"Just pretend you're talking to your dad."

She shot him a surprised glance, and he answered with a smile. "Fine. But don't do anything dangerous or illegal while I'm on the phone."

"That's why you agreed to let me drive, remember?" Good thing, too, because at the speed Glenn was driving on the suburb streets, they were already going ten miles over the limit. Lucky Victoria had agreed to let Cillian drive her car so she wouldn't be the one stalking Glenn or breaking any traffic laws if they had to follow him.

Cillian tried to keep a safe distance behind Glenn so he wouldn't notice them. The curator might change his plans if he knew he was being followed. But it was a tricky balance, staying close enough to track the many turns on the quiet streets while avoiding being spotted.

By the time Victoria ended her call with Willis, they were driving on busier roads. Good for staying hidden but harder to keep a bead on Glenn's car.

"You and Willis had quite a long chat." Cillian tossed her a grin.

"At least he didn't sound annoyed." She lowered the phone to her lap. "He's sending some officers in this direction. You probably heard I told him our location, but they won't know precisely where to go when we keep moving like this."

"Can't help that." Cillian kept his gaze locked on the silver Mercedes as Glenn switched to the right lane just before halting at the red stoplight. "As soon as we figure out where he's going, we can call it in."

"That's the freeway entrance ahead."

The light turned green. Glenn took off but was slowed by another car in front of him.

A sign along the road announced the freeway ramp on the right.

"Yep." Cillian checked over his shoulder. The right lane was packed with cars.

"He turned on his signal light. We need to get over." Urgency tightened her voice.

"You got it." He angled the front bumper of the car between two slow-moving cars in the right lane.

Honks answered the maneuver.

"Cillian."

"You said I needed to get over." He smiled, ignoring her disapproving glance as he focused on threading the needle between the cars.

The line moved forward. The cars separated rather than crash into him as he forced his way between them.

"It's too late anyway." She craned her neck to see around the line of cars in front of them. "He's already entering the freeway. I see him on the ramp."

"No worries. I'll catch up."

She jerked her head toward him. "Cillian, be careful."

"Can't let this guy get away, Vicks."

"I would rather be alive to see the capture."

He chuckled as the line of cars moved forward. Almost at the ramp. "You'll be safe. I won't let anything happen to you." He gave her a look to show how much he meant that.

She met his gaze, her mouth in a tense line.

He pulled his focus back to the road. The cars ahead finally started to accelerate on the ramp. "But you might want to hold on."

As soon as he hit the freeway, Cillian darted out from behind the cars in front, weaving across traffic to reach the fast lane.

Victoria gasped.

Better give her something to think about. "Let me know when you see him."

"As if we can see anything but a blur at this speed." At least she wasn't too scared to deliver a spunky comeback.

He grinned, keeping his eyes on the road as he pressed the accelerator.

"Wait. I think I see him."

Cillian glanced in the direction Victoria stared.

The silver Mercedes drove in the far right lane of the six-lane freeway.

"Cillian, I know where he's going."

"Where?"

The signs posted above the freeway answered his question. The airport exit was one and a half miles ahead.

"Call the lieutenant. Glenn cannot get on a plane." If he did, he could fly anywhere in the world. And they would never catch him.

Cillian didn't tell Victoria, but whether the police got there or not, Glenn was going to be stopped.

"Yes, he is now at the airport." Victoria reminded herself to breathe, pressing the phone to her ear as she spoke with the officer who had said he would direct the squad cars that had been dispatched to apprehend Glenn.

At least Cillian had finally slowed from his death-defying speed on the freeway. Now only two vehicles separated them from Glenn's silver car as he took the airport roads to the departures area of the airport.

The roads split ahead. The signage labeled one route as *Short-Term Parking* and the other as *Long-Term Parking*.

Glenn swung onto the long-term parking road.

"He's headed for the long-term parking lot." Victoria reported the update to the officer.

"Got it. We have two squads almost there." The officer's tone stayed calm and normal. Almost too cavalier for the circumstances. "I'll send them to long-term parking."

"Looks like he's not planning to come back anytime soon." Cillian's remark was laced with a serious tone he hadn't had before.

She scanned his profile.

A muscle twitched in his jaw.

Her stomach tensed. She ended the call with the police officer, lowering the phone to her lap. She stared at Cillian. "What are you going to do?"

"Nothing."

She started to pull in a relieved breath—

"If the police get here."

"Cillian..."

He followed Glenn as the curator drove through the full parking lot, likely trying to find a stall.

"Aren't we too close?"

"Not so worried about that at this point." Cillian's resolve clenched her chest.

Glenn pulled into an open stall, the only one in the near vicinity.

Cillian braked behind him and shoved her car into park.

He pulled off his seatbelt and pinned Victoria with a stare so fierce, it almost frightened her. "Tell the cops where we are and stay in the car, no matter what."

"Cillian, wait for the pol—"

Her last word was cut off in the slam of the driver's door behind him.

She rolled down her window to hear. Cold air billowed in, but she barely felt it. Every facet of her focus was riveted on Cillian.

He approached Glenn's car at the same time the curator emerged from the driver's side. "Going somewhere, Glenn?"

The curator froze, staring at Cillian. "You stay away from me." Panic twisted his tone.

But Cillian kept walking toward him.

"I mean it!" Glenn's shout carried to Victoria and beyond. "You stay back!" His hand reached into his coat pocket as Cillian kept approaching.

She tensed. A museum curator wouldn't be carrying a weapon, would he? She opened her mouth to call out a warning to Cillian.

Before she could, Cillian lunged at the curator, hitting him low on the hips.

The men disappeared between the parked vehicles.

She scrambled out of her car and ran to where they'd fallen out of view.

Grunts reached her on the wind as she stopped at the rear of the vehicles, her gaze landing on Cillian and Glenn.

Cillian was on top of the older man, but Glenn kept struggling.

They seemed to be battling for control of his hand.

And the gun he held there.

Victoria's heart stopped.

Glenn grunted and strained against Cillian, managing to pull his arm down, angling the gun toward Cillian.

A shout of warning surged up Victoria's throat. But she held it back. She could distract Cillian at the wrong moment.

*Lord, please help him restrain Glenn. Don't let him get shot.*

Cillian abruptly sat up and launched a punch, landing the blow sidelong into Glenn's face.

Glenn's arm and body went limp, the gun dropping to the pavement.

Breath returned to Victoria's lungs. She went to the men, her pulse still racing. "Is he unconscious?"

Cillian grabbed the gun and sat up, twisting his head to see her behind him. "Think so." He breathed hard with the words, a cloud of air forming in front of his face. "You're the expert, Doctor."

A siren sounded.

She pivoted toward it.

Two police cars made their way to them on the road that led to the long-term parking lot. Where Cillian had proven himself a hero, once again.

He rose to his feet and came close to her. He put his arm around her waist, his warmth and strength seeping through her coat as they both watched Glenn, lying unmoving on the ground.

As if of its own accord, her head tilted to rest on Cillian's chest.

Praise the Lord, it was over.

# CHAPTER
# THIRTY-THREE

Mission accomplished. Cillian had ended two threats against Victoria. The threat of death posed by an unlikely murder suspect and the threat of arrest by a vindictive police detective would no longer haunt her.

Cillian sat on the sofa in Victoria's living room, watching the woman of his dreams as she perched on the edge of the armchair's cushion and texted her siblings.

The steady red light of her ankle monitor peeked out from beneath the hem of her pants. The cops should've taken that off right away when they'd arrested Glenn. But Detective McCully had claimed he couldn't until the court order was reversed or ended.

Cillian would need to check into that tomorrow. McCully was probably just hoping he could still hang the murder rap on Victoria somehow. He sure had seemed put out over needing to arrest Glenn instead.

"There." She looked up from her phone, her hazel eyes finding Cillian. "Hopefully, that will prevent any disasters at dinner. None of my siblings will be arriving as early as I plan to, though Hank is likely home already." Stress creased her forehead. "In theory, now that they know the killer has been apprehended, none of them will be tempted to discuss the matter in front of our father."

"Great." Cillian's tone probably showed too much of his ambivalence. He couldn't care less if her father was disturbed at his birthday dinner.

She glanced at her watch. "Oh, my." She stood. "I need to get going. I need to tell Sydney about dinner in the refrigerator, and then I'll change."

"Did she seem a little weird to you when we got here?"

Victoria met his gaze. "I thought so. Anxious, perhaps. I'm not sure why." She gave him a weak smile. "Well, thank you for everything today."

His mouth twitched with the urge to grin. "Is that your way of saying you want me to leave now?"

She glanced away. "I'm no longer in any danger, and I do need to get ready."

"You just don't want me to see you in the dress." He let the grin loose.

A blush colored her cheeks even as she shook her head in exasperation.

The buzz of his phone interrupted the fun exchange. He sighed and grabbed the device off the coffee table.

*Marsha Faint.*

The plaintiff in the malpractice suit against Victoria's father. What would she want?

"Sorry." He lifted the phone as he got to his feet. "I have to take this."

"Of course. I need to go anyway." She walked out of the room, saving him from needing to move somewhere private to take the call. She probably thought he would leave her house now, but there was no way he was going to miss the chance to see her looking even more beautiful and dressed up than usual.

He pressed the phone to his ear. "Mrs. Faint, good to hear from you."

A pause.

"Are you the one who came to my house, asking about Dr. Weston?"

"Yes, ma'am. Cillian Doherty."

"Is your grandmother going to sue him for malpractice?"

"She's still trying to figure out if she should. She doesn't have much money, and her health isn't good." Adding more reasons for Mrs. Faint to feel sympathetic wouldn't hurt.

"Well, I feel this is the right thing for me to do then. I need to tell the truth about what happened."

He waited, anticipation building in his chest.

"Tell your grandma it could be dangerous."

"Dangerous? How would it be dangerous?"

She paused again. "Is anyone there with you?" Her voice grew quieter, even more cautious.

"No, ma'am. Please tell me what kind of danger my grandma could be in."

"When I had a lawyer sue Dr. Weston, I started getting phone calls." She stopped again.

"What kind of calls, Mrs. Faint?"

"From a man. I don't know who he was. But he said I should drop the lawsuit if I didn't want to get hurt. Things like that."

Whoa. Had Weston really stooped to threats and intimidation? He wouldn't have made such calls himself, of course. Probably hired someone.

"And then one night, I'm sure there was someone sitting in a car across the street, watching me. I told my lawyer to drop the suit the day after that. I don't have anyone to protect me."

Poor woman. The heat of anger pumped through Cillian's torso. What a coward Weston was, hiring thugs to scare a lonely old lady. "Did you report any of this to the police?"

"No, my lawyer was concerned I didn't have enough evidence to do so."

Cillian clenched his jaw. Maybe the lawyer had been paid off by Weston, too. "I'm so sorry that happened to you, Mrs. Faint."

"I just don't want the same thing to happen to your grandma. I've never been so frightened in my life."

"Thank you, ma'am. I appreciate your kindness in telling me. I'll pass the information along." To Dr. Weston himself.

"Good. It's just not worth going through that."

"You're probably right. Please let me know if there's anything I can do to help you now or in the future. You have my number."

"What a sweet boy. Your grandma must be so proud of you."

If he actually had one.

"Take care of her and yourself, young man."

"Yes, ma'am, I will. You have a good night."

He ended the call and slid the phone into his back pocket. Tension twisted his muscles. Maybe he should go to Henry Weston now, birthday dinner or not, and confront him with what he'd done to the sweet old lady. For intimidating and threatening her into keeping silent about the malpractice. Which he was clearly guilty of, since he'd resorted to such tactics to keep her quiet.

Cillian ground his teeth together as he stared at nothing in Victoria's living room. He'd hoped to find dirt on Weston this way, but the truth of it was dirtier than even he had expected. Victoria's father was worse than he'd thought. How would she take learning that he was guilty of malpractice and threatening an elderly patient?

Pushing a hand through his hair, Cillian blew out a breath. He had the leverage he needed now. But should he use it?

The truth could hurt Victoria pretty badly. And she might not thank him for exposing it. If he worked her father the right way, Henry Weston would meet Cillian's demands to keep the truth from everyone, including his family. Cillian could get Weston to stop controlling Victoria, and she would never need to know why or hear of her father's potentially criminal actions.

But it was a risky play. It could go sideways and have the wrong effect on Victoria.

She was trusting Cillian a lot now as he tried to help her do the right things. She'd even joined him in trailing and capturing Glenn, despite her fear of disobeying the police and irritating her father.

It was another great sign that she was pulling away from Henry Weston, getting free from his hold bit by bit as Cillian helped her to do so.

Yeah. He didn't need to use his leverage over her father yet. He'd keep it in his back pocket to pull out if necessary. He wasn't going to let Victoria waste any more of her life in the doctor's control. But things were looking very good right now, and—

"Cillian? Are you still here?" Victoria's voice carried in front of her from the hallway where she appeared, Sydney trailing behind her. "Oh, good."

His thoughts exactly. Or more like *wow* and *incredible*.

Victoria Weston was the most beautiful woman he'd ever seen no matter what she wore. But the formal green dress she'd changed into took her natural attractiveness to a whole different level. The floor-length dress had long sleeves and a wide, curved neckline that revealed only her slim neck and a hint of her shoulders before modestly draping her slim figure, hinting at her curves and highlighting her undeniable femininity. She looked like a queen.

He opened his mouth to say so.

"Sydney wants to tell us something together." Victoria's serious tone held an edge of urgency that stopped him from voicing his admiration.

He managed to drag his gaze from her and glance at the short girl in a tank and sweatpants that stretched around her pregnant belly.

"You've both been so nice to me, and I know you want to help. And your brother said it would really help me." Sydney paused, her eyes widened and her face a little pale. "So I want to tell you what you've been asking."

The sentence didn't quite make sense, but he got the gist.

"We do want to help you, Sydney. You can trust us." Victoria touched the girl's arm.

"Okay." Sydney took in a deep breath as she intertwined her fingers and held her hands under her chin. "His name is Lawrence Massey."

The girl had Cillian's attention now. "That's the name of the baby's father?"

She nodded.

"Is he married?" Cillian might as well ask while Sydney was in a sharing mood.

"Yeah. That's why he didn't want me to tell. He's going to get a divorce."

Poor, gullible kid. Taken advantage of by an adult who was supposed to be a man but was instead a child rapist. One who needed to get his comeuppance for that.

Cillian swung his gaze to Victoria.

Her face had turned whiter than Sydney's and her eyes even larger. Did she know the father of Sydney's baby?

---

Victoria's heart rate beat an unhealthy rhythm in her chest as she tried to find the air that had whooshed from her lungs at Sydney's declaration.

But she couldn't say anything negative or alarming in front of the teen. She swallowed. "Thank you for telling us. I know that took courage."

Sydney nodded, her expression and the way she tangled her hands together indicating she was still uncertain and apprehensive. "What are you going to do?" Her gaze darted from Victoria to Cillian.

He watched Victoria with his eyebrows lowered. He would

certainly have perceived her alarm, given how in tune he seemed to be with her emotions recently.

Victoria answered for them. "I don't know yet."

"Could you just try to have him call me or text? I want him to know when I have our baby." Sydney rested her hand on her round stomach and the new life housed there.

The poor girl. She still loved the man who had manipulated her into this life-changing situation through lies and deception. She still believed he would come for her.

Victoria's heart squeezed. "We can try."

"Okay." The girl nodded and reached for her hair, twisting a clump between her fingers. She was clearly still anxious.

"Why don't you go visit Max for a while? He's in my bedroom, and I think he'd like some company since I was gone so long today."

"Oh, sure." Sydney smiled and spun away to hurry up the hallway where she disappeared into Victoria's room.

"You know the guy?" At least Cillian had waited until Sydney was out of sight. But she could still be within earshot.

Victoria walked toward him, and he took the hint, angling sideways so she could pass him into the living room.

He followed her to the center of the space and folded his arms across his chest.

How much should she say? Cillian was so set against her father, and Dad certainly wouldn't want her dragging him into this. "I don't know him personally. But he's a friend of someone I know."

"I see." Cillian's eyes held enough skepticism that it was obvious he knew she wasn't revealing everything she could. "Well, we'd better get going."

"Going? Where?"

"To confront this loser."

"What? We can't do that."

He lowered his arms and stepped closer to her, stopping with a few feet between them. "We have to, Vicks. You do realize this guy is guilty of statutory rape."

"Yes, I know that. But that means we should report him to the police, not confront him at his home."

"You mean your buddies, the cops?" Cillian smirked. "Come on, Vicks. Even a good police force would say there isn't enough evidence to charge the guy."

She moistened her lips and looked away. He was unfortunately correct. There would be no evidence, certainly not this long after the crime. It would be Sydney's word against a prominent, successful CEO of a huge company. But it wasn't right to let the man get away without any punishment for his horrible crimes.

"I know you want this guy to pay as much as I do."

She jerked her gaze to Cillian. "We can't do that. I won't be part of any violence."

He chuckled. "I like the way you think. But I wasn't going to rough the guy up. Not yet, anyway."

She narrowed her eyes. "This isn't amusing."

He grinned. "Somehow you make everything fun, Vicks."

A shiver trickled down her spine at the look in his eyes that changed from teasing to something intense and hot.

"You're gorgeous in that dress, by the way. Totally worth waiting for."

*Worth waiting for.* Did he intend a double meaning in that remark?

Goosebumps raised on her arms, thankfully hidden by the thin sleeves of the velvet dress. She dug in her dry throat for her voice. "At least it covers the ankle monitor."

"Oh, it does a whole lot more than that."

Her pulse tumbled. If he kept looking at her like that, she—

Wait. Was he trying to distract her and charm her into his new harebrained scheme? She pressed her lips together. "Even if you don't intend to do Lawrence Massey any physical harm, we can't confront the man. It wouldn't help Sydney."

"Sure, it would. We might not be able to get enough evidence for the cops to arrest him, but jerks like this are cowards. All it would take is letting him know *we* know what he did. His reputation would be on the line. He's married, and he didn't want Sydney to tell anyone, so he clearly has a lot at stake if this news gets out."

Victoria checked the clock on the wall. "Oh, my. It's nearly five o'clock."

"Which gives us an hour to go to this Massey guy's house. He's probably home this time of night, especially with the blizzard coming." Cillian suddenly stepped beside her and took her elbow, tugging her forward toward the garage. "Do you know where he lives?"

"Cillian, no." She pulled away.

He stopped and stared at her. "Are you going to tell me what's really going on? Just how close are you to this guy?"

Heat flushed her face, fitting both her initial embarrassment and the rush of frustration that followed. "I told you, I don't know him personally."

"Oh, I get it. Is he a pal of your dad's?"

She chose her words carefully before she answered. "My father knows him, yes."

"Perfect." A smile curved Cillian's mouth. Not the reaction she'd expected. "That gives us even more leverage. With you there, we can pressure him to do the right thing."

"Absolutely not. I can't go and confront one of my father's friends. They're members of the same country club."

Cillian's eyes narrowed. "I'm surprised at you, Vicks." The disappointment in his tone scraped along her conscience. "Don't you want this guy to take responsibility for his child and Sydney?"

"Of course, I do. But I need to think through all the repercussions. My father is already so upset with me. He would not want me to accuse one of his friends and a country club member of something so awful. The scandal could taint him, as well. Or Massey could phone him and tell him that I confronted him. He could call him tonight." The thought pinched her throat. "During the birthday dinner."

"Vicks, come on." Cillian moved close, leaving only inches between them as he cupped her upper arms with his warm hands. "I know you." His gaze delved into hers, holding her captive. "You're not the kind of woman to put reputation or even risk to yourself before helping people in need. Especially a teen mom and her baby girl." He leaned his head closer to hers. "We can't let him dump Sydney and the baby. We can't let him get away with this scot-free."

He was right. Preserving the reputations of people like Lawrence Massey only allowed them to keep hurting others. And even her father's preferences did not supersede the calling of Christ to help those in need, like Sydney and her baby.

She tightened her jaw and met Cillian's searching gaze, so close to hers that she barely found her voice. "You're right. We need to help Sydney, if we can, and at least show Massey that he has been found out." Perhaps doing so would prevent him from doing the same to another victim.

"Good girl. Let's go get him." The approval in Cillian's eyes and his broad smile calmed half of the apprehension that twisted her stomach.

It was much easier to demote her father's priorities in her mind than it would be to face him at the birthday dinner if he found out. Lord willing, he wouldn't have a clue.

# CHAPTER
# THIRTY-FOUR

"WHAT EXACTLY ARE you going to say to him?" Victoria whispered the question to Cillian as the Masseys' maid or housekeeper—whatever she was—closed the door to go find her employer.

Cillian gave her a grin. "These things just come to me in the moment."

Did she realize how close she was to him as they stood on the top step of the grand pillared entrance to the mansion? Maybe it was the cold or her nerves that made her press so near that her coat sleeve brushed his, but Cillian wasn't going to miss the opportunity.

He slid his arm behind her waist. "Don't worry. We're doing this for Sydney. Somebody has to make this guy take responsibility."

She nodded, her mouth in a tight line. But she didn't pull away.

The door swung open, and a man appeared, scanning them with blue eyes.

Lawrence Massey looked exactly like Cillian had expected. Fifties with thick graying hair cut in a modern style that said he still thought he was attractive to young women. About five eleven and in decent shape. Dress shirt and navy pants that had likely paired well with his overpriced suit jacket before he'd taken it off to relax at home. With the wife who had no idea he was playing around with teenage girls.

Or maybe she did know. His money or power could be enough to keep her quiet and locked in to the marriage.

"I remember you." The player gave Victoria a smooth smile. "Victoria, isn't it? You look so much like your mother."

Her frame tensed beneath Cillian's arm.

Great. The guy had known her mom. Hopefully, that wouldn't make her want to go soft on him.

"Please, come inside." Massey stepped back, gesturing with his hand for them to enter.

Cillian let Victoria go in first. This was perfect, coming with someone Massey knew and trusted.

He was already letting his guard down, clearing the way for a strike to his conscience. If he had one left. If he didn't, Cillian was just as willing to use the leverage of public exposure or legal charges.

"My wife and I were about to sit down to dinner. I don't think you've met her yet, have you?"

Victoria returned his smile, though she shot a quick glance at Cillian. "I don't believe I've had the pleasure. But I'm afraid we're in a bit of a hurry this evening."

"Oh." His gaze went to Cillian.

"Forgive me." She lightly touched Cillian's arm. "This is Cillian Doherty, a friend of mine. Cillian, this is Lawrence Massey."

Cillian extended his hand, and Massey took it in a strong handshake. But something flickered in Massey's eyes as their gazes met. Did he sense Cillian was a threat?

He shifted his attention to Victoria. "What brings you by on this cold night?"

"We need to discuss something rather difficult with you, I'm afraid." She might be nervous about doing this, but even Cillian couldn't tell now. Her posture was perfectly straight, as usual, and she looked Massey in the eye as she spoke with a kind but unwavering tone.

"What might that be?" Massey crossed his arms over his chest, like he sensed he wouldn't like where this was going.

"Sydney Morris has been trying to reach you, and she says you haven't returned any of her messages."

Massey froze without changing his posture. Only his eyebrows moved, immediately scrunching toward each other. He stared at Victoria for a few beats.

Cillian would let him sweat it out for a bit.

"I have no idea what you are talking about. Who is this, Sydney, did you say?" His denial would be more convincing if he'd stayed immobile. But fear battled the eyebrow lift he attempted and pinched the corners of his mouth. And his eyes widened ever so slightly. He was panicking but trying to think, trying to strategize.

"Like she said, we don't have much time." Cillian's turn. "So let's cut to the chase and skip through the denials. We know you had an affair with this sixteen-year-old girl and got her pregnant."

"Will you keep your voice down?" Massey hissed the words as he looked over his shoulder toward the doorway that must lead to wherever his wife was waiting for him.

Good. With any luck, she'd be within earshot.

"I'll consider it, if you agree to support Sydney and your daughter, at least financially." Cillian stayed at full volume as he pinned Massey with a stare.

"I already told you," Massey flipped his focus between Cillian and Victoria, "I don't know anything about this pregnant girl, and I have nothing to do with it."

*It.* Revealing use of language to detach himself from the situation.

"And I told *you*, we know you have everything to do with this unwed teen mom and her child. Are you seriously going to reject your own daughter? You know Sydney's pregnant with a girl, right?"

Massey glared at him, dropping any effort to appear friendly or calm. "I don't know who you are, but you had better think very seriously about what you're accusing me of. I have the best attorneys money can buy, and I will destroy you."

Cillian stepped closer to the player. Looked down at him. "I'm shaking in my boots."

Massey met his glare, then pulled back, aiming his anger at Victoria. "I can't believe you would be involved in something like this. Trying to smear my name, a friend of your father's, with malicious lies. He's going to hear about this."

She paled a shade but didn't flinch. "Mr. Massey, I would never attack you or try to ruin your reputation with lies. We're only asking you to do the right thing. I've been helping Sydney and your unborn child. They're staying at my house right now because her mother evicted her. She and your daughter would be homeless and in danger if not for the kindness of others. Doesn't that concern you?"

"What concerns me," Massey's voice quivered with the fury his eyes shot at Victoria, "is that a Weston would come into my home and accuse me of something so heinous and untrue. What have I ever done to you or your father that you would try to destroy my marriage and my life?"

"Mr. Massey, that's not—"

"But I guess I shouldn't be surprised." Massey's stance widened, as if he was setting up an attack. A verbal one? "After all, you are suspected of murder."

She closed her mouth, surprise and dismay tightening her features.

"I assumed you were innocent, since you're a Weston. But now, I can see why the police would think you have the capacity for cruelty."

"That's enough." Cillian stepped between the jerk and Victoria. "This isn't about her, it's about you. And you don't have a moral leg to stand on. You manipulated an innocent teen girl by conning her into believing you loved her, just for your own pleasure. So you could use her and throw her away. Her and your own daughter." Cillian moved closer to the loser, shooting daggers at him with his eyes. "Only the worst excuse for a human being would stoop that low."

Massey looked up at Cillian, fear flickering in his eyes as his features clustered like he was trying to hold his position. But he caved again, backing farther away this time. "Get out." He pointed toward the door. "Both of you, get out of my house right now, or I'm calling the police." He jerked his gaze to Victoria. "And we all know you don't want that."

"Actually, Victoria has been cleared of all suspicion now that we captured the real murderer." Cillian gave the jerk a satisfied grin.

"Cillian, let's go." The tug on his arm drew his attention to Victoria.

"Not until this guy is ready to man up."

"No, now." She switched to pushing, shoving Cillian's arm to try to move him toward the door. "We're sorry to have bothered you." She threw the polite apology over her shoulder to the heartless player.

Anger surged through Cillian. Was she really going to placate a worm like Massey?

"You'd better not tell anyone about this." Massey delivered the statement as a threat.

Cillian swung around Victoria, facing the jerk. "Oh, I plan to tell everyone. Starting with your country club, your board members, and anyone else I can think of. Maybe a few news outlets."

"Get out!" Massey's screech echoed in the foyer.

Cillian grinned. "Bet your wife heard that."

"Cillian, we've done enough. Please." Victoria grabbed his hand this time. If she'd done that the first time, he might've gone along with her.

He let her tug him out the door as he returned the grip. Her hand felt so at home in his, so slim and perfect.

Until she let go and yanked her hand out of his. She

marched ahead through the snowflakes that must've started while they'd been inside.

He quickly caught up as she hurried to her car, parked in the Masseys' driveway. "That went great."

She stopped so quickly, Cillian almost smashed into her. She stared at him. "What?"

"That was great. He may not have agreed to help Sydney yet, but he will. Now that he knows we know all about his dirty secret, he'll be more willing to play ball next time. Especially if we can get more leverage. Maybe a witness of some of the times he met with Sydney or—"

"Enough." Victoria's tone, sharper than he'd ever heard her use, stopped him cold. She swung her hand toward the mansion. "That was the most humiliating thing I've ever done. It accomplished absolutely nothing except for creating potential embarrassment for my father and the country club and breaking up a marriage."

"Now, hold on." Frustration heated Cillian's chest. "If any marriage is broken up, Massey's the one who did that when he started sleeping around with teen girls. And your dad? Really? I know you'll do whatever he wants, but does he really mean more to you than an unwed teen mom and her baby?"

Her cheeks turned red as she glared at him. "How dare you? How dare you insinuate I don't care about Sydney and her child?" She pivoted and stalked to the unlocked car, going to the driver's door.

But Cillian had the key fob in his pocket, since he'd driven. He followed her, walking around to the passenger door for now. He slid his legs into the cramped floor space as Victoria pulled another key fob from her purse. Of course, she would have a spare with her.

She started the car, then reached for the gearshift.

He laid his hand on her slim arm. "Vicks, wait." He couldn't lose her now. Couldn't let her slip back into her father's control. Not when she was getting so close to breaking free.

She finally looked at him, hurt and anger mixing in her beautiful eyes.

"Do you ever wonder how life would be different if you and I had stayed together all this time? If you'd chosen me instead of your dad?"

She looked away, staring out the windshield. The line of her jaw tightened.

He made himself wait. Let her think. She had to have wondered. Had to have wished, like he had, that they hadn't broken up.

"I made the decision. It was my idea to break up. My dad didn't even know about it."

---

Victoria felt Cillian's stare as she pulled her arm away from his touch.

His intake of air filled the cold silence of the car. "That can't be true." Hurt tightened his voice.

She closed her eyes. She didn't want to hurt him, but he needed to know. Needed to stop hoping and interfering. She needed to reestablish the boundaries she should have kept from the moment he'd stepped back into her life.

"Why?"

She steeled her resolve and forced herself to face him. But she nearly winced at the confusion and pain in his eyes.

Cillian never showed pain. Not to anyone but her. And now she had to hurt him once again. But it had to be done.

"Why do you think, Cillian? I left my dying mother to go out with you." Her throat swelled with emotion, pinching her tone. But she had to keep going. "She died alone." Tears blurred her view of him. She looked away, catching the tears before they could fall far.

"She died in her sleep, Vicks. You couldn't have saved her. You said she'd been peacefully sleeping for days. She was comfortable at home with hospice coming in during the day. You were all just waiting for her to pass."

"I don't know if she did die in her sleep." She threw him a glance. "That's what I told everyone, but she could've awoken and looked for me when I..." her throat swelled, "wasn't there."

"You were only gone half an hour, tops. You felt so guilty for going out with me, you wanted to go right back, remember?"

"That was thirty minutes too long. I never should have let you talk me into going out that night." Just as she shouldn't have followed him to confront Lawrence Massey. Would she never learn?

"So it's my fault she died?" Simmering anger laced the question. That was more like Cillian. But he was only trying to defend himself, his reflex when hurt.

She sighed. "No, it's mine." She met his gaze. "That was my decision, too. But I never should have left. And I've had to live with the knowledge that I let my mom die alone. But I couldn't possibly keep seeing you. I couldn't take the chance that I would again allow you to persuade me to do something wrong."

"You were a fifteen-year-old kid, Victoria. You shouldn't have been the one having to sit by your mom's death bed day and night." His eyes flashed, but his frustration wasn't entirely aimed at her. "That burden never should've been put on you. It was too much. You were exhausted. I saw it. You needed a break."

"I needed to be there for my mother."

"And since you weren't, you have to pay for it for the rest of your life?" His raised voice bounced off the walls of the car. "By sacrificing everything for your family?"

As if that were a bad thing. Answering irritation rushed through her torso. "No, I choose to honor my mother by doing what she would have wanted, by holding her family together and making sure her children thrive."

"And making her husband happy at all times? Is that part of the slave-labor penance, too?"

Victoria blinked, trying to absorb the sting of his words. He couldn't have just said that to her. "I never should have let you back into my life." She reached to shift the car into reverse.

"Victoria, wait."

She paused, her heart pounding against her ribs.

"What about you? Wouldn't your mom want *you* to be happy and thrive, too? To find someone you love and be free to make your own choices?"

A resurgence of moisture stung her eyes. She would not cry over him again. Not in front of him or anywhere else.

"That's all I care about, Vicks." His voice softened, the anger gone. "I still love you. I've always loved you."

The words found the vulnerable spot in her heart and pierced the old wound that had never healed—the place once occupied by Cillian Doherty.

She closed her eyes against the pain.

"We've wasted too much time already. Too many years. Let's not waste another second." The tenderness in his tone stung like salt in the wound.

Oh, how she wished the situation were different. That her mother was alive to somehow persuade Dad to approve of Cillian. That Victoria had been mature enough all those years ago to demonstrate more Christ-likeness and better explain the Gospel instead of giving him her heart and adoration.

"Come on, Vicks. I know you love me, too. Let's leave all this behind and build the life we were meant to have together."

"I can't."

A heavy silence, thick and unbearable, filled her car.

"Because of him?" It was an accusation, raw and angry. But he had no right to put her in this position again. To make her choose again.

This time, she would not make the wrong choice. She swung her head to meet his anger head-on.

Hurt swirled in his eyes, too.

She swallowed back the remorse that climbed up her throat. She lifted her chin. "I will not destroy my family." Destruction was exactly what would happen if she crossed her father in such a severe way. He would never forgive her, would cut her off, wouldn't allow her to have contact with her siblings. Some of them might be led to cross him, too, because of her, perhaps choosing her over him. Their family would be in shambles. And her mother's legacy, the only thing Victoria could still do for her, would be ravaged.

"I can't believe you want to stay under your father's thumb for the rest of your life." The disbelief and anguish in Cillian's voice matched his expression. "That you'd choose him over me. Again."

*Father, please help me stay strong. Help me to do the right thing.*

The silent prayer worked like a shield against her heart's desire to soften, to end the hurt she was causing Cillian. And to admit that despite being a grown woman who knew better, she'd started to love him again.

She steeled her jaw. He could not persuade her this time. "I choose to do the right thing." She finally shifted into reverse and drove away from Massey's house.

She would drop off Cillian at his apartment and return to the task God had given her—to care for her family as her mother would have and live a peaceful life of obedience and faith. And she would never see Cillian Doherty again.

# CHAPTER
# THIRTY-FIVE

CLINKING SILVERWARE and the swirling winds of the blizzard outside the windows were the only sounds in the dining room at Henry Weston's birthday dinner.

Victoria forced down one more swallow of her barely touched pappardelle.

Robert, sitting kitty-corner to her position at the foot of the table, gave her a tiny, sympathetic smile.

"The pappardelle and bruschetta are really great, Vicki." Hank's compliment drew her gaze down the table to where he sat at their father's right, opposite Treese. "You always make the best I've ever had." His smile, though bigger, was just as inhibited as Robert's.

"Except for mom's." Treese leaned past Spring and Torin to see Victoria. "But yours is second."

"I know mine can't compare with hers. You're right." Victoria's attention returned to her father.

He'd eaten most of the veal, mushroom pappardelle, and bruschetta, on his plate. But judging from his demeanor, he'd only done so to have a task, a means to avoid looking at Victoria or speaking to anyone.

He was never chatty, but in recent years, his mood had

lightened at his birthday dinners. He would regale his children with stories of his triumphs as a youth, a student, and a surgeon. Then he would ask about his children's work and education, remarking with approval on anything they were doing well and encouraging them to reach greater heights.

Tonight, he glowered at his plate without a word.

Victoria should be grateful he was silent rather than voicing his obvious displeasure. But her stomach was creating more knots by the minute as the tension emanating from him increased.

Should she apologize for getting arrested? No, not in front of everyone. That would only bring up the very topic that was best to avoid.

"I thought I was going to slide right off the road." Hank's laugh and chuckles from the others drew Victoria's attention to the story he must have been telling for a bit already. "But I remembered Westons don't miss Dad's birthday dinner, so no blizzard was about to stop me."

Robert laughed. "That's the spirit."

Hank grinned. "And it worked, too. I think that snow was afraid of me." He glanced at their father. "Or maybe just afraid of Dad." Hank tacked on the addition to his joke with a jovial tone, but it was a risky remark. Especially this evening.

Their father lifted his head and looked at his favorite child.

Hank's smile grew shaky. "Just kidding."

Victoria jumped in before their father could misdirect his wrath onto Hank. "Dad, would you like your cake now?" She'd baked his favorite German chocolate cake that Mom had always made for him and prepared it with candles in the kitchen. Victoria removed the cloth napkin from her lap and started to rise.

"No." The steel in his tone made her immediately sit as her heart seized.

All eyes went to their father.

"What I would like," he dabbed his mouth with his napkin before setting it beside his plate, "is to know what on earth possessed you to harass an esteemed member of the Green Hills Country Club at his home with that reprobate I told you never to see again." He lifted his gaze with the final words, piercing her across the length of the table with a degree of barely bridled fury she hadn't seen in years. Certainly not directed at her, not even when he'd reprimanded her for being questioned by the police.

"I—" Panic spiked through her. But she knew how to calm her father, how to meet his expectations and please him. She knew how to calm his stormy waters. *Lord, please help me.*

Her father respected strength and intelligent acquiescence. She met his gaze and fought for a steady tone. "I'm so sorry you heard of the meeting characterized in such an inaccurate light. I can assure you there was no harassment, only a discussion. I was trying to help a young girl who was the victim of that particular man."

Dad's eyes narrowed. "Define what you are implying by 'victim.'"

She glanced at her siblings, all of whom stared at her. They already knew of the situation, but not the identity of the guilty party. Except for Robert.

He gave her a small nod, a gesture of encouragement her heart grabbed for strength.

She returned her focus to her father. "She's a teenager with whom Lawrence Massey had an affair. She's now pregnant with his child."

"Whoa."

"Oh, my goodness."

Hank's and Spring's reactions overlapped one another.

"If your story is true, you have no business becoming directly involved with this girl." Dad's features relaxed slightly, shifting into his usual calm expression as the pent-up anger receded.

*Thank you, Lord.*

Perhaps Victoria would get a chance to explain so he would understand. "With all due respect, her own mother evicted her from the only home she has when she's about to have her child."

"Precisely what I suspected. We don't involve ourselves with the class of people you are dealing with."

Victoria stared at him. She shouldn't be surprised. He'd always placed inappropriate value on wealth, so-called class, and social standing. But to hear him admit his bias so bluntly, especially when learning the identity of the culprit, hit her with disappointment and shock.

"I sincerely hope," he leveled her with a warning look, "you are not about to tell me you allowed her to stay in your home."

She took in a breath through her nose. Calm strength. "Yes. She's temporarily staying with me, so she'll have a roof over her head when her baby arrives."

His gaze darkened as his mouth tightened. "I'm surprised at you, Victoria. You will have this girl removed from your house immediately. Do you realize the damage this is doing to your reputation? To this family's reputation?"

"Now hold on." Torin aimed his confident interruption at her father. "We're talking about statutory rape, sir. If it's true and could be proven. The girl is a victim, not the criminal." Thank the Lord for a police sergeant, soon-to-be family member, who wasn't afraid of their dad. But she knew Torin tried to stay out of family dynamics as much as possible while Spring was trying to repair her relationship with their dad.

"I'm aware of that." Dad's fingers flexed beside his plate, a clear sign anger was simmering and building inside. It would explode if Victoria couldn't calm him down. But she couldn't agree to cast Sydney and her baby out on the street, or even into different housing. She'd promised Sydney she could stay.

"I can't believe you would say this girl isn't worth helping because of her 'class.'" Spring bobbed quotes in the air with her fingers as she stared at their father. "The man who did this to her is in *your* class. He's your friend, a member of your own country club, probably from a *supposed* good family." Her voice elevated with each word. "And he's married!"

Victoria sent her a look, trying to warn her to stay out of this. It would ruin her attempts to smooth things over with their father.

Irritation clustered in harsh lines on Dad's brow. "He is not a friend, merely an acquaintance. He obviously misrepresented himself and does not belong at the Green Hills Country Club. I'll see to it that he's thrown out. But that does not change the damage Victoria is doing by becoming involved. I give hundreds of thousands of dollars to charity every year for this sort of thing." He swung his gaze to Victoria. "Give to a charity to help her, but you will stop your involvement with her immediately, is that clear?"

Her heart pounded in her ears. She couldn't agree to that. It wouldn't be right. But if she didn't, if she crossed Dad in front of everyone, the results could be catastrophic.

*"I can't believe you would want to stay under your father's thumb for the rest of your life."*

Cillian's words echoed in her mind. Was he right? That she acquiesced to her father when she shouldn't? If Cillian were here now, he would be ripping into her dad for his unfeeling harshness and cruelty.

"I'm sorry, but I can't do that." Her bold response seemed to come from someone else. "It wouldn't be right."

"Unacceptable!" Dad abruptly stood, his chair squealing on the floor as it slid back.

Her heart lurched into her throat, somehow continuing to thump there as she stopped breathing.

"No wonder you've gotten yourself arrested for murder, your face and name plastered all over the news." He waved a hand in the air as if gesturing to the media outlets. "I knew that Doherty boy would ruin you. I don't know who you are anymore." He pointed a finger at her. "You have dragged the Weston name through the mud. You are destroying the reputation I've worked my entire life to build for all of you."

Every accusation pierced her ribs, finding a bullseye in her heart. Her limbs trembled. She could only stare at him, that finger, the glare of disappointment and wrath.

"That's enough, Dad."

She numbly saw someone rise on her left.

Robert?

"Being accused of murder was not her fault. And now she's trying to do the right thing to help someone in need. You have no right to blame her for either of those or pretend she is purposefully tainting your name."

Robert should stop. He should sit down. He had a peaceful relationship with their dad. She couldn't be the reason for ruining that.

The grim possibility helped her find her voice. "Robert, please sit. It's all right."

"No, it's not." Hank's voice was louder than normal, tightened with emotion. He swung his head toward their father. "I can't believe you."

"Hank, stop." She had to do something. Hank was in enough hot water with their dad as it was right now.

"No, I won't, Vicki." He shot a glance at her before facing their dad again. "I can't believe you would accuse Vicki of hurting our family when she's done nothing but keep us together and happy our whole lives. She just wants to help everyone, including you. She was falsely accused of murder," Hank flung his hand high into the air, "and you don't even care about how scary that must be for her or how unfair it is. Your own daughter!"

"You had better hold your tongue." Dad's tone was cold as ice. "You forget who you're talking to."

"Dad, he has a point." Spring jumped in again. "And especially about Sydney. I can't believe it doesn't bother you that your friend did that to an innocent girl. How can you honestly say we shouldn't help her and her baby?"

"That's not what he said." Treese's sharp tone sliced the air as she glared down the table at Spring. "You all need to leave Dad alone. He's totally right." She switched her angry gaze to Victoria. "You're not helping Sydney. You're hurting her by telling her not to get an abortion. It'll ruin her life."

"Treese!" Shock pulled the exclamation from Hank. "How can you say that? That not killing her baby will ruin her life?"

"Henry, Jr." Their father's hard voice cut through their battle. "That is hardly a medical opinion. You will need to redefine your opinions or keep them to yourself if you are to succeed as a physician."

"Maybe I don't want to do that." Hank crossed his arms and dropped his gaze as he muttered the response.

"The point is that we are all allowed to have our own opinions and should be allowed to make the choices we decide are right as individuals." Robert somehow maintained his even psychiatrist's tone as he looked at each of them. "But none of us should blame each other or try to force anyone into thinking as we do."

"We don't need your psychobabble, Robert." Treese spewed out the putdown. "Victoria messed up, and she should apologize to Dad and stop making a bigger mess out of everyone's lives."

Spring and Hank jumped to Victoria's defense at the same time, leaning toward Treese as they started a shouting match.

Victoria's stomach churned. This couldn't be happening. They were turning against each other. Picking sides. At Dad's birthday dinner.

Her family was self-destructing before her eyes.

And it was her fault.

She had to stop this. She would gladly apologize to her father.

But he wouldn't be satisfied with that. He'd want her to reject Sydney, suddenly withdraw from her life when she most needed support and love.

But she had to do something. "I'll get the cake." She made the announcement in a loud voice as she rose from the chair.

Robert tossed her a glance but then entered the verbal fray, trying to calmly help the others deal with their conflict more peacefully. But they weren't listening to him any more than Victoria.

She went to the kitchen anyway, guided by a blind, Pollyanna hope that cake and candles would somehow halt the disintegration of her family in the next room.

Her phone dinged from the pocket of her purse on the counter. A text message.

Desperation, like the captor's overwhelming need for escape, drove her to go to her purse and pull out the phone.

A text from Sydney. Ironic timing. What did she—

Victoria's blood froze.

*Lawrence kidnapped me. He says he'll kill me unless you come. No cops or he'll kill me. Please help. He'll text you the address.*

Lawrence Massey? Why would he kidnap Sydney?

Oh, no. Was it because Victoria and Cillian had confronted him? Had they caused this?

They must have. They'd pushed him into desperation so extreme that he felt the only way out was to kidnap Sydney. And to lure Victoria there to eliminate her, as well.

The horrible shouts pierced the wall, finding her in the kitchen. She couldn't go in and tell them, tell her father she was going to help Sydney in direct defiance of his orders. Crossing him had started all of this.

And Torin was there. It would be like telling the police.

She might need to involve the police if it looked like this situation was as dire as it seemed. But she didn't even have an address yet. She would start out and decide what to do once she received the text with the address.

Grabbing her purse, she paused, looking through the doorway as the angry barrage of accusations and insults from the other room pelted her like bullets aimed at her heart.

The pull to stay kept her feet rooted to the floor. To set things right, to restore peace to the family once again.

But the unbridled tempers flaring, shouting at their father,

Treese yelling at the others—their father trying to regain control—the damage was too great to be undone.

She wouldn't be able to fix this by letting another family die. She had to try to save Sydney and her baby.

She typed a reply. *I'm coming. Tell me where to find you.*

Slipping the phone into her purse, she hurried to the foyer and snatched her coat from the closet there.

The shouts were quieter in the foyer. She could almost imagine it had all been a nightmare.

She slipped her arms into the coat and went to the door as the angry voices caught her again.

No. The nightmare was very real.

Drifting snow and blowing flakes met her outside. She made herself keep moving, plunging one foot and then the other into the deepening snow as the strong wind pressed into her, slowing her progress. She wouldn't be able to get to Sydney quickly in this weather. Neither would the police.

But she should still call them. She wasn't equipped to handle a desperate man like Massey on her own. As soon as she received the directions, she would—

Was that a crunch in the snow behind her?

She turned to look.

A burst of pain split her scalp.

Darkness claimed her.

# CHAPTER
# THIRTY-SIX

CILLIAN STOOD BY THE WINDOW, staring at the blizzard that seemed to be a reflection of his own insides at the moment. The turmoil of emotion swirling inside him could easily rival the blustering snow and wind that whooshed and moaned against the window.

How could Victoria do this to him? To herself?

She was thirty-one years old. A full-grown woman with strength and independence she hadn't had as a kid. How could the same woman who faced Cillian down and directed her strong-willed siblings with spunk and confidence choose to live a life controlled by someone else?

How could she go running home to her dad again? For his birthday party, of all things.

Frustration cinched Cillian's muscles.

This couldn't be it. He couldn't have lost her to her father's control again, after all this time.

But she didn't even seem to want to be free.

That was common among victims. He knew that from experience.

That had to be it. She must have become so used to her dad's bullying, to being controlled by him, that she was scared to live without it. Or didn't realize how much better life could be if she escaped her dad's subtle form of abuse.

Cillian would not leave her there, even if she didn't yet realize she was in trouble. He loved her too much to let her live like that, no matter how many times she pushed him away. She didn't know what she was doing.

He wouldn't let her or her dad stop him. He'd use all the leverage he had to end her father's bullying, of Victoria and the rest of her family, once and for all.

He had the leverage now, thanks to Marsha Faint.

Cillian turned from the window, pacing to where his phone sat beside his computer on the desk by the wall. He should try to find more evidence to back up Marsha's claims, but there wasn't time for that. He needed to get Victoria away from her father now, before she pushed Cillian away even more and got sucked completely back into her father's manipulation.

The threat of Cillian's information from Marsha should be enough to shake a guy like Henry Weston. Sure, he was tough and used to bullying everyone to get his way. But he also cared a whole lot about the Weston name and his reputation. He'd do pretty much anything to protect that.

Which gave him a weakness. One Cillian could exploit with Marsha Faint's story and what it revealed—that Dr. Henry Weston was actually guilty of malpractice. Why else would he have risked illegally intimidating the woman to keep her quiet?

But Cillian would have to wait until tomorrow. Wouldn't do him any good to break up the birthday dinner, as much as his sense of justice would love for him to do that. The leverage would lose its power over Henry Weston if his kids heard about their dad's malpractice. He wouldn't want anyone, including his kids, to know the truth.

His top priority would be to keep the truth from coming out, which would be the only way Cillian would get him to agree to back off of Victoria and let her live her own life. To be who she wanted to be, and to spend her life with the person she chose. With Cillian.

He'd go to Dr. Weston's clinic first thing tomorrow morning.

Cillian gripped the chairback, fighting the desire to forget caution and strategy and go end this now.

Tomorrow morning. Then Victoria would finally be free.

He couldn't wait.

A vibrating sound jerked his attention to his phone. It shook and slid across the smooth desktop.

He grabbed it. Would Victoria be texting him to apologize? Maybe she'd changed—

*This is Lawrence Massey.*

What in the world? How did Massey get Cillian's number?

Another text came through on the heels of the first.

*I've got Sydney. If you want to see her alive, come alone to 1518 Phoenix Boulevard. No cops or she's dead. You've got twenty minutes before I kill her.*

Cillian clenched his jaw as he stared at the message. Hadn't seen that coming. Massey seemed much too cowardly to try anything like a kidnapping or abduction. And luring Cillian there? Did Massey hope to shut him up? Permanently?

There was something weird about it. Something didn't fit.

Why would a guy so afraid people would find out he'd impregnated a minor suddenly be brave enough to commit murder? Desperation made people do crazy things, but...

Cillian could figure it out later. Right now, the clock was ticking.

Twenty minutes to drive all the way to Phoenix Boulevard would be impossible in this weather. But he had to try.

He grabbed his jacket off the sofa where he'd tossed it and hurried at a jog out of the apartment to the exit stairs at the end of the hall. It'd be faster to dash down two flights of stairs to the parking garage than wait for the sluggish elevator.

He pushed through the heavy steel door to the stairs and paused a split-second to dial the police station on his phone.

He tapped the button for speaker and gripped the phone in his hand as he ran down the stairs.

No cops? Massey had to think Cillian was an idiot. The police were the only chance of reaching Sydney and Massey in time and with weapons.

"Gealanden Police Dep—"

"Put me through to Lieutenant Willis. He knows me, Cillian Doherty. It's an emergency."

"One moment please."

Grating electronic music signaled the woman had put him on hold.

He reached the bottom of the second flight and slammed the door open to the parking garage. At least he wouldn't have to dig out his jeep from accumulating snow.

He ran to his stall where he'd parked the jeep, brake line repaired just in time.

The music finally stopped as he reached the driver's door.

"Lieutenant Willis here."

Fire seared the back of Cillian's head.

He slowly blinked. Why couldn't he see anything but darkness?

He shut his eyes, then opened them again. Narrowed them, peering into the darkness.

This couldn't be the parking garage, and he was lying down on something. Had he been knocked out, and he was just waking up now?

He lifted his head.

A bolt of pain surged through his skull, answering his question.

Massey must have been waiting for him in the garage and jumped him from behind. The guy was a lot smarter than Cillian had thought.

What was that sound? Like a moaning or a whirring. The floor beneath him was firm but not hard or cold. And it was vibrating.

Was he in a vehicle? The back of a truck or...

He felt the floor with his palm. It was covered with something fuzzy. Like the interior lining of a trunk.

He wasn't tied up. That was good. But he was definitely being driven somewhere.

If this was a trunk, there should be a release latch he could pull. Unless Massey had thought to remove it.

Cillian reached for the trunk lid above his head. Nothing but air met his fingers. If this was a trunk, it was the biggest one he'd ever seen. If he could see it.

He straightened his bent legs, stretching out until his shoes hit something solid. Then he got to his knees and crawled in the other direction. Reached another wall there. But they were too far apart for a trunk.

SUVs and vans had that same kind of floor lining, too.

So, Massey had come prepared with a large vehicle that had cargo space. Seemed awfully strategic for a panicked reaction to Cillian's threats to expose the man.

Wait. If Massey wanted Cillian out of the way to keep his secret, would he want to eliminate Victoria, too?

Alarm and anger collided in Cillian's chest. Massey had better not have touched a hair on her head. At least she wasn't in this vehicle. Maybe he wasn't going to mess with her, since she was a Weston.

Victoria. Just the thought of her was apparently enough to make Cillian remember her lilac scent.

The aroma of her, or the memory of it, drifted to him, triggering an ache behind his ribs.

A moan came from the darkness.

Much too close to have come from the driver. And Massey didn't smell that good.

Cillian wasn't remembering her.

Victoria was here.

# CHAPTER
# THIRTY-SEVEN

A THROBBING ache pulled Victoria from sleep. She opened her eyes.

At least, she thought she'd opened them. But she couldn't see anything.

Why was her room so dark? There was always some light from—

"Vicks?"

Cillian. What was he doing in her room?

Alarm spiked through her, and she sat up.

The pain in her head sharpened. She gasped.

"Easy. Don't try to move fast."

She turned toward his voice, but she could only see a dim outline of what appeared to be his head.

"Don't worry, your eyes will adjust. I think he must have the back windows covered with something. Though maybe the snow is blocking the streetlamps and city lights anyway."

Cillian's words jumbled in her mind like babble.

She blinked, hoping to rush the adjustment process as she tried to organize his statements and her thoughts in her mind. "Are you saying we're in a vehicle of some kind?"

This had to be a dream. A very peculiar one.

"Yeah, I think it's a van. Do you remember how you got here?"

Did she? She tried to ignore the spikes of pain that seemed to shoot from the back of her skull to her forehead. She didn't recall going to bed before this dream, actually. She hadn't said goodnight to Max or—

She hadn't been sleeping. She'd been walking through snow to her car, in a hurry, worried. The text.

Her breath caught as she recalled the message. "Sydney. Is she all right?"

"I don't know. I assume you got a text? I got one, too, from Lawrence Massey."

The memory returned sluggishly. "I received one from Sydney. She said he would kill her unless I came."

"And don't bring the cops? Yeah. I was on hold waiting to tell Willis when I got clocked from behind."

Victoria reached to touch the back of her head. A large, painful bump swelled on the back of her skull. "I was apparently knocked unconscious, as well."

"Massey must've been waiting for you, then came and ambushed me at my place. He took my phone. Did he take yours, too?"

She peered into the darkness. A pointless exercise. "It was in my purse. I assume he wasn't courteous enough to bring that along for me."

"Seems weird, doesn't it? That Massey would resort to abduction and...whatever he has planned for us?"

"We pushed him too far. We never should have confronted him." Her words ricocheted back at her.

Dad. He'd been angry with her.

Her foggy brain slogged through the effects of the blow, trying to retrieve the memories.

Her father glared at her from the head of the table.

Treese accused her of hurting Sydney.

Robert, Hank, Spring—they all defended her.

The raised voices ping-ponged against the walls of Victoria's mind, stinging each time they hit.

Oh, no. They'd all been fighting at Dad's birthday dinner. Because of her.

"…now we see how right it was to show Massey we know what he did. But what I don't get is the leap from cowardly abusing teen girls to this." Cillian's commentary drifted past her in the darkness like a distant, mismatched echo of the much louder voices of her family in her head.

*"No wonder you've gotten yourself arrested for murder, your face and name plastered all over the news."* Dad's accusation rang in her ears. That was it, the real reason he was so angry. Not her involvement with Sydney.

It was that she'd become a criminal. Branded as one for all his friends, acquaintances, and patients to see. His perfect reputation had been destroyed by her.

*"I knew that Doherty boy would ruin you. I don't know who you are anymore. You have dragged the Weston name through the mud."*

More than anger had flashed in Dad's eyes with those words. Disappointment and—

"Whoa." Cillian's remark drew her gaze toward him.

She could see a clearer outline of his face now and a flicker of some bit of light catching his eyes.

"I didn't see it before." Shock lined his tone. "This wasn't a spur-of-the-moment break of character for Massey."

She blinked, but it didn't help her see Cillian better. Not that it mattered. Her mind and aching heart were focused elsewhere. With her family's—

"It was him. All along."

She brushed aside Cillian's interruption to her thoughts. How could she have risked such consequences to her family, to everything she'd dedicated her life to since Mom passed?

"He was the one trying to kill us. The threatening note, the shooting, the car that tried to run you down. All of it was Massey. He was trying all along to silence you, and then me when he saw I'd met Sydney, too. He knew we could find out what he'd done and would expose him. Especially with you being a Weston."

Cillian let out a half-laugh of disbelief. "Man, were we off on that. We assumed it had to be Glenn since he killed Briscoe. I wonder which one sabotaged my bike. Could be Glenn was telling the truth when he said he didn't know anything about it."

Only part of Victoria's mind seemed to grasp what Cillian was saying. Massey may have been the one trying to kill her. But what did it matter? It made no difference to the most precious, important treasures in her life. She had still damaged them beyond repair.

*"I cannot believe you would bring shame on our family in such a way."* Dad's sharp gaze appeared before her eyes more vivid and painful than the darkness.

*"You all should leave Dad alone. He's totally right."* Treese's ready defense of her father as she had stood between him and her siblings, pinched Victoria's ribs. Treese would never be reachable to Victoria now or to the God she represented.

*"I can't believe you."* And Hank. Oh, sweet Hank. *"You don't even care about how scary that must be for her or how unfair it is. Your own daughter!"*

Victoria shut her eyes, but she was too late to stop the tears. They slid down her cheeks.

Hank had always loved their father, idolized him even. And now he'd turned against him, for Victoria's sake.

*Oh, Lord. Please forgive me.* The inward prayer squeezed from her shriveling heart.

Why had she kept pushing Detective McCully when he'd told her to stay away from the investigation of Thomas's death? If she had done what she usually did—gone along to get along—than none of this would have happened. She would never have been questioned, arrested, suspected of murder. Dad wouldn't have had reason to become so angry with her. Her family would still be getting along, living and thriving in peaceful relationships with each other. Why hadn't she listened and followed the instructions of the police?

Cillian. He'd convinced her to keep pressuring the police when she'd known better. She'd let him persuade her again and lead her into another disastrous mistake.

How could she have done that? Had she learned nothing from letting her mother die alone?

A sob rose in her throat, nearly choking her as she swallowed it down.

Mom. *Oh, Mom, I'm so sorry.* The cry of Victoria's heart seared every fiber of her being.

Mom would be so ashamed. So disappointed.

It was bad enough Victoria had let her die alone. But now she had failed to do what her mother would have wanted most of all—to do everything Mom would have for the Weston family. Above all, to keep the peace between Dad and all the siblings.

Victoria hadn't merely tried and failed, she had been the one to launch the direct attack on that peace when she'd crossed Detective McCully and then, far worse, her father. He'd told her, after McCully had questioned her, to stop being involved in the investigation. Why hadn't she obeyed him as she usually did? She knew not to cross him.

All she would have had to do was adhere to what her father wanted, as Mom had always done, except when she'd become a Christian.

Then Victoria had come to Christ, too, from Mom's secret talks and nighttime reading of the Bible when Dad wasn't around to stop her.

Victoria's Christianity made this error even more grievous.

*"Blessed are the peacemakers,"* Christ said.

As a Christian, she was called to make peace. And by following her mom's exceptional example, she'd kept peace among her family and others for sixteen years. Until today. When she had obliterated her mother's legacy of peace and love in her family.

They were all against each other now. Divided. Some opposing each other and most turned against their father.

Victoria was probably going to die tonight. And she was leaving behind four brothers and sisters who would never understand that their father did love them. They would never know how much their mom had wanted them to love him and each other. They would never realize how much Mom had wanted them to know Christ.

Victoria's heart cracked under the weight of what she'd done, of what she'd destroyed, of the grief for the mother she had lost and failed to honor.

A gulping, tearful gasp escaped her control.

*Forgive me.*

---

"Victoria?" Cillian leaned toward her, reaching for her arm. She had gasped like she was in pain. "Are you okay? Is it your head?"

"I'm fi—"

The vehicle jerked, like Massey hit the brakes.

Cillian froze with his hand on Victoria's forearm. Listening.

They'd stopped moving.

A slam. Maybe the driver's door.

Footsteps broke through the walls of the van. Shoes crunching on snow.

Cillian squinted at the darkness. There had to be something in the van that he could use as a weapon. He could see much better now, past where Victoria sat with her legs stretched in front of her to a solid wall that must divide the front seats from the cargo area.

Nothing but floor and the walls of the vehicle met his searching gaze. No weapon.

Well, a fist had always been enough for him. He'd have no problem handling a wimp like Massey.

Cillian scooted toward the doors. A good double-legged kick should be enough to knock the coward on—

The doors swung open, letting in a rush of cold air and the dark night, brightened only by snowflakes swirling all around.

Cillian stared into the white-flecked darkness, his knees drawn in toward his chest, ready to kick their abductor.

But the man stood too far back. Aiming a gun.

Cillian lifted his focus from the weapon to Massey's face.

"Warren?" Victoria's shocked one-word question escaped at the same time Cillian registered the face of Warren Morris. Sydney's brother?

The lanky teenager stood in the snow in his usual blue jacket and dark jeans, the gun shaking in his bare hand as he pointed it at them.

"Warren? What are you doing?" Disbelief twisted Victoria's tone.

"You made me do this." He aimed his gaze at her, his lips working. "It's your fault."

What? The kid had gone crazy. "I don't know what's gotten into you, Warren, but why don't we just talk this out?" Cillian scooted toward the bumper.

"Freeze." The kid had watched too many cop shows. But Cillian paused. Warren was just edgy enough to pull the trigger, on purpose or by accident. "Don't move."

Cillian lifted his hands, palm out. "Okay. But you don't need that gun. We're all friends, remember?"

"You're not my friends." He jerked the gun barrel at them. "You've messed up my whole life." He looked at Victoria. "Everything was going great until you wouldn't leave it alone."

"Leave what alone, Warren?" Her voice was gentle. Kind. To a kid who might shoot her. "Do you mean Sydney?"

"No. No." Warren blinked away the snowflakes that landed on his eyelashes. "The old man."

The kid had lost his mind. What old man was he...

Realization lit in Cillian's mind. "Thomas Briscoe?"

"I didn't mean to kill him. It was an accident. He was supposed to be asleep."

Cillian looked over his shoulder at Victoria.

She'd turned to face Warren head-on. Her gaze met Cillian's, shock lifting her eyebrows.

Cillian swung his head back to Warren. "*You* broke into his house?"

"Just to take some stuff. He was filthy rich. Never could've used all that money, but I needed it. We needed it. For Sydney and me. And her kid." Warren's voice sounded more and more strangled. He needed to calm down or he'd shoot them without even meaning to.

"And then Thomas heard you and woke up." Cillian offered the prompt for the confession. Maybe the kid would lose some tension if he got the truth off his chest.

Warren licked his lips. "I heard him on the stairs. He was gonna see me, and then I'd wind up in jail. I couldn't help Sydney from there."

Or enjoy the fruits of his criminal labor. Cillian kept the observation to himself as he nonchalantly eyed the kid's loose grip on the gun, his weak stance.

"I had to make sure he didn't see me."

"But you didn't mean to kill him. Only to knock him out, as you did with us." Victoria's tone was so understanding, it nearly made Cillian sick.

Good thing the practice he got by hitting Briscoe had helped the teen figure out how much pressure to use, or he could've accidentally killed Victoria and Cillian already. As it was, they had more than a fighting chance.

Cillian would need leverage to launch himself from the bumper of the van into Warren before he—

"Don't. I see that." Warren pointed the gun more directly at Cillian instead of Victoria.

"See what?"

"You were going to try something." He glanced for a split second at Cillian's hands.

He must've planted them more firmly as he'd gotten ready to jump at the kid.

Warren was sharper than he seemed, even with his obvious nerves.

"Wasn't doing anything, man. Just sitting here, listening to your confession."

Warren smashed his lips together, his eyebrows clustering. "Get out. Both of you."

Good. Permission to get on his feet. Cillian stood, then turned to help Victoria slide out of the van.

He leaned toward her as he reached for her arms, his face close to hers. Close enough to see the moisture coating her cheeks that hadn't yet been touched by snow.

She'd been crying.

His gut clenched. Had being abducted and kept in the back of the van scared her so badly? It would scare most people. But she was so tough all the time, he hadn't thought to consider she might be frightened.

His jaw clenched as he gently gripped her arms to help her to the ground. He met her gaze, trying to say without words that they were going to be okay.

But there was something different in her eyes. Not fear. More like a deep sadness and a distracted detachment that made it seem like she was somewhere else, thinking about something else.

He turned around to face the punk who'd made her cry, ready to jump him at the slightest opportunity.

But Warren had backed up much farther, out of range of a lunge, keeping the gun trained on them. "Start walking." He tilted the barrel toward the front of the van. "That way."

Cillian touched Victoria's elbow with a slight tug to show she should walk in front of him. He didn't know what waited ahead. But he wasn't about to let her be the one with the gun or the killer at her back.

Cillian followed close behind her, peering into the thick,

blowing snow. The visibility was ridiculous. Couldn't see more than ten feet ahead, even on foot.

At least they had a tailwind going this direction. But to what? To where?

Looked like a road beneath their feet. It was packed down enough that it must have been plowed and driven on at some point during the storm. Now fresh layers of snow obscured any visible sign of tire tracks.

A dark blur peeked through the falling snow to the left. Trees? Looked like a forest, or at least a thick stand of trees lining the road.

Had Warren brought them to some obscure location to shoot them? Maybe hoping it'd be a long time before anyone would find them in the snow.

Victoria stumbled.

Cillian reached for her arm, steadying her.

She felt cold through the sleeve of her coat. The dressy, navy blue coat was long, but probably not lined with much. She wouldn't last long out here in that and the thin velvet dress. But hopefully, she wouldn't have to. Cillian would—

"Stop right there." Warren's command grated like nails on a chalkboard, but Cillian halted with Victoria, immediately spinning toward the punk. No way was he going to let Warren shoot them in the back. He wasn't going to let the kid shoot Victoria at all. No matter what he had to do.

Maybe he could start by finding out more of what Warren had in mind. "What's your plan, Warren? If you shoot us, everyone will know we were murdered."

Victoria tensed beside Cillian. Was she scared?

His arm twitched with the urge to wrap around her. But Warren probably wouldn't like that. And Victoria might not either, given their last conversation.

"They're going to think you got into an accident."

Cillian stared incredulously at the kid through falling snowflakes. Maybe he'd lost his mind. "An accident? With bullets?"

Warren pushed shaking fingers through his short hair. "I'm not gonna shoot you. I'm just gonna leave you here. Everyone knows you ride that thing in the winter." The hand holding the gun swung toward the punk's left, like he was gesturing toward something.

Cillian peered through the snow. Nothing but the side of the road. Maybe. Hard to tell where the road started and ended when everything was white.

Not everything.

A large, dark object caught his attention. Looked like something a little lower down than the road. In the ditch?

He risked taking a step toward it, the angle of his body showing Warren he wasn't headed for him.

His bike. Cillian's motorcycle lay on its side, half-buried in the snow. He pivoted to Warren. "You brought my bike out here?"

"Wasn't hard with this company van and the ramp."

Of course. The van must belong to Warren's employer. The kid had a more strategic mind than Cillian would've guessed.

"When they find you, the cops will think you were both riding, and you lost control in the snow. Then you froze out here."

Cillian shot a glance at Victoria.

She looked half-frozen already, her arms wrapped around herself and her lips turning blue.

His ribs pinched. He had to get her out of here. "Come on, man. You don't want to do this to Victoria. She's been so nice to your sister. She's taken her in. Sydney depends on her. What are you going to tell Sydney if you hurt Victoria?"

"She won't find out."

"She knows you, man. She'll figure it out."

"Then she'll understand. I'll tell her the truth. That you made me do this."

"I'm not the one holding the gun, Warren."

"Not you. Her." The kid veered the weapon slightly more toward Victoria. His eyes narrowed. "It's all your fault. You were the one to make the police think it was a murder. And then you kept trying to figure out who did it."

"The cops would've done that anyway, Warren." Cillian tried to draw the teen's growing intensity away from Victoria.

"No, they wouldn't." The punk kept his focus locked on her as frustration pitched his voice higher. "They didn't have a clue. I kept trying to scare you off, but you wouldn't stop. If you'd just gone along with things and let it go, if you'd just backed off, I wouldn't have to kill you."

Oh, man. None of that had been Victoria's choice. Cillian had pushed her to stay on McCully. He'd persuaded her to follow up leads, tail suspects, keep forcing the police to investigate.

If he hadn't done that, they wouldn't be in this situation. Victoria never would've become Warren's target. Wouldn't have nearly been killed by him shooting at her and trying to run her over.

Wouldn't be here, about to—

"Oh, and don't bother trying to get your bike running. I took enough parts out to make sure it can't be fixed."

"Don't do this, kid. They'll figure out it was you. It'll ruin your life."

"They didn't figure out I'm the one who killed that rich guy yet. They arrested that other dude."

"Exactly, man." Cillian switched to a friendlier tone. "You're in the clear."

Warren shook his head. "He'll get off. Rich people always get off. They'll believe him when he says he didn't do it." The punk glared at Victoria again. "I knew you'd figure it out soon. Figure out how I knew you worked for him. Sydney told me you work in those rich neighborhoods."

Cillian inched toward Warren as he continued, staring at Victoria.

"All I had to do was follow you until I found the right house. An old man, no dogs, easy fence to climb. Nobody with him at night. Should've been a sure thing. Until you stuck your nose where it didn't belong."

Only two feet more, and Cillian could dive for the gun.

"I'd never have to do this if you'd left well enough alone."

Now.

Cillian bolted toward Warren.

A shot boomed, exploded through the storm.

Cillian braked.

The kid meant business. Lucky the shot missed. But why was his mouth open, his eyes wide with…horror?

Cillian angled back to see what Warren was staring at.

Victoria lay on the ground.

"Vicks!" He sprinted to her, dropping to his knees in the snow. "Talk to me. Are you hit?"

He scanned her coat, her dress.

Snowflakes fell on her, instantly melting on her stomach. Where dark liquid seeped through her green dress around a hole in the fabric. The size of a bullet.

Panic seized him. "Vicks!" His gaze dragged from the blood to her face.

Her eyes were huge, staring up at him. "I think I've been…shot."

No. This couldn't be happening. The denial reached his lips. "No. No, no, no." He grabbed the front of her coat and pressed the material against the wound. Had to stop the bleeding.

Warren was supposed to shoot him, if anyone. Why hadn't he shot Cillian?

"Can't you aim that thing?" Cillian launched the furious shout over his shoulder.

But Warren wasn't there.

The sound of an engine starting reached Cillian's ears. The van. Their only transportation. Only way to get help.

Cillian jumped to his feet and sprinted to the van.

Warren was turning it around, jerkily, moving forward and back in the deep snow.

Cillian grabbed the driver's door handle.

It was locked.

He pulled. "Warren! She needs help!" He pounded on the window.

Warren swung his head away from him, managing to turn the van around as Cillian trotted alongside.

Warren hit the gas. The tires slipped in the snow. Maybe he wouldn't get traction.

"Warren, stop! At least call a doctor!"

The van moved forward again, finding a grip in the snow.

Cillian grabbed the side mirror and the door handle, hefting himself onto the running board to ride along.

But that wouldn't help Vicks. He couldn't leave her there. And he might never be able to find her again.

The van picked up speed.

Cillian let go. Dropped to the ground.

He spun back.

Oh, no.

The thick snow blocked his vision. He couldn't see her.

"Vicks!" He jogged in the direction she must be. Where he thought he'd come from. "Vicks! Answer me!" He stopped. Listened.

The howling wind answered.

No. What had he done?

Why had he pushed her into this? Why had he made her investigate killers and suspects and antagonize the police? If he hadn't, Warren wouldn't have dragged her out here to...

Cillian's hand went to his head as horror steamrolled through him. He pivoted in every direction, desperately searching the white darkness for some glimpse of her.

Of the woman he loved. The woman he'd tried to save. The woman he'd led to her death.

# CHAPTER
# THIRTY-EIGHT

SHE'D NEVER WANTED any of this.

Cillian trudged through the snow, scanning the white wall that shifted around him as it blew. Almost seemed pointless, trying to find Victoria in this storm. But he had to try. He owed her that much.

She hadn't wanted to keep looking for Thomas's killer, to insist the police listen to her, to keep chasing down new suspects and leads. She hadn't wanted to do any of the things that had made Warren target her.

And when he had started the threats—the shooting, trying to run her over—she had wanted to quit.

*"I said that's enough. We have to stop."* The memory of Victoria at the pregnancy center, when Cillian had walked in after his bike crashed, hit him with a pang behind the ribs. *"We need to stop investigating and trying to find the killer. This has gotten far too dangerous."*

What was it she'd said after that? This wasn't an adventure involving only him.

*"You need to think, to consider how your actions will affect others."*

And he'd ignored her. Told her that's why she'd needed to wait for him so he could keep her safe.

*"Cillian, you aren't listening."*

*"I am listening. I'm going to make sure you're safe until this guy is locked up, so you don't have to worry about a thing."*

If he could eat his own words now, if that would somehow help, he would in a heartbeat. What a dolt he was. What a jerk, not listening and forcing her to do what he wanted when he knew she didn't agree, when he knew she thought it was too dangerous.

Oh, no. His thoughts echoed back to him, and he heard them more clearly. Saw himself for the first time.

He was a bully.

He was like her dad.

Shock hit Cillian harder than the wind, stopping him in his tracks. His throat swelled with disbelief. And disgust.

He fought against bullies. His whole mission in life, his career, everything he did was about freeing victims from people who abused power to get what they wanted. People who manipulated and controlled others.

But somehow, sometime, maybe even while trying to beat the bullies, he'd become one himself.

Memories from his childhood and beyond shifted quickly through his mind. He'd been able to see what the adults around him couldn't, from as early as he could remember. He saw what drugs were doing to his mother, how she sold herself to the addiction. He saw how she abused and used him to get more supply. He'd known that the men who came in and out of their lives were using her, too.

But he'd been too smart to let them bully him. And he'd decided he would never let anyone else go through what he had. Because he knew what was right.

He knew how to tell when a kid was lying or the adults were. He knew how to use leverage, intimidation, or persuasion to outwit bullies at their own game. He'd freed so many kids from the abuse and control of people in power. He had a perfect record since becoming a social worker.

Didn't matter how he got that, did it? As long as he was in the right, doing the right thing, it was all good.

But had he always been right? The Mason Blunt case leaped to his mind.

Cillian had freed Mason from the control of a stepfather who had left the boy stranded in the ocean to teach him toughness. Mason had been wearing a life jacket that, combined with a kind stranger who had come along and brought Mason to shore in a boat, saved the boy's life.

Once Peter Blunt had realized how much trouble he was in, the stepfather became apologetic, promising Cillian he wouldn't do anything like that again. A far cry from Peter's initial boasting about his tough-love discipline when Cillian had first visited the family.

Cillian couldn't risk Peter would gain a judge's sympathy with his temporary, probably manufactured remorse. So he had gotten in Peter's face, challenging his ego and masculinity until the man dug-in again, defending his abusive childrearing tactics in front of the judge.

What if Cillian had taken a page from Victoria's book? Could he have found a more peaceful way to create positive change for the Blunts, one that wouldn't have broken up their family?

How many other times had Cillian run roughshod over others to secure the end goal he'd determined was best for everyone?

Those other times didn't matter so much right now. The one that mattered most, the person who mattered most, had been Cillian's victim.

Was it too late to do anything about it? To make it right? If he could find Victoria, he would set her free from himself, from his own desire to control her and orchestrate her life the way he wanted it to go.

But could he actually do that? He didn't know how, wouldn't know where to begin. He needed to be with her more than anything in the world. So much so that he'd tried to force her into the future he'd wanted for them.

It wouldn't be much of a future if she were forced and manipulated into being with him. And it wouldn't be any future at all if she...wasn't alive. Because of him.

He started forward again. At least he thought it was forward. Hopefully, in the direction he'd originally come from.

But what if he was wrong, and he'd gotten turned around in the near-zero visibility? What if it was too late? He couldn't make it right if he couldn't find her.

Frustration and desperation rose in his chest until it exploded out of him in a groan, a yell that echoed back to him from somewhere in the storm.

*"You could have it, too, Cillian."*

Victoria's voice came to him on the wind, as if answering his cry, flying to him to touch his aching heart.

*"Christ in you, changing who you are. If you truly want to be better, you could ask Jesus to save you, and He will make you a better man, a better person than you could imagine."*

He had called it a crutch, that faith of hers. The declaration of a bully afraid he would lose control over her. It seemed he'd been wrong about that, too.

*"He'll guide you through life and help you to know the best way to live. He'll give you hope for the future."*

The memory of her words cut deep into his heart, maybe into the soul he didn't really believe he had until now. He and Victoria might not have any future, thanks to him. It was probably too late to change, to become the better man she had wanted him to be.

If he could see her again, he'd ask her how to do what she said, what she meant by asking God to save him. But God wasn't in the business of helping people like him, bullies who tried to control innocent people like Victoria and lead her into disasters like this.

According to Victoria, God did help her.

"God? If you're listening, lead me back to Victoria so she doesn't have to die." More arrogance again. What could he do even if he reached her? Obviously, no one was driving out to this remote location in the blizzard. And he was no doctor.

He nearly tripped in a thick patch of snow. Deeper than before. He must've strayed into the ditch. He should angle back up to the road.

He trudged a few more feet.

Wait.

Dark colors streaked through the white that covered everything else.

His bike?

His pulse jumped into his throat. Victoria had been close to the bike. On the road just above.

*Please, God. Let her be there. Let her be alive.*

---

*"Mom?"*

*Victoria shielded her eyes with her hand. It was so bright. The light hurt her eyes, but she couldn't look away.*

*She knew that silhouette.*

*Mommy.*

*Her long black, wavy hair cascaded around her shoulders as she walked out of the light, toward Victoria. She smiled.*

*The smile found Victoria's heart, infusing it with warmth. But the pain there didn't lessen. It was still broken.*

*"Mom, I'm sorry."*

*Mommy reached her hand toward Victoria. "I'm here. I love you."*

*But she was too far away. Too far to touch or be touched. Too far to fix what Victoria had done.*

"Vicks?"

A touch on her shoulder.

Was Mom closer now?

But no. She wasn't there. The bright light was fading.

A rushing sound reached Victoria's ears.

Something shook her. Was she in an earthquake?

"Victoria, can you hear me? Honey, you've got to wake up. Please."

The voice was familiar. Deep.

Cillian? But why did he sound scared? And sad.

"Come on, Vicks. Please, don't leave me. We all need you." The anguish in his tone attached to something deep inside her, pulling her to him.

She must be sleeping. She tried to open her eyes.

"Vicks? Did you just move? Come on, honey. You have to tell me how to get right with God."

She cracked her lids open.

White blurs scattered in front of her vision. But beyond that was his handsome face. Cillian.

"Vicks." He smiled, though his brows drew together over his coal-black eyes. Moisture seemed to glisten in those dark orbs. "I thought that might get you to wake up."

She blinked slowly. They seemed to be outside in winter.

He was above her, cradling her head in one hand while the other felt like it was on her shoulder. Or was her head actually in his lap?

She couldn't tell for sure. She felt so numb. "What—"

"Warren shot you."

Shock rolled through her at the statement. But perhaps she was already in a state of shock in the medical sense. That could account for the numbness. Though the cold was also likely inducing that symptom.

The boom of the gun as it fired jolted in her memory. She'd thought he had shot Cillian. But then, she'd felt the pain in her abdomen. Or perhaps more toward one side.

Relief had quieted any alarm she might have felt. Cillian was unharmed. That was all that mattered.

Cillian seemed to be pressing something against the area of the wound.

Her coat?

She tilted her chin downward to look. Yes, her coat and his

leather jacket layered over the top of it. But that meant he wasn't wearing a jacket.

She aimed her gaze up at his face. "You'll freeze." The words sounded weaker with her voice than they had in her head.

"Cold never bothers me, remember?" His mouth tugged up at one corner.

Always so stubborn, even to the end.

And this was the end. Her mind was fully awake now, with complete access to every detail that had brought them there.

Including the decimation of her family by her own hand, by her own mistakes. And that would be the last time she would ever see them all, at least in this life. They would be left with the division and dissension she'd created when she had abandoned peacemaking for confrontation, acquiescence and obedience for rebellion.

"Lord, please forgive me." The prayer escaped as a whisper that was snatched and carried away on the wind. She would see Him soon, face to face. She knew He did forgive her. Christ had paid for all her sins when He died in her place on the cross. But oh, how she wished she could have left her family with the peace, love, and faith that their mother had passed on to her.

"Vicks, I promised God I would ask you if He let me find you." Cillian's low tone drew her focus to him. "How do I get right with God?"

She stared at him. Did he mean that? Perhaps her body's shock had drawn her into another dream.

"You should see your face." He grinned, but the curve of his mouth weakened quickly, the corners of his lips tucking as he watched her. "You'd better tell me quick, Vicks."

He started to disappear, darkness moving in to hide him from view.

"Vicks, don't you want me to go to heaven?" A shake brought Cillian back.

Or must have made her open her eyes. She hadn't realized they were closing.

He moved his head side to side. "I can't believe you, Vicks. Here you've always wanted me to come to Jesus, and now when I want to, you go to sleep."

She blinked. "If you really mean that, I'll stay awake."

"That's the spirit." He smoothed her forehead with his hand. "Are you going to tell me how to get right with God?"

"Well," her eyelids started to droop, but she forced them open, "you need to understand the problem. God made us, but then we sinned. And because we rebelled against Him, there's enmity, a divide between us and God. We're always against God and deserve only wrath from Him for our sin."

She stopped, her breath falling behind her thoughts. "That's why God sent His Son, Jesus Christ, who gave Himself up for us, died for our sins to make peace between us and God. The Bible says, 'in Christ Jesus you who once were far off have been brought near by the blood of Christ. For He Himself is our peace.'"

He Himself is our peace. The Peacemaker above all peacemakers was Christ, would always be Christ. And people had killed Him for it.

"But what do *I* have to do to get right with Him?"

She barely heard Cillian's question as the truth dawned. Jesus hadn't always done as He was told by people, He hadn't gone along to get along. He hadn't obeyed all the manmade rules of the pharisees or even the law enforcement and lawmakers of the time when He'd walked the earth.

He had obeyed and followed only God. That obedience had included confronting people in their sin, calling out hypocrites, and driving out evildoers from God's house of worship.

"You don't have to do anything." Wonder flowed through her body, the only thing she could feel as it filled her soul. "Jesus did it all. He brought peace between me and God, between you and God."

"I don't need to do anything?"

She smiled up at Cillian, his forehead lined with adorable, confused furrows. "Do you trust in God? Do you believe Jesus brought peace between Him and you by living a perfect life and dying to pay for your sins?"

The lines smoothed as Cillian met her gaze for several seconds. "Yes. I've really blown it. I did this to you, Vicks." His gaze lowered, drifting toward her wound. "I turned into a bully who pushed you into doing what I wanted. Just like your dad. I've become the very person I've been fighting against my whole life. But I don't even know if I can change. I need God's help. I need him to change me, like you said. If you were to..." Emotion strangled his voice.

He took in a breath. "I can't live with this, knowing what I've done, how wrong I've been." Was that a tear, tracking down his face? His cheeks were already moist from the snow melting on them. But this was larger.

She reached toward his face to wipe the tear away. But for some reason, she could only lift her hand close enough to brush one fingertip against his chin.

He captured her hand in his. "I was listening to you, Vicks. I don't want the eternal condemnation you talked about. And I can't live with this guilt. I'll never be perfect, but I want to try."

"You don't have to. You'll never be able to be good."

A shaky smile curved his lips. "Always the bad Doherty boy, huh?"

"No. None of us can earn our way out of God's judgment. We can't do it. That's why Jesus did it for us. He already made peace for you, Cillian. And your contrition, your sorrow for your sins now, He did that, too. He's giving you the repentance and faith to believe in Him, to put your trust in Him forever."

Exactly as Jesus had done for Victoria. And His example, even above her mother's, was the one she should have been following all these years.

She'd forgotten that Christ came to make peace between God and man but also to bring division between families—as some came to faith and others didn't—to bring judgment on sinners, and to oppose those who did wrong.

Oh, how foolish she had been in her approach with those in authority, especially her father.

She'd thought she had clear boundaries and that she would only obey people in authority as long as they didn't tell her to do something wrong. But she had enabled them to continue doing wrong themselves, making it easier for them to do so because she didn't challenge them or stand in their way.

By never challenging her father's selfish requirements and demands on his children, she had become a participant in his wrongdoing. She'd become so much a part of ensuring that his desires were met that she had become as guilty as he was. No wonder Spring had remarked during her rehab that she thought Victoria was like their father.

Yes, Christians were called to be peacemakers, but never to ignore evil. Bringing true peace meant emulating Christ—confronting people, in love, about their sin, and challenging them to change, to repent and come to Christ. How different the Weston family might look now if Victoria had followed Christ's definition of peacemaking instead of her own.

"I guess this is what it feels like to be you, huh?"

She peered up at Cillian.

A new brightness filled his eyes, a light of hope and happiness she'd never seen there before.

"What'd you call it?"

"Belonging to Christ. Peace…" Her eyelids closed as her voice weakened.

"Oh, no you don't, Vicks. I'm happy to go to heaven with you when the time comes. But we aren't done yet, do you hear me?" Movement jostled her body, something like corded ropes under her.

Was she rising off the ground? Was this what dying felt like? Perhaps she was flying away, to heaven.

She would see Mom there. And Cillian, too, if he couldn't find a way out of the storm.

But most glorious of all, she would see Jesus. Oh, how her heart yearned to set eyes on her Redeemer.

His peace washed over her as He brought her nearer, so much nearer to Himself.

# CHAPTER
# THIRTY-NINE

"I'LL NEED your help with this following God thing, Vicks." Cillian hefted Victoria higher against his chest as he trudged through the snow, carrying her in his arms. "You'd better stay with me, or you know I'm going to mess it up."

Her eyes were still closed, her breathing shallower than before. Her face was so pale.

But he kept talking to her. Had to give her a reason to fight, to keep going.

But until when? He didn't know where he was going. Hopefully in the direction Warren had taken off, back toward the city, toward help.

The snow still blew so thickly in the darkness that he couldn't see any houses or streetlamps. Nothing that could lead him to a phone or people.

"God, you know I'm new to this whole thing of asking you for stuff. But Vicks says you don't need my help to do whatever you want. And I know you must love her a lot. So could you do your thing and send some help?"

Cillian glanced down at her terrifyingly pale face as he pushed his legs to stride faster. Should he be putting pressure on the wound again to stop the bleeding? He'd done that for several minutes, but he couldn't just sit there, watching her die. He had to try to get help.

"Did you hear that, Vicks? I just prayed. And I even kind of admitted you were right about something. I'd love to hear what you have to say about that." The attempt at humor stuck on the lump in his throat. "Please, God. I can't lose her."

A sound, somewhere beyond the constant swooshing of the wind, touched his frozen ears.

Crunching?

"Hello?" His call was swallowed up in a snowy gust.

Yeah. It was crunching. But steadier and louder than footsteps.

Light. A soft glow, breaking through the wall of snow.

The light grew brighter, whiter, coming closer.

His heart raced. Was that—

Headlights. The hood of a red vehicle appeared, driving toward him. A pickup truck. Was that Hank's pickup?

"Over here!" Cillian shouted, unable to wave with Victoria in his arms.

The truck slowed, skidded to a quick stop.

Both doors opened, and two men dropped out, running toward Cillian and Victoria.

"Vicki!" Hank's alarmed call cut through the wind at the same time Cillian recognized his silhouette.

Robert ran beside him, both of them reaching Cillian in seconds. "What happened?" Robert glanced from his sister to Cillian.

"She's been shot."

"What? No." Anguish twisted Hank's voice as he reached for her. "Where's the wound?"

Cillian blinked at him. Right. He was a med student. He could help. "Her stomach, I think. It's in the abdomen area."

"Lord, please help Vicki. Help us." The prayer spilled from Hank as naturally as breathing as he peeled back Victoria's coat to see the bloody patch of clothing. His gaze met

Cillian's. "Get her in the truck. I'll sit in the back with her and do what I can. Rob, you drive."

Surprise filtered through Cillian at Hank's sudden switch from the laidback, youngest child to take-charge leader.

They hurried to the pickup where Hank hopped into the back seat of the extended cab. Robert helped Cillian transfer Vicki to Hank as gently as possible.

A moan emerged as they set her on the seat, halfway onto Hank's lap.

The sound of pain cinched Cillian's chest. He shot Hank an alarmed glance.

"It's a good sign." Hank gave him a nod, then aimed his gaze past Cillian to Robert. "Let's get out of here. Fast. Go to Rampart Memorial Hospital."

Robert ran around to the driver's side as Cillian yanked open the passenger door and landed on the seat.

He twisted to see Victoria while Robert turned the truck around. "How is she?"

Hank didn't look up from examining the area of the wound. "How long ago was she shot?"

Cillian paused, trying to figure it out. "I'm not sure. Feels like hours. But probably isn't."

"Looks like the bleeding has slowed. And the bullet didn't enter the stomach. Could've caused shrapnel damage, though, and it could've damaged other organs. I can't be sure. But she isn't as far gone as she should be by now if the bullet had damaged something vital."

Hope coursed through Cillian's torso. Was God going to let her live?

"You did a good job trying to keep her warm with your jacket and stopping the bleeding." Hank met Cillian's gaze. "Thank you."

Cillian jerked a nod. "I'd give my life for her. I'm..." He looked away. "I'm so sorry she caught the bullet instead of me."

"Who shot her?" Robert's tone was harder than Cillian had ever heard from the even-keeled psychiatrist.

"Warren Morris."

"Who?" Hank's question sounded behind Cillian.

"Sydney Morris's brother."

"That doesn't make any sense. Why would he want to hurt Vicki or you?"

Cillian twisted his head to see Hank. "He killed Thomas Briscoe, trying to rob him. He didn't like Victoria and me looking for the killer. Thought we'd figure out it was him."

"So he tried to get rid of you before you could." Robert's jaw clenched as he stared into the snow that streaked like strips of white lightning shooting at them in the headlights.

"Yeah. I'm…sorry." Cillian glanced down at his hands, the feeling slowly beginning to return to his fingers with a burning sensation. "It's my fault. Vicks never wanted to do any of that investigating and pushing the police. When Warren started trying to kill us, she said it was too dangerous. I made her keep going."

A hand suddenly clamped down on his shoulder from behind.

Cillian glanced back at Hank, the guy's long arm stretched over Victoria in his lap. "If you think that, you don't know Vicki. She's a strong woman of God."

A small smile cracked through the anguish squeezing Cillian's heart. "Yeah. She is."

"We'd better call the police." Robert's grim comment jerked Cillian's attention to him. He reached into his jacket pocket and pulled out a phone, extending it toward Cillian. "Find the last number in recent calls and ask for Lieutenant Willis."

Cillian took the phone and woke up the screen. "What's going on?"

"He dispatched some squads to come out here when we located you. But they should reroute to the hospital now."

"How did you find us?"

"Vicki's ankle monitor."

"Wow." Cillian had forgotten all about it. And his annoyance that she'd had to keep wearing the thing even after she'd been cleared. "Willis actually shared her location data with you?"

"Only because our dad got on the phone to ask him for it." Hank's answer came with a sardonic tone.

Whoa. Cillian never thought he'd want to thank Victoria's father for anything. But now he owed Dr. Henry Weston his life and Victoria's. If they could get to the hospital on time.

"Can you step on it, Rob?" Hank's urgent question spiked fear through Cillian again. The med student was worried about Vicks.

Robert shot Cillian a sidelong glance before returning his attention to the snowy road. "You can see how we beat the police here. My little brother has an adventurous, race car driver streak."

"Right. The police." Cillian looked down at the phone in his hand, navigating to the list of recent calls. "I suppose they'll want to talk to me and Vicks." That must be why Robert wanted them to come to the hospital.

"I was thinking they'll want to grab Briscoe's real killer."

"At the hospital?"

"Yeah." Robert kept his focus on navigation as he answered. "Sydney texted me. She was trying to get ahold of Vicki to tell her she's having the baby. That's when we noticed Vicki had left our dad's."

"We went outside to see if we could catch her," Hank picked up the story like a smooth handoff, "and we saw her purse in the snow."

Robert nodded. "Her car was still there, along with tire tracks from another vehicle."

"We knew something was wrong, so we called the police right away."

Cillian glanced back at Hank. "Good thinking. But what makes you think Warren is at the hospital? He drove us out there to leave us for dead. I don't think he'd go back to town and see his sister."

"Sydney said he was driving her to Rampart Memorial."

Cillian stared at Robert. "You're kidding."

"Not a bit."

"Okay. I'll call Willis." Cillian put the phone to his ear and was quickly transferred to the lieutenant. First time the man sounded pleased to hear from Cillian and didn't question anything he said about Warren being the real murderer or that he was currently at Rampart Memorial with his sister.

If he hadn't just dropped her off and left.

Cillian ended the call and looked at Robert. "Willis said he's sending the cops to Rampart with more backup."

"At the moment, I'm more concerned with getting Vicki there on time." Hank's tone carried a warning that sent a shiver through Cillian. "Faster, Rob."

Robert pressed the pedal harder, earning a slide from the tires. But he steadied the truck and kept driving at the same speed.

"I know neither of you are praying men, but you might think of saying a prayer for Vicki."

Cillian jerked his head toward Hank in the back, dropping his gaze to Vicks.

Her face was so pale, lifeless.

"I'm a praying man. Now." His gaze found Hank's.

The younger guy's eyes widened. Then he gave Cillian a single nod.

Cillian took in a breath. "God, Vicki would say you already know what's happening here. Save this beautiful, amazing woman. Please, heal her." The prayer emerged awkward and halting at first, but Cillian kept going. He would do anything for her. Give his life if he could. But all he could do now was this—pray to the God she'd always wanted him to believe in. And he did believe now. With all his aching, worried heart.

So he prayed all the way to the hospital, only stopping when Robert careened into the recently plowed parking lot.

The red letters, *Emergency Department*, glowed above the entrance where three squad cars were parked, lights flashing.

No cops in sight. Maybe they'd gone inside after Warren?

"Keep an eye out for the Warren kid." Robert braked beside one of the squads, close to the entrance.

Cillian would love to nail the punk who had shot Victoria. But she came first. "I'll get help." He jumped out of the truck and sprinted to the building, the automatic glass doors opening too slowly in front of him.

"Help!" He glanced around, looking for a nurse or orderly.

"This way." Robert grabbed his arm, then let go as he darted around the corner to the left.

Cillian hurried after him, spotting a desk just ahead with two women in scrubs behind it.

Robert reached the desk first. "We have a female gunshot wound victim in critical condition in our vehicle just outside."

"Orderly!" One of the women waved at a man coming out from a corridor, and she hurried around the desk.

The other nurse had picked up a phone and was saying something over the PA system that Cillian didn't try to make out.

"Show us where she is." The first nurse looked at Cillian as the orderly she'd called grabbed a stretcher on wheels parked by a wall.

Cillian glanced back at Robert. Looked like the other nurse had him filling out some sort of form on a clipboard. Lucky he was a family member. Or was that God's doing, too?

Cillian spun away, tabling the question for another time as he led the orderly and nurse out of the hospital to the pickup. He helped the orderly transfer Vicki from Hank to the stretcher, then stayed glued to her side as they wheeled her into the building.

More hospital staff met them at the door, walking quickly alongside the stretcher as they threw medical terms and numbers back and forth.

They turned to the right at the corner, no one trying to

push Cillian away from Vicki, which would've been impossible.

"Stop!" A man's shout echoed in the corridor.

A guy ran straight at them.

Tall and skinny. Blue jacket. Dark jeans.

Warren.

Cillian bolted into action, running at him.

Warren froze, eyes huge as he stared at Cillian.

He had him.

Cillian dove at Warren. Too soon.

The kid dodged.

Cillian fell to the ground, his chin smacking against the hard floor. He scrambled to his feet as the pursuing cops ran toward him, too far behind to catch the fugitive.

"Warren!" Cillian sprinted after the punk.

Warren headed right for the doctors and nurses surrounding…Victoria.

If he hurt her again—

He suddenly stopped. Next to Victoria's stretcher.

The nurses and other staff moved into Cillian's path, forcing him to slow as they tried to get away from the fleeing criminal.

"Victoria?" Cillian pushed through the panicked people who blocked his view of Victoria as they jabbered in confusion and chaos.

His vision of Warren and the stretcher cleared as he reached the other side of the medical staff. All except for one orderly who lingered on the opposite side of the stretcher from Warren. Why wasn't the orderly rolling Victoria away?

Then Cillian saw it.

Victoria's arm reached out from the stretcher, her hand on Warren's wrist as he stood there, unmoving.

Cillian snuck closer, not wanting to spook the punk.

"I thought I killed you." Warren's tight, frightened voice reached Cillian's ears.

"No, Warren." Victoria's weak tone was harder to hear as

Cillian got within a couple feet of her shooter. "I know you didn't mean to shoot me."

The orderly on the other side of her stretcher looked at Cillian, his eyes signaling he was ready to act.

Cillian held up a hand to keep him back. If they made the wrong move, Warren could grab Victoria.

"Sydney needs you, Warren." Victoria's words grew even weaker. "Do the right thing. God will forgive you if you're sorry for what you've done. So will I."

Inches behind Warren, Cillian grabbed his arms, pulling them behind the kid's back as Victoria's hand fell away.

The punk didn't fight Cillian. He kept staring at Victoria, whose beautiful eyes had shut again as her arm hung limp.

Two police officers appeared behind Cillian and reached for Warren.

Cillian gladly transferred the kid and went to the incredible woman who had rallied just enough to stop the bad guy from getting away. He gently lifted her arm to rest on the stretcher again. "A little help here!"

The nurses and other staff, distracted by the police pulling Warren away to cuff him, snapped to attention and returned their focus to Victoria.

The stretcher moved, and Cillian started to follow. But a hand grabbed his shoulder, holding him back.

"They've got this."

Cillian turned to see Hank standing next to him and Robert a few feet away, watching his sister get carted off.

"Well, them and God. She's safe in His hands."

Cillian swallowed. It was going to take some getting used to. This trusting God thing. But it was like Victoria had said, he couldn't really do anything right on his own. He'd gotten the killer's identity wrong and put Victoria in harm's way through his stubborn belief that he knew best. About time he let someone much wiser take the lead.

*God, show me how to stop pushing everyone around to get my way. Help me to do things Your way instead.*

He would need all the supernatural help he could get with that. Because now, more than ever before, he wanted nothing more than to spend the rest of his life with Victoria Weston. To love her forever.

But actually...this was different. He felt the change deep in his heart.

He finally loved her enough to let her choose. And whatever she chose, to love him or not, he would keep on loving her to the end of his days.

# CHAPTER
# FORTY

FUNNY HOW A SHIFT in perspective changed everything. Leaving Victoria in God's hands and leaving the choice of their future up to Him and Victoria unexpectedly made Cillian feel lighter.

For the first time in months—years, actually—his brain didn't need to work on plotting how he was going to force her father to let her go. And how he was going to charm her into leaving Chicago to spend her life with him.

Cillian stood at the edge of the emergency department waiting room where the open space met the wide corridor. He could see better from there, keeping watch for a doctor or nurse who might have an update about Victoria.

But the lightness, the restfulness that seemed to emanate from his soul stayed throughout the long hours of waiting after the nurses had reported Victoria would need emergency surgery. Instead of his usual restlessness and need to do something, take some action, he wasn't anxious as the Weston siblings arrived at the hospital to wait the long hours together with intermittent hushed tones and silence. When Torin, Hank, and Spring took turns praying out loud, Cillian grew even calmer, their prayers soothing the anxiety about Victoria's condition.

Cillian had never waited so well in his life.

Victoria would laugh if she could see him now.

*"I can be patient."*

What a cute look she'd given him when he'd said that. And when she'd quipped, *"That would be the first time."*

He'd responded by saying maybe it was worth waiting for, meaning *she* was worth waiting for.

No maybe about it.

Movement in the hallway caught his attention. Could be another false alarm. He'd gotten his hopes up every time one of the nurses or doctors passed by.

But this man was pulling a surgical cap off his head. Maybe a surgeon? He angled directly toward the waiting room.

"Guys." Hank signaled to his siblings as he rose from the chairs to join Cillian.

The short man stopped in front of them, surveying the crowd. "Are you all the family of Victoria Weston?"

"Yes, sir." Hank nodded.

"I'm Dr. Britton, the surgeon who operated on Victoria. She's out of surgery, and I expect a full recovery. The damage wasn't as severe as we'd feared."

The words shot deep into Cillian's heart, flooding him with more happiness than he'd ever felt in his life.

He didn't hear much else, only that she wouldn't be able to see visitors until tomorrow.

"Praise the Lord." Spring's words echoed the gratitude that threatened to bust through Cillian's ribs.

He would see Victoria again. Get to hold her, tell her how much he loved her.

If she let him. The reminder curbed his enthusiasm. She could still say they couldn't be together. Still reject him. After all, her father still didn't approve of Cillian and never would.

If Victoria chose to part ways once again, if she asked Cillian to leave her life forever, he would do it. Even though the idea sucked the air from his lungs and left him with a hollow pain.

But either way, he would be grateful that God had saved her life. And that he'd get to see her again, even if it was for the last time.

He and Victoria's siblings lingered at the hospital for a while longer until they were told they should go home and return the next day.

But Cillian couldn't leave. Not even when Spring mentioned that he might want to change and shower before seeing Victoria. She had a point. He probably looked more than a little scruffy.

But he couldn't leave. He had to know. Had to find out what their fate would be. What his fate would be. He had to see her before her father could forbid it or have her moved somewhere Cillian wasn't allowed to go.

So he waited. Slept a little in the hard chairs. Stretched and walked when the growing anticipation of Victoria's decision messed with the calm relief he'd felt before.

"Are you Cillian Doherty?" A female voice jerked him to a halt in the middle of pacing. He spun toward the woman, apparently a nurse, judging from her garb and nametag. "Yes, ma'am."

"Thought you must be." She smiled. "Victoria's awake, and she asked to see you."

Cillian's chest swelled. She'd asked for him before anyone else? That had to be a good sign.

"Take this hallway, then turn right and look for Room 212. It'll be on your left."

"Thank you." He forced himself to stay at a quick walking pace as he started in the direction she'd pointed. But his feet, his heart, had other ideas. He sped up, reaching a jog as he turned right into another hallway. He scanned the room numbers that counted up to…

212.

He hurried to the closed door. Rapped on it. Probably way too hard.

A muffled voice said something from inside. Victoria?

She'd better have said he could come in because nothing could stop him right now.

He pushed open the door and walked inside, frantically taking in the room until—

There. Victoria lay in a bed around the corner to the left, her upper body propped partially upright, allowing him to see her face.

Gorgeous, incredible Victoria. Her auburn hair fell free to her shoulders, making her look more beautiful than ever.

"You look worse than I feel." Sarcastic humor laced her comment, matching the slight curve of her mouth.

He walked to the bed, a grin stretching across his face as his heart thumped against his ribs. "I thought I was the one who was supposed to be the thrill-seeking risk-taker. And here you go, getting shot."

She started to chuckle, then winced, her hand closing on the sheet by her side.

IV cords connected to a needle that entered the top of her hand. All humor seeped away as the memory of the worry, the anguish of thinking she might die, came back to grip his chest.

He had to touch her, had to know she was really there, alive and well. He carefully reached for her fingers, scooping his hand under them. "I thought I was going to lose you."

She tightened her fingers around his. "I know. I thought I might lose you, too."

Did that mean she didn't want to lose him? That she wanted him to stick around? His breathing shallowed. But he was getting ahead of himself. There was something else he had to say first. "Vicks, I have to apologize."

She lifted her eyebrows, apparently too tired to cock one like she usually did. "If I recall correctly, you were apologizing the last time we spoke, out in the blizzard."

He gave her a shaky smile. "I guess I have a lot to apologize for. But here's one of the biggest ones." He took in more air and met her gaze. "I'm sorry I convinced you to leave your mom and go out with me that night. It was wrong."

She watched him, her expression not easy to read under her heavy lids that hid part of her eyes. "You saw I was hurting and tired. You wanted to help. I know that."

"But I should've helped by sitting with you at your mom's bedside. I should've taken a shift, watching her so you could get some rest. There were a lot of things I could've done to help instead of adding to your burdens in the worst way possible. Instead of only doing what I wanted." He dropped his gaze to her fingers as he brushed his thumb across her knuckles. "And because of me, you've had to carry the burden of that night alone for sixteen years."

"No. Not in the way you might think." Her surprising response jerked his eyes to hers. "I rarely thought about that night until you came back."

He winced. Another problem he'd caused her with his abrupt return.

"I repented for what I'd done, and I knew the Lord forgave me. I thought I'd left it behind. But when you returned, it all came back."

"Vicks, I'm—"

"No," the skin bunched between her eyebrows, "you made me realize I hadn't left it behind. I apparently had a harder time believing my mom could forgive me. I wanted to fix what I'd done by stepping into her shoes and carrying on her legacy."

"She was a wonderful woman. She even liked me." His remark earned a small smile. "Not a bad example to follow."

"True. But she wasn't perfect. I put her on a pedestal and followed everything she'd done. I emulated her example of what I thought was peacemaking instead of seeking God's truth about peace. You helped me see that."

"I did?"

"Yes. You helped me see how wrong my father was. That

night when he said those awful things about you…" She turned her head an inch to look away. "I didn't stop him. I didn't confront him and tell him how wrong he was." She slowly brought her tired gaze back to Cillian. "Like you would have done for me. Or for anyone who was being wronged." She blinked, slowly.

For a moment, he wasn't sure her eyes would open again.

Then they did and fastened on him. "I'm sorry, Cillian. Will you forgive me?"

He squeezed her fingers as he leaned toward her. "Of course. As long as you forgive me, too."

Her lids drifted shut again.

"Victoria, I love you. I want to spend the rest of my life with you."

Her eyes stayed closed. Her breathing slowed, evening out like she had gone to sleep.

Pulling up a chair, he sat beside her bed and gently cradled her hand in his.

What he needed to say could wait. As long as he could stay with the love of his life, he would wait forever.

# EPILOGUE

*ONE MONTH LATER.*

"I thought you said Robert sent you in here to fetch my cheese tray, not eat it all." Victoria sent Hank a teasing smile as another slice of cheddar disappeared into his mouth.

He finished chewing in record time and grinned at her over the generous island in Robert's large kitchen. "You know, now that you're a wealthy heiress, you could afford to bring two cheese trays."

She chuckled. "Yes, I'm sure that was Thomas's intention in entrusting me with his fortune."

"What do you think he wanted you to do with it?" Hank's expression turned more serious, but his hand drifted toward another slice.

"I haven't figured that out yet. Nor do I know if I'm going to live there or what I'm going to do with his money, to answer your next question. I'll give much of it to Christian charities and mission work, but I haven't determined the best way to go about that yet. I want to make sure I'm a good stewardess of the gift Thomas left me."

Hank nodded. "You totally will be." Another slice entered his mouth.

"And you are stalling. You'd think you never eat."

"I'm a poor starving college student." He mumbled the unconvincing defense around the stolen cheese in his mouth.

"Who has the semester off and lives in a mansion with our father." She moved toward him on the near side of the island, shooing him away with her hands. "Go. Take the tray into the living room while there's still some cheese left for the others."

"So possessive about your cheese." He laughed as he trotted out of the kitchen, leaving her laughing, too, as she turned to wash her hands in the sink.

"Dad's here."

Victoria glanced over her shoulder to see Spring wheel into the kitchen, her eyebrows lifted with either surprise or trepidation. Victoria dried her hands on a towel and faced her sister while she processed the news. "I didn't think he would come."

"Neither did I." Spring halted her chair next to the island in the spacious layout that allowed for her wheelchair.

"Did Robert tell him Sydney and Mariah would be here?"

Spring shrugged.

"And Cillian?"

"Nope." Robert breezed into his kitchen, wearing a dress shirt and slacks that he'd donned in case their father decided to attend the celebration. He grinned at Victoria as he set the salad bowl and two used glasses on the counter beside her. "You said you wanted him to come."

She narrowed her eyes at him, but her lips tugged at one corner. "Not under false pretenses, Robert."

"He knows I'm hosting a party to celebrate your recovery. Nothing false about that." He grabbed a hunk of spinach from the bowl and stuffed it into his mouth.

"I wouldn't have thought that would be enough to make him leave work or the house to go anywhere on a Friday night." Spring's matter-of-fact statement drew Victoria's gaze. "No offense, of course."

"None taken. But, yes," Victoria transferred her gaze to

Robert, "I did hope he would come. I need to speak with him."

"Want backup?" Spring quirked an eyebrow.

Victoria smiled at the sweet gesture. "Thanks, but Cillian has already agreed to provide that."

"Ahh, I see." Spring shot a conspiratorial look at Robert as they both grinned.

Heat rushed to Victoria's cheeks, though it was hardly a secret at this point that she and Cillian were...involved. In the weeks that followed her surgery, he'd barely left her side at the hospital and then at her home. Kathleen had stayed overnight those first evenings of her at-home recovery, but Cillian had helped care for her needs so often during the daytime that even Max had come to love him, too.

The implication of her thoughts sped her heart rate. Yes, she loved him. She had for a long time. But she hadn't told him yet. She'd expected him to ask her, to talk about their relationship and their future. But he hadn't broached the subject at all.

She might think his feelings for her had changed, that he no longer loved her. But his attentiveness and the way he wordlessly expressed his love for her through his actions every day made it clear that he still loved her, perhaps more than ever.

"Cillian's in the living room." Robert's remark pulled Victoria from her thoughts. "I assume that's who you're thinking about, given the dreamy look on your face." He gave her another classic Robert grin.

"Victoria never looks dreamy, Robby. She's far too mature and practical for that." Spring giggled.

"Ah, you're right." He tapped his bearded chin with a fingertip as he pretended to study Victoria. "Contemplative then?"

"You two." Victoria pursed her lips, more to hold back a laugh at their antics than to curb their teasing. "I believe it's time for me to leave the children and find the adults." She crossed the kitchen and went to the doorway.

"Never run from your feelings, Vicki." Robert's attempt to sound like a serious psychiatrist collapsed into laughter with Spring.

Victoria chuckled as she continued into the hallway, walking the short distance to where the wall fell away and opened to the large living room.

She scanned the people there, her gaze magnetically drawn to Cillian first, as usual. My, he looked handsome in his charcoal blazer layered over a black turtleneck that perfectly complimented his dark coloring and broad-shouldered physique.

His gaze found hers across the space, his mouth tugging up at the corner. Since he was speaking with Torin, Victoria only smiled, then continued to look for her dad.

There he was. Dad stood with Treese near the modern fireplace, discussing something Victoria couldn't hear.

Treese laughed, picking a bit of nonexistent lint off his black blazer. Their father never allowed anything to blemish his deportment. But Treese was the only one who could behave so familiarly with him, and she always took advantage of it.

Victoria regretted the thought—or rather, the resentful edge to it—as soon as it passed through her mind. It was an unbelievable blessing that her siblings had returned to getting along with each other and to their former relationship status with their father. That meant Robert was still effortlessly staying on Dad's good side, Hank was trying to bear the weight of his expectations, Spring was planning to patch things up, and Treese was still his princess.

Their father, for his part, had seemed to decide to let pass the things his children had said against him, at least for now. He seemed remarkably unchanged and unaffected by it, which was perhaps the most surprising development of all. Hopefully, he wasn't merely suppressing his true feelings—anger, resentment, or hurt—only to have them explode at a later date or inform his treatment of the children who had confronted him.

The appearance of peace felt tenuous, fragile, and artificial. But such had been the so-called peace that Victoria had created during most of her siblings' lives. If, or when, the veneer fell away, she was prepared to respond differently than she had in the past. She would speak the truth in love, even to her father, instead of guiding her siblings to please him at any cost. When he was wrong, she would speak out and try to prevent any further harm to her family, some of which she had unintentionally facilitated.

But at least for the present, the birthday dinner disaster hadn't had as much of a damaging effect as Victoria had feared. Except with Treese. She'd barely spoken to Victoria since, losing her smile and sense of humor whenever Victoria entered a room.

And she noticeably kept her distance from Sydney and her new baby during the party this evening.

Victoria swung her gaze to the armchair tucked into a corner of the room where Sydney held her daughter in her arms. It was so kind of Robert to invite her to the celebration, especially given her unwitting involvement in their family's division and her brother's violence.

Sydney looked up, and Victoria headed her way.

Victoria paused by the empty chair angled to face Sydney's. "Mind if I join you two?"

Sydney shook her head with a bright smile. "Sure." She looked down at her sweet daughter. "Mariah's sleeping." The wonder in the young mother's tone warmed Victoria's heart. What a gift to have been a part of keeping this mother and daughter together.

Victoria leaned closer to see the baby's perfect, tiny features. "She's so beautiful."

"Isn't she?" Disbelief and love lit Sydney's face as she

studied her baby. "Warren says she looks more like me than Lawrence."

Victoria paused before answering, not wanting to misstep and cause any hurt.

Sydney's gaze jumped to Victoria's face as her mouth rounded. "Oh, I'm sorry. I shouldn't have mentioned them."

Victoria gave her a gentle smile. "No, of course you can mention them, Sydney. Warren is your family, and I know you still miss Lawrence."

"Not really." The girl lifted one shoulder. "I mean, he'll always be Mariah's dad, so there's that. But I'm getting it now. Robert's helping me with all that stuff. I know Lawrence never loved me." She nodded slowly. "I'm okay with that."

"That's wonderful, Sydney. You know I'm here, as well, whenever you need to talk. And God is even more available than I am. Bring your worries and cares to Him, and He'll help you."

"I'm doing that more now. Kathleen talks about that in Bible study. I think it's really helping. I'm starting to feel... different about things."

"I'm so glad to hear that." What a hopeful sign that Sydney was still in Kathleen's Bible study, which the girl had joined shortly after moving into the room that had opened up at Life Pregnancy Care Center. Bible study participation was mandatory for the residents, but it sounded like the Lord was creating in Sydney a desire for Him and His Word. Perhaps soon, He would also give Sydney new life in Him.

"I'm starting to get how you could forgive Warren." Sydney's tone grew more serious as she met Victoria's gaze. "Even after he tried to kill you. And he did kill your friend." Her mouth pulled into a frown. "I still can't wrap my head around it. That he'd do anything like that."

Victoria reached to cover the teen's hand where it rested on Mariah's blanket. "I know. I'm so sorry for the grief this is putting you through. But it wasn't your fault. It was Warren's decision to do those things."

Sydney bit her lip and nodded.

"Have you seen him again?"

The teen took in a deep breath. "Yeah. I visit him every week. I'm the only family he's got, and he was there for me when I messed up. Mom doesn't want anything to do with him either now."

"I'm sure he appreciates seeing you."

Warren would have a long wait in jail before his case would come to court. Victoria's dad had said the District Attorney assured him they would get a conviction and likely life in prison for the litany of crimes Warren had committed.

"He's really sorry about what he did." Sydney's expression shifted to one of surprise. "Hey, did you know Cillian visited him? Warren couldn't believe it."

"Yes, Cillian told me."

"Warren was afraid he was going to yell at him or something."

Victoria smiled. Cillian had told her that he'd shared the Gospel with Warren, telling him how his sins could be forgiven, and he could be set free, even while in jail. Warren hadn't come to faith yet, but Cillian intended to visit him again.

"I plan to visit Warren, too, now that I'm feeling better." Victoria still had residual pain from scar tissue and a generalized weakness from inactivity, but she would keep at her recovery program and return to full strength soon.

"Wow, really? That's super nice."

"You know what I always say."

"It's not you." Sydney smiled. "It's Christ in you."

"Exactly." Victoria gave the girl's hand a pat, then swiveled her head to check for her father before he could duck out.

He wasn't apt to stay long. There he was, already walking toward the entryway.

"Leaving already, Dr. Weston?" Cillian's question halted her father.

"I'll talk to you again later." Victoria touched Sydney's

shoulder as she stood and brushed past to hurry toward Dad and Cillian. As unlikely and volatile a pair as one could wish to see. And more alike than either would care to admit. Though Cillian's realization of those similarities, in the negative aspects, may have saved his life, sending him to the feet of Christ.

Victoria came alongside Cillian, drawing her father's guarded stare. "Dad, could I speak with you in the other room, please?"

He transferred his gaze from her to Cillian, then back again. "I only have a few minutes."

"Wonderful. Let's go in Robert's office." She hooked her arm through Cillian's, glancing up at him as they led the way to the office located off the foyer.

He placed his hand on hers where it rested on his arm, the loving, confident expression in his eyes reassuring her and giving her strength.

Thank the Lord they had learned that Marsha Faint, the woman who had sued her father for malpractice, had not actually been intimidated or mistreated by anyone. Cillian had told Victoria about his investigation and his intentions to use the findings against her dad to help her. But he'd learned that poor Mrs. Faint suffered from schizophrenia and had conjured the entire story while off her medication. Without that information, Victoria and Cillian might have had to hold an even more difficult conversation with her dad. Although this one would be quite hard enough for Victoria.

She walked to the center of the office, then turned with Cillian to face her father.

Dad stepped inside the doorway and stopped, folding his arms across his chest. "I suppose this is where you two tell me you're getting married, whether I like it or not."

Victoria shot Cillian a startled gaze.

But he simply grinned at her and then her dad. "Hadn't gotten quite that far yet, but now that you mention it—"

"Cillian." She reached her other hand over to squeeze his

forearm. That was not what she'd said she was going to discuss with her father. And Cillian was supposed to be a silent supporter during this conversation.

He pressed his lips closed, but a twinkle still lit his eyes as he looked down at her.

She returned her focus to her dad. "I need to tell you something that you should know. I didn't tell you before because of the havoc I knew it would cause our family. But now, I believe it's time that you know what happened." She drew in a breath, meeting Dad's measured gaze.

Cillian put his hand on hers again.

"Sixteen years ago, the night Mom passed away, I wasn't with her as I let you believe."

No reaction. Dad didn't even blink.

"I had gone out with Cillian. We were only gone for thirty minutes, but when I returned..." Her throat closed. Or perhaps the lump expanding there filled the space.

Cillian released her arm and slid his around her back instead, anchoring and holding her.

"When I returned, she was gone. I hoped she passed in her sleep, as I told you she did. But I can't know for certain because...I let her die alone." She forced herself to keep a steady gaze on her father. "I'm so sorry, Dad."

He watched her—silent, immovable. It was such a similar expression to the one he'd given her that night, when she had dried her tears and found him in his office to tell him his wife had died. Did that mean she had hurt him all over again? That the pain of this confession was as great as the grief he'd felt then?

"It's good to see you on your feet again."

She stared at him. Disbelief seemed to paralyze her brain. Hadn't he heard what she had shared?

Of course he had. This was Dr. Henry Weston, the brilliant, world-renowned neurosurgeon who was also the most intelligent man she knew.

And he'd just said so much that she'd nearly missed it.

He turned away and left the room.

"Did you hear that?" Victoria pivoted in Cillian's arm, facing him.

"Yeah." He glanced past her to the door. "Weird reaction."

"No." She put a hand on Cillian's chest. "He was saying he cares about me. That he still cares." A smile lifted her mouth as relief and hope spilled through her. "That he forgives me."

"He said all that?" Cillian's eyebrows scrunched with incredulity.

"Yes." She beamed her smile up at him, placing her other hand on his chest, as well. "He did."

"He didn't even blink or anything when you told him, though."

"I know. I think he knew."

"He knew?"

"Yes. All this time, he knew." She shook her head. Why hadn't he said anything to her that night? She would've expected him to be furious she had left, especially that she had left with Cillian. He must have at least been disappointed in her for leaving her mother and disobeying him. But he hadn't said a word. He hadn't removed any of her responsibilities and had fully trusted her to become like a mother to his children.

A few weeks ago, when Victoria had returned home to finish healing from her bullet wound, Hank had told her that their dad had overseen her care at the hospital. The night of the shooting, he had phoned Dr. Britton, the best trauma surgeon in Chicago, to ask him to drop everything on his night off and go to Rampart Memorial Hospital to perform Victoria's surgery. During her recovery, Dad had also often called the hospital to check in on her healing and care.

She wasn't surprised that he'd watched over her essential needs from afar. That was his way with his children, his way of loving them.

But to learn he had known what she'd done that awful night of Mom's death but hadn't blamed or confronted her about such a failing was an unbelievable gift. The discovery lifted a burden off her shoulders that she hadn't fully realized she'd been carrying.

"You know, I think there might be more to your old man than I thought."

The humor in Cillian's voice drew Victoria's full attention to him. "Oh?"

"Yeah. Like when he guessed we wanted to tell him we were getting married." Cillian closed both arms around her back, cradling her. "That's the best idea he's ever had."

A flush of warmth rushed to her cheeks.

"There it is." Cillian brushed his knuckles ever so gently against her cheek. "I love it when you get flustered." His voice dropped to a whisper that sent a shiver up her spine.

Then he dipped his head, touching his forehead to hers. "I'll wait forever for you, Victoria Weston. But it's your choice. If you want me to, I will even leave. But you know how I feel. What I want." He drew in a ragged breath and lifted his head, his gaze staying locked on hers. "What do you want?"

She looked deeply into his dark eyes, the pools of the most intense love she'd ever seen. "I want you, Cillian. I love you. I want to spend the rest of my life with you."

A broad, joyous grin split his face, and he wrapped her in his arms, lifting her off the ground as his lips met hers in a kiss that left her breathless and blushing.

When he finally ended the kiss and lowered her back to the floor, Cillian was breathing as hard as she was. His eyes roamed her features. "Now that was worth waiting for." He brushed a loose strand of her hair behind her ear. "Want to do it again?" His slightly wicked grin spiked a thrill through her.

"I think we had better join the others." She stepped back, but slipped her hand into his, threading their fingers together.

"Yes, ma'am."

As soon as they crossed the entryway and rejoined the others in the living room, Spring's eyes grew wide. "What were you two up to?"

Oh, my. Victoria reached for her bun. Was it disheveled from Cillian's fingers?

"You're red as a rose, Vicki." Robert's teasing smile said it all.

Mortification rose in Victoria's chest. What an example she was setting for—

"That's because we just got engaged!" Cillian's announcement drew whoops from Hank and Robert and congratulatory exclamations from the others as they gathered around.

As Victoria returned their hugs and cherished their joyous response, her gaze found Cillian's. In that moment, he seemed to be thinking what she was.

This was God's timing, not theirs. They were together at last, exactly when they were supposed to be, ready to embark on a future with each other, walking with the Lord.

And in His providence, not a moment of their lives or their love story had been wasted.

Turn the Page for a Special Sneak Peek of
WINDY CITY WESTONS, BOOK 3

---

# WATCHED

---

PREORDER NOW

# EXCERPT OF WATCHED

The office building was quiet, seemingly empty as Robert passed other closed office spaces on his way to the elevator.

He took several more slow, calming breaths in the nearly silent elevator as it carried him down from the sixth floor. The doors opened, and he stepped out into the lobby that looked much larger without the daytime bustle of people.

Phil Davis glanced up from the book he was reading behind the front desk.

"Hey, Phil." Robert lifted a hand in a still wave to the security guard as he walked by. "How's the thriller?"

"Terrifying." Phil's deadpan made Robert grin.

"Don't let it keep you up all night."

Phil chuckled. "It better." Good answer, since the guard had to stay alert for the overnight shift. He frequently joked that was why he read the scariest books he could find. "Have a good night."

"You, too." Robert pushed through the glass door that would lock behind him and stepped out into the still darkness, brightened by lamps overhead.

Only a few other pedestrians shared the sidewalk, and light traffic moved along the street. Two hours earlier, the sidewalk would've been packed with people coming and going from the offices and businesses in downtown Gealanden. The large Chicago suburb wasn't as busy and congested as Chicago's downtown, but it had enough traffic to make the office location a good one. Even if it did require parking his car in the garage a block away.

Not really a problem on a cool spring evening like this one. It was a perfect night for taking a walk and releasing his stress from the confrontation with Jackson.

He needed to focus on Carrie. And Wendy, Randall, Sabrina—all patients he'd helped that very day. He'd made their lives better with his knowledge and skills. He'd helped improve their mental health, which would enable them to have happier lives.

Yeah, he was getting his groove back. Despite the weird thing with the lost appointments. Though why Jackson made such a big deal—

"Weston."

Robert started as a man stepped into his path. He'd subconsciously registered someone loitering by the corner of the office building, but it was pretty normal to have a few smokers or homeless people hanging around downtown. This guy knew his name.

"What do you think you're doing?" The man's aggressive question sent Robert's sympathetic nervous system into action.

Epinephrine circulated through him, pumping his heart and tensing his muscles. Hopefully an overreaction. He breathed in through his nose as he quickly assessed the man.

Sixties, trucker-style baseball hat, scruffy stubble like he hadn't shaved in two days. Stress in his stance, the curl of his fingers in and out of a fist by his side. The other hand was stuffed in his right jacket pocket.

Why? Did he have a weapon in there? The hair on the back of Robert's neck stood on end. "How can I help you?" He kept his tone calm and worded the question carefully. "I don't believe we've met."

The man grunted. "No, we ain't met. But you know my wife real well." His emphasis on *real well* was not a good sign.

But since Robert had never had an affair with anyone's wife, the guy was going to need to be more specific. "Who might your wife be?"

"You know. Betsy." The man's mouth worked like he wished he was chewing on Robert.

"Betsy Richert?"

"You know another Betsy you're carrying on with?" The man spit on the sidewalk in front of Robert's feet.

Robert resisted the urge to back up out of pure disgust.

Angry, resentful, irrational. And maybe had something in his pocket. The man was dangerous. Just as Betsy had described her husband.

"You must be Paul, Betsy's husband." Reaffirming the man's relationship to her might help.

He swore. "You bet I am. And you're never gonna forget it again."

"I swear to you that I have never had an affair with Betsy, and I have never seen her as anything other than a patient." Robert stared unblinking at the man. Hard to make direct eye contact since he couldn't see Paul's eyes in the shadow cast from the bill of his cap. "I have never had inappropriate dealings with her or any other patient."

"That so?" His other hand went into his opposite jacket pocket.

Robert tensed.

"Then how do you explain this?" Paul whipped his hand out and lifted it in the air, something white between his fingers.

"I'm sorry, I don't know what that is."

"Yeah, right. Like you don't know what you wrote on this card for *my wife*."

"Is it an appointment card? I give those to all my patients, Paul."

He held up the card to his face, presumably to read it. "Can't wait to see you tomorrow night. R."

What in the world? Robert had never written that on an appointment card for Betsy. He hadn't even given her one.

The cap bill lifted as Paul looked up. "I knew you two were messing around. You're all she ever talks about. But nobody touches my wife. Nobody." He took a step toward Robert.

"Now hold on, Paul." Robert raised his hands, palm-out, as a peaceful gesture that he also hoped would stop any forward movement. "I don't know where you got that card, but I didn't write that." He would know if he'd given Betsy an appointment card. He didn't give her cards because they met on the same day every week.

"My wife doesn't see you at night. She goes in the afternoon while I'm away working so she don't have to work."

"Exactly." Robert nodded calmly, trying to defuse the anger increasing Paul's volume. "That's why I never would have given her a note like that." Unless she had said something about going on vacation and needing to switch to an evening this week. No, that was Tammy.

"Nice try. I ain't that stupid. That's how I know it's personal. You're planning to see her real *inappropriately*, you slick snake oil salesman." Paul retracted the pocketed hand.

This once, Robert wished he wasn't always right.

Paul held a gun, aimed directly at Robert's chest.

**His mind is a steel trap. He didn't know it could trap him.**

Robert Weston became a psychiatrist to heal people's minds. He can't lose his. But if the strange occurrences of forgetfulness and confusion continue, he may not be able to hide the truth much longer. When his psychological issues put his life in danger, he must face the reality that the genetic nightmare he fears inheriting has seized him.

Attorney Monty Montgomery knows she doesn't like Robert Weston. His expert testimony once ruined her client's case. She didn't realize the psychiatrist isn't only wrong but also completely unreliable. How can she defend him against a malpractice suit for the insurance company that hired her when he's clearly incompetent?

Robert and Monty have bigger problems than they know. Someone has a mission. A mission that won't be stopped until somebody ends up dead.

Is everyone a pawn in the lethal game, or is Robert's failing mind playing tricks on him? Even with the help of the Weston siblings, Robert and Monty may need a mind smarter than theirs—the mind of God—to escape this twisted game alive.

Shop *Watched* at
JerushaAgen.com

JERUSHA AGEN
INTROVERTED

GUARDIANS UNLEASHED
"Fast-paced suspense at its best."
- DiAnn Mills, bestselling author of Concrete Evidence
JERUSHA AGEN
RISING DANGER
JERUSHA AGEN
HIDDEN DANGER
JERUSHA AGEN
COVERT DANGER
JERUSHA AGEN
UNSEEN DANGER
JERUSHA AGEN
LETHAL DANGER
JERUSHA AGEN
TERMINAL DANGER
GuardiansUnleashed.com

# ABOUT JERUSHA

Jerusha Agen imagines danger around every corner but knows God is there, too. So naturally, she writes romantic suspense infused with the hope of salvation in Jesus Christ.

Jerusha loves to hang out with her big furry dogs and little furry cats, often while reading or watching movies.

Find more of Jerusha's thrilling, fear-fighting stories at www.JerushaAgen.com.